THE BLANCHARD WITCHES

HOUSE OF DUQUESNE

MICAH HOUSE

This is a work of fiction. All of the characters, organizations and events portrayed in this novel are either products of the author's imagination or used fictitiously.

The Blanchard Witches: House of Duquesne

First published 2021

Published by Kendrell Publishing, Birmingham, Alabama

Edited by Crystal Castle

Cover design by Paul Palmer-Edwards

ISBN: 978-1-7365086-7-1

LCCN: 2021924974

This book... the hardest to write because so much happens... is dedicated to my editor and new friend, Crystal Castle. I could never have gotten this far without you. You have not only helped me make the stories better, but you have also taught me so much about storytelling itself. This one is for you.

CONTENTS

Blanchard Family Tree

Names in italic originated from an alternate dimension

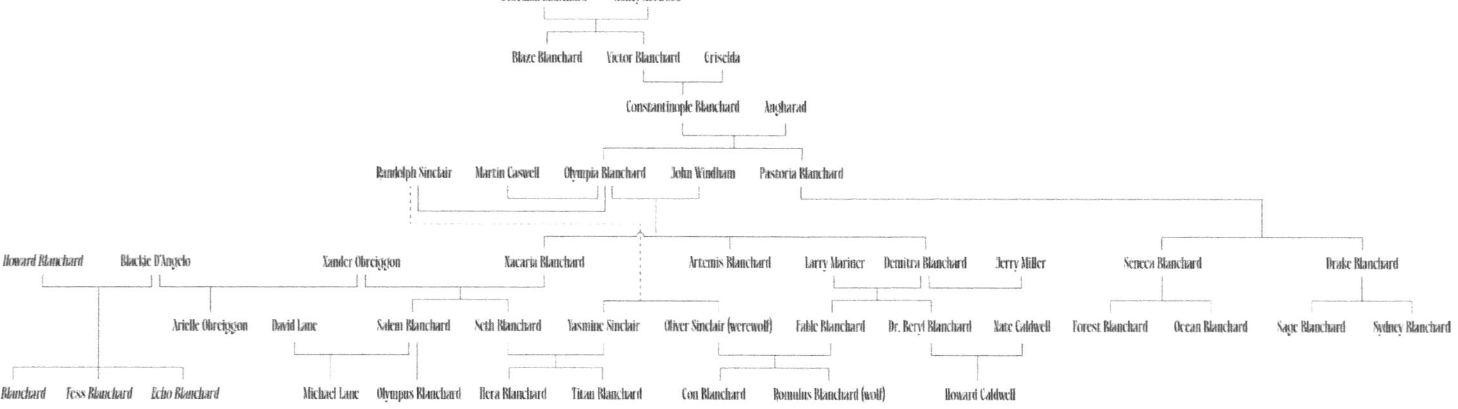

D'Angelo Family Tree

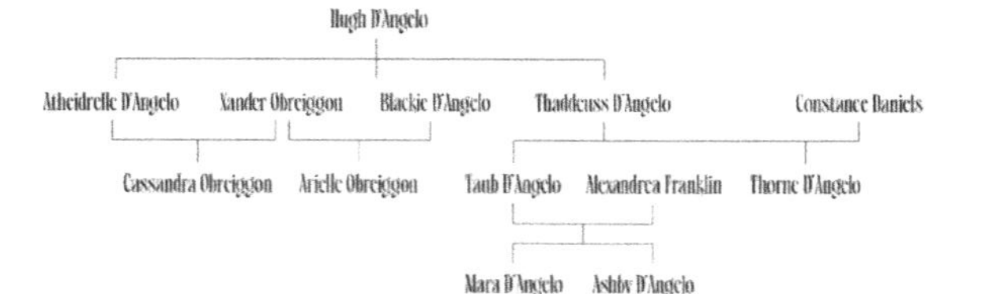

CHAPTER ONE

Birthday Boys

Blanchard House had its usual summer adornments. Olympia Blanchard's rose garden was all abloom in pinks, yellows, and deep red—still maintained with loving care by her daughters. The gardenia bushes fragranced the air around the porch while the confederate jasmine vine stemming along the walls of the pool patio in the side yard perfumed the lawn as if invisible hands were spraying from a bottle. There were other adornments today—more frivolous. Along the balustrade of the porch and tied to the benches around the many picnic tables, balloons of all colors, bright and cheerful, floated in the air. A large number 7 made of wood sat in the front yard, shaped like a giraffe and painted with bright orange spots. The banner stretched over the roof of the porch read *Happy Birthday Rom and Con.*

The tranquility of the 100 acres of Blanchard land was interrupted with the noise of twenty children all running amuck across the meadow. The field looked like a small circus had come to town. Three medium sized bouncy houses, one shaped like a ladybug, one shaped like a bunny rabbit, and one shaped like a dog, complete with floppy ears, held the attention of some of the children. Flanking the meadows other side was a small carousel with eight ornately carved horses spinning slowly in circles to the delight of the six kids riding. Beside the merry-go-round was a long inflatable tunnel replicating a caterpillar which a couple of children were crawling through. And crowning the end of the meadow stood a two-story inflated slide which the rest of the children were climbing as if it were Everest to experience the four-second escape down to the grass. Hera Blanchard was leading this charge with her band of friends—mostly boys—and she wasn't doing a fantastic job of being less bossy, as Miranda had cautioned her.

Miranda Perkins was standing at the refreshment table with Fable Blanchard, her eyes fixed on Hera and her hand gestures making sudden stops and starts as if she were trying to decide whether to scold the child or let her behavior slide.

"She is a tyrannical little thing sometimes," Miranda murmured to Fable. "But normally she's so closed off and keeping to herself I don't know whether to get on to her or not. At least she's finally interacting with other children besides her cousins."

"I'd let it go. Let her have her fun. I was bossy at her age too."

Fable was keeping an eye out on her son Romulus. Though it was equally his twin brother Con's birthday, it was Rom which Fable worried about most. Con was charging off to the next jumpy house with his circle of friends, while Rom was simply circling the meadow, running as fast as he could while two other children squealed in delight chasing him. Fable's eyes kept moving from Rom to the parents of the party guests. She hoped they all finally understood that Rom was no threat, and their children were in no danger.

Romulus Blanchard was a wolf. He was also Constantinople Blanchard's actual brother and Fable Blanchard's legitimate son. But of course, no one except family knew that. The people of Daihmler Alabama all knew about the Blanchard family's pet wolf and how he was supposedly quite docile. In fact, Romulus was practically Daihmler's town mascot. Everyone who passed him on the street stopped to say hello and stroke him under the chin. But the people of Daihmler had no idea Romulus and Con were Fable's sons from a liaison with a werewolf almost eight years ago. Their father was evil and the Blanchards ultimately destroyed him. But his legacy lived on in his sons. Neither son possessed a drop of their father's malevolence, but they did carry his curse. Luckily, The Natural Order of things worked its magic, splitting the curse and dividing the beast—one brother human, one brother animal, but both brothers humane.

In the distance Salem Blanchard was sitting under a shady pecan tree feeding a slice of cake to her nephew Titan. Hera's brother was two years old and really liked cake, particularly strawberry cake. Salem's own baby, Olympus was inside having a nap. At least he was supposed to be. She had not seen her sister Arielle in a while. That usually meant Arielle was upstairs in Salem's room playing with her nephew when he was supposed to be sleeping. Salem didn't mind. Arielle had not been in their lives when Salem's first child was alive. Seeing Arielle take such interest in Olympus and her brother Seth's children Hera and Titan, made Salem happy.

Seth was on the lawn too. Talking with a couple of fathers of other children. Even from the shade of the tree Salem could tell Seth was forcing himself to participate.

Seth's heart was not yet healed from the loss of his wife months ago, and though he had finally stepped back out into life, it was a baby step.

Under the shade of one of the three large oak trees in the front yard, an old man was hard at work grilling hot dogs and hamburgers. Artemis Blanchard was with him, happily filling a platter of empty buns when the meat was ready. Behind her was a small line of children and a few parents awaiting their lunch.

"I can't thank you enough Skillet for volunteering to help out today." Artemis told the elderly man who also worked as a cook for her restaurant in town.

"I just love children," Skillet said, placing two perfectly charred hot dog wieners onto a paper plate of buns she held outstretched for him. "Now, you know Con has done told me he wants his hamburger with a sliced-up hotdog on it too, so when he gets up here, I'll need a sec to cut one up for him."

Artemis passed the hot dog plate to the next child in line and began placing open buns onto a fresh paper plate. "He's a demanding thing," she laughed, tossing her long black hair back over her shoulder out of the way. "And I have seen Romulus sneaking up to you three times already for a hot dog."

Skillet chuckled as he flipped the burgers and dashed them with special sauce he used at the restaurant. "That boy cracks me up. Got an appetite like a—well, wolf."

Artemis smiled, although it seemed peculiar to her how Skillet referred to Rom as "that boy". Almost as if he somehow knew there was an element of humanity inside Romulus. She shook off the thought. There was no way anyone outside of the family could know the Blanchard pet wolf was actually a Blanchard. It wasn't uncommon for people to humanize animals in their speech. Still, Skillet was a perceptive old cuss.

A car was pulling into the driveway, one no one in the family recognized until the person in the passenger seat stepped out. Madam Zelda with her outlandish lime green skirt with hot pink trim and a bright yellow blouse stepped out onto the lawn, assisted by the woman who had driven her, her daughter Sarah.

Artemis stepped away from the grill and met them in the driveway. "Sarah, I haven't seen you in ages. You look fantastic!"

"No, she don't!" Zelda quipped, grabbing hold of Artemis' arm for stability. "You're just bein' nice. Sarah knows she's just as fat as she ever were."

Sarah turned pink and looked to the ground in that mousy way she always did when her mother berated her. "Hi Artemis. Good to see you again."

Artemis presented an exaggerated smile hoping to distract from Sarah's humiliation.

"You have got to start visiting us more often. We miss you." Artemis clutched Zelda's arm tightly and whispered into the old woman's ear, "Would you stop coming down on her so hard. She doesn't have to be humiliated every time you open your mouth."

"She don't have to be, but sure makes me have a better time." Zelda guffawed.

As Artemis led Zelda to a picnic table to sit down, Demitra scurried up to Sarah and gave her a gentle embrace. "Is she feeling any better?"

Sarah frowned and shook her head. "No. That's why I drove her today. Melinda and I feel that she shouldn't be driving until things improve."

Demitra gave an attempt of a laugh, "I'm sure that went well."

"Like a hailstorm over a glass roof." Sarah replied. "Oh, she says she's fine but look at her. She's getting so pale. And those heart flutters she keeps complaining about. But every time I try to get her in to see Doc Mackleson she refuses."

Zelda heard the exchange and mouthed loudly from the table, "I done told you Beryl was my doctor. I ain't a'goin to nobody else."

"But Beryl isn't here anymore." Sarah argued.

"That ain't my fault. I ain't the one who done decided she ortta be God."

Demitra smacked her hand into her forehead and gave a commiserate wink to Sarah.

Back in the field Tess and Trix were overseeing some of the children at play since not all the parents opted to stay for the party. Like most parents will, they seized the opportunity to ditch their kids to someone else's supervision for some much-needed rest or errands.

Tess was watching a child enter the caterpillar's mouth. She could see the indentions on the side walls of the long balloon as the child traversed through the caterpillar's belly making its way to the end. As the child found the end of the run and began climbing out, Tess clasped her sister's wrist and gasped. "Trix. What does that look like to you?"

Trix focused her eyes on the end of the caterpillar's tail and immediately saw what Tess was referring to. The red inflatable caterpillar's tail end was a peachy color. As children pulled themselves out of the end it made for a rather startling picture.

"That looks like a vagina giving birth!" Trix shrieked as another child crawled out.

Tess doubled over in laughter, still holding Trix's arm, "It really does. It's like that thing is birthing kids left and right!"

Across the yard Echo was coming outside holding the birthday cake—an extra-large sheet cake Artemis had spent the better part of last night making. Arielle was beside him, holding Olympus of course. As they made their way to the center picnic table where all the children were now running with a fervor, Demitra's husband Jerry was coming across the field from the inflatable area holding Con's hand with Romulus trotting eagerly beside him.

Con took the center seat at the table while Rom stretched up on his hind legs beside him placing his paws on the tabletop. Fable could see the fascination in the eyes of the other parents as the birthday boy and his pet wolf faced the cake.

Jerry led the sing-along of the Happy Birthday song as the gathered children joined in. At the end when he sang "Happy Birthday dear Con and Romulus, Happy Birthday to you," Fable noticed a couple parents slanting their eyes to one another. She witnessed a neighbor from a few miles down who fancied herself a friend of and expert on the Blanchard family, whisper to them, "They rescued that sweet baby cub right around the time little Con was born. It's so cute how they always celebrate their birthdays together."

Fable sent her an appreciative wink and refocused on the blowing out of the candles, which only Con could successfully perform. Fable felt a familiar pang she often felt in public situations when outsiders were near. When the boys were born her grandmother Olympia warned her that she would always suffer when seeing her two sons treated so differently in life. And it was true. Rom was just as much a Blanchard as anyone else, but no one would ever know. Fable could tell that Rom sensed the difference and sometimes she thought she could see him becoming saddened over the fact. Yet when weighing everything realistically, Fable had no reason to feel melancholy about it. Things ended up being far more positive than she ever dreamed could be that night she birthed her baby wolf. Romulus was beloved in town. And though there might be inequities between the two brothers, Rom had a splendid life.

Jerry cut the cake for his grandsons and the rest of the children. Even as he laid the paper plate with Rom's large, frosted piece on the lawn, he knew the poor wolf would be throwing it back up in about half an hour on the other side of the house. Wolves generally do not digest strawberry cream cheese frosted cake very well. But there was no way he was going to snub the child. Once all the children had their slices, the adults began coming forward for a piece. Everyone in Daihmler knew one of Artemis Blanchard's cakes was not to be skipped. Even diabetic people would have taken the chance.

"Go grab me a piece a'that cake, Sarah." Zelda bellowed from the next table.

Sarah did her daughterly duty and returned with a small piece for her mother, who sent her back for a more appropriate larger slice. As Zelda heartily ate the cake Sarah grimaced at Artemis. Artemis nodded her head in understanding. In Zelda's current state of health cake was probably not the best thing for her but arguing with the old woman would be far worse.

The party began to wrap up shortly after the birthday cake, as the parents who'd dumped their kids on the Blanchards returned to collect them again and the parents who were present through the party understood it was time to wind down and head for home. It was such a rare treat to be able to spend time at Blanchard House that no one really wanted to leave. Generations ago the Blanchards were perceived as mysterious and sinister with their secrets and cliquish cloistering together. Nowadays the family was well known for their kindness and generosity—and more than a few people reported their suspicions around town that the Blanchards had stepped between them and disaster more than once.

Old Skillet cleaned up the grill and rolled it back to the pool deck where it usually stood. Artemis was walking his way to thank him once again when she saw him bending down on the lawn to scratch Rom's head and give Con a goodbye handshake.

"You be good boys for Skillet now. I'll be seeing you fellas soon."

Artemis tried to give the old man a handful of cash for his afternoon of assistance, but the old man refused. She understood. He had no family of his own and any opportunity to be around other people was a welcome distraction. This was why he was perhaps the most beloved employee at The Cobblestone restaurant.

As Skillet drove off and the final guests left, all those remaining on the lawn were family, Sarah suggested to Zelda that it was time they returned home as well. Zelda wasn't too keen on the idea.

"You go on," she said. "I'm fixin to kick back in that porch rocker and take me a nap. I'll get Fable or Tess or somebody to run me home after dinner."

Sarah looked aghast. "Momma, you haven't been invited for dinner."

Zelda shot her an indignant smirk, "Girl, I'm always invited to dinner. Gonna see if'n I can get Arty to rustle us up some pork chops or maybe fry us some chicken."

Artemis grinned and kissed the top of Zelda's head. "I'll make you whatever you want."

Zelda slowly and shakily raised herself from the picnic table with her two unsteady hands. She wobbled slightly and Artemis steadied her. "Fine. I'll go on up to the porch."

But Zelda didn't quite get to the porch. She had no sooner reached the end of the third picnic table when suddenly she felt woozy and stumbled. Thinking fast, Arielle thrust her hand in a crossing motion in Zelda's direction and propelled the picnic table bench under her backside as Zelda began to sink to the ground. As Zelda plopped onto the bench, Echo rushed toward her to catch her from tilting backward off it to the ground. Sarah ran to her mother's side.

"I'm okay, I'm okay," Zelda scoffed. "Just old and my foot stepped in a hole."

"I don't see any holes." Sarah pointed out.

"Then get your eyes checked girl, ain't nothin' wrong with me." Zelda's words were not convincing. She may have been acting as ornery as usual, but her face appeared frazzled. Scared. "Maybe you should just take me on home. Don't wanna risk stepping in another blame hole. Y'all tell Romulus to stop diggin' up the yard."

Romulus lifted his head as if he were insulted. Demitra reached down and patted his side. Seth and Echo helped Zelda to the car. As Seth went to close the passenger side door, the old woman looked up at him from her seat. It was only a moment—a split second—but never in his life had Seth seen frailty in her eyes as he did now. He reached down and gripped her shoulder. She lifted her shaky left hand to place over his. They said nothing to each other. Zelda simply gave a sharp nod which Seth returned before closing the car door.

Artemis and Demitra watched as Sarah and Zelda rode away down the drive. "I'm very worried about her." Demitra admitted.

"Me too."

CHAPTER TWO

Friends at Lunch

Blackie D'Angelo envied the ease with which her friend Nacaria could arrive places. Blackie herself had to experience the monotony of starting her car, backing out of a drive which butted against a busy street in the city of Birmingham, waiting for traffic to provide her room to enter, and hope the car air conditioning cooled things off before her make up ran. And that was all before she traversed the congested streets getting to the Five Points district where she waited in line to turn her car over to a valet to enter Che Fon Fon, the restaurant they'd chosen for their lunch date. Nacaria, on the other hand, simply had to get her husband Xander to touch her arm and propel them both through time and space until they appeared in the women's bathroom of the restaurant where Blackie was waiting, securing the door from anyone entering while Nacaria materialized. Once Nacaria popped into the bathroom of Che Fon Fon, Xander kissed her goodbye as he kissed Blackie hello and he returned in a zap back to his estate in Charleston. He'd return once his wife texted that he could pop back to retrieve her after lunch. Returning to the table Blackie already obtained for them, the two lifelong friends began to catch up on the goings on of their lives.

"I have been dying to know how everything is progressing with the triplets," Nacaria admitted as they took their seats and ordered glasses of white wine.

Blackie sighed through a proud smile and answered, "It has been a transition, I'll be honest. At least on my part. Tess, Trix, and Echo act as if they already know me, even though the woman they remember as me was never actually me. But it doesn't appear to make much of a difference to them. I suppose Barbara Blanchard and I are alike enough that it's just a big reunion for them."

"And for you?"

Blackie frowned slightly, "Difficult. I was just getting accustomed to Arielle knowing I was her mother and now I have three other children. But I like them, Nacaria. I like them so much. They really are remarkable, especially considering everything they have been through."

Everything they have been through. It was quite the understatement. Everything they had been through consisted of growing up in an alternate reality where vampires had taken over the world—and slaughtered or imprisoned most of it. The triplets had lived like action movie warriors, fighting to survive every day. They lost their mother to a vampire nest. They lost their father when good old Howard Caldwell was accidentally propelled into their reality and usurped their real father, Howard's doppelganger. It was only at a Blanchard family cookout two months ago when Blackie's arrival brought the shocking revelation that she was the doppelganger of their long-lost mother. The triplets shared Howard and Blackie's DNA, thus making them technically their biological children. Howard jumped in with both feet at playing Dad, but he'd had more time to adjust. Blackie was still acclimating to the role.

"I can tell you," Nacaria replied with a reassuring smile, "It isn't easy adjusting to life with grown children when you have missed their entire childhoods. "But it will happen. You will carve your spot out in their lives."

"If anyone can understand it's you." Blackie winked. "You've managed to build quite a beautiful relationship with your children and grandchildren."

Nacaria smiled appreciatively but then pointed out that Blackie's son and daughters would acclimate more quickly than Salem and Seth. Salem and Seth were raised by Artemis during the years Nacaria was imprisoned in Dredmore Asylum witch's prison. When Nacaria returned home she found herself at odds with the bonds and history her sister shared with her children. This wasn't the case for Blackie. Tess, Trix, and Echo had been raised by Blackie's doppelganger in an alternate world. Even though Barbara Blanchard and Blackie D'Angelo were two different women with different life experiences, they were in essence the same person. In fact, the triplets were having very little difficulty connecting to Blackie as their mother. They'd always known her. It was Blackie who was having to adjust to three strangers who turned out to be her biological children.

"Speaking of adjustments," Blackie said, moving the subject in another direction. "Is everything still harmonious at Blanchard House with my newfound children in the mix?"

Nacaria beamed, "Completely. Of course, I'm off in Charleston so I don't get home too often, but from what Artemis and Demitra tell me, things are great. Everyone has come to love the triplets. And of course, Xander and I hear nothing but joy from Arielle. She is over the moon."

Blackie smiled at the thought of her daughter experiencing such happiness. She'd waited a long time for it. "It is all quite ironic when you examine it." Blackie remarked. "Arielle grew up so alone. She and Cassandra were never close. Atheidrelle regarded Ari as something to despise. She rather enjoyed crushing her spirit. When Arielle found Salem and Seth, I was elated for her. Finally, she had a family. And now, with the addition of the triplets, Arielle is related to everyone! Not only are Salem and Seth her sister and brother, and she has finally built a relationship with Cassandra—but now she has Echo, Tess, and Trix. Arielle has a plethora of siblings."

"So much has changed for us all." Nacaria agreed. "Xander and I are happier than either of us ever had a right to be. And speaking of Cassandra—she and I have grown quite close. I cannot believe sometimes she is the same person who held me prisoner for months. With her mother dead and gone, Cassandra has truly experienced a metamorphosis."

Blackie didn't return as bright a smile as Nacaria would have expected. But then again, Blackie never enjoyed a mention of her evil sister Atheidrelle. Too much bad blood lay there to ever move past.

As orders for lunch were placed and a couple additional glasses of wine poured, the friends moved the topic into other areas. Nacaria talked about Xander's desire to return the Oleander plantation back to a producing tea plantation again. Decades ago in his father's time, Oleander was quite prosperous in the tea industry. Now that Xander had relinquished his seat on the council of witches to his daughter Salem, he had nothing but time on his hands and wanted to start again.

Nacaria also shared her accomplishments in making strides to enter Charlestonian society. Becoming Mrs. Obreiggon opened quite a few doors for her, and she was enjoying being part of something outside of the world of witchcraft. She had joined a patron of the arts league. She also spearheaded a charity to help impoverished Charlestonians from the poorer side of town to send their children to college. Furthermore, Nacaria had orchestrated a movement to remove statues depicting Confederate soldiers as war heroes from Battery Park. Of course, Charleston being Charleston, her latter endeavor failed miserably. But at least she tried.

Blackie listened happily, taking much joy in seeing her friend so fulfilled. But of course, whenever one speaks of the good in life, the bad must soon follow.

"I don't get to see my sisters as often as I would like," Nacaria divulged. "Xander and I pop home sometimes on Friday nights for family dinner, but lately the dinners have been put on hold."

"Why?" Blackie asked.

"Zelda."

"What's wrong with Zelda?"

The delicate, timeless features of Nacaria's face stiffened slightly as she revealed, "Zelda is dying. Her heart is wearing out quickly."

Blackie did not know Zelda very well but was saddened by the report. She knew the colorful gregarious character was a fixture in the lives of the Blanchard family. And Zelda was one of the last true heroes of their time. Too few people remembered just how many times she and Olympia and Pastoria Blanchard saved the world, or at least some of it, back in their youth.

"Can nothing be done?" Blackie asked. "A healing perhaps?"

Nacaria shook her head. Zelda was old, far too old to expect a healing witch to keep her living unnaturally. If Beryl were still around it might be easier, but at some point, every witch must accept their time to go.

"Demitra and Artemis are with her round the clock these days." Nacaria continued. "It's going to be hard for everyone, but especially them, when Zelda's time comes."

"How is Seth these days?"

"Better," Nacaria said sadly, "But only moderately. After Yasmine died, he shut down completely. But Xander was able to snap him back a little. At least he comes out of his room now and interacts with his children. But he is not the same. I fear he never will be."

CHAPTER THREE

Farewell, Old Friend

Artemis Blanchard and her sister Demitra were taking shifts during the day to be with their old friend, Madame Zelda. Zelda's first heart attack came by surprise that August, shocking everyone. By the time the second attack came in early September, the venerable woman knew her time was drawing near. She recovered, as they all hoped she would, but she had been left winded, lethargic, and empty of the bountiful zest for life they had always known Zelda to have. Her daughters, Sarah and Melinda, took loving care of their mother every night, but neither was able to miss work during the daytime. The daily help the Blanchard sisters gave had been a blessing.

Zelda insisted on remaining in her home while she awaited death to come. Her inability to leave her bed made round-the-clock care necessary. Artemis and Demitra rotated days while Melinda and Sarah rotated nights. Of course, outside help would have been possible. The Blanchards had plenty of money to hire any help needed, but neither Artemis and Demitra nor Sarah and Melinda had any desire to turn Zelda's final moments over to a stranger. She was one of their own, and they would take care of her until the final breath. That final breath was coming more sooner than later. When Sarah heard her mother's lungs making what old southerners called "the death rattle", all four women sat vigil round the clock that day in late September.

None of this would have been necessary if Demitra Blanchard's daughter, Beryl, were still around. Beryl had been a witch with a remarkable power to heal the sick. She had spent her life helping people, but now when one of their own—practically a family member—needed healing, Beryl was beyond reach. She had evolved. Transcended. Beryl had become God, or at least one of whatever beings existed out there who had become much too enlightened for the mortal world. However, it was doubtful Zelda would have accepted Beryl's help had Beryl even been around. Demitra's great-grandson, Echo, possessed the ability to heal, although not always reliably, and Zelda refused his offer during one of her moments of mental clarity, insisting she would face her natural fate gracefully.

"It's getting closer," Demitra said aloud without meaning to. Possessing the power of clairvoyance, she could sense Zelda's light dimming. Demitra looked over to her sister on the other side of Zelda's bed. "This is hard. We just lost Aunt Pastoria and now this. How do we say goodbye to old Zelda?"

Artemis wiped a tear from her cheek as she swiped back a few strands of her long black hair. "By giving her the dignity she deserves."

Sarah and Melinda were seated at the foot of their mother's bed with the Blanchard sisters sitting at Zelda's side. The four women all reached out to clasp one another's hands, the shared love for the old woman uniting them. The four of them had always known each other. They had grown up together, but Zelda always preferred the company of her best friend Olympia Blanchard's children to her own. Sarah and Melinda never resented the Blanchards in their mother's life, and now seeing the dedication the Blanchard sisters were showing their mother at the end, they understood the admiration was mutual. Artemis and Demitra truly loved their mom.

"It is the end of an era, isn't it?" Sarah commented. "Olympia's gone. Pastoria is gone. Now Momma's dying. All that talk of their youthful adventures they bored us to tears with is over. They had a sisterhood we never really understood."

"And now the last sister is going to join them," Artemis smiled. "I don't know what I'll do without Zelda. It's like losing Mother all over again."

Demitra grinned. "Zel really stepped in after Mother died, didn't she? She always had our backs."

Melinda gave an involuntary chuckle. "I think you guys got the best in her. Sarah and I, not so much. Oh, she loved us, but it was you girls she felt the closest to."

"I bet that hurt," Artemis whispered. "I'm sorry."

"Oh, don't be!" Melinda smiled. "Sarah and I were never gonna live up to what she expected. Momma had too much action in her life with your mother and the rest of your family than we were ever gonna be able to provide. She needed that adventure. Sarah and I were pretty boring in comparison. Frankly, I'm grateful she had y'all."

Zelda began to stir in the bed. Her craggily wrinkled face twitched as one eye slowly raised open. She looked confused at first. Opening her other eye, she scanned the room as she tried to sit up. It proved too much effort, and she sank back into her pillows, her eyes still open as she grinned.

"My girls," she said. "All my girls."

"You need to rest, Momma," Sarah cautioned.

"Like hell," Zelda scoffed. "What am I restin' for? To do a pole dance? I'm fixin' to die. Let me see my girls one last time and say my peace."

Artemis wiped Zelda's face with a cool cloth and gently stroked her magenta-colored bangs from her eyes. She leaned down and kissed the old woman's cheek and assisted her to sit up. Zelda gave her a weak but thankful smile and looked out to the end of her bed to her daughters.

"I did love you two fools, you know."

"We know, Momma," Melinda replied.

"I know I ain't never said it, least not enough, but I'm mighty proud of you girls."

"Really, Momma?" Sarah gasped with joy.

"No, not really," Zelda replied in her candid Zelda way. "Why you gotta always press me on these things when I'm a tryin' to be nice? I am just tryin' to say you mean a lot to me. You and Melinda here did right by me in my old age, and I guess I shoulda been better to you all these years. Don't go through life frettin' over what we coulda been better at. You were good girls. And I love you both very much. That's all you gotta take through life after I go."

"We love you too, Momma," Sarah said.

Zelda looked over to Demitra. "You and me sure had some scuffy spots didn't we, Demmy? But you know I love you. And don't let this go to your head, but I reckon you're about the best Mother I have ever seen. I wish I'd been half a momma the way you have been to your girls. And now the way you see after Howard and his chil'ren...and your grandyoungens from Fable. You're all right, kid. You keep tending to your family. Outta all three of Lympy's girls, you're the most like your momma."

Her words brought tears to Demitra's eyes. Demitra kissed the old woman's hand and held it to her cheek. Zelda turned her attention now to Artemis. For a moment she said nothing as she battled a round of coughing. Her heart began to skip here and there from the impact of it. Zelda could tell it was going to stop beating very soon. Finally, she recovered enough to speak to Artemis.

"It's all on you now, Arty," she grinned. "You ain't got me here no more to back you up. This is where you figure out that your momma knew 'xactly what she was doin' when she put you in charge of the family. I'm so proud of you and the woman you are. I could bust. Keep this family a'goin. Keep the Blanchards strong like all the ones who came before you did. I love you. But I ain't really gotta tell you that."

"No, you don't Zelda," Artemis said with a cracked voice. "I know. I know."

Zelda sat quietly for a little while. Her eyes were closed but she was not asleep. Zapped of energy from her goodbyes, she needed to lay still and wait for whatever was coming. She did not have to wait very long. She felt it. Like a vibration beginning from inside her. Opening her eyes, she could see the four women around her bed watching her intently. She knew from their expressions that they knew her time was here. But she didn't really need them to know that. She could see it for herself as the bright glowing form grew larger at the foot of her bed behind her daughters. Zelda knew they could not see what she saw, but that did not make it nonetheless real.

Zelda squeezed Demitra's hand, "She's here. I see her."

"Who, Momma?" Sarah asked, "Olympia?"

"Naw," Zelda said, smiling brightly. "Beryl's here."

Demitra sat straight up in the chair, turning to look behind her in hopes of seeing her eldest daughter's presence. She could not see Beryl. Whatever Zelda was seeing it was obvious that only Zelda was entitled to see it.

"I ain't got words," Zelda muttered, mesmerized by the sight only she could see. "You come to get me, Beryl?"

Sarah, Melinda, Artemis, and Demitra looked at each other. Nothing had changed inside the bedroom. No bright light, no phantom wind rushing past. No sounds emitting from the ether. But Zelda was clearly experiencing something extraordinary.

"I'm fixin' to go with Beryl now. Y'all won't believe what she is now. She's come to take me home. She says Lympy's waitin' for me with your Daddy. Y'all won't believe what I see. Beryl. She's magnificent."

Slowly Zelda's eyes dimmed as her body relaxed into lifelessness. She was gone. Madame Zelda was dead. No one said a word for a long time. Although a deep sadness prevailed in the room, also in the room was an astounding sensation that they had just witnessed Zelda moving on to the next life, escorted on the arm of God. How could they bring themselves to cry over Zelda's departure? Zelda was now with Beryl. And her beloved Lympy.

CHAPTER FOUR

The Consort

The week leading up to the Consort meeting went by in a fury of hustle and bustle. Decades had passed since the Blanchards hosted one of the Witches Association events and Artemis was determined to make Blanchard House shine. Her mother would have appreciated that. Over the last couple of weeks, Olympia's flower beds and vegetable garden had been infiltrated by rabbits. Artemis was not about to have hundreds of fellow witches wandering the grounds only to balk at the shoddy garden her mother once took so much pride in. Fable took care of things. Walking out to the edge of the field behind the house, she used her mind to summon reinforcements. Within a few minutes several bucks with beautiful, pointed antlers emerged from the woods and approached Fable.

"I need you guys to guard our garden, please. Rabbits and gophers—you know, the usual culprits. If you will stand guard for the next few days and keep our gardens lovely, I will let you have first pick from the vegetable garden the very next day after our party."

The deer made a bow of their heavy heads. The Blanchard family took astonished pleasure every day after watching from the porch as at least one, sometimes two, deer stood sentry alongside the gardens, chasing off any animal who dared try to pilfer. Sometimes Romulus joined the deer and chased the rabbits back off into the fields. Once or twice, he caught one, but his mother scolded him and warned him he was not allowed to kill the furry creatures. The boy in Rom obeyed, but the wolf in him seemed to slink away with an "Aw Mom!" kind of attitude.

Construction crews were on site most of the week building the necessary structures required to host such an elaborate event. Using his powers to control the weather, Seth made certain the rainy forecast skipped the Blanchard property keeping the workers from any delays. Blanchard House was a madhouse of preparations. The family did what they could themselves and hired out the more strenuous tasks. Artemis replaced the old, summer blooms from the beds and hanging baskets around the long front porch with fall flowers. Although she was never a fan of mums, she had little choice but to line the porch with them. Seth and Echo did not enjoy being the designated weed pullers and planters of new shrubs. Fable, Salem, Arielle, Trix, and Tess had not enjoyed getting the house spruced up either. Luckily, Arielle took care of all the exterior windows on the house using her knack for floating, soapy sponges into the air along with a hose to wash them clean.

Artemis Blanchard stood in the yard on the day of the Consort, surveying the house and the land around it making sure everything was perfect before the guests arrived. Blanchard House shined like a new penny, and the lawn and gardens were a showplace. The Blanchard family was ready to host the Autumn Consort.

The cars began their descent onto Blanchard land as the sun began to set, sending its final rays of reds and golds over the horizon. Parking attendants from Artemis' restaurant took the cars from guests as they pulled down the driveway, relocating vehicles out of site in the east meadow. Guests entered the grounds through an arbor of blooming moon flowers, making their way to the lawns where a series of elaborate canvas cottage tents were set up. Each tent was extravagantly appointed with lush fabrics, floor rugs, velvet couches, coffee tables, dining tables, hanging art, and bright lighting fixtures. Included in every tent was a fully stocked bar with bartender as well as a food station where the best cooks from The Cobblestone restaurant whipped up an array of offerings for the varied tastes of the many Consort members. The chefs were being overseen by Artemis' right-hand man, Skillet. The colorful old man had worked at The Cobblestone through three different owners. Artemis liked him. With no family of his own, all the staff at the restaurant were his children. Artemis knew the feeling.

"Miss Artemis, this place sure does spruce up real nice," Skillet said, approaching his boss. "And our cooks sure are making up a feast."

"Well, I know I can leave everything to you, Skillet, and enjoy my party. You'll keep it all running smoothly."

"You know I will, Missy," Skillet's bright toothy smile filled his face. Artemis recently paid for new dentures for the old man and ever since he smiled ear to ear when he spoke. "I done told the waitstaff to feed the fat people first. Fat people gotta be fed first else they get real anxious and start poking up some trouble."

"I don't believe we have a great many fat people coming tonight," Artemis smiled.

"I worked a party once for a plus-size actor guild. Lordy, the main course was running late and before you know'd it those folks done turned on the skinniest fat one and darn near yanked her hair out cause she ate the last shrimp cocktail on the tray. She left that party crying, dress all torn, and a busted lip while everybody else sat down to eat their beef wellington."

Artemis snickered at the old man. Skillet had a story for everything. As she watched him return to one of the tents to monitor the staff, she thought of Zelda. She wished Zelda could be here tonight. She began to greet her guests as they were arriving. So many faces she had not seen in years. It seemed to Artemis that many Consort members who may have long skipped Consort meetings were all coming out for this one. Perhaps all it took to rouse these sporadic association members into attendance was for the Blanchards to be hosting a Consort. The notion made Artemis feel proud. She was certain Olympia would be. There had been other Consort meetings in the past, hosted by other families, which were more ostentatious or elegant, but no one could deny that the Blanchard family succeeded in creating an intimate environment, richly appointed to make every guest satisfied.

"How much did this cost you guys?" Blackie D'Angelo asked her friend Artemis as she studied the layout with its many elaborate tents, bars, food stations, and bands playing softly in the background.

"I honestly don't know," Artemis admitted. "I sent the bills to Howard's office. From the red-faced emojis he texted me yesterday afternoon, I can assume it amounted to more than he expected to pay."

Blackie laughed and slapped her friend's arm. "And how is my ex-husband from another reality doing these days?"

Artemis gave a wink and said, "You can ask him yourself. He is going to be here tonight. Didn't the children tell you?"

Blackie shook her head, "The first couple of times I spent with the triplets they tried matchmaking to bring us together. But I think I have finally made it clear that Howard Caldwell and I are total strangers and not going to become the couple they remember from their childhood. I think the triplets have finally allowed that dream to die. For now, we are just working on establishing some sort of relationship with one another—not an easy task considering they share my DNA, yet I never gave birth to them."

"At least you're not a year younger than your grandson," Demitra Blanchard quipped from behind as she sauntered up. She gave her friend a welcoming hug.

Life for the Blanchards, as well as Blackie D'Angelo, had taken quite a turn several months ago when a spell gone awry hurled several family members to the past and back again, upending the family timeline. The result produced an array of changes to the Blanchard family's lives. Demitra was now the grandmother of longtime family friend and financial manager Howard Caldwell. Howard was now the father of three adult children—new Blanchards previously unheard of. Triplets Tess, Echo, and Trix were still getting to know their father and after only just discovering their biological mother from their original timeline, was none other than Blackie D'Angelo, they were all doing their best to bond. It was quite a confusing situation for everyone to navigate, but so far it was going well.

On the porch of the house, had one been observing, Nacaria Blanchard Obreiggon would have been seen materializing on the arm of her husband Xander, with his daughter Cassandra. Xander, having the power to zap to any location he desired within the blink of an eye, had little need for driving—especially considering the Obreiggons were coming from their home in Charleston. Nacaria was dressed in a lavender silk, Halston-style gown. Her golden, almost platinum, blonde hair curled at the waist and over one eye. Older generations would have likened her to Veronica Lake, but by today's standards she was incomparable. Cassandra Obreiggon looked very much like her mother had when she was still alive, however Cassandra lacked the icy wickedness. Xander was still quite a handsome man with wavy, light-brown hair and a proud gait. He'd changed over time. Once he'd been mousy and slack-shouldered when bound in marriage to his previous wife.

Nacaria sent her husband and stepdaughter out onto the lawn to mingle while she darted into the house to find her children for a quick hello. Salem was upstairs in her room, feeding her infant son, Olympus, when her mother bounded in.

"Give me that baby!" Nacaria exclaimed. "I've missed him so much."

"Mother, you were here for dinner last week."

"Has it been that long?" Nacaria smiled as she lifted her grandson into her arms.

"Grandma!" squealed young Hera Blanchard from the hallway as she saw her grandmother in her aunt Salem's room. Behind Hera trotted her toddler brother, Titan.

Nacaria knelt to welcome all her grandchildren into her arms. For a moment she felt a sense of deep gratitude. There had been a time not too many years ago when she never would have imagined any of this being possible. Now she had everything. Married to the love of her life, close with her once estranged children, and beloved by her grandbabies. Nacaria Blanchard Obreiggon was completely happy for the first time in her life.

"You two come back here!" called a voice down the hall. It was Miranda Perkins. Miranda had been living with the Blanchards for several months. A refugee from another reality where her world was devoured by vampires, Miranda lived at Blanchard House now as a kind of self-appointed nanny to the children.

"Miranda, we want to see Grandma!" Hera squealed.

"Yes, I know," Miranda smiled at the little girl. "But Grandma and Aunt Salem have to get downstairs to the party. You, your brother, cousins, and I are going to watch a movie in the upstairs den and have some delicious snacks."

Nacaria shrugged to her grandchildren. "Miranda is right. I really do need to get back downstairs."

"When can we go to the Consort, Grandma?" Hera asked.

Nacaria patted her granddaughter's head and stroked her lovely brown curls. "When you're older and big witches. For now, you best go back with Miranda. Grandma will come kiss you in bed before she leaves tonight, I promise you."

Nacaria watched Miranda escort the children away. She felt a hardness in her throat as she saw Hera trot away, looking back behind her to blow Nacaria a kiss. Little Titan was barely able to keep up alongside them with his little feet. Hera looked so much like her mother, except for Seth's eyes. And Titan, he would never even remember his mother. Nacaria ached for them. Losing Yasmine was a hard blow to everyone, but for those children it would now mark their lives forever.

Outside on the lawn the many members of the Witches Association had all arrived and were now mingling before the meeting began. Tess, Echo, and Trix clung closely together, unsure of themselves among all the strangers. Blackie was nearby, talking with past Queen of the Consort, Ursula Craven. Seeing the triplets feeling out of place, she ended her talk and made her way over to them.

"Mom!" Echo exclaimed, giving her a peck on the cheek.

Blackie blushed. "I am still getting used to that."

She gave the girls a hug and linked arms with her "children". Blackie D'Angelo normally lived a life of quiet solitude. Not many friends and never a serious lover. The childhood home she escaped left its indelible mark on her, directing her to the welcome isolation she created. Discovering a few months ago that in another life—another reality—she had loved a man, been married, and birthed three children, came as quite a shock to her system. These children *remembered* her—remembered growing up with her love and protection. The fact that she had no knowledge of them at all did not lessen their affections for her, so Blackie was doing her best to make space in her life for three grown children she was inexplicably biologically connected to.

"We never had anything like this at home," Tess whispered. "It's overwhelming."

"Stick close to me, and I'll guide you through it," Blackie smiled reassuringly.

For all her years keeping a distance from people, Blackie had to admit to herself that she rather liked these kids. She didn't even mind very much that the story of their origin into her life had spread through the witching world and was now known by practically everyone. She was proud to be considered their mother. Tess, with her shoulder length honey blonde hair, looked far more like her grandmother, Beryl Blanchard, than she resembled Blackie. But Trix—Trix was a different story. She looked exactly like her sister except for darker brown locks, but her strong willed and fearless personality, that was Blackie all the way. And of course, the boy, Echo. He was his own kind of man, but there was no denying he had Blackie's crow-black hair.

Howard Caldwell approached, looking even more nervous than his children were. He had acclimated to his new offspring much easier than Blackie, but he had not yet managed to accept himself as a blood bonafide witch. This world was all still quite new to him. Howard presented Blackie with a glass of chilled champagne.

"Thank you," she nodded. "You appear to be as unsettled as these three."

"I've never seen anything like this before," Howard confessed. "I know I am supposed to be here because it is somehow necessary for the Blanchard Coven, but to tell the truth I'd rather be home watching the basketball game. I'm really only here because Artemis made me come."

Howard only learned in the past few months that not only was he a Blanchard, but he was also a witch. Both took him by complete surprise. Now standing on the lawn amid hundreds of witches gathered for their Association meeting, he felt more out of place than at any time in his life.

"But isn't it great to be all together again?" Tess beamed, leaning her head onto Howard's shoulder.

"Tess forgets reality sometimes," Trix, the more outspoken one, replied. "*We* are having a reunion, but do you two even really know each other very well?"

Blackie raised one of her perfectly shadowed brows and answered, "No, not at all. I believe Howard and I may have met once or twice decades ago in passing when Nacaria and I were young, but until you three came along we had no tangible affiliation."

"Boy we do now," Howard chuckled.

Across the lawn Fable nudged her cousin Seth and directed his attention toward Blackie and the others. "That is the weirdest thing I may have ever seen. And I gave birth to a canine."

Seth sniggered. "Who would ever have imagined those two would get together in life and have kids, even in an alternate universe?"

"You think they'll fall in love in this world?"

Seth shook his head. "No. Howard has always been in love with Aunt Artemis. I don't see him falling for Blackie D'Angelo."

"Well, he can't be with Artemis now. Not since he is her grandnephew." Fable paused, taking a sip of her cocktail before tilting her head, elbowing Seth in the arm and adding, "But you married your cousin, so who knows?"

Seth flinched a little at the joke. It was funny, but he did not like to be reminded of Yasmine. It was still far too painful. Of course she was never out of his thoughts, but those thoughts were private. Somehow speaking her name aloud took his internal pain and hung it around his shoulders like an anchor. He turned his attention to the lawn entrance and directed his Fable to follow his gaze. "Look who's here! Our other half!"

Entering the lawn underneath the arbor of moonflowers, walked the Mobile branch of the Blanchard family. Seneca Blanchard and his brother Drake headed the pack with their respective children Ocean, Sage, and Sydney following behind them. As with most Blanchard reunions, Seneca and Drake split off in the direction of the cousins they grew up with; Artemis, Demitra, and Nacaria while the younger trio waved to Seth and Fable as they headed their direction.

"Ocean! Sage! Sydney!" Seth exclaimed, hugging his cousins and passing each one over to Fable.

"Seth," Sydney said, clinging to him tearfully. "I was so sorry about Yaz. I wanted to come, but Daddy said y'all had enough going on. I've thought of you and the kids every day."

"Thanks, Syd," Seth smiled uncomfortably.

"We've been thinking about you guys too," Fable frowned. "Especially now. Tonight's going to be hard on you, I know."

"I never expected life to be so empty without Grandmother," Sage confided. "But then again, you guys know all about that kind of thing. I still can't believe both she and Aunt Olympia are gone now."

Fable nodded, wiping a solitary tear as she agreed, "Everything is so different. This place is full these days, but still so empty with Olympia and Beryl gone. And now Zelda."

"We are definitely getting older I guess," Seth nodded. "We are now the middle generation. Never saw that coming!"

"Speak for yourself, cousin," Ocean laughed. "You are the ones with kids. The three of us are still the babies of our family!"

"Keep thinking that," Fable mocked. "You're all out of college now. That's pretty adult. Soon you'll be having kids, too, and you'll feel as old as we do."

"Not me!" Sydney stated. "I have too many cases of abandoned kids or children in terrible homes. All my caregiving attention goes to children already on this earth who need me."

"That's right!" Fable remembered. "You're a full-fledged social worker now. I bet you see a lot of horrendous homelife situations."

"It's heartbreaking," Sydney said. "I oversee programs I was able to institute to try and help, and that pretty much eats up all of my time."

"Sounds like you love what you do despite the awful side," Fable noted. "Can't pay well though."

"No, it doesn't," Sydney said. "But thanks to your grandmother tricking my grandmother into thinking she inherited a natural gas field, our family has enough income to supplement the shortfall."

Seth and Fable looked at each other in confusion. "We have no idea what you are talking about," Seth said.

Sage slapped Seth on the shoulder and grinned. "Good old Aunt Olympia. She finagled some kind of deal where our grandmother thought our granddad left her some land with gas on it. Everybody in our family knew it was Olympia's doing, except our grandmother. Pastoria would have never taken it if she knew her big sister bailed her out of financial ruin."

Fable winked at Seth. "Hecate sure was full of surprises."

...

Inside one of the elaborate adorned tents, Artemis and Seneca Blanchard stood at the bar awaiting two Cosmos being made by one of her staff. Their conversation took several pauses as fellow witches passing by stopped to offer condolences to Seneca or to offer congratulations to Artemis for such a successful Consort party. Taking their drinks to an empty high-top table in the corner, the two cousins finally found a little privacy.

"How are you handling being coven leader now?" Artemis asked him.

"It's a great deal more responsibility than I was previously aware," Seneca said. "I never knew just how much information a coven leader has that the rest of us never knew about."

Artemis smiled brightly and laid her hand atop his. "Finally!" she exclaimed. "Someone I can talk to who understands! We never knew any of this stuff before. We were living in a blissful ignorance I now realize."

"I know, right?" Seneca grinned. "All the secrets we are now in on and still have to keep from the others!"

"Yes!"

"I had no idea my mom and your mom were such badasses in their day," Seneca whispered. "They literally saved the world a few times."

"It is crazy what you find out when the responsibility lands on your shoulders," Artemis commiserated. "Now you and I have each other, Seneca. We can talk about it all together, and we can turn to each other when we need advice or help. I had no clue how much Mother and Aunt Pastoria had to shoulder."

"You know about the vault, don't you?" Seneca said in a low voice.

"Yes! Mother told me about the secret second vault before she died."

"So did mine!" Seneca gasped. "I was blown away. She said she had never seen it but knew where her father built it. Of course, if I ever have need of it, I would obviously clear it with you first. It is in your house after all."

"Yes, but Blanchard House belongs to all Blanchards. Even though we live here, and I technically own it, these lands are just as much yours and your family's as any of ours."

"Thank you for that," Seneca smiled. "And thanks for allowing Mom to have her remains buried here in the family cemetery. At least what will be left after the cremation and after we take the bone dust. It was her wish to return home."

"This was her home for a long time," Artemis said. "She should be here. In the end, I suppose we will all be here."

. . .

The sounds of the party reached across the meadow, breaking the tranquility of the somber family graveyard where Ocean Blanchard stood inside the iron gates staring down at his brother's grave. The wind shifted slightly, muting some of the drifting chatter and music. He heard a crunch from a ground twig behind him and turned around to see who had followed him.

"I'm sorry," the young woman said, her brilliant red hair shining under the moonlight. "I didn't mean to invade your privacy. I just felt like I should talk to you."

Ocean had never met her before but certainly knew who she was. "Arielle."

Arielle examined Ocean Blanchard more closely; he looked so much like his brother, only a little taller and broader shouldered. He shared Forest's wavy hair, only Ocean's was black, not brown, and longer—chin length. He looked like a surfer.

"I wanted to express to you how sorry I am for your brother's death. I still feel partially responsible."

Ocean shook his head. "You weren't."

Arielle sat down on the little bench by Forest's grave. It was at that moment Ocean noticed none of the other graves had a seat beside them. Obviously, Arielle came out here a lot. She pushed a few strands of her long, red hair out of her eyes and tucked them behind her ear. The look of sadness upon her face made Ocean temporarily forget his own grief. He took a seat beside her.

"It was my mother—or rather the woman I believed to be my mother, who possessed my body and killed him."

"Again, that was not your fault," Ocean repeated. "You were in love with him?"

Arielle sighed and looked off into the distance. "I was well on my way. If given more time, I think Forest and I would have had a life together. Our romance was so brief. I still have trouble measuring its impact on me."

"How so?"

"It wasn't like we were Seth and Yaz or anything as deep. Like I said it was the very beginning of something. Sometimes I feel guilty that his death didn't devastate me, though I did grieve and still do. But now I feel more like the custodian of his memory. His life was cut short so young. He didn't have a wife or children. I feel like it's up to me to keep honoring him and the brief time he walked on this earth. I can't let him disappear from people's memory. So, I make sure to remember him every day and come out here when I can to honor his existence even if there is nothing to show he was once here."

"I think that's beautiful, Arielle," Ocean said quietly. "But know he is remembered at home by us. I understand that here it's like he was just passing through this branch of the family's experience. But Forest left his mark with us in Mobile. Still, I appreciate how you try to honor his life."

Arielle looked up at Ocean and asked, with misty eyes, "Did he ever mention me to you?"

Ocean gave a surprising chuckle. "Oh yeah. He was really into you. I think it was as you said, it was the start of something. Not technically in love but well on its way. I used to tease him about it when he called me."

"Tease him?" Arielle replied. "About me?"

Ocean blushed. "I would ask him how his little mermaid was. I remember once when you two went out to dinner in Charleston. He told me you guys had lobster and shrimp. I asked him, 'You mean you made her eat her friends?'"

Arielle looked confused. She didn't get it. Ocean nudged her arm, "You know... The Little Mermaid? Ariel? You even have the same color hair."

"Oh. I never thought about that."

"Really?" he said in surprise. "Kids didn't make fun of your name in school?"

"I wasn't around other children often," Arielle answered.

Ocean was surprised. His childhood in public school was filled with friends and regular childhood activities. "You didn't have friends?"

"No," Arielle replied. "My first real friends were the Blanchards."

"Well, please consider me your friend now," Ocean smiled. "I think Forest would have liked it if you and I became friends. You and I are the keepers of his memory."

Arielle liked that thought. She gave Ocean's hand a gentle squeeze and excused herself back to the party. She knew he needed some time alone with his thoughts and his brother. She felt a little lighter as she trekked back to the gaiety and commotion of the tents. Ocean had absolved her of the guilt she'd carried. If Forest's own brother did not blame her for his death, perhaps she could stop blaming herself so much.

CHAPTER FIVE

Ashes to Ashes

The Autumn Consort meeting of the Witches Association began. In the freshly mowed field behind Blanchard House, seven circular rows of chairs were situated around a center circle where the five Council members and the king sat facing each area of the circle. The two branches of the Blanchard family sat together, along with Zelda's daughters, Melinda and Sarah. Their group filled a great expanse of three rows. Demitra placed herself next to Howard and the triplets so that each of them was within a lean's reach to whisper words of assurance in case they felt ill at ease. Nacaria sat at the end of a row beside her son, next to her husband—bridging the transition to the Obreiggon family's section where her husband and two stepdaughters sat. Arielle Obreiggon was paying little attention to the king and mostly waving and smiling at her sister, Salem, seated at the Council table. Salem had become a member of the governing witches council a few years ago, and it always thrilled Arielle to see her seated among them.

King Geoffrey finished recounting the association's old business and was wrapping up new business. "Are there any other member requests to be made before we move forward?"

Artemis stood to address the Council. "Your majesty, Council members—as the head of the Blanchard Coven of Daihmler I would like to officially add new members to our coven roster."

King Geoffrey, already knowing what she was going to say, as almost everyone among them did, nodded to Artemis so that she could continue with the necessary formality.

"The Blanchards request new members to our coven be recorded and accepted into the Witches Association."

"Name your new members," Geoffrey asked.

Artemis looked lovingly to the nervous faces of her new relatives. Demitra leaned forward and gave the triplets a supportive shoulder squeeze. "Howard Caldwell Blanchard." Artemis leaned forward and tugged Howard's arm to direct him to stand up. He did. "Tess Blanchard." Tess joined her father standing before the Council. "Beatrix Blanchard."

"Trix," Trix corrected as she stood with her sister and father.

Artemis grinned and continued, "Record her as Trix, please. And lastly Nathan Blanchard, record him as Echo."

Old family friend Brimford Uding winked at the new members and made the notations in the official journal. The congregation clapped for the new additions to their association as Howard and the children returned to their seats.

King Geoffrey resumed the meeting. "If that concludes any member's requests, I will now turn the meeting over to Council member Salem Blanchard."

Salem stood up from the Council table and addressed the audience. "Tonight, we sadly have to dispose of the remains of two of our most beloved Consort members. Would the representatives of those families please stand and address the Consort?"

Seneca Blanchard stood along with Zelda's eldest daughter Sarah. Both requested the Association allow the cremations of their deceased loved ones. Both also officially requested the Blanchard family allow the remains to be interred in the Blanchard family cemetery. Artemis stood to grant the requests.

The meeting of the Consort was adjourned. While the Consort members returned to their drinks, food, and gossip, Artemis led the Council and the family members of the deceased witches to a patch of land just beyond the family cemetery. The two pyres of kindling were already in place side by side, ready for the bodies of the dead to be placed upon it.

Artemis stood with Sarah and Melinda, clutching their hands as dear old Zelda was marched forward—carried by Seth and Howard—lovingly laid atop an elaborately-woven thatched bed decorated with exotic flowers as colorful as the old woman had been in life. The men placed the bed gently atop the wood piling.

Ocean and Sage carried their grandmother, Pastoria, upon a similar bed to be laid upon the second pyre. Pastoria's sons and grandchildren stood before her body as the lit torch was tossed by Drake onto the oil-soaked wood. Artemis stood with Zelda's daughters as Seth tossed Zelda's torch onto her pile. It was Zelda's wish for it to be him. Her daughters had no protests. They understood their mother's special kinship to the Blanchards. No one said a word as two of the most beloved witches in Consort history were returned to the ash from which they came.

Once the bodies were aflame, Artemis led the families back to the shelters on the lawn to await their bone dust to be collected and presented to the family members. Seth and Ocean had each volunteered for those jobs. Ocean, out of respect to the grandmother he loved, and Seth out of affection for the dear friend who would always have a special place in his heart.

"I'm gonna miss betting on football games with you," Seth said to the ash as he scooped it into a large jar. "You're with your *Lympy* now. Pastoria is too. The three of you are together again. We love you, Zelda. We will never, ever forget what you mean to this family. Thank you, old friend. We never had a better one."

...

Nacaria and Xander watched their son from afar as he and Ocean began to bury their loved ones' remains in the Blanchard family graveyard. Blackie walked up and stood beside them.

"Seth was close to Zelda it seems."

"Very," Nacaria nodded. "They had an interesting relationship."

Xander gave his ex-sister-in-law a gentle hug and commented, "How are you finding motherhood?"

Blackie half laughed and replied, "I was just getting accustomed to Arielle knowing I was her mother, and now I have three more."

"Well, Ari is over the moon about having a new brother and two new sisters!" Xander exclaimed. "It is all she talks about. And the fact that she and Echo now work together in Howard's office makes her even happier."

"That's what Nacaria was telling me at lunch a couple of weeks ago," Blackie told Xander. She was about to comment on how well it pleased her, but she suddenly caught sight of something she hoped she would never see. She turned to Xander to see if he saw it as well. He did. His face reflected his displeasure. Across the lawn, the triplets were being approached by the last person Blackie ever hoped they would meet.

"I have been so anxious to make the acquaintance of the three of you," said a dark, almost sinister looking man with a short trimmed brown beard and hair.

"Really?" Trix asked. "Who might you be?"

"I am your uncle," the man replied. "I am Thaddeuss D'Angelo."

Before anyone had a moment to digest the information, Blackie sailed in to situate herself between her brother and the triplets.

"What are you doing here, Thaddeuss?"

"It is a Consort, isn't it my dear little sister?"

"Last time I checked you had withdrawn from the association."

"Things change," Thaddeuss smirked. "As these three are the best testimony to. My word, Barbara, three new D'Angelos. You've done well."

"These children are not D'Angelos," Blackie countered. "They are Blanchards."

"Only by half," Thaddeuss sneered. "The rest of their blood flows through our veins as well. Imagine, witches who possess both Blanchard and D'Angelo blood. What a combination."

"Stay away from my children," Blackie warned. There was a fierceness in Blackie's tone which took the triplets by surprise. Whatever animosities ran between Blackie and her brother ran deep.

Tess, Trix, and Echo didn't understand what was happening, but more than the discomfort of the situation, they were pleasantly shocked to hear themselves addressed by Blackie as *her children*. It made them feel a joy they had not known they'd been without.

"I have no reason to cause distress to your children, Barbara. They are my nieces and my nephew. I only want to get to know them better."

"My name is Tess," the more generous one smiled, extending her hand.

Blackie pushed it back and reprimanded her. "This is not a man you need to know."

Thaddeuss smiled with amusement. "Your mother has never been the most courteous member of our family, my dear."

"I went through a lot to get away from you and all the D'Angelos," Blackie said threateningly. "Do not come near my children or you will live to regret it. Remember, I know much and so far, I have kept it to myself. But if you come for my children, all promises are nullified."

Thaddeuss stood for a moment stone-faced, locked in an eye battle with his sister. Then the moment broke its intensity as he presented a coy smile and bowed to the four of them. As he backed away, he looked back to his sister. With what sounded like either a private joke or a targeted threat, he simply recited, "Too many secrets in the House of Duquesne."

"What the hell was that supposed to mean?" Echo asked.

"Pray that you never have to know," Blackie answered softly.

CHAPTER SIX

Cleaning Up

If the setup for the Consort had been a whirlwind of noise and chaos, the tearing down of it was almost worse. At least while setup was going on Artemis had the fun of decorating the tents, but with it all coming down she simply retired to the porch, watching from the rocking chair. She was still exhausted from the party and let the work crews handle deconstruction.

Echo and Seth were dragging trash bins to the edge of the long driveway for the garbage men to collect on Monday while Arielle was removing the garlands of flowers which had lined the front fence the night before. She didn't understand how the garlands could have been so beautiful the day before and look so ragged now. No one was really meandering around the fence last night. She guessed some of the animals living in the woods must have nibbled at the garlands in the night. Taking a break from their work, she, Seth, and Echo plopped down on the wooden Adirondack chairs under the oaks with plastic tumblers of iced tea.

"Last night was something," Seth commented, wiping sweat from his brow.

"Speaking of last night, "Echo mentioned. "Do either of you know who Thaddeuss D'Angelo is?"

Arielle made a curious face, wondering why her brother would be bringing him up. "He's my uncle," she said. "Yours too, now that I think of it."

"He really seemed to upset Blackie last night."

"Yeah," Seth said. "Blackie doesn't like her family too much."

"Why?" Echo asked, picking a damp paper drink napkin off the bark of the nearest tree where it somehow had become stuck last night.

"I have no idea," Seth said. "I don't know much about any of them, except they were my father's first wife's relations. The D'Angelos don't like me and Salem, for obvious reasons."

"Ari," Echo asked his new older sister. "Do you know anything about any of that?"

"Some," she replied. "But Daddy did his best to steer me clear of them. I only really ever knew Uncle Thaddeuss because he would come to our house to see my mother—or who I believed was my mother, I should say. But I didn't encounter the other D'Angelos very often."

"There are other D'Angelos?" Seth asked in surprise. The thought never occurred to him.

"Oh, yeah. Thaddeuss has a wife and a couple of children. There is also a cousin I knew when I was little. Her name is Mara. She has a sister I believe who is much younger. I think there's another cousin or two. I don't really know how anyone is connected or even most of their names. I don't know if I'd even recognize any of them if I even saw them."

Echo propped his foot on the end of his chair and asked, "What is the House of Duke Kane?"

Arielle's face hardened unexpectedly.

Seth noticed the change in her. "*Duke Kane*? Like an English Duke?"

Arielle shook her head, "No, it's in Charleston, not far from Oleander. Duquesne. D.U.Q.U.E.S.N.E. It is where the D'Angelo family lives."

"Well, what is it like?" Echo pushed.

"It is an awful place," she answered. "I have only seen it a few times. I was little, but it was enough to give me nightmares for days. The house is a mess. It even looks evil."

"Thaddeuss said there were *too many secrets*. What did he mean?"

"It's a poem," Arielle explained. "A poem written about the house. We were not allowed to associate with most Charlestonian children. We always kept to ourselves on Wadmalaw Island, but every once in a while, I'd be around other kids and they all knew the poem. I don't know all of it, but a few lines go something like:

(Something) (Something) farthest from light
And answers are why you can't sleep at night
Old family wealth (something) old family name
And too many secrets in the House of Duquesne."

"What the hell?" Seth cried.

"That's a poem?" Echo remarked.

"I guess," Arielle said. "I think it's more of a legend. Something people say—kids mostly. I remember in grade school some girls picking on me because my mother was born in the House of Duquesne. It's kind of like this big, haunted house boogeyman thing in Charleston."

Echo would hear about the house again later in the day. Reporting to work at his father's office in town, Echo thought he would be alone. Arielle had the day off, and Howard was away at meetings out of state for Sinclair Industries business. Echo was just settling in at his desk when a knock rapped at the outer door. Standing before him stood none other than Thaddeuss D'Angelo himself.

"Mr. D'Angelo," Echo said with a dash of confusion to his voice. "What can I do for you?"

"I am Uncle Thaddeuss to you, son," Thaddeuss grinned. "I only wanted to pop in and attempt to get to know you better before I depart for home in the morning."

Echo stood rather formally and extended his hand out of politeness. "I am not sure why you would want to," Echo stated as Thaddeuss shook hands. "But please sit down if you'd like. I don't have much time to spare. I came in to work late. I was needed at home this morning."

Thaddeuss took a seat in the chair opposite Echo's desk where Echo returned. Glancing around the modest design of the small office, Echo could tell his uncle was not impressed with the surroundings. Thaddeuss returned his attention to his nephew. "I imagine so," he replied. "Your aunt threw quite the event last evening. I am certain there was much to clean up."

"I'll say."

Thaddeuss leaned forward onto his crossed leg and looked earnestly into his nephew's eyes. "I feared that your mother may have given you and your sisters the wrong impression of me last evening. It is my fervent hope to repair old family ills, and I could think of no better way to begin than by making the better acquaintance of my only nephew."

Echo eyed him suspiciously but decided to give him the benefit of the doubt. "May I ask what caused the bad blood between you and Blackie?"

"Blackie," Thaddeuss smirked. "I will never get accustomed to her rudimentary nickname. Barbara and I have unfortunately never been especially fond of one another. I blame our father for that. Your grandfather, Hugh D'Angelo, was a difficult man. I am afraid early in life he pitted his children against one another. Barbara was always, it seemed, the lesser in his heart than the rest of us. Perhaps because she was never too interested in playing his games. My other sister, Atheidrelle, and I unfortunately yearned for his acceptance in ways your mother did not."

"That sounds very sad," Echo replied. "That he would pit his children against each other."

"Yes," Thaddeus agreed. "Has your mother never talked about her childhood?"

Echo got up from the desk and situated himself in the chair beside Thaddeuss. He wanted no distractions. This was all new information to him, and he wanted to hear every word.

"Mr. D'Angelo—"

"Uncle Thaddeuss, please."

"Er-Uncle Thaddeuss," Echo corrected. "You may not know this, but our connection to your sister is kind of accidental. We just discovered a few months ago that we share her DNA."

"I am aware of the peculiarity of your connection to my bloodline. However, I assure you the ties are authentic. The Barbara of your world is the same genetic makeup of the Barbara D'Angelo of this world. Therefore, you and your sisters are genuine D'Angelos by birth."

"Yes, I am aware," Echo replied. "But because this is all so new to all of us, I haven't known Blackie long enough to learn much about her history. As for now, we are all just getting used to each other. The same with Arielle. It isn't easy being the only brother in the family."

"No, it isn't," Thaddeuss grinned, seizing upon this one common thread between them. "It is made even more difficult when you have a father who values daughters less than sons. Barbara was at quite the disadvantage from the beginning. I realize that now. I was arrogantly unsympathetic to her condition in our youth. I would like to make amends for that."

"I hope the two of you can."

"It is my great hope you will meet my family—your family—one day soon. It would make me overwhelmingly pleased and perhaps it might help mend fences."

"I'm not sure," Echo stuttered. "That would need to be discussed with my sisters, and with Blackie."

"You are welcome at the House of Duquesne at any time. Now I will leave you and allow you time to work. I thank you for this time, Nathan—Echo."

"I appreciate your reaching out," Echo said, extending his hand once again. After a parting handshake and a pat on the arm, Thaddeuss withdrew himself from the office, leaving Echo with much to consider.

...

"No!" Tess said sternly over the Blanchard family dinner table after Echo recounted the visit. "Blackie warned us about him."

"But he seemed pretty friendly," Echo countered. "He didn't have to make the effort to come see me. But he did. I believe him when he says he wants to mend fences within his family."

Artemis spoke up after dabbing the corner of her mouth with a napkin. "I'd caution you against taking people at face value. At least D'Angelos. I have never really known Thaddeuss, but my mother distrusted that family immensely."

"We trust Arielle," Trix pointed out. "And she grew up with them."

"Yeah, but I didn't go around that part of my family very often," Arielle said. "My father didn't trust them or like them very much. And I am not much of a fan of Thaddeuss."

Fable added her two cents as she wiped gravy off Con's cheek. "Keep in mind Blackie ran away from all of them. And we all know what a monster Atheidrelle was. I'd be careful before putting too much stock in his talk of family unity."

"I was only telling you guys what he said," Echo defended. "That's all."

"He's up to something," Arielle said. "I'm Blackie's kid, too, and he has never had much use for me."

"Regardless," Demitra said next, "None of this has to be decided tonight. But if you are asking your great grandmother's opinion, I line up with Arielle. I wonder why Thaddeuss showed up at the Consort and why he has chosen this time to try and repair family rifts. Think on that."

CHAPTER SEVEN

Family Ties

Oleander plantation stood back from the main road on Wadmalaw Island, hidden away behind generations old iron gates. The large oaks lining the driveway bowed their heavy ancient limbs as a gentleman kneels to his lady. Thick Spanish moss dropped like lacy curtains from boughs veiling some of the beauty of the formal gardens beyond from passersby. Taub D'Angelo had not been to Oleander in decades, perhaps not since boyhood, even though it lay only a few miles from his own home. The D'Angelos rarely left the House of Duquense, but this excursion had become necessary.

Pulling his dark green Mercedes before the steps of the front porch, he took in the beauty of the house. Standing three stories tall, its magnificence seemed misleadingly small compared to his own home. Yet its thick white columns and sharp angled capitals provided a crisp, stark contrast to the gray forbidding stone of the D'Angelos' house. On either side of Oleander's square façade curved bay wings filled with windows. Within one of those windows on the lower floor, he could see a blonde woman standing with a white curtain sheer pulled back. He assumed this was his uncle's new wife, whom he had never met and didn't care to.

The front door opened for him without need of knocking. Taub's cousin Cassandra greeted him politely as she escorted him inside to a cheerfully appointed sitting room off the entrance hall. He glanced around at his surroundings. Though it had been years since his last visit, he knew right away almost everything had been changed.

"The place looks rather different," Taub commented.

"Yes," Cassandra smiled. "Isn't it brighter and cheerier? Nacaria restored the place to what it was in my grandmother's time. She removed the dark and moody elements Mother preferred. I suppose Mother wanted it to more resemble...well... where you live." She felt embarrassed.

"Yes, the House of Duquesne is a bit somber I suppose," Taub smiled back graciously. "White beams and sunlight would be dreadfully out of place there."

Cassandra directed him to sit down and be comfortable. She already prepared coffee for them and had it waiting in shining silver on the coffee table. Taub thanked her for the thoughtfulness and poured them both a cup.

"You'll forgive me for saying so, Taub, but I was more than a little surprised when you asked if you could pay me a visit."

Taub nodded with a blushing grin and conceded, "I know we haven't been close in recent years. However, we once were when your mother would bring you to the house on her visits. I remember how we used to play along the twisty halls and try to find undiscovered rooms. We had fun together as children."

"We did, I suppose," Cassandra replied cautiously. "But what brings you here now?"

Taub's face took a more serious turn as he answered her. "I need your help, cousin. My wife, Alexandrea. She had a brain injury several years ago which left her in a kind of vegetative state. She can move—walk, I mean. She can sit. She can eat, when directly fed by another hand. But her mind..."

"I don't understand."

"It is as if she is a great big doll you can dress up and feed, yet she does not think. She does not speak. She only exists."

Cassandra frowned. Taub's wife's condition sounded disheartening. For a moment she felt ashamed that she was not aware of any of this. The two families had become distant over the years since her mother, Atheidrelle, died. Cassandra had spent those years in self discovery—coming to terms with the damage done to her psyche by her mother. Where Cassandra had once been a rather dark soul, she'd found light and shed the machinations instilled in her from birth.

"I'm very sorry to hear about your wife," Cassandra said. "I remember hearing Dad talk about an accident, but I am ashamed to say I know very little else about it."

"It hasn't been easy on me," Taub admitted. "She was extraordinarily beautiful, still is. My pride and joy. I loved her very much."

"I'm sure you did," Cassandra said, patting his hand softly. "Your children? How are they handling things?"

Taub blew on his coffee and took a first sip. His eyes slanted slightly as if frustrated. "Mara is defiant as ever. I see very little of her these days. Ashby was despondent over her mother. She already had issues before the accident. She is a touch autistic. I had to remove her from school and bring her home. She has tutors now."

"Ashby is how old?" Cassandra asked.

"Thirteen," Taub replied. "Mara started the College of Charleston last term. I do not see her much these days. She has a place in town where she lives during the school week, but I always insist she return home on weekends. Although I cannot be sure how often she really does."

"You don't know?"

With a head tilt and lifted brow, Taub reminded, "You know the house. Who can tell where anyone is within those walls? If she does not join us for dinner, I have no real way of knowing."

Cassandra felt sympathy for her cousin. Obviously, his life had not been easy these last years. Again, she felt guilty for not having stayed in touch with her mother's family. "How can I help you, Taub?"

"I would like to hire you," he replied. "I know you do not need the money; the salary would simply be a formality. But you see, Alexandrea's last nurse left quite suddenly and without explanation. Between you and I, I believe she ran off with the gardener's assistant, who also disappeared."

"Surely there are nurses you could enlist to take over the care..."

"People don't like to live out here on the island, so far away from the pulse of the city. And you know as well as I do, the House of Duquense doesn't put anyone's soul at ease. But you, Cassandra, you have training as a nurse. You've even worked at Dredmore Asylum."

The mention of Dredmore sent a wave of humiliation and regret through Cassandra Obreiggon's spirit. That seemed so long ago, and her motives had been less than humanitarian at the time.

"I'm afraid my time at Dredmore was not something I'm very proud of," she said. "In fact, it almost cost me my freedom. The Council of Witches planned to confine me to Dredmore as an inmate because of the things I did."

"I know all about that," Taub said with a wink. "I also know you were operating under Aunt Atheidrelle's wishes then. None of that alters the fact that you have a nurse's training. You are also well acquainted with Duquesne House. I do not think it will scare you as it has so many of the others I have hired. More importantly, you are family, Cassandra. I trust my wife's care in your hands."

"I don't really know what to say."

"Think about it," Taub implored. "That is all I ask. Perhaps try it out on a one-month trial run? I need someone to look after Alexandrea. She needs not only care, but a person who might help her get better. Doctors say that is not possible. But what do they know? Please consider it."

...

Alexandrea D'Angelo was seated in a cushy chair on the balcony of her room overlooking the marsh when Taub came in to see her later that evening. The blackness of the night and the blackness of her long, silky hair blurred her against the backdrop of the trees and swampy waters. Still, he knew she was there. She was always there this time of night. The staff would have positioned her in her usual place to watch the sun disappear into the South Carolina glades.

He went to her and placed a firm hand upon her shoulder. Any other woman might have flinched from surprise. She did not. She was unable to even register his presence as her blank eyes stared unblinking into the darkness.

"I have found a companion for you, my dear. A new nurse. It is my cousin, Cassandra. She has not accepted the offer yet, but she will. I added a little potion to her coffee from the compartment within my ring. It should aid her to be extra sympathetic to our needs. You will have proper care, and my father will be incredibly pleased when he returns home. Cassandra Obreiggon may be exactly what we need."

He stood a few moments, quietly looking over the murky waters lining the lands which had been a part of his family for hundreds of years. Every so often he remembered the way he and his wife had once traversed those waters in a paddle boat in the beginning of their romance. It was a long time ago, but he did remember. But that was before. Before Alexandrea was changed. He had truly loved her then. He didn't now. But she had her uses. A means to an end.

"The D'Angelos will own this world one day soon," he said mostly to himself. "It is within reach. Only a few more pawns to move before we have unending power. Cassandra will be such a pawn. I am almost certain I will receive her acceptance of my offer by morning. It won't be long now before all are restored to the House of Duquesne."

CHAPTER EIGHT

A Night Out

The last time the Blanchard's second generation was able to go out and have a little fun, they had been the youngest generation. Life had taken Salem, Seth, and Fable on quite the roller coaster over the years, and so when Trix suggested they all go out for a night of bar hopping, their immediate reluctance was vetoed by the aunts.

"Go," Demitra implored them. "All of you need a night out—a night to cut loose and enjoy yourselves. Artemis, Jerry, and I will watch the children."

"Oh, I'll be here," Miranda said. "I can watch them."

"No, you are included in this," Artemis replied. "You almost never leave this house except for the carpool line. You, Salem, Seth, Fable, Arielle, Tess, Trix, and Echo are going out tonight. That is an order."

"I don't want to go anywhere," Seth frowned. "It wouldn't be right."

Artemis walked over to her nephew and placed her hands gently around his neck. "Son, you need this. You can still grieve Yasmine. Having a little fun once in a while does not undo your love for her. I want you to go."

"Yeah, Seth," Echo said. "I can't be the only guy with these crazy girls."

Demitra gave a stern look toward Echo and his sisters, then she pointed a finger to Fable. "Remember, they are not familiar with things, and they are not of drinking age. They are 20 years old, and I hold you responsible for them, Fable."

"Why me?"

"Let's just call it payback for everything you put me through at their age."

It was decided that Bounce, the newest night club in Tuscaloosa, would be the destination for the evening. Most bars in Tuscaloosa and Birmingham were strictly 21 and up, but being a college town, Tuscaloosa had more underage offerings. Trix heard about Bounce from some co-workers at the restaurant.

The Blanchard crew were dressed for a night out as they paraded in line down the foyer stairs toward the door. Trix led the way in a strappy light blue, low cut, short length mini dress. Tess was dressed more conservatively, but still femininely, in a short sleeve floral print dress. Fable dressed like the old days, despite Salem warning her "you are too old to still dress like that". Fable didn't care. Her black mini skirt and halter top was once her *lucky* outfit. Miranda and Salem were dressed more as if they were going to a church bake sale than a club. Light colored jeans and a blouse. Seth dressed as Seth always did. Khaki shorts and a green polo. With his sandy blonde hair, he still looked like he might have been in college, even if he was 31 now. Echo proved to have a style of his own, dressing in black jeans with a tight gray t-shirt which accentuated some upper body muscles not everyone in the family really knew he had. Around his waist he wore a black garment that might have been a light jacket tied at a slant. No one really knew.

"Are you wearing a skirt over your jeans?" Seth asked him, walking out the door.

"No, I'm not."

"Is it a waist cape?" Fable asked.

"It's a black asymmetrical kilt," Echo explained. "It's in style. I bought it last week."

"It's a skirt," Tess laughed as she pushed him out the door.

Demitra waved them all goodbye from the porch as they piled into two cars. "Don't forget, Fable...the triplets are not to drink."

"I know, I know," Fable called back as she got into the driver seat of her Jeep.

"So, we *really* can't drink?" Trix whined.

"Oh, you're totally drinking," Fable smiled. "Just wave to your grandmother and nod."

. . .

To everyone's surprise there was a line at the Bounce door—an unusual occurrence for Tuscaloosa. However, Trix appeared to have connections, or perhaps it was her cleavage that did the trick. The doorman let them all through. Later she claimed to have offered him a free meal at the Cobblestone if he'd allowed them in. Tess still believed it was the cleavage though.

The club was packed. Music thumping all around as happy, flirty faces moved like ants searching for the next leaf to carry up the tree. It took a little while for everyone to get their drinks. Fable performed a mirage spell on the triplets' driver's licenses so that anyone checking them would believe they saw an earlier birthdate. Soon everyone had a drink and were situated in the middle of the main room.

"What now?" Seth asked. "I've forgotten how to do this."

"Yeah, it doesn't seem as much fun as it used to," Salem agreed.

"You never had fun, Salem." Fable smirked. "You and Beryl were too busy keeping constant watch over Seth, me, and Yaz."

"Well, I have a friend meeting me tonight," Salem grinned. "So, I have built-in entertainment."

"Who are you meeting?" Seth asked.

"Miles Thorsby," Salem answered. "My business partner. He's wrapping up a meeting nearby and said he'd meet me here to go over the details."

Fable gasped and smacked her cousin on the head, "You're having a business meeting at the nightclub! Damn, Salem. You did get old."

"Well, I'm not old," Trix said, giving a nearby man a wink. "Excuse me while I leave the geriatric set to find more stimulating company."

Trix crossed the room with a walk which turned more than one head. Within seconds she'd made the acquaintance of the man in her line of sight, who was now laughing with her and leading her to the dancefloor.

"Well, *wholesome* never was one of her attributes," Tess commented.

Miranda looked as uncomfortable as she felt, nervously sipping her cocktail with her eyes toward the floor. Seth took notice and lifted her elbow, guiding her over to a nearby empty table. He sat with her and said nothing, only exchanging a mutual nod of discomfort in the situation. The others meandered over to them and stood by the table, observing the crowd.

A girl was looking their way and soon she gathered the courage to cross over to them. She smiled politely and commented to Tess on how she liked her dress. It was clear by the way she kept side-eying Echo her real reason for the compliment was a possible introduction.

"This is my brother, Echo," Tess said politely.

"Hey," Echo said flatly.

"Hi," said the girl. "I'm Jessica. Aren't you in one of my classes? Maybe it's poli sci?"

"I'm not a student," Echo said without emotion.

Jessica did not let it stop her from trying. "I could swear I know you from somewhere."

"Could be," Echo said. "I've been somewhere before."

Jessica feigned a mild laugh to shield the embarrassment of the rejection. Before too long she made her excuses to walk away.

"You were really rude to that girl." Fable scolded him. "She liked you."

"I wasn't interested," Echo replied.

"Well, you could have been nicer." Tess gasped.

Echo shrugged indifferently.

"Really, men!" Fable sighed. "Do you know how hard it is to walk up to a guy you really like and make a move? It is very hard."

"It's not so hard," Echo said, staring off to the crowd. "See."

Suddenly Echo walked away toward a group of people congregated by the pool table. Astonished Blanchard eyes watched as he approached a very attractive, very muscular man who was shooting pool with a few other guys. The man took his shot and then took immediate notice of Echo. He must have liked what he saw because he passed the pool stick off to a buddy to finish the game as he and Echo walked to the bar for another drink.

"Um...Did y'all know Echo was gay?" Seth asked his family.

Tess stuttered a moment, her eyes as round as saucers, and finally said, "I never really thought about it. Maybe he and Amelia really were just friends."

"Amelia knew he was gay," Miranda divulged. "We both did. You and Trix didn't?"

"No!" Tess exclaimed. "That is a pretty important detail we should have known."

"Does it change anything?" Fable asked her niece.

"Of course, not," Tess answered. "I don't care. But I wonder why he never said anything. I hope he knows it wouldn't make a difference to us."

As the evening went on, Salem's companion Miles showed up, pulling her to a private table in the corner where the dance floor sounds were more muffled. From the looks of things, they were not talking much business. Seth felt very out of place without Yasmine. Had she been alive, the two of them would have been dominating the dance floor. His feet didn't feel much like dancing these days. Miranda felt as out of step with society as Seth did and the two of them mostly sat and talked about the children.

"There is a parent/teacher conference Monday," she told him. "Do you think you might go, or would you prefer me to?"

"Any trouble at school?"

"No, nothing like that," Miranda clarified. "It's just a check-in with the teacher to see how Hera is doing. She's doing just fine, by the way, but it's mandatory. It shouldn't take longer than fifteen minutes."

"I'll go," Seth replied. "I guess I need to show the school my daughter does has a father at some point." He sipped his beer and looked into Miranda's eyes. "I am grateful for all you've done to help with my kids. I've been a mess. I'm glad they've had you to pick up my slack."

They looked back out across the bar in silence, each trying to find a distraction from the mistake they had made in coming out tonight. Tess had found a few other girls she knew from work to hang out with, and the pack of them were twirling each other around the dance floor. Seth watched her from afar, admiring her youth and energy. He remembered when he and his cousins would while away the nights dancing. Tess reminded him very much of Beryl at that age.

Trix was now seated at a table surrounded by guys, each one vying for her attention as if she were Scarlet at the barbeque. Fable was shooting pool with some guys she'd met, and from the looks of it, her group of college boys was into older women. Suddenly, Seth caught sight of Echo heading toward the door with the guy he'd been dancing with. Seth bounded up and headed them off.

"Where are you going off to?" Seth asked.

Echo looked confused and a little embarrassed. "We're heading out. This is Paul."

"What's up?" Paul nodded.

"I think you'd better stay here with those you came with," Seth advised.

Echo began to blush. "Seth. It's fine."

Seth turned to Paul and firmly asked, "How old are you?"

"Twenty-seven. Why?"

Seth gestured toward Echo, "He's only twenty."

"So?"

Seth was getting angry. "So, he's not going with you."

"You his boyfriend or Daddy or something?" Paul quipped.

Seth's brow furrowed as he reddened around the temples and cheeks. "Do I look old enough to be his father?"

Paul shrugged. Seth wanted to knock his lights out.

"Echo, you came with us, and you'll leave with us."

Echo asked Paul to go wait for him by the bar so he could have a private word with his cousin. Once Paul was out of earshot, Echo faced Seth and threw his hands up in confusion.

"Dude! What's up with this?"

Seth leaned in and gripped Echo by the neck. "What's up is that you are barely a legal adult. Not to mention everything in this world is new to you. Do you have any idea what that guy has on his mind if you leave here with him?"

Echo smirked and replied, "Yeah, I know what's up."

"Oh," Seth said condescendingly. "You're a big man now. My mistake. So, you've done this before?"

Echo's arrogance waned a little as he lowered his eyes and answered, "Well, no. But everyone has a first time."

Seth placed his hand on Echo's shoulder and said, "Well this isn't going to be yours. Not like this. Not with him. And not tonight."

"Why does it matter to you? You're a guy. You know what it's like. I need a little...attention."

"Yeah, well you're getting the same treatment I'd give any one of my siblings or cousins. My job is to look out for you—your wellbeing and safety. And tonight, you are staying here."

Echo wanted to push it further, but he knew to do so would mean having to fight Seth and he didn't want to fight Seth. He wasn't even sure if he could win a fight with Seth. Instead, he went back to the bar and stood with Paul. Seth watched him presumably explaining why he couldn't go. Seth went back to the table and sat back down.

"You are a very good dad," Miranda smiled.

"I can't even believe I did that," Seth said. "I was his age and believe me I left with a lot of girls."

"Had it been a girl, would you have let him go?" she asked.

Seth thought for a moment and rubbed his face. "I don't know. Good point. Maybe it's different because he wants to leave with a man. That's probably not fair I guess, but I still feel protective."

Miranda laughed and said, "I guess his friend threw in the towel, he's leaving."

Seth looked up to see Paul leaving the bar alone. Another man followed behind, but Seth wasn't sure if they were together. Something felt off. Seth bounded up and followed them outside. Paul was crossing the street to a truck parked on the curb. He stood by it as if waiting for something or someone. The other guy was rounding the side of the building out of sight. Seth followed him. Turning the corner of the club's exterior wall, Seth confirmed his suspicion. The strange man was morphing, turning back into Echo. Echo turned around to start for the road to meet his friend at the car.

"How stupid do you think I am?' Seth said sternly. "I know you have the ability to alter your appearance."

"C'mon, man!" Echo whined.

"Get your ass back inside and stay where I can see you square on at all times... unless you want me to kick your ass in front of this whole damn place."

CHAPTER NINE

Man to Man Talk

Echo was lounging in a hammock tied between two trees in the apple orchard. His foot was dragging the ground as he listened to his Spotify through his headphones. His eyes were closed. As Seth lifted the headphones off his ear, he jumped from surprise.

"What now?" Echo asked. "Gonna lecture me for being a whore just because I have some natural needs?"

Seth shook his head and sat down on the ground beside the hammock. "No, I want to apologize for interfering last night. You are basically a grown man and can make your own choices. But last night you were about to make a bad one, and I want to talk to you about why it was."

"Because I'm into guys?"

"Not at all. You're attracted to whoever you're attracted to. I don't care whether its guys or girls. But you are new to life here, and you aren't fully aware of the dangers."

With a dismissive eye roll, Echo replied, "For instance?'

"For instance, this is Alabama." Seth began. "Not everyone here is accepting or kind. There have been cases of cruel frat boys posing as gay just to lure some unsuspecting innocent guy out to be beaten."

"That guy last night wasn't like that?"

"Maybe he wasn't. But it does happen occasionally."

Echo made a face. "Seth, I'm a witch. I think I can handle myself."

Seth slapped his hand onto Echo's knee and raised his voice a level, "Yes, but you shouldn't have to. And there are a lot of guys out there who aren't blessed with powers who get attacked every day simply because they are different."

Echo nodded, dropping the attitude. "I understand."

"There's more," Seth continued. "You hinted last night that you've never been with a guy before."

"There weren't really many romantic options where I came from," Echo replied.

"I know. Now you have many. I want you to make correct choices."

"I already have a father, Seth."

"Okay," Seth said. "Want me to call Howard over here and you and he can have this discussion?"

Echo sat up, "No!"

"Then that's what cousin Seth is for," Seth grinned. "Look, I know this is embarrassing. I also know that I don't understand what your feelings are like because I'm not the same. But I had an uncle Larry once, and he made it his job to teach me the things about being a man that Aunt Artemis couldn't. I'd like to pay that forward and help you."

"How?"

"By warning you," Seth replied. "When your time comes, I want you to feel appreciated and safe. I don't want you giving yourself away just to get it out of the way. Remember you are a man with dignity and honor. Your body shouldn't just be handed to anyone. And remember any partner you have should be a man with dignity and honor. Do not abuse that. Treat them with respect while you are also respecting yourself."

"Okay, I get it. Don't be a whore," Echo said. He paused for a moment and then confided to Seth, "There is a guy at Artemis' restaurant I like."

"Have you asked him out?"

"No," Echo said, turning red. "He's like this perfect thing. I know he has tons of experience. I have none."

Seth understood better now, "So last night you thought you'd gain some experience?'

"Maybe."

"That's the wrong way to go about it," Seth said. "My first time was with my first girlfriend. It was special, and we took our time. She died, and after she died, I stopped caring about myself and my dignity, and I made a lot of mistakes I wish I hadn't. I hurt a lot of girls who didn't deserve to be tossed away the way I did."

"I'm not a girl though, Seth," Echo said. "Just because I'm attracted to men doesn't make me a girl. I have a guy's impulses and emotions. I can hit it and quit it and not be hurt."

"Until you fall for the one guy who just wanted the one thing but you wanted more," Seth noted. "Talk as cavalier as you want, but you do still have a heart. And it can be broken. I only want you to be aware and not give yourself away to people who don't deserve the honor."

"Okay," Echo said. "Got it."

"Now," Seth said. "Do you know about condoms?"

"Oh my God."

"I don't know what they had in your reality. Do you know about condoms?"

"Yes, I do."

"Good. I bought you some and put them in your room," Seth revealed. "You know about HIV?"

Echo was silent. Then he told the truth. "Not really. We didn't have that. Or maybe we did, but when the world is devoured by vampires you don't really learn much about diseases. But I've heard it mentioned since I've been here."

"Okay," Seth smiled. "HIV is a sexually transmitted disease anyone can get, but it is pretty prevalent in the gay community. It can cause your cells to attack your body and render a lot of damage. You prevent HIV with condoms. Always wear one and have your partner wear one. But sometimes that doesn't happen. I know from experience; you get in the moment and just take the chance. So, I want you to go to the medical clinic in town and ask the doctor there to prescribe something called Prep for you. It isn't 100 percent effective in prevention, but it will add a layer of protection for you."

"Okay. I will," Echo said, wishing this conversation would end, but also realizing Seth had imparted some important information he otherwise would not have known.

"All right," Seth said, standing up. "Good talk. Thank you for listening to me. And we are the only men in this house. If ever you need my help, my advice, or you think you are in trouble you come to me. I will always be here for you, Echo."

Echo stood up and said thank you.

"Wanna hug it out?" Seth asked.

Echo laughed and opened his arms, and they hugged for a second, but then Seth pulled back and looked into Echo's eyes, "Shit! We covered sex, but do we need to have the drugs talk?"

"We don't," Echo grinned.

As Seth walked back to the house, Echo felt something he hadn't really felt before. It was a kind of deep comfort. There truly was someone else in his life besides his sisters, someone young enough to relate to him who truly cared about his well-being. Embarrassing as it was, Seth's talk made Echo feel grounded and safe.

CHAPTER TEN

Cassandra Nightingale

"I don't think this is a good idea, my dear," Xander warned his eldest. "You have worked hard to distance yourself from your mother's influence. Going to live in that house with Atheidrelle's family unnerves me."

Cassandra could not deny his right for concern, but she still couldn't release herself from the feeling it was her family duty to be there for her cousin during this time of need. "Everything you say is correct," she admitted. "But I believe Taub really needs me, at least for a little while. I'll be alright. I don't feel like I can say no and feel good about it."

Xander made a disapproving face and looked to his wife for backup. Nacaria lent him a supportive smile. Without words the two of them seemed to have an entire conversation about the matter in only a few seconds of shared glances. Nacaria shook her head and gripped her stepdaughter's hand.

"I have confidence in Cassandra," Nacaria told Xander. "She has cleansed her mind of her mother's brainwashing, and I think it is because she is such a good person now that Cassandra feels it necessary to help her cousin out. Besides, it's not like she's going very far."

Cassandra smiled Nacaria's way, appreciative of the backup.

"The House of Duquesne might just as well be a thousand miles away," Xander replied.

"Dad, I'll be alright. I promise." Cassandra assured. "You know how I feel about you and Nacaria. Even if I am walking into an enemy camp, there is nothing Thaddeuss can do to make me turn against the two of you. I love you both very much."

"And we love you, Cassandra," Nacaria smiled. "And we trust you."

"But if anything happens which causes you to feel the least unsafe, you come home immediately," Xander said.

...

As Cassandra drove up the long, winding drive to her mother's ancestral home, she felt as if the forest around the road were staring at her. The night was dark and the moon only a crescent, illuminating nothing. She attributed her unease to the setting, but still she could not shake the feeling the trees bore eyes. The house came into sight under the starry, but almost moonless night. The few lighted windows scattered across the many floors of the mansion looked like beady eyes as she pulled under the long portico in front. Cassandra felt like a stereotypical horror movie character as the thought crossed her mind, *the house knows I'm here.*

She was met at the door by Crenshaw, the butler, and Mrs. Pendleton, the housekeeper, as she switched off the engine of her car. She knew these two foreboding characters very well, but it dawned on her she'd never come here at night before.

"Welcome, Miss Obreiggon," Crenshaw smiled, extending a hand to guide her up the stone steps to the door. "I'll have one of the servants take your car to the garages and bring up your bags."

"Thank you, Crenshaw," Cassandra nodded as she went inside.

No one from the family was waiting for her as she entered the massive entrance hall. Mrs. Pendleton took her immediately upstairs. Traversing the wide marble staircase, Cassandra realized she had never ventured upstairs before during her few visits here. The second floor offered a confusing situation. Instead of a grand landing as she expected, they entered a small vestibule containing several corridors reaching in all directions like arteries leaving a heart. Looking beyond the thick, velvet drapes framing each doorway, Cassandra saw that almost every corridor twisted and turned chaotically. The house seemed to be one, large catacomb.

"Confusing, isn't it?" Cassandra observed.

The housekeeper gave a slight chuckle and replied, "I confess even I don't know how many rooms there are."

Cassandra followed Mrs. Pendleton to the third floor to her patient's room. Though no one seemed to be at home, Cassandra could faintly hear voices echoing along the limestone walls. The house was vastly different from her memory by night. It was frightening enough by day. As Cassandra and the elderly woman traversed the many winding corridors to Alexandrea's chamber, Cassandra felt her senses intensifying. She could still hear distant chattering and the feeling of being watched was oddly stronger indoors.

"Is anyone home?" she asked the housekeeper. "I hear people talking."

"Some are home, I'm sure. Some are not. You know these old houses—especially this one—sounds travel rafters and mortar." Mrs. Pendleton swung the door open, and Cassandra saw her cousin's wife seated in a high back red velvet chair. She was staring out the window, but at what, Cassandra could not see.

"Alexandrea," she said, approaching her. "Do you remember me? I'm cousin Cassandra. It has been a few years since we last saw one another. I've come to take care of you."

Alexandrea's eyes fluttered slightly, but she gave no real response. Taub had been correct in his depiction of her as a large doll. She was alive but nothing else. Mrs. Pendleton walked to a large oak paneled door at the end of the room and opened it.

"Your room is here through this connecting door," she told Cassandra. "I'd advise you enter your room always through Mrs. D'Angelo's chamber. Your bedroom door connects to an entirely different corridor which adds another few minutes to access from the stairs."

"I'd forgotten how confusing this house can be," Cassandra replied. "I've only been here a handful of times. And I don't think ever upstairs. I am sure to get lost quite a bit until I get my bearings."

Mrs. Pendleton gave her an ominous look and said, "Oh, dear, there is no getting your bearings in this place. I have been here all my life, and I lose my way often. This house changes."

Cassandra didn't mean to laugh when she said, "How can a house change? It's simply a large place with many corridors that look alike."

"You know about this house and how it came to be," the housekeeper asserted. "This house has a mind of its own." The woman walked back across the room toward the door they originally entered before adding, "I will bring you up a tray in case you are hungry. The family has already dined. Breakfast is served at 7 a.m. in the breakfast room. I'll send a maid to guide you there in the morning."

"Thank you."

As the door closed behind the housekeeper, Cassandra returned her attention to her own bedroom. It was as large as Alexandrea's and similarly decorated. The wood-paneled walls had breaks in them where a two-toned navy velvet wallpaper broke the hardness of the wood. In Alexandrea's room, the paper was burgundy red. A large, four-poster bed was set back into its own alcove with a bank of windows surrounding it. On the right side of the window bank was a door to a balcony which seemed to be shared with Alexandrea's room. Heavy antique furnishings filled the cavity of the room reducing some of its largeness. Cassandra was accustomed to this design. It was how her mother had tried to decorate Oleander in her day. Seeing this room gave Cassandra a new appreciation for the lighter, more cheerful remodeling Nacaria gave to Oleander. Cassandra turned to go back to Alexandrea's chamber and stopped in her tracks. She hadn't noticed before. Perhaps it was because she'd walked right past upon entering, but hanging on the wall of where she'd come in was the life-sized portrait of her mother. Atheidrelle Obreiggon loomed over the room as overbearingly as she had loomed over Cassandra's life. It struck Cassandra as a little ironic that the sight of her own mother would make her shudder when most of her life, she'd clung to her mother's side as a protégé would their idol. But Cassandra knew better now. She knew what her mother had been and what her mother had tried to turn her into. Perhaps there was a part of Cassandra which still loved Atheidrelle a little, as any reasonable child would, yet she feared her more than anything. And now Atheidrelle's eyes stared piercingly down onto her as they had all her life until a few short years ago.

Cassandra returned to her cousin's bedroom and sat beside her on a little stool. She didn't know what else to do. As she sat in the quiet of the room, she realized she wasn't exactly certain how her being there was going to be of any help. It then occurred to her that there might be a witch with the power to heal Alexandrea. She wondered why Taub had not reached out to the Consort. Then again, Beryl Blanchard had been the only witch with healing abilities Cassandra had ever known. It was a rare talent. It was possible Taub didn't know anyone.

"She can't be healed," Taub said entering the room. She had not heard him enter, and it startled her. She also had not previously known her cousin had the ability to read other people's thoughts.

"I had a witch come who possessed the power of healing, but for whatever reason it did not help. My wife's condition is a human frailty I know, still I am hoping that having you here—a witch with medical knowledge—might be the key to restoring her to me."

Cassandra was about to reply when she observed her cousin withdraw a syringe from his pocket and approach his wife's chair. Without saying a word to Cassandra, he injected Alexandrea's arm with the medication. Her eyes fluttered from the prick of the needle. Taub then lifted her by the arm to beckon her to stand. Cassandra joined him, taking the other side of her and helped him lead her to the bed.

"If you will see to her changing into her nightgown and lay her down for the night, I would be most grateful."

"Of course," Cassandra replied. "Taub, may I ask what it is you injected her with?"

"It helps her rest through the night. It won't do for you to be up all hours looking after her. We keep her sedated at night and during the day with a lighter dose."

"I don't understand."

"She tends to wander," Taub explained. "Part of your duties will be keeping her in your vicinity at all times. You will exercise her daily. Long walks around the grounds. She likes the statue garden. But you must watch her. She will meander off if allowed. Her mind doesn't know what it's doing. She can obey simple commands. She can use the bathroom if you sit her in there twice a day, although you'll have to assist her after. You'll have to bathe her and dress her and feed her."

"It sounds almost like advanced Alzheimer's."

"It is very similar, I suppose. But it is my sincere hope this condition is temporary while her brain heals."

"I see."

"So how do you like your room?" Taub asked his cousin. "There are many other empty ones available if you find it unsatisfactory. I just felt that you'd want to be nearest your patient."

"It's a fine room," Cassandra replied. "I was a little surprised to see the painting there however."

"Oh, yes! Aunt Atheidrelle," Taub smiled. "Father thought you might like it in your room to make you feel more at home. It's one of the few pieces your mother had we were able to return to the House of Duquesne after her...death. It typically hangs in one of the gallery halls with the other D'Angelos. Father had it moved to your room yesterday."

"He didn't have to go to such trouble," Cassandra said. "It can go back to the gallery where it belongs."

Taub made a face and shook his head slightly, "Better let Thaddeuss have his way on this one. It was meant to be a thoughtful gesture. He thought so highly of your mother he expects everyone else does as well. You don't mind it so much, do you? It's just for a little while."

Cassandra gave in. "It's alright. I'm used to seeing it. I wouldn't want to insult Uncle Thaddeuss' kindness."

Taub left Cassandra alone with Alexandrea again while she dressed her in a lovely light blue silk gown. As Alexandrea sat upright on the edge of the bed, Cassandra brushed her long hair. She was exactly as Taub described her, like a great big doll. Yet something about her condition didn't jive. Cassandra couldn't wrap her head around what it was exactly bothering her. Possibly the explanation of this condition seemed too convenient. Too easy. A brain condition. No cognitive function. Yet Taub could find no witch who could heal her, and still he held hope his wife would recover one day. It made little sense. But nothing in that house made much sense. Cassandra resigned herself to following her cousin's orders—for the moment—until she could figure out the real picture.

CHAPTER ELEVEN

Halloween

The crunch of the dry, brown leaves underfoot made for a noisy carpet along the sidewalks of the Daihmler streets. The Blanchard children ran fast through picket fences and swinging gates to welcoming homes ready with bowls of candy.

"Trick or treat!" shouted Hera and Con in unison as Fable and Miranda watched from the walkway.

"Oh, what a beautiful princess you are!" Mrs. Dryersdon smiled, handing Hera a handful of chocolate bars.

"I'm Glinda, the good witch," Young Hera corrected the kind lady.

"Well of course you are!" Mrs. Dryersdon replied. She leaned close to the child's ear and whispered, "All Blanchards are good witches."

She turned her attention next to Con, dressed as a cowboy. He smiled brightly and opened his bag for his offering. She dropped an equal amount of candy bars into his bag and patted his head.

"Where is your special friend tonight?" she asked Con.

Con knew what she meant. She was referring to Romulus. Everyone in Daihmler knew about the wolf that lived with the Blanchards—the wolf who was always Con's companion. Con gestured toward his mother, "Over there."

Mrs. Dryersdon strained her eyes to see through the darkness. Just under the lamppost, she made out Fable, Miranda, and the shape of a large animal. "There you are!" she cried. "I have something for you as well, boy."

Cautiously, Romulus began to creep toward the door, looking back at his mother for reassurance. Fable nodded and told him it was safe. Romulus sprang forward in excitement but stopped himself from appearing too excited. He did not want to frighten the kind woman.

"I went by the pet store and bought you a special bacon flavored rawhide treat,

Romulus," Mrs. Dryersdon said, extending the unwrapped jerky for him to take in his teeth. Rom gave a grateful simper and a slight bow before returning to his mother's side.

"Thank you, Mrs. Dryersdon," Fable shouted. "That was really thoughtful of you."

"Well, he's practically one of the Blanchard children too," the woman smiled as she readied herself for the next oncoming batch of children strolling along the sidewalk, headed for her door.

Miranda took Hera's hand, and Fable took Con's as they ventured forward to the next house. It pleased Fable how many people in town regarded Rom as a kind of town mascot. Though there were still some in town who feared the rumors circulating about the Blanchard family, those who had lived in Daihmler for generations harbored no fear of them. Everyone had some personal experience from life where a Blanchard came to their aid either supernaturally, or simply as a good neighbor. The Blanchard wolf had somehow become a cherished piece of the town's colorful tapestry.

The lighted jack-o'-lanterns lining porches made the night all the more special for the children as every house they went to seemed to join in on the spooky spirit of the occasion. Fable watched with a mother's grateful eye as the children enjoyed the same adventures she and her cousins had at their age. She hoped her sons would have as memorable a childhood with their cousins as she had with her own. Titan and Olympus were still far too young for trick or treating but in perhaps another two years all of them might do this together. Fable thought back more on her early years. The fun she, Beryl, Seth, Salem, and Yasmine had was something she wished for Con, Rom, Hera, Titan, and Olympus.

"This is Mrs. Asher's house," Fable told the children. "I'll go with you on this one."

Fable accompanied the children to the door where the middle-aged Mrs. Asher greeted them dressed as a lady pirate. She marveled at the princess (everyone assumed Hera was a princess) and the cowboy's costumes. They were not store-bought fare, Demitra and Artemis had sewn well into the wee hours of the morning to finish them.

"Here are some lollipops for you two cuties," Mrs. Asher said, dropping candy into the children's bags.

"And I have something for you, too," Fable replied, handing over a small vial sealed with candle wax. "My Aunt Artemis made this for your migraines. One drop into a glass of water every morning should do the trick. And..." Fable shooed the children back toward Miranda and Rom waiting at the gate. "This is from me, for Mr. Asher's nausea."

Fable withdrew a small bag of marijuana from her pocket and tucked it into Mrs. Asher's hand. Mrs. Asher looked as if she might cry from the gesture. Fable simply nodded in understanding and squeezed the lady's hand gently.

"There are some rolling papers in there too. Once he comes home from his chemo treatments, have him smoke two or three drags and then put it out until he needs more. If you run out of this before his next session, just text me. I'll get more and run over to you."

"You are the dearest people," Mrs. Asher wept. "Thank you so much. It has been such a trying time."

"I only wish my sister were here to help him," Fable frowned. "Unfortunately, she moved away."

On the next block stood the Wilmont house. The Wilmonts had gone through quite an ordeal a month before, which was rather obvious from the still charred oak tree and the bright new timber on the left side of their house. That end of the house was still under construction from the fire which ravaged it weeks before. Luckily, the rest of the house was saved and soon the repairs would be completed. Mr. Wilmont was on the porch handing candy out to a few Pokémon costumed children when he spotted the Blanchards coming down the sidewalk.

He bounded off the porch and ran to his gate. With arms outstretched he shouted down the street, "Come on, boy! Come here Romulus! Come to me!"

Romulus Blanchard sprang forth charging down the sidewalk and leaping straight into Mr. Wilmont's welcoming arms. The man lifted the young wolf into the air and laughed as Rom's long tongue covered his face with affection. Sitting Rom back down, Mr. Wilmont began rubbing the wolf behind the ears and patting his back happily. Romulus was the Wilmonts' personal hero. On that terrible night when the fire was at its fever pitch and all looked lost, it was the Blanchard family wolf who came bursting through the picture window, waking the family from their sleep. Romulus dashed through the flames and grabbed little Ellie Wilmont from her bed, dragging her to safety outside. Mr. and Mrs. Wilmont would never forget his heroics and credited their daughter's life to his bravery. If anyone in Daihmler ever had a concerning word about the wild animal who lived with the Blanchard family, they'd better never speak it in front of a Wilmont.

"How are you tonight, Mr. Wilmont?" Fable called approaching.

"Splendid, Miss Blanchard, splendid. The house is almost finished."

Hera and Con ran up to the porch where Mrs. Wilmont was now handing out candy. Mr. Wilmont was too distracted with Rom, who he now led to the porch where he had a special bag of cooked steak strips ready for his special friend.

Fable thought back to the night when the boys were born. She remembered being so afraid her animal son would be shunned, feared, perhaps even hunted. Her grandmother shared that worry. She wished Olympia could see the way things turned out. She wished Olympia could witness the sincere affection the people of Daihmler felt for the Blanchard wolf.

. . .

Back at Blanchard House Salem, Tess, and Arielle had their hands full with their own trick or treaters, and other visitors. The Blanchards were known to hand out the best treats in town. Cookies, cupcakes, candy, chocolate fudge. The children of Daihmler begged and pleaded with their parents to drive them out to Blanchard House. Parents argued that doing so would limit the amount of trick or treating time the kids would have, but Daihmler children were all too happy to forgo a few extra Laffy Taffys in their treat bags if it meant they'd get even one of Artemis Blanchard's chocolate chip cookies.

"I have never really experienced Halloween like this before," Tess observed. "I mean, we all heard about this tradition, but it died a long time ago in my world. This is fun. I like handing things out to happy kids."

"We get them most of the night," Salem said. "Until about 9, then we turn the lights off."

The three of them stayed on the porch. There was no need to go inside because the steady flow of cars pulling in offered no time to return indoors—unless it was to refill the platters of treats. On the table beside the treat platters sat a basket of glass vials. Each labeled for its specific function.

A woman and her daughter got out of their car and approached the porch as they saw other parents and children walking away. Several other people were lining up directly behind her to take their turn at the Blanchard porch.

"Trick or treat!" cried the little girl dressed as Wonder Woman.

"What a beautiful superhero you make!" Arielle exclaimed, handing her a wrapped candied apple.

Salem made eye contact with the mother and gave a smile of permission.

The woman spoke, "It's my H U S B A N D," she spelled out to keep her daughter from understanding. "I think he's interested in someone else."

Salem nodded and fished through the basket of vials until she found one labeled LOVE. She placed it gently into the woman's open palm. "Empty the entire contents into his coffee, along with one drop of your own blood. He will only have eyes for you for at least six months."

The woman hugged Salem before darting away with her daughter. The next woman in line had a similar situation. The man after her had lost his job and needed a luck potion to find a new one. The man after him was too red-faced to tell Salem his problem, but she smiled understandingly as she placed a vial labeled ERECTILE ISSUES in his hand.

Tess returned from the kitchen with three glasses of margaritas and handed one to her sister and one to her cousin. The tiny break between cars was over now as bright headlights flashed along the side road headed their way. It looked to be about six more vehicles.

"Wow," Tess commented. "It never ends does it?"

"Well, it's the night most people feel less awkward asking for potions," Arielle explained. "I remember my second year in the family, I worked this porch with Yaz for like five straight hours I think."

"Speaking of Yaz," Salem said. "Is Seth still out in the graveyard? Or did he go back inside through the kitchen?"

"I think he's still there," Arielle answered.

"He wasn't in the kitchen," Tess said. "GG and Jerry are watching a movie in the den, so I doubt he's up there."

Salem looked out over the dark lawn toward the family cemetery but couldn't see very far. "Y'all tend to the trick or treaters for me for a while. And listen out in case Olympus or Titan wake up. I'm going to check on my brother."

The wind was kicking up a chilly wall as Salem made her way through the iron gate of the Blanchard family cemetery. Scattered along the graves were the remains of the little pies and cakes lain there earlier in the day as offerings to their dead. No one believed their deceased relatives ate the treats, but it was tradition. And the birds, squirrels, and deer rather appreciated it.

Seth was laying on his back across his wife's grave with his eyes closed. For a moment, Salem thought he'd perhaps fallen asleep there. She nudged him with her foot to see. He opened his eyes immediately.

"I'm awake. Just laying down with Yaz for a bit."

Salem sat on the graying grass beside him. "I miss her too. All the time."

"I know I should have taken Hera out myself tonight," Seth began. "But somehow I felt like tonight I needed to be with Yaz. I always spent Halloween with Yaz. Our anniversary."

"I get it. It's the first one without her. You can start a new tradition with your kids next year. Titan will be old enough to go out then. I'm sure Miranda is showing Hera a fun time."

Seth gave a deep sigh before admitting, "I'm not much of a father these days. But I will be better. Dad helped me figure that out. I just needed tonight with her, you know?"

"I do."

Seth sat upright and glanced around at the many headstones. Each illuminated by a votive candle beside their treat offering. "We sure have a lot of people out here, don't we?"

Salem sighed and shook her head. "We do. We've lost a lot of loved ones." She gently stroked her own husband's headstone beside Yasmine's. "David. Yaz. Uncle Larry. Granddaddy Sinclair. Aunt Pastoria. And dear Zelda. It's filling up."

"You ever think about it?" Seth asked. "Like really think about life in that way. For example, Olympia's parents are here. Blaze is here. People we once knew nothing of other than a name on a headstone. But David, Yaz, Zelda, the others—they are who we are connected to. But our kids won't know them. To our kids they are just names on a stone. And one day their kids will see our names out here and we won't mean anything more to them either."

Salem laughed, "Well, with Olympus able to cross time there's a really good chance our future generations may show up in our lifetimes at some point. However, I do know what you mean."

"We've had quite the gamut of tragedy haven't we, sis?"

Salem leaned her head on her brother's shoulder. "We certainly have. But we are stronger for it. And we need that strength for our children. It's their time now. Our job is to just pave the way."

"Happy Halloween, Salem."

"Happy Halloween, Seth."

CHAPTER TWELVE

The Turn of Fate

November arrived and with it came a bevy of work in Howard's office. Echo was busy at his desk going over the gains and losses for the month on client investments. Most Caldwell Financial clients were his and Arielle's concern now. After Yasmine's death, Howard had to take over all responsibility for Sinclair Industries for the Blanchard family. Olympia Blanchard had left her husband's corporation to Yasmine upon her death and after Yasmine's demise it passed to her children. Howard had always handled Sinclair matters, but now with the only actual Sinclair deceased, all the company's demands fell to him. He was currently at the company headquarters in Chicago meeting with the CEO over board matters. Keeping the Blanchard family empire running kept him away from the office fairly often these days. Having Arielle and Echo there to handle local accounts made things easier on him.

Echo was lost in gains and losses of client investments for the month when Arielle gave a tap at the office door. "There is a Mrs. Williams here to meet with us. She's a possible new client."

"Do we have time to take on new accounts?" Echo asked his half-sister.

"She's pretty insistent we meet with her," Arielle replied in a low voice so that Mrs. Williams didn't overhear. "She says she desperately needs our help."

Echo came out of the office and introduced himself to the potential new client. He, Arielle, and Mrs. Williams went into the small conference room. As they took their seats around the table, Arielle remembered not too long ago in the old office space when she and Howard only had two rooms to work out of.

"What may we do for you Mrs. Williams?" Arielle said, beginning the meeting.

"It's rather simple," the lady began. "My brother Curtis died recently and willed his chain of boat repair businesses to me. Obviously, I know nothing about boats.

I'm looking to sell the business and was told that Howard Caldwell was the best at negotiating price and handling the transaction."

Echo looked confused. "Your brother had a boat repair company here in Tuscaloosa County?"

Mrs. Williams laughed, "Oh no! I'm sorry I should have been clearer. His garages—do you call boat repair places that? They are all located on the coast. The headquarters is in Charleston."

"Charleston?" Echo replied in surprise. "That's funny, I have heard a lot about Charleston lately."

"I'm actually from there," Arielle smiled.

"Really?" Mrs. Williams seemed delighted. "That truly is wonderful. You see, I am not familiar with the area at all. I also am not familiar with business either. I was a schoolteacher until I retired last year. What I need is someone who can sell these three businesses for me and handle all the legal and tax matters associated with them. I'm happy to pay whatever fee is standard."

"I suppose we could do this," Echo stated. "It doesn't sound too complicated or time consuming."

Once Mrs. Williams was gone Arielle turned to her brother with excitement. "How fantastic! We are almost finished with monthly statements and can easily take a week off to fly to South Carolina. I can see my Dad and Nacaria, and you can see where I grew up. We'll stay at Oleander."

"I suppose I could pay a visit to uncle Thaddeuss while we are there."

"Thaddeus!" Arielle exclaimed. "I don't know if that's wise. But if you decide you want to, I'll go with you. It's always better to have backup whenever you deal with a D'Angelo."

...

Daihmler Elementary looked nothing like it did when Seth had been a student. The antiquated red brick building with air conditioner units poking out of each classroom's long rectangular windows was no more. The building was sparkling new now with contemporary angles which looked more like Frank Lloyd Wright might have designed it. The red dirt playground with the tall iron bar jungle gym was now covered in soft faux rubber mulch, a tire/rope climbing pier and plastic swings in place of the black rubber padded ones that used to rub off on children's clothes.

Seth pulled at the front door to enter, but it wouldn't budge. It was then he noticed the sign: PRESS BUTTON TO ENTER AND SIGN IN AT DESK. In his day, the school was never locked. Aunt Artemis popped in any time he had forgotten his lunch or got in trouble with his teacher. Both were often.

In the entrance way, a fountain sat recessed into an alcove lined behind with large mosaic tiles in colors of teal, orange, and wheat. Each tile bore a specific donor's name. Instantly he spotted the largest teal tile in the center inscribed with *The Blanchard family*. He had forgotten about that. Artemis donated a hundred thousand to the fund when the school was rebuilt a few years ago. Or had he technically donated it? He wasn't sure. Howard handled the Sinclair fortune, and Artemis handled Howard. Seth did not concern himself with Yasmine's money or Olympia's. It was all family money, and Artemis was the head of the family.

He stopped by the front desk where an overly-happy-to-be-there lady greeted him and gave him a visitor tag to pin to his shirt. He didn't. Then he made his way to Hera's classroom for the parent/teacher conference. It took him a minute to find the way. He realized he had not been to her classroom once since she began school.

Opening the classroom door, he saw that—like the school itself—nothing was as it had been when he was a boy. This kindergarten class looked more like a Gymboree franchise. Brightly colored with cushy chairs, pristine round kid-sized tables. Toy bins, workstations, and an art corner complete with little easels and paint shelves. Mesmerized by the classroom itself, Seth was startled by the teacher when she spoke.

"Hello, Seth."

He knew that voice. He turned around to see her.

"Oh my God," he gasped in surprise. "Vanessa."

Vanessa Collins smiled and came forward to give him a hug—not something she did with every school father. He hugged her back welcomingly. It had been years since he had seen his old girlfriend, not since the night they broke up. The night she helped him realize he was in love with Yasmine.

"I was wondering when you'd start participating in Hera's school life," Vanessa smiled. "I'm glad to see you."

Seth felt ashamed. Hanging his head, he replied, "Yeah, I have been kind of MIA."

She patted his hand gently, bending her chin to make eye contact with his bowed head. "It's understandable," Vanessa offered generously. "I was so sorry to hear about

Yasmine. She really was a very kind person."

"Thank you," Seth replied. "I still can't believe this. You are Hera's teacher?"

"Yes, that's me," Vanessa said, gesturing for him to sit down at one of the little tables. He looked rather funny sitting in the tiny student chair.

"How did I not know this?"

"Why should you?" she asked. "Miranda enrolled Hera, and she is the person I correspond with. Frankly, I wasn't aware Hera was yours until a few weeks after school began. I knew with the last name Blanchard she had to be related, but I thought perhaps Miranda was a cousin I never knew about, and Hera was her daughter."

"Miranda is a family friend," Seth explained. "She looks after the children for us. She's been a lifesaver since...since I lost Yaz."

"She's a great ally to the school," Vanessa informed him. "She volunteers for everything. She chaperones on field trips, helps with school bake sales, she's even on the annual fundraising committee."

"I didn't know," Seth frowned. "I guess there's a lot I don't know about anymore. I'm just now getting back to living again."

Vanessa felt her heart ache for Seth. Despite the many years since their courtship, she still felt a fondness for him. She could remember those days well, back when Seth had no problems bigger than getting his two gym workouts in each day. Thinking back on that younger version of him, with his way of never taking anything seriously other than muscle gain, she hurt for him now. Life had not turned out the way he planned, and it showed. He was still quite handsome. Still well-built even though Vanessa could tell he hadn't been to a gym in ages. But the worry lines on his face, under his eyes. This man had suffered. She hoped maybe he was climbing out of that suffering now.

"If you ever need a friend, Seth, I'm here. I'm here for you, and I'm here for Hera."

"Thank you," he said. "Is she okay in school?"

"Oh, Seth, she's a wonderful child! Very bright," Vanessa smiled excitedly, then to lighten the mood she added, "I am sure she gets that from her mother."

That comment brought a grin to Seth's face.

Vanessa went on, "She gets along well with other children and never gives me any trouble—except for her powers."

"Powers?" Seth repeated unsure how to respond.

Vanessa Collins laughed and shook her head. Grabbing his hand and giving it a friendly squeeze, she said, "Oh Seth, I know all about her powers. I realize when we dated you tried to keep all your family's secrets from me, but this is a small town. Everyone knows the rumors about the Blanchards. The moment I saw Hera levitate up to a tree limb to get a ball down, I knew I would have my hands full. Don't worry, no one saw her besides me, and she and I had a long talk about how some things she can do at home she shouldn't do at school."

"Uh, okay," Seth stammered. "Thank you. Sorry about that. I appreciate you looking out for her. I bet that's hard to do, considering you and me...and Yaz. Our history."

Vanessa could see that he felt guilty over all that. She wanted to ease his conscience. "Seth, that was a lot of years ago. And truthfully, you didn't do anything wrong. You were always very good to me when we dated. It was not your fault you were in love with someone else. You didn't even know yourself until I pointed it out to you. As for Yasmine...I only knew her briefly, but she was always a kind and loving soul. I couldn't dislike her if I wanted to. I feel honored that I get to teach her child now. I get to look out for her little girl for a few hours each day."

Seth looked at Vanessa with tears in his eyes. "You do more than I do. I've just crumbled. I can't even spend time with my children without breaking down."

Never before had she known Seth Blanchard to display real emotion. When she had known him, he kept himself closed off to anything too deep. She suspected then his childhood had been difficult. He had no parents and lived with his grandmother. He kept everything so superficial then. Seeing him fragile and teary eyed, nearly broke her heart now.

"Hera has been through a lot for a child so young," Vanessa said. "She represses a great deal. I think she feels more than she lets on. I am glad you are getting back involved. She needs her daddy."

"I'm trying," Seth said. "I figured out I have to try."

"Know that I am here if you need a friend," Vanessa told him. "And I will continue to be there for Hera whenever she needs me."

"She's very lucky to have you as her teacher," Seth said. "We both are."

CHAPTER THIRTEEN

Blackie's Fear

Standing atop the parapet of her home overlooking the city of Birmingham, Blackie D'Angelo could feel the evil wind coming for her family. The knowledge had not required Arielle's call to alert her to its presence. She could feel it inside her bones. The wickedness she spent most of her life trying to escape was finding a way to reassert itself, and it wanted to claim her children.

Below her, coming up the hill she could see Arielle's car stopped at the traffic light. Blackie made her down the five cylindrical flights of stairs to the bottom floor of the massive house which had once been an abandoned apartment building until Blackie renovated it into her own reclusive mansion. Now Quinlan Castle loomed over the city—a landmark, owned by the mysterious woman no one suspected was a witch. Arielle was already waiting for her in the parlor when she came in.

"Hi, Mom," Arielle said, giving Blackie a kiss on the cheek. "What was the emergency? I have a lot to do before Echo and I leave town, but you made it seem so urgent that I come see you."

Blackie minced no words, addressing her feelings right away. "I do not want you to go to Charleston."

"Why?" Arielle asked. "I'm from there. It's home."

"It is not Oleander I am concerned with," Blackie warned. "It's the House of Duquesne."

The House of Duquesne again, Arielle thought to herself as she looked into her mother's concerned eyes. Considering that house was one which Arielle had managed to ignore her entire life, and only visited a few brief times in her youth, it was becoming a rather prolific topic of conversation as of late.

"Is this because Uncle Thaddeuss paid Echo a visit?" Arielle asked, taking a seat on the large, overly stuffed velvet sofa. "Echo is just curious. He wants to pay a visit to meet the D'Angelo clan, and I told him I would go with him. But it will only be one day. The rest of the week Echo and I are working to close a sale for a client."

"Why would a client from Alabama have dealings in Charleston of all places?" Blackie cautioned, taking a seat beside her daughter. "Too coincidental. I think this is one of Thaddeuss' schemes. I wouldn't be surprised if he arranged this whole matter as an excuse to get you to Charleston."

Arielle made a face. "Why would he do that? Seems like a pretty big, complicated ordeal just to manufacture a reason to get us to visit."

"And not at all unlike my brother to do so."

Arielle was confused. It all seemed like a bunch of manufactured drama in her opinion. "But for what purpose? How could meeting your family be so big a deal that he'd orchestrate a fake sale?"

Blackie closed her eyes and took a deep breath. She was almost shaking with anxiety. "There is much you do not know about my family."

Taking hold of Blackie's hand, Arielle urged, "Then tell me."

"I can't," Blackie sighed. "If I were to tell you everything and I am wrong about what I fear, you can never unknow. I must wait until things are clearer. The secrets dwelling in the House of Duquesne should remain unknown until there is no other choice."

"I promise if anything happens, I will call you," Arielle vowed.

"And I promise you if anything happens, I will be near to help," Blackie stated. "I have a townhouse on Broad Street. I believe I will return home for the duration of your stay. The two of you will be with me in downtown Charleston. There will be no need to visit the island."

"I think Echo wants to go to the island. He seems interested in knowing the D'Angelos."

"That is the very thing I fear the most," Blackie replied.

It was late in the night, a couple of hours after her daughter had gone, when Blackie rang up Xander Obreiggon in Charleston. She told him it was urgent that she see him and Nacaria. Shortly after midnight Blackie's two best friends popped into her living room by way of Xander's power to travel great distances in a flash.

The moment Nacaria materialized in Blackie's house she could see by her friend's face just how distraught Blackie was. Rushing to her side she exclaimed, "Blackie, what's the matter? We are here to help in whatever way we can."

Blackie wasted no time expressing her frantic concerns. "Thaddeuss is trying to get my children to the House of Duquesne."

Nacaria exchanged glances with her husband. Both seemed to accept their friend's worry as legitimate, yet it also seemed rather premature to be so worked up. Nothing had actually happened. "Okay," Nacaria said gently rubbing her friend's arms. "Granted the D'Angelo family aren't our favorite people, but it doesn't sound exactly life threatening."

"Oh, but it is," Blackie said intensely, staring directly into Nacaria's eyes. Nacaria had never seen Blackie so afraid. Blackie D'Angelo was well known for her unflappable demeanor. Always the right word, the right movement, and had ice in her veins when under pressure. But right now, she was verging upon hysterical.

Xander approached his former sister-in-law. "Blackie, I have never really understood the goings on of that house. Atheidrelle went there often but typically alone. I have done my best to keep my distance from that family. But you are clearly disturbed by something, something you are not telling us. Perhaps this is the time to elaborate."

"I can't," Blackie sighed. "You must trust me. This is a terrible idea. If they get their hands on Echo, then it won't be long until they claim Tess and Trix as well."

Nacaria lifted her hands to Blackie's face, her thumbs caressing her cheek before removing them to the back of Blackie's head, stabilizing it to look at her directly. "Blackie, you must share your burdens with us. You know we love you. You know you are safe with us. You, me, Xander...we share far too much history of friendship to fear we would ever turn against you. Please. Please tell us what is going on. What are you so afraid of?"

"What isn't there to be afraid of, Xander?" Blackie cried. "Don't you remember when Atheidrelle possessed Arielle? She tried to kill our daughter and take over her body so that she could live again and destroy the Blanchards."

"But that's ancient history, Blackie," Nacaria said. "We destroyed Atheidrelle. We killed her."

"Did we?"

Nacaria stepped backward involuntarily. She didn't like the way Blackie said that.

Xander was beginning to feel afraid now, he needed answers. "Blackie, you must tell us what has you so upset?"

Blackie's eyes were glistening from the tears she forced herself not to cry. Stealing her emotions into an inner cage so as to not break, she simply replied, "There are too many secrets in the House of Duquesne."

Xander began pacing the room. The fear emanating from his friend was beginning to truly scare him. "Tell us those secrets, Blackie," he urged. "If not to unburden yourself, then tell me for the sake of my own children. Two of my children are D'Angelos. And Cassandra is there now helping out with Taub's wife. I deserve to know what's going on."

"Cassandra is there?!" Blackie gasped. "Cassandra has moved into the House of Duquesne?"

"Yes."

"It might be too late then," Blackie said cryptically. "Cassandra is exactly what they need. They'll use Echo and the girls for other purposes."

"You're scaring me, Blackie," Nacaria gasped. "What is going on?"

Blackie was now the one pacing. For no reason at all she lifted a fringy pillow from a nearby settee and began running her hands nervously along the border of golden braids. Finally twisting the delicate pillow between her two hands she tossed it back where it belonged.

"There is too much," Blackie replied. "Too many things going on. Too many secrets. Cassandra and my children would only be one part of it. The house is evil. The house is alive. The house is the battery. The house is the gateway."

"The gateway to what?"

But Blackie said no more. Suddenly she was trembling. Violently. Xander ran forward to brace her with his hands, trying to hold her steady but the force of her convulsions was stronger than he was. She fell back into Nacaria. Nacaria wrapped her arms around her friend and sank to the floor with her, where Blackie began to thrash ferociously while her eyes rolled back in her head.

"Xander! She's having a stroke! Zap us to St. Vincent's Hospital!"

Nacaria sat by Blackie's bedside in the hospital through most of the night. Xander wanted to call Arielle, but his wife advised waiting until they knew more. It was just before dawn when the doctor sat down with the Obreiggons and explained Blackie's condition.

"She will pull through. However, she can't move her right side at present, and she is unable to speak."

"Oh no!" Nacaria gasped. "But she *will* recover?"

"I think so," the doctor said. "She is a strong woman and obviously takes exceptionally good care of herself. I think she will fully recover in time, but how much time that will take is undeterminable right now. I'd like to keep her here for a day or two for observation and testing."

. . .

When Arielle got the call that morning, she woke Echo, Tess, and Trix and the four of them raced to St. Vincent's Hospital in Birmingham. Nacaria met them in the rotunda and caught them all up to speed about the stroke.

"I spoke with the doctor, and he said that her children may go in to see her two at a time. She's in Room 337."

Arielle went in first with Echo. It was strange for them both to see her in such frail condition. Blackie was typically a regal force of strength. Seeing her unconscious, drawn to one side, gave her a vulnerable characteristic none of them had ever seen in her before. Arielle sat quietly holding her hand. Knowing her better than her siblings, Arielle was not as ill at ease as Echo seemed. Though she had only discovered Blackie was her mother a short time ago, she'd been her aunt all her life, and they'd shared a special connection. Yet Echo and his sisters only recently met their mother. Even in perfect health there remained an air of unsureness when in her presence because they were all practically strangers. As Echo looked down at his mother, realizing yet again that this was actually his mother, he couldn't sort the many feelings in his heart.

"She will be fine," Arielle said, patting his arm. "She's strong."

Echo didn't seem convinced. It troubled him to see her this way. It brought up way too much pain he worked hard to forget. "I lost her once already. Another lifetime ago. I don't want to lose her again this time."

"You won't, Echo," Arielle smiled. "Believe me. I know our mother. A little stroke won't be the thing that takes Blackie D'Angelo down."

Tess and Trix took their turn next. Both were as equally uncomfortable as their brother had been. This was especially the case when a nurse popped in to check Blackie's vitals and made idle chit chat about how worried they must be about their mother. The nurse attempted to be personable, asking simple questions about her patient, but the girls had no answers. They knew so little about their mother, but how could they explain that to the inquisitive nurse? Luckily for them the nurse was so struck by the identical twinness of Tess and Trix (other than their hair color) that this dominated the brief conversation while she was at work with her patient.

That evening Arielle drove them to Blackie's house, Quinlan Castle, on the mountain side overlooking downtown Birmingham. The triplets were in awe of the stately old worldness of the renovated structure. The thick stone walls, heavy tapestries, the parapets, and the battlements atop the roofline fascinated them. Blackie's housekeeper was reluctant to let them in with her mistress unable to offer permission, but Arielle argued her way in, pushing past the Aunt Bea from Mayberry lookalike.

"I am her daughter. You know this, Ms. Lindstrum," Arielle said authoritatively. "These are her other children. This is our mother's house, and we will be staying here until she is released from the hospital. Make us up four guest rooms. We would also like something to eat if you have anything to prepare."

Mrs. Lindstrum did not like it, but there was little she had the power to do. She disappeared into a corridor, presumably to the kitchen although Arielle realized she had never seen Blackie's kitchen before and wasn't quite sure where it even lay inside the large house.

"This place is massive," Echo announced as he walked through the gothic entrance hall into the front parlor.

"It's crazy big for one person," Arielle said. "I think she feels more at home here because it's the closest thing Birmingham has to what she grew up in. The House of Duquesne is similar to this, but about a hundred times bigger."

"How rich is she?" Trix asked, eyeing the artwork and sculpture around the room. "Or is that tacky to ask?"

"She's our mother," Tess replied. "I don't think it is all that tacky."

"I have no idea how wealthy she is," Arielle admitted. "The D'Angelos have always been enormously wealthy, yet I have never learned how they became that way. It's always been an avoided subject."

Ms. Lindstrum fed Blackie's four children with a feast as if she had expected them. Perhaps she had. She showed them to their rooms before retiring for the evening herself. Tess and Trix slept in bedrooms opposite Blackie's master bedroom, while Arielle and Echo took two rooms on the floor above because Echo was insistent he stay in the room with the balcony facing the city's Vulcan statue on the mountain. It was eerily quiet in the house as they all closed their doors for bed, except not everyone went to sleep.

Trix crept out of her room shortly after midnight and made her way across the hall to Blackie's room. Closing the door behind her, she clicked on the light switch and began to look around. Her mother's room was elaborately designed in shades of Tiffany blue. A large four poster bed sat on a riser in the center of the room with three steps surrounding the platform on all sides. Along the walls, between the tall windows overlooking the city, hung paintings, mirrors, and sketches from what Trix assumed must be famous artists. Two double doors stood on a far wall, and as Trix pulled them open she was startled at what she found behind them.

"Tess! What are you doing in here?"

Whirling around in surprise at being caught, Tess replied rather red-faced, "I suppose the same thing you are doing. Snooping."

Trix laughed and nodded. "I am ashamed to admit it, but we know so little about her. I couldn't help myself. When else will we have free access to our mother's home?"

"I know," Tess replied. "I feel like a total creep, but I want to know so much more about her—about us. I found myself unable to sleep thinking about this golden opportunity we have."

Trix went further into the enormous dressing room/closet. "Have you found anything interesting, other than these amazing clothes? Look at these dresses!"

"Girl, wait till you go through that door over there. It is another entire room full of only shoes."

The snooping expedition morphed quickly into a game of dress-up as the girls tried on multiple evening gown and shoe combinations from their mother's closet. They felt like little girls playing in their mother's room, only this time the clothes fit them—and probably cost more than they would ever earn in their lives at the restaurant.

"I wonder if there is a jewelry closet," Trix said as she fiddled with a few cabinet doors. "Yes, there is! Look at these necklaces, Tess!"

Tess rushed over to a set of built-in drawers which her sister was opening. Dozens of jeweled necklaces clasped around velvet necks lay inside the deep drawers. They found rings staggered in rows in the drawers beside it. Trix saw the most beautiful ruby she had ever seen in her life and reached to lift it from its place. As she did the velvet board holding the line of rings lifted slightly.

"Is there another stash underneath?" Tess asked, helping her wedge the board of rings out.

Beneath the rings was something else entirely. Something unexpected and rather puzzling. Photographs. Old photographs. There were at least a dozen or more. Most were black and white or sepia, although there were a few color photos that looked to be from the late 1970s. None of the pictures were modern by any means.

"Do you suppose they are of family?" Tess asked Trix.

"Possibly. Look at this one. It looks a little like Blackie, doesn't it?"

Tess turned the photograph over and read the name printed on the back. "Deidre D'Angelo. I suppose she was a distant relation."

"This blonde woman is gorgeous," Trix noticed. "It's a color pic. She looks a little like you. Says her name is Wilhelmina Jackson."

"So, this is where you two are!" Arielle shouted standing in the doorway of the closet. "I went to find you to see if you needed anything, and you weren't in your rooms. What are you guys doing in Blackie's closet?"

Tess frowned and replied. "Prying. Don't get mad at us. We weren't going to steal anything. We just wanted to know a little about our mother and figured why not seize the moment."

Arielle was not happy with her sisters, but she also couldn't help but understand a little. She told them it was all right as long as they put everything back where they found it and went back to their rooms.

"Arielle, before we go, do you know who these people are?" Trix asked, holding up the photos.

"Oh, I've seen these faces before in some of my mother's—pardon me—my aunt's old family albums. That man is Uncle Thaddeuss. That man was Grandfather Hugh. And that black headed girl is Blackie when she was in grade school."

"It says Deidre D'Angelo on the back," Trix pointed out.

"No," Arielle replied. "That's definitely Blackie. I believe Deidre D'Angelo died when she was very young. Hit by a car I think."

"Why would this have the wrong name?" Tess asked.

Arielle shrugged dismissively. "I don't know. Maybe it's a simple mistake. Maybe they looked alike. What does it matter?"

Tess lifted the photo of the young blonde woman. "Do you know this person?"

"Unfortunately, I do," Arielle scowled. "That was my mother. Sorry—again I keep making that mistake. It is still all new to me, too—Blackie being my actual mother. That picture is of my aunt, who raised me as her daughter. That is Atheidrelle D'Angelo Obreiggon."

"This is Atheidrelle?" Trix said. "I've wondered what she looked like. She was gorgeous."

Tess looked skeptical. Flipping the photo over, she commented, "If it is a picture of Atheidrelle, then why does it say Wilhelmina Jackson on the back?"

"It does?" Arielle questioned, taking the photo from her sister's hand. She read the writing on the back. "It does say Wilhelmina. I wonder why. This is definitely Atheidrelle. She would have been about 19 here. Just shortly before she met my father."

"Why would our mother have a drawer full of photographs with wrong names written on them?" Trix pondered.

"Are they all labeled incorrectly?" Arielle asked.

"Didn't you say this was Uncle Thaddeuss?" Trix asked, holding up a photo of a young man.

"Yes, that's absolutely Thaddeuss. Much younger but definitely Thaddeuss."

"It says Malcolm Jackson on the back."

CHAPTER FOURTEEN

Blackie's Recovery

The elaborately gothic dining room of Quinlan Castle made for a fitting setting as Blackie's daughters filled their brother in on the findings of the night before. Ms. Lindstrum disappeared upstairs to make the beds after serving their breakfast and though their voices echoed throughout the tall walls and ceiling of the room, the siblings had privacy.

"You're saying the two of you rummaged through our mother's private things in the middle of the night?" Echo scolded, crunching on a dry piece of toast.

"That isn't the point Echo!" Trix snapped. "It's what we found that is very mysterious. None of the photographs had the correct names written on them."

"So."

"So? Doesn't that seem odd to you?"

"Not particularly," Echo said. "Someone could have accidentally written names on the wrong photos. I bet if you kept looking, you'd find a picture of the real Deidre D'Angelo with Blackie's name on it. Somebody made a mistake."

"Shouldn't Blackie know her own picture when she sees it?" Tess chimed in, tasting the scrambled eggs. They needed salt.

"You don't know Blackie did the writing," Echo pointed out. "Maybe some old looney aunt we never met mislabeled them years before Blackie took them from a scrapbook to keep for herself. There are a hundred explanations."

"Possibly," Tess said. "But it is weird."

Arielle was quiet. Staring off blankly at her plate as she picked off the fatty pieces of her bacon strips. She always liked to eat those last because she thought that was where the flavor lay.

"What do you think, Arielle?" Echo asked. "You know her better than any of us."

"I don't know what to make of it," Arielle admitted, eating the meaty pieces of the bacon first. "Your explanation sounds the most likely. But I can't help but get the feeling there is something else. Maybe it's just because I grew up knowing how foreboding the family estate was. I almost never went there. The few times I did, I was scared to death. Noises everywhere, whispers in rooms no one else was in. The house kind of moves itself around inside. Like one visit I ran across a trophy room in a particular area of the house. But the next time I was there the room was in a totally different location. I found the original location, but there was just a wall there. It is a crazy place. So, keeping that in mind, finding mislabeled photographs only adds to the mystery. I'm sure there are simple explanations, and if we found those pics at Blanchard House, I'd just say someone messed up on the names. But with the D'Angelos. Almost anything could be true."

"Do you think Wilhelmina Jackson and Deidre D'Angelo are doppelgangers or something?" Tess asked.

"Maybe they can change their appearances the way Echo can. Maybe that's where Echo gets that ability?" Trix suggested.

"Like I said," Arielle replied, now eating her fatty bacon pieces. "Almost anything is possible with that family."

"Well, this just makes me want to go there even more," Echo announced. "Arielle and I have to go to Charleston on business next week. If Blackie is okay that is. I'm thinking now we should take Uncle Thaddeuss up on his offer to stay with him."

"I don't think that's a good idea," Arielle said. "Blackie was upset when I told her we were going. In fact, she had decided to go with us and open her house on Broad Street. We were going to stay there."

"I don't think Blackie is going to be able to do that now," Echo noted.

"We could still stay at her place," Arielle said. "Or Oleander, my home, is just a few miles away."

"I wish we could go," Trix stated. "I wonder if we could? Tess, do you think Artemis would let us off work?"

"I think we should stay here. Blackie may need us. Echo and Arielle can snoop around Charleston and tell us if they find anything out."

Arielle zoned out for a moment then came back to herself. "I feel so strange. Just talking about that place. Seeing those pictures. All my mind can think about is that old poem..."

Seized with an idea which didn't occur to her before when Echo originally asked about the poem after the Consort, Arielle pulled her cell from her purse and made a fast internet search. It only took her a few moments before she found it.

"It's here!" she exclaimed. "Somebody posted the poem on a Charleston Haunted History page."

"Read it!" Echo begged. Arielle proceeded,

"You e*nvy the line but know not the shame.*
You know not what lurks in the House of Duquesne.
Covet the wealth, ancestry, and pride
But shun the house with the evil inside.

Forged in greed and a price paid too high,
Stands the house in the marsh, where all good things die.
Souls there are lost and sins there reside,
In the house on the marsh where all skeletons hide.

Truth is best left farthest from light,
And answers are reasons you can't sleep at night.
Old family wealth laced with old family name,
Mixed with too many secrets in The House of Duquesne.

"Well, that's scary as shit!" commented Echo. "What the fuck?"

"The D'Angelos are one of Charleston's best mystery stories," Arielle divulged. "Lots of old tales about people disappearing around the house. Ghost stories. All kinds of things. Of course, that was years ago when Charleston was cut off from most of the world. People don't really talk about any of that now. But back in the day it was considered a scary family to associate with."

"And we all have that blood flowing through our veins," Tess noted. "That's disturbing."

...

The siblings visited their mother at St. Vincent's Hospital that morning and were pleased to find Blackie doing rather well under the circumstances. Though she remained paralyzed on one side and unable to speak, they could see from her eyes she was happy to see them all.

"You had to know we'd be here," Arielle smiled, holding Blackie's hand. "The second Nacaria called us, we flew here. We are staying at your house until you can come home."

Blackie attempted to smile. She hoped they could tell. She liked the idea of her home being filled with her children. She gave Arielle's hand a squeeze. Tess walked over to the bed and withdrew a hairbrush from her purse and began to spruce Blackie up a bit. Letting go of Arielle, Blackie reached her good hand up to gratefully caress Tess' arm.

Tess patted Blackie's hand and said, "I know we don't know each other very well yet, but I think I know you well enough to know you like to always look your best."

Blackie nodded slightly and closed her eyes as the soft brush stroked her long, black hair. A stray tear fell down her cheek. Arielle asked her what had her upset. Blackie couldn't communicate it well. With her good hand she kept touching her face where it was paralyzed.

"I think she wants to see herself," Trix deduced. "I don't know if that's a good idea right now."

Blackie's eyes looked pleadingly at Trix.

"You are still a beautiful woman," Trix said trying to soothe her fears, "But right now your face is a little drooped. But that's a temporary thing."

Blackie touched her face again and looked up with her big black eyes. She wanted to see for herself.

Arielle did not like the idea and said so. Echo looked around for a mirror in the room but could not find one. Tess removed a small compact from her purse but then felt reluctant to open it.

"Momma," Arielle calmly said. "I think you should wait. It is not that bad, but you don't need to see it right now. It might upset you."

Blackie shook her head defiantly.

Echo placed his hand on Blackie's head and let his fingers stroke her scalp affectionately. "Blackie is a grown woman," he said. "She isn't a child. If she wants to see herself, I think she has that right. She probably thinks things are much worse than they actually are."

Blackie darted her eyes to her only son and blinked. She was grateful he understood. Echo closed his eyes. He began to vibrate slightly and then his form shifted its composition. Within the flash of an eye, Echo had morphed himself into Blackie. Her drawn and twisted face stared down at her. His arm contorted and his neck tilted. He looked as she did after the stroke. Blackie stared a long time at him. She began to cry from the one good eye. Echo morphed back into himself and then tossed his hand toward Tess. Suddenly Tess morphed into Blackie! Arielle and Trix, and Tess herself were shocked by the trick.

"I learned that I could morph other people too!" Echo exclaimed. "I've been working in the magic room with Artemis! I can change myself or anyone else!"

He then stepped over to Tess—who now looked exactly like their mother. Echo placed his finger on the drawn side of her face. "Look, Mom, it's only this area that drooped. It's because these muscles are paralyzed. But the second they aren't this will spring right back up. That's all it is. Just this one paralyzed muscle here. Don't be upset. It's all going to heal. You will be just as beautiful as ever. And if by some crazy chance you don't heal, I can just cast your old face on you, and no one will know the difference."

The thought eased Blackie's mind. She grabbed his hand and shook it in thanks. Echo released Tess back to her normal self and that was that...except his sisters still being flabbergasted that he could now change anyone into anyone else within his presence.

The doctor came in while they were all assembled and gave his orders. Blackie could return home but would need daily rehabilitation therapy. He had no calendar date for her full recovery but acknowledged that one was highly likely if she followed his orders. Blackie could do no more than listen as the doctor spoke mostly to the four young people in the room. It was the first time in a long time that Blackie D'Angelo listened while decisions were made for her. Only this time she did not feel as powerless as in her younger days. She kept reminding herself that these were her children and that they cared about her, which gave her a sense of security. She did not even mind that much that they were all speaking for her.

"She will do everything you ask," Tess said. "My sister and I will stay with her and look after her."

"And we will personally see that she is at her therapy appointments every day," Trix added.

"How do we need to feed her?" Tess asked. "I assume she cannot open her mouth or chew."

"I will leave detailed notes for you on how to care for her," the doctor said. "It shouldn't be too difficult."

After the doctor left the room, Trix looked down at her mother. "Tess and I will not leave your side. You will be just fine. But you are going to follow orders. Blink to agree."

Blackie raised her left brow in consternation.

"I said blink to agree. This is no time to be stubborn."

Blackie blinked and tried to smile again. Trix undoubtedly inherited her toughness. Blackie admired that. She glanced toward Arielle and Echo and raised her brow again.

Arielle understood the meaning.

"We have to go to Charleston for a week or two, but we will come back as soon as possible," Arielle said. "I'd cancel the trip altogether, but you appear to be in good hands with the girls."

Blackie suddenly looked afraid. With her left hand she clutched Arielle's wrist. It was a warning. She did not want them to go.

"Mother, we have to go. We will be okay. Daddy and Nacaria are there. If we have any trouble with the D'Angelos, we only have to call Daddy. Besides, we are there on business. I doubt we will even have much time to see anyone other than our client."

Blackie did not look reassured.

Echo stepped forward and looked at Tess, "Do you think—what if I tried—"

"To heal her?" Tess asked. "I don't think so, Echo. You are not very skilled with that talent. Last time you tried to heal someone they only got worse. I think you need way more practice on animals before you attempt to heal our mother. We will trust the doctors and therapists and Artemis. Blackie is strong, and she will recover the regular way pretty quickly I imagine."

Blackie motioned for something. With her left hand she made a writing gesture. Tess figured out what she wanted and withdrew a small notepad and pen from her purse. Blackie tried to write something but being right-handed her left was rather uncooperative. Tess lifted the notebook up to see what she had managed to write. It was almost illegible.

"From what I can tell she's written, 'No Duquesne.'"

Blackie blinked repeatedly.

"Don't go to the House of Duquesne?" Trix asked her.

Blackie blinked again.

"Okay," Echo complied. "You just rest and stop worrying about us. Okay?"

Blackie blinked again.

Walking out of the door toward the hospital elevators Arielle turned to her brother and asked, "So we aren't going to the house after all?"

Echo smiled, "Oh, we are totally going. There is just no need to worry her while she recovers."

CHAPTER FIFTEEN

School Father

The Daihmler Elementary School field trip to the Birmingham Zoo needed parents to assist with the children. Vanessa Collins was rather surprised when she received the email from Seth Blanchard saying he would be happy to volunteer to help oversee the kindergarten class on the trip. Truth be told, Fable bullied him into it—partly because he needed to take a more active role in his daughter's life and partly because if she was going to volunteer to help in her son's class then she wanted Seth there for company.

It was a pleasant November day, not too warm nor too cold. Perfect for walking around a zoo all day. The children were running all over the place, but there were enough parents around to keep the classes well corralled. Hera had friends at school—something Seth never really considered before. She seemed to be the ringleader with a cluster of little girls. He liked seeing that. In his own childhood he only really had his cousins as friends. Seeing his child popular made him happy. Hera had been through so much. She needed friends. Of course, her cousin Con had his own posse of boys, but Seth enjoyed seeing that Con always seemed to know where Hera was and what she was doing, as if he were looking out for her. Just like Seth used to do with Fable and Yasmine.

"I cannot believe we are the parents now," Fable said, walking up next to Seth at the elephant enclosure. "I remember you, me, and Yaz running around here while Mom and Aunt Artemis were the ones standing in the background with the other parents."

"Time does march on."

Fable looked behind her to where the teachers were standing together watching over their groups. "So, Vanessa seems pretty happy to have you here today," Fable smirked. "Does the schoolteacher still have the hots for you?"

Seth snarled, "I haven't given it much thought."

"I know," Fable frowned. "It's still so soon. But I am so glad you came. It's time you got back into living again. Maybe one day you'll fall in love again."

Seth made a face. "I doubt that. When you love once, perfectly, I don't think you love again."

"You never know," Fabel replied. "Like you said. Time marches on."

Seth propped his leg onto the bottom rail of the enclosure fence and stared out over the large sunken domain of the majestic African Elephants. "That's just the problem," he said, mostly to himself. "What do I do with all this time that is marching on? Days go by. Weeks go by. Months. I still think of her every single day, all day. I can't breathe without her. There's too much time ahead of me filled with days without her in them. Sometimes I think I'll go crazy. Remember what your mother once told us, 'Grief can drive you crazy if you've loved deeply enough.'"

Fable leaned her head onto his shoulder as she squeezed her arms around his sides. "I know. I miss her every day. Life without Yazzy and life without Beryl. It is just too much to take sometimes."

Seth bumped his head affectionately into the side of hers and replied, "I forget about you. I get so caught up on feeling sorry for myself because I lost my wife, but you lost your best friend and your sister on top of that."

"And I still can't wrap my head around why Beryl left."

"That is still so crazy," Seth snickered.

"As if I wasn't always the problemed child anyway," Fable sneered. "Now my perfect never-did-anything-wrong big sister got elected God!"

Fable sighed as she watched the younger elephant clasp the tail of the older elephant, both trudging along in the dusty, arid environment meant to reflect their place of origin. She thought of her and Seth. They were sort of holding the other's tail as they trudged through life now. "We are quite the lonely pair."

"But we have each other," Seth grunted. "You know you're my best friend, right?"

"I do. Same here."

When lunch time came, the class went outside of the zoo to eat their lunches on the picnic tables in the little wooded area beside the parking lot. Children unpacked brown bags full of fresh fruit, pretzels, parfaits, carrot sticks, and a few homemade sandwiches. Fable unpacked a wicker basket full of fried chicken. The moment the aroma of chicken wafted across the air, teachers, parents, and students were clamoring for a piece. Fable had brought plenty. She had never been one of those parents that believed a carrot stick or piece of celery would ever satisfy a child's hunger. She'd ordered dozens of pieces of chicken from The Cobblestone Restaurant. Enough for anyone who wanted some.

"This is the best fried chicken I have ever tasted," cried Billy Herron's mother.

"Wow. This is fantastic!" shouted Mr. Williams, Claire's father.

"Do you know how much I've longed for some of Artemis Blanchard's fried chicken?" Vanessa declared, removing a piece from the basket. "Losing this chicken from my life was one of the worst parts of our relationship failing," she said, winking at Seth.

"I knew you were only with me for the food."

"You know it," she smiled. Suddenly her eyes grew larger, as she waved her hand toward Fable, unable to speak with a mouthful of chicken. Quickly chewing it, she swallowed hard and said, "Oh Fable, Milo Goin's family are vegetarian! He doesn't eat meat!"

Fable looked over at the hungry child downing his third piece of chicken and quipped, "Well he gives a really good impression of a carnivore."

After lunch, the children walked to the bear habitat and watched the three black bears at play. The kids loved watching the animals rolling a small bike tire around and licking insects off one another. While the bears were entertaining the kindergarten children, Fable was speaking with a parent. The parent was eager to have the renowned vet's advice because her cat was due to have kittens any day, and she didn't know what to do once it started giving birth. Their conversation was interrupted when Con came over and began tugging at his mother's shirt.

"Mama is talking, honey," Fable told her son. Con persisted.

"Mama, I think something's wrong." The little boy pointed toward the bear confinement.

Fable turned to look at what her son was so concerned over and saw that one of the bears was pawing playfully with something between its feet. The closer Fable walked to the glass, she could see that an innocent rabbit had somehow happened into the bear exhibit and found itself being thrown around by a playful bear.

"Oh, no!" Fable sighed. She looked around to see if anyone else was watching. She had to do something to help the poor creature.

"Don't hurt him," she said to the bear. The bear looked in her direction and cocked his head to the side in confusion. He bellowed a short call as he stared her way. "Yes, I understand you," she said. "I'm asking you to let the rabbit go please."

The bear bellowed again. The mom Fable had been speaking with walked up to the glass beside Fable with a puzzled look on her face. Fable didn't have time to worry about her presence now, she had to help the bunny. The bear made another sound.

"I understand," Fable told the bear. "But you get plenty to eat, and this rabbit hasn't harmed you. Will you let it go for me, please?"

"You really *can* talk to animals," the mom said quietly as to not allow the others to hear her.

"I've heard stories about why you are such a great veterinarian, but I didn't believe them. You're a regular Dr. Doolittle!"

Fable smiled politely, placing a finger to her lips to signal the woman to keep mum. "I have to help this bunny. Will you shield me?"

The woman nodded obligingly and turned her back toward Fable to keep her out of view from the others. Fable watched as the bear scooted back away from the rabbit. Fable focused her mind and sent out a call. Within seconds an owl appeared overhead, swooping down into the bear enclosure. Fable and the other mom watched as he gently lifted the rabbit with his talons and rose from the enclosure to drop the poor injured creature into Fable's arms.

"If I hadn't seen this with my own eyes!" the mom exclaimed.

"Please," Fable whispered. "Our secret, all right?"

"Oh yes, absolutely. What will you do? Take it to your clinic?"

"First, I need to talk to it and see what's hurt. Then I should probably turn it over to the zookeepers. It is a zoo bunny after all."

Fable discovered the bunny's leg was broken, and she found the proper zoo attendant to hand it over to. The mom was more than thrilled to have been a small part in such a rescue and the newly shared secret she held with Fable endeared her even more to the vet.

Fable successfully avoided detection with the rabbit incident, but her desire to remain discreet about her family and their powers became harder to hide as the day went on. As Vanessa led the children into the woodland exhibits, things became a little hard to explain. One by one the school children passed by the hyena habitat, the lemurs, and the foxes, pausing to see the different creatures. But just as Con passed by the fox enclosure, everything went a little crazy.

Children in line behind Con began buzzing with excitement which drew the attention of the rest of the children up ahead. Within moments, all the parents and teachers directed their focus to whatever was happening in the back of the line. Everyone circled back and soon a crowd of Daihmler Elementary students and adults were gathered in a cluster watching the foxes. All seven of the coppery colored animals in the enclosure had stopped their activity and were now lowering themselves on their hind legs—bowing to Fable's son.

Fable was rendered motionless, in shock, unsure what to do. Seth was up ahead in line with Hera but the moment he caught sight of what everyone was staring at he rushed to his nephew. Directly across from the fox enclosure, the coyotes in their enclosure were following suit. Hind legs up, front legs lowered, heads to the ground, the canine animals were showing their deference to the young boy standing between the two habitats. And every human saw it happen. Seth scooped Con up in his arms and walked him away. As Con departed, the animals raised themselves and sat, heads all turned, watching the boy disappear up the hill in his uncle's arms. Their king.

Later that afternoon at school, as the final parent left with their child, Seth was about to leave with Hera when Vanessa placed her hand on his arm to stop him.

"Interesting day."

"Yes, it was," Seth grinned.

"A lot of parents had questions, but of course I dismissed it as just an odd coincidence. But they have all heard the rumors about the Blanchards. If Hera or Con experience any repercussions from this—you know, parents telling their children not to play with them—I'll call you."

"Thank you, Vanessa," Seth smiled. "I'm sorry. I guess maybe Fable and Con should not have attended a zoo trip. We didn't really think that one through all the way—considering their animal connections. Now if you take the kids to a skating rink, I think we're golden."

Vanessa laughed. "I think it'll be forgotten eventually. Besides, you can't live in Daihmler and not know about the Blanchards."

Seth gave a funny smirk, remembering something from a long time ago. At first, he wasn't going to speak it, but then decided it was not disrespectful. "I recall trying really hard a long time ago to keep you and your father from learning about the Blanchards. That didn't work out too well."

Vanessa blushed beneath a small smile, "No it didn't. My father was not very keen on us dating."

"And what does he think of you being my child's schoolteacher?"

He meant it to be a playful remark—one they might both laugh over. But Vanessa did not laugh. She went rather silent, reflective. A sadness crossed her.

Seth approached and placed his hand gently on her shoulder. "I'm sorry. Did I say something wrong?"

Vanessa shook her head and returned a more genuine smile this time. "No, you didn't. It's just that my father and I do not speak anymore. We haven't had a relationship in several years."

"I'm so sorry."

"He's a difficult man, as you know. I finally had to choose to remove him from my life."

Seth did not know how to reply to her statement, so he didn't. He just gave her shoulder a squeeze.

"It has been good to see you again, Vanessa," Seth said. "It really has. I'm glad you are still in Daihmler."

"Me too."

CHAPTER SIXTEEN

Blanchards in Charleston

On their way into Charleston, Echo and Arielle drove past one of the satellite locations of Williams Boat and Outboard Repair. They decided to explore the facility the following day once they'd met with Mrs. Edna Williams, the new owner, and could have a look at the books and value of the assets. Since it was Echo's first time seeing Charleston, Arielle took him downtown before heading to Wadmalaw Island, where Oleander was located. The old-world majesty of the city was unlike anything Echo had ever seen, especially considering he was born to a mad world overcome by chaos and destruction. Charleston was a wonder of beauty to him. If one could tune out the window displays of modern shops and boutiques and imagine a bygone era of village haberdasheries and merchant markets, it was like stepping back in time. None of the structures had been altered in hundreds of years.

"This is beautiful," Echo marveled, driving by on Broad Street. "It's like no one has torn anything down and built anything new."

"They haven't," Arielle explained. "It's an ordinance. Nothing can be demolished. Everything you see has been here since probably the revolution. Notice the church steeples?"

"Yeah, you can see a lot of them."

"Nothing can be built higher than the steeples. It was how people knew where the churches were located," Arielle said, continuing her history lesson. "It's a great city. Not a lot to do, but very historic."

"Many witches here?" Echo asked.

"Tons. You wouldn't believe it. Although not very many here in the city proper. Most witches chose to live out on the islands."

"Like your family?"

Arielle nodded. "Yes. John and James Island are populated with several families, but ours reside on Wadmalaw. There is also Kiawah, Folly, and Morris. Folly is my favorite though. The beaches are amazing, and it's a really fun beach town."

Echo continued driving until he reached the turn onto East Battery. It did not take long before he was compelled to pull the car over and walk the sidewalks of the bay to take in the breathtaking sight of the mansions lined in a row facing Battery Park and the ocean.

"These remind me a little of Blanchard House, only some are way cooler," Echo noted. "And there's no land."

"The fronts are smaller you'll notice," Arielle said. "The majority of the homes stretch back longways. That's because homes were taxed on the dimension of the frontage. So, everyone built thinner fronts and really long houses. Let's go on and get to Oleander. Traffic will be packed soon on the road to the island."

As Arielle steered the car down the long road into Wadmalaw, Echo was enthralled from the views outside the car window. Monstrous oaks lining each side of the roadway hung heavy with Spanish moss laden limbs. They stretched their thick arms across the roadway to the other side where other oaks did the same—as if trying to embrace yet falling only a few feet short of reaching. Echo felt as if they had driven into another world.

When they reached the gates of Oleander, his entrancement continued as the tall white mansion loomed ahead crowning the shadowy landscape.

"This house is beautiful," he gasped. "It looks like those we saw on the water in town. Just a little bigger."

"This was a tea plantation back in the day. One of the largest. The Obreiggons have been here forever."

Nacaria heard them arriving and met them at the bottom of the porch steps. "I am so happy to see you two," she said, giving hugs. "Xander is in town at the moment but should be back any time now. And dinner is almost ready. I bet you are both starved."

Arielle enjoyed being home again. It was a feeling she once never believed she would experience. But with Atheidrelle long gone and Nacaria's presence adding much needed warmth to the house, home felt like a home. Echo enjoyed the tour his sister gave him of the property. He stood silently back for a few minutes as she placed flowers on the grave of Salem's infant son. Xander and Nacaria laid out a magnificent spread for dinner of roast beef and all the trimmings. But the conversation quickly turned to more serious matters.

"Daddy," Arielle began. "I know we are here on business for Howard, but we are also hoping to solve a little mystery. I was hoping you might shed some light."

"What mystery?" her father replied.

Arielle withdrew her phone from her pocket and flipped through screenshots until she came across pictures she'd taken of the snapshots found in Blackie's room. "Who is this a picture of?"

"That's your mother," Xander said. "I mean, Atheidrelle."

"Are you absolutely sure?"

"Of course, I am. She was that age when we met. I know my own first wife's face."

Nacaria took a glance at the screen and agreed, "Yes, that was how Atheidrelle looked at around 20."

"I found this photo among others in Blackie's bedroom," Arielle informed them. "They were hidden away. The photo has a name written on the back, but it isn't Atheidrelle's. It said it was a photo of someone named Wilhelmina Jackson. Any idea why it said that or who she was?"

Xander thought for a moment before replying, "The D'Angelos had some distant cousins who were Jacksons. I think they were all from Mount Pleasant. I wouldn't swear to it though. I can't say why her name is on this picture, but the photo is definitely of Atheidrelle."

"Perhaps it was a mistake?" Nacaria suggested.

"Maybe," Arielle replied. "But there were other photos, all mislabeled. One with Thaddeuss labeled Malcolm Jackson and one of Blackie labeled Deidre D'Angelo."

"Deidre D'Angelo died years and years ago," Xander said. "Way before I met the family. But it was all over the papers then. Car wreck I believe. I think she was Hugh D'Angelo's niece."

"It's strange," Echo said. "Multiple pictures with the wrong names written on them. We are hoping to get to the bottom of it."

Xander looked concerned. "Don't go poking around in that family," he warned. "This isn't a game to play. The D'Angelos are sinister. I'd stay as far away as possible."

"Well, they are actually our family," Echo noted. "I personally am curious. While we are here on business, I plan to visit them."

Xander's face flushed. "I wish you wouldn't," he cautioned. "I avoid them at all costs."

"Isn't Cassandra there?" Arielle asked.

"Against our wishes," Xander explained. "She felt the need to help Taub, but I won't rest a night until she's back in this house."

"Well, it will be good to see her while we are here," Arielle said. "I don't think a quick visit to the D'Angelos will cause any harm. Echo is pretty eager to know more about where he comes from."

With a stern look toward Echo, Nacaria wiped her mouth with her napkin and set it aside. "You come from Beryl Blanchard," she reminded him. "You come from my sister Demitra. You come from Olympia. Isn't that sufficient?"

Echo offered a polite nod but replied, "Yes. I love the Blanchards. I am proud to be one. But I still want to know more about my mother's people. It doesn't erase my loyalty and affection."

"Just be cautious son," Xander said. "For your sake, and my daughter's."

The following morning Arielle and Echo met with Edna Williams at Williams Boat and Outboard Repair. Once they had the preliminary back and forth over the price she was hopeful to get and they talked about the realistic price according to the assets, Echo and Arielle made inspections of the several locations on the islands. It was a rather dull day, but the commission Howard's company would receive from the sale was going to be substantial. They decided to break for lunch a little after 1 o'clock, and Arielle drove them to her favorite place in Charleston, Leon's.

"This place is known for oysters and fried chicken," she told him. "Do not tell Artemis, but their fried chicken is even better than hers. I always have it."

"I'm totally getting one of these Rosé slushies," Echo grinned. "I don't care if we're still working."

Arielle raised one eye, "You know you are not 21 yet."

Echo grinned mischievously, "That's what having a really cool big sister is for."

Waiting for the waitress to come take their order, Arielle and Echo were distracted by a heated conversation happening at a nearby table. The bustle of the restaurant kept them from hearing everything being said, but it was a tense interaction. They could only see the man—young, sandy haired, chiseled cheeks, good looking. The young woman was seated with her back to them. All they could see of her was her gorgeous, full-bodied coffee-colored hair.

"I told you it is over," the man said, raising his voice. "I don't know why we had to meet. We settled this weeks ago. I don't want to see you anymore."

"I don't accept that," the young woman challenged.

"You have to accept it! I don't want this relationship to continue."

"Why?" she asked. "Have you found someone else?"

He sighed and shook his head in frustration. "That has nothing to do with it."

"Then you have."

Arielle and Echo made silent surprised faces at each other. A few other diners who also were overhearing this tense conversation exchanged wide-eyed expressions with Arielle and Echo. Arielle mouthed the word *Awkward*.

"Yes, there is someone I am interested in," the man said angrily. "We have been out a few times this week, but she isn't why I broke up with you. What you and I had was not that serious."

"It was serious to me," the young woman countered. "Is there some reason why you can't care for me the way I care for you?"

The man leaned closer to her over the table and with all seriousness in his tone answered, "Frankly, I am a little afraid of you. You are intense—scary at times."

Both Arielle and Echo, now far too invested in the rest of this exchange, strained to hear the girl's response. When it came it was a little desperate, and surprising. She told the man, "Then I'll take the fear until the love can grow."

The man reared back in his seat in utter bewilderment. His voice was elevated when she cried, "I think you're crazy. I really want you to leave me alone." With that he got up, tossed some cash on the table to cover the check, and left the restaurant.

The young woman sat there alone for the next several minutes. The waitress came over to Arielle and Echo's table to take their order. As she stepped away, they noticed the young woman who had just been dumped rise from her chair to leave. Getting a better look at her now, they noticed she was eerily beautiful. Her shoulder length hair cascaded down her back like black mink, and she had the most piercing green eyes. Her skin was alabaster, and she was wearing the reddest shade of lipstick Arielle had ever seen. As Arielle stared, the young woman's eyes met with hers. She paused, as if recognizing her. The woman approached the table.

"You don't remember me, do you?"

Arielle looked puzzlingly at the girl, half embarrassed she might suspect they eavesdropped, but also curiously trying to place where she knew her from. "Did we go to school together?" Arielle asked. "Please forgive me, I've been away from Charleston a while."

"We are cousins. Second cousins, actually. My father is Taub. I'm Mara D'Angelo."

"That's right!" Arielle exclaimed, rising to give an awkward hug. "Oh, it must be seven or eight years now since we last saw each other. This is my brother, Echo."

"Also, my cousin," Mara smiled, shaking his hand. "I have heard about you from my grandfather, Thaddeuss."

"Won't you join us?" Echo politely invited. He felt ashamed now for having been on the man's side now that he knew the girl being dumped was his cousin.

"Only for a moment," Mara said, sliding into an empty chair. "I just had a terrible argument with my boyfriend. I am afraid I am not great company. However, I am so pleased to see you again, Arielle and to meet my newest cousin."

Arielle frowned as she placed a concerned hand on Mara's, "We heard some of that conversation. I'm sorry things ended badly."

Mara made a bemused face and said, "Oh that wasn't the end. We go through that kind of thing all the time. With us it's never really over."

It seemed pretty over to me, Arielle thought to herself but out of politeness, said nothing.

The awkwardness of the moment felt heavy, causing Echo to change the subject. "We are hoping to pay a visit to your grandfather and meet the family while we are in town," Echo informed Mara. "But I'm glad to know you first. I'll have one friend I already know when I meet the D'Angelos."

Mara's expression changed to one more morose. "I may be the only friend you'll have in that house," she remarked. "Please let me know when you plan to visit so that I can make certain to be there—to help you through any difficulties."

"Difficulties?" Echo repeated.

"My family are not the kindest of people. In fact, they despise your mother. I have no idea why they are so eager to meet you. Be wary of them."

"That seems to be a general consensus among everyone we've talked to," Echo remarked.

Arielle was curious about something Mara said and decided to ask. "You said we should let you know when we plan to visit so you can be there. Don't you live at the House of Duquesne?"

Mara gave a sly wink and answered, "I am supposed to live there on weekends. During school I stay in a little apartment I rent over the garage of a house on Church Street. I rarely return home if I can help it. I try to limit my time at the House of Duquesne."

"May I ask why?" Echo replied.

"You'll see when you visit," Mara said. "The family. The house. The things that go bump in the night there. I have never felt comfortable in that place, and the moment I was old enough to get away from it I did. However, if I hope to retain my generous allowance from my father, I must give the semblance of still living there."

Arielle was confused. "No one knows you don't live there anymore?"

"You know the House of Duquesne, Arielle," Mara commented. "Who would have any idea I wasn't somewhere inside it? I have my bedroom. I pay a maid to muss the bed every weekend morning, flush toilet paper so the rolls decrease, toss clothes around—you know, so the more talkative servants think I've been there."

"I have never heard anything so weird before," Echo stated. "To go to such lengths. Couldn't you just leave in the open and live on your own?"

"Not in our family," Mara replied. "D'Angelos never leave. In fact, I never understood how Aunt Blackie managed to get away until the truth came out about you, Arielle. Then I realized she must have bargained with Grandfather and Atheidrelle for her freedom. Anyway, I have taken enough of your lunch time. Here is a card with my number on it. Text me when you plan to visit, and I will be there. Good to meet you, Echo, and to see you again, Arielle."

As Mara left Arielle made a face at her brother. "See? That family is peculiar."

CHAPTER SEVENTEEN

Blackie's Stubbornness

Blackie D'Angelo blinked vigorously in defiance at her physical therapist. The more he tried to move her right arm and leg, the more she expressed her frustration in the only way that she could.

"Ms. D'Angelo," he told her. "I have to try and determine your range of motion. I understand this is uncomfortable, but it must be done."

Blackie gestured with her left hand as if wanting to write something. He offered her a pen and held a clipboard before her where she scribbled in broken handwriting, *Heal myself.*

"You can't heal yourself. You need therapy."

Tess had been standing in the doorway observing and decided it was time to step in. Walking over to the table where Blackie was laying, she shook her finger in her mother's face and clicked her tongue. "Stop acting like a spoiled child, Mother," Tess scolded. "This man is here to help you. And whether you like it or not, you and I are repeating these same exercises at home this afternoon and tonight."

Blackie pointed her weak finger at the clip board.

"You can't heal yourself on your own. And you really have no say so in this. Until you can walk and talk and tell me to go to hell, I am in charge of you. You are going to get better if I have to yell at you every single day. Now stop being so prideful and follow orders."

That evening when Trix took over for Tess, Tess recounted their mother's stubbornness. Both sisters understood how hard it had to be for a woman as independent as Blackie D'Angelo to admit vulnerability and accept help. But whether she liked it or not, she was a stroke victim, and she was going to have to be patient while she recovered in the normal way...just like everyone else in the world. This was one time that being a witch was not going to give her an advantage.

Trix repeated the exercises on Blackie that evening. Blackie didn't fight them this time, giving in to the way things were at the moment. Trix said very little during the exercises. She understood that talking unnecessarily to someone who could not respond, especially someone like Blackie, only made her feel even more helpless. Or worse, childlike. Trix was very much the same. She respected her mother's need to feel in control even if she wasn't. And during the silent exercises, Trix's mind wandered back to old times, in another dimension, when she had been the patient after falling off a ravine and breaking her leg mid-flee from vampires. Her mother, the other Blackie—Blackie Blanchard—had helped her regain movement of her leg in much this same way. Trix had been just as stubborn then as Blackie D'Angelo was being now. Trix looked at Blackie's features while she lifted her arm and leg into different positions. She looked so much like the mother of Trix's childhood. Trix sometimes forgot that they were in fact two totally different people. She felt a pang of remorse for somehow forgetting her own mother too often these days because her doppelganger was now in her life. How do you mourn someone who is still with you? Yet she wasn't, not really. Trix had two mothers now, and she wasn't quite sure how to reconcile the differences between the women when there weren't really much of a difference at all between them.

...

Midmorning, Artemis found Miranda laying on a quilt under the grape arbor reading a storybook to Titan, Rom, and Olympus. The boys seemed more interested in wresting the book from her hands to chew on than hearing the story. Rom was not interested in the book at all, too preoccupied swatting at a nearby butterfly. Artemis laughed a little to herself at the sight.

"I believe they are a little too young to appreciate a good book," she said, joining them on the ground.

"I know," Miranda smiled. "But I like to stimulate their minds whenever I can."

Artemis tilted the book to the side to read the cover. "The Little House. I used to read this to their parents. It always made me cry. The little house in the country, slowly being choked to death by progress and growth as the city grows around it. Then it gets hauled out of the chaos and placed back onto another countryside where it is happy again."

"Reminds me of my life," Miranda replied. "Out of chaos and back to tranquility."

Artemis liked that she drew that similarity. She often wondered what Miranda felt inside. "You do enjoy it here, don't you?"

Miranda pulled the edge of the book from Olympus' teeth. "I truly do. I sometimes forget what it was like where I came from. You all have been so good to me. I feel like this is my home."

"It is your home."

Titan took a swat at Olympus; angry he had taken the book into his own hands. Miranda gently reminded Titan that we do not hit other people. Then she patted Romulus and gave him permission to chase the butterfly as long as he did not harm it. The young wolf took off over the grass after the escaping insect.

"You are so good with them," Artemis said. "We all appreciate what you do around here."

Miranda blushed and changed the subject. Artemis recognized the woman's self-deprecating aversion to compliments. "Have you heard from Echo or Arielle?" Miranda asked.

"No, not yet," Artemis answered. "Howard should be returning in a week, so I expect they will be back in the office shortly after that. I'm afraid our family's business keeps him moving at a swift pace these days."

"Is it strange that he is a part of your family now?" Miranda asked. "Or is that really too personal a question?"

Artemis chuckled. "Oh sweety, the Blanchards have few personal secrets. But to answer your question, it was at first, I suppose, but perhaps not when I really think of it. Howard has been a part of us for all his life. All our lives. Like you are now, he was a part of this family despite whether he was blood tied or not. Turns out he was blood related the entire time, but that did not change very much from our vantage point. I think he had the lion's share of getting used to things."

"Is it true you and he were once engaged?"

"Yes, it is." Artemis laughed again, privately recalling those long-gone days. "Obviously now it makes more sense as to why my mother was against our marriage. I had not understood that then because she'd always loved Howard. Now it is pretty clear."

"Sorry I'm so curious," Miranda apologized. "I guess I like hearing about your family because I've really been missing my sister lately."

"It is hard to feel alone, I imagine," Artemis said gently. "We never have had to worry about that around here. I had my sisters. The children had each other. And now these little ones have each other to grow up with. I hope you know you have us as well. You'll never be alone if you don't want to be."

"I do know that. I appreciate it more than you know," Miranda said. "And I do feel part of the family. Well, as much as a non-magical person could."

"Well, you are in good company with Howard and Jerry. And of course, Yasmine was like you. She had no powers other than the two times she was pregnant. It seems we Blanchards always have a few non magical family members around."

CHAPTER EIGHTEEN

The House of Duquesne

Time seemed endless after the car entered the wrought iron front gates. The winding, stretching drive beneath the canopy of trees, heavy with foliage, defied the afternoon sky by blotting out the sunlight, casting midnight shadows along the road. Nothing could be seen beyond the barricade of oaks and brush and patches of vines. Echo rode in the passenger seat speechless as Arielle drove to the house.

"It's like a world to its own."

"It really is," Arielle replied. "I think they have about as much land as the Blanchards, but every bit of it is dreary. I don't know if there is a single patch of land where sunlight consistently falls."

"It's like a swampy forest."

The car eventually moved from the darkness into a broader scope where minimal light could shine through to illuminate the great house. Arielle instinctively braked although she did not know why. The two of them sat staring up at the creature waiting before them.

"It's atrocious," Echo gasped. "I hadn't expected it to be so...hideous."

"Menacing is the word," Arielle corrected.

The house was unlike anything Echo Blanchard had ever imagined possible. Its walls of stone and hard brick, neither in any discernible pattern, seemed clumsily pieced together. Mortar was haphazardly dispersed between each layer as though a blind man had sealed the walls. The shell of the house extended so widely and deeply that it seemed to Echo to be not one house, but many pressed together in chaos. There was no defining number of floors visible. Some areas appeared to be two stories tall while others stretched to at least five. Balconies were tossed in at random without thought or balance. One or two alarming towers rose in the background behind pitched rooftops and spires. The house had no symmetry. No theme. Windows did not align with others that appeared to share the same floor, nor were the windows of the same style. It was a combination of too many architectural fashions, constructed with a clashing arrangement of every imaginable material. The House of Duquesne was a cancer sprouting out of the dank marshlands, scarring whatever morose beauty these lands might have once possessed.

As Arielle continued the drive toward the house, Echo could not turn his eyes away from the fascinating disorder. Windows unaligned, doors placed several stories high where no balcony stood to catch whoever passed through them. The D'Angelos had to be wealthy. There was no doubt about that. The estate, though ghastly, was no poor man's home. Repulsive as it was, the house itself was like a castle. But Echo could not rationalize who on earth would build a house as horrifying as this.

The car slowed to a stop beneath a stone portico flanked with what looked like devils for gargoyles on the roofline. Two elaborately carved wooden doors, moorish in design, stood before them atop three large stone slab steps. While Echo was still taking it all in, the doors opened where Mara stood to greet them.

"Welcome to the House of Duquense."

Mara led Arielle and Echo into the entrance hall. Unlike the exterior of the house, the entrance hall was magnificent. Mahogany walls with dozens of intricately carved panels lined the room. A colossal spiral staircase of marble twisted to the floor above, its iron railings further embellishing the already impressive feature. Regal and colorfully stained glass hovered in sections overhead in the foyer to form a domed ceiling. The stained glass depicted a pastoral scene which slowly changed colors to depict the changing seasons. The floor was a heavy dark stone, and Arielle's heels clicked atop it as they strode inside.

"This is surprisingly beautiful," Echo exclaimed as he allowed his lungs to breathe in the fragrant botanicals coming from the large urn of freshly cut flowers in the center of the hall.

"Quite different from outside, isn't it?" Mara commented.

"Very," Echo nodded.

"It is rather nice in places here and there," Mara agreed. "Then when you least expect it, it startles you again."

"Where is everyone?" Arielle asked.

"They are in the main Drawing Room having pre-dinner drinks," Mara said. "I'll take you there."

Echo whispered in his sister's ear as they followed, "Do you know where that is?"

"I don't know if I've ever been in there," Arielle said. "There is a library I was in once and something called the evening room. But mostly I played outside the few times I was ever here."

Mara led her cousins to a hall behind the staircase. The hallway was long, a gallery of sorts, with paintings of what Echo and Arielle assumed were long dead relatives. They thought they might see portraits of Thaddeuss, Atheidrelle, and even Blackie by the time they reached the end, but they didn't reach the end. Halfway through the hall, Mara grasped the frame of a portrait depicting a tall man in a bowler cap and dandy suit. Pulling it forward she revealed a secret door in the wall.

"Wow!" Arielle gasped. "Are all the paintings secret doors?"

"No," Mara answered. "But there are surprises all around. Some I'm sure I still have never discovered. I don't know how many hidden passages there are. But this is the quickest way to the drawing room. At least it was the last time I went in there. The house changes sometimes."

"Changes?" Echo repeated.

Mara seemed far too casual in her reply, "Yeah, sometimes doors aren't there anymore. Halls disappear. New ones sprout up. You get used to it."

As they continued following Mara, Echo turned to his sister and mouthed with wide eyes, *You get used to it.*

As they maneuvered through a new hallway, Arielle and Echo saw a slender staircase ahead. As if she felt them noticing it, Mara gestured toward it and said, "That stair goes up about 25 steps and then takes you back down again, and you end up back on the portrait hall. It's a big waste of time, don't ever use it." They continued moving ahead as the sound of voices began to be audible.

"Must be close," Echo said. "I hear them."

"We are close," Mara said. "But that doesn't mean anything. You hear voices all over this house. I guess it's haunted, although no one has ever said so."

She opened a paneled door and led them into the drawing room. Before Echo even noticed the people inside, he noticed the room itself. It was excessively large and rectangular. It reminded him of a documentary he watched on European castles. It was like a grand gallery where olden day people at court milled about gossiping as they waited their turn for an audience with the king. Long couches sat in several arrangements providing multiple conversation centers. One large fireplace—large enough for four men to stand inside—stood fireless against the back wall. The walls were papered in richly colored fabrics as if they had been covered with tapestries. End tables held overflowing flower arrangements and lush rugs spread across the parquet floor.

In one of the centermost furniture arrangements, a group of people was gathered with cocktails in hand. Echo immediately recognized Thaddeuss D'Angelo who was now looking up to see them. His chiseled, bearded face gave a large smile as he came forward to greet his guests.

"Arielle, my dear. And Echo, my boy! I am so pleased you could come tonight. I have been so anxious to acquaint you with your family. But where are your sisters? I was hoping to see everyone tonight."

"Tess and Trix are in Birmingham with Blackie," Echo explained. "She's had a stroke and they are taking care of her."

"What a shame," Thaddeuss frowned unconvincingly. "My poor sister. I will cast a spell for her speedy recovery."

Arielle suddenly saw her sister standing up from a chair and rushing toward her. "Cassandra!" she shouted.

The two embraced. Arielle had not expected to be as glad to see Cassandra as she was. Perhaps it was the frightening feeling of the house or perhaps it was because they had only managed to finally become close over the last few years. Whatever the reason, Arielle felt safer now.

As Thaddeuss pulled Echo by the arm to meet everyone else, Arielle had a short moment with her sister. "How are you? How are things going here?"

"It is so strange, Ari," Cassandra whispered. "But so far I've had no problems. I just feel like there is something happening all around me all the time and cannot figure it out. This place is so weird." The sisters joined Echo as introductions were being made around the room.

"I want you all to meet our newest family member, Echo Blanchard," Thaddeuss said with a hand on Echo's shoulder.

Echo felt a little less anxiety as Thaddeuss' comforting hand patted his back. He felt like he really was being presented at court, but by the king himself no less. A woman came forward. She looked sophisticated. Radiant. Her reddish-brown hair had two cool gray streaks rising from each temple, curving down to her cat-like cheekbones.

"I am Constance D'Angelo," she introduced with a smile. "I am Thaddeuss' wife."

"Very nice to know you," Echo said.

"Hello, Arielle," Constance said past his shoulder. "It is wonderful to see you again. You have grown into a stunning young woman."

"Thank you, Aunt Constance."

"This is my son, Taub," Thaddeuss said next as Taub D'Angelo stepped up.

"It is good to meet you, cousin," Taub nodded. "I believe you already know my daughter, Mara. And this is my other daughter, Ashby."

A younger girl around thirteen gave a slight bow and smiled brightly. She had blond hair, unlike Mara, and seemed like an average—albeit well mannered—child. Echo immediately liked her. Arielle did not remember her but figured she must have been quite little when Arielle had last been there, and the D'Angelo's were not known for keeping their children close.

A handsome young blonde man stepped up next. He had long hair that reached down to his shoulders. Echo almost laughed when he introduced himself as Thorne D'Angelo, Thaddeuss' other son. At first Echo thought he'd said his name was Thor, quite fitting since he looked very much like the movie superhero of the same name.

"You're Thorne?" Arielle asked curiously.

"Yes," Thorne replied. "Do you not remember me, cousin?"

"No, it's not that," Arielle stumbled. "You just look different from when we were little."

"Well, it has been a long time ago," Thaddeuss replied.

Constance gave a soft laugh and placed her hand on her son's arm, "And my son has decided to indulge a look I don't quite approve of with this long hair."

I remember Thorne D'Angelo as being dark headed, Arielle thought to herself. Cassandra seemed to know what she was thinking and discreetly shook her head, tilting it slightly toward Taub as if to say, *he can hear you if you are thinking something.*

Dinner at the D'Angelos house was a feast. Echo and Arielle dined on lamb with apple chutney served on delicate china. The antique silverware and crystal must have cost more than Echo and Arielle made in a year. The dining room which adjoined the drawing doom was similarly designed with two large gothic chandeliers hanging over the long, oak table. Windows comprised two of the walls and must have been open because the sheer lace covering them trembled lightly in the breeze as the sound of crickets chirped beyond.

"Tonight is a special treat in many ways," Constance said over dinner. "Not only do we get to dine with the two of you, but since she arrived Cassandra has only dined with us once."

"I don't like to leave Alexandrea alone," Cassandra said politely. "Had one of the maids not offered to relieve me, I wouldn't be here tonight. But I couldn't pass up seeing my sister."

"How are you settling in here?" Constance asked Cassandra. "Do you require anything to make your stay and your job easier?"

"I'm getting along fine," Cassandra replied. "The doctor is coming tomorrow, so I am looking forward to officially meeting him and discussing treatment options. So far, we have only spoken by phone. Other than getting lost a few times in the house, things are well."

"This house," Echo commented before he could stop himself. "It really is something."

Thaddeuss laughed. "It is an unusual place to say the least. But it is home."

"Why is it so...unusual?" Echo asked. "Or is that rude?"

"Not at all dear boy," Thaddeuss smiled. "It's a natural question. One we have had to answer many times over the years. It is actually quite an interesting story. Quite famous in Charleston."

"I'm not sure I even know that story," Arielle admitted. "Mother never talked to me very much."

Thaddeuss began the tale, telling it as if it were a ghost story he'd memorized word by word long ago sitting by a campfire.

"Emmerick Duquesne was a good farmer, a genius in the cotton industry. Seizing an opportunity to purchase a small shipping company, Emmerick thought he could profit from shipping his goods himself as well as provide new income from the venture. He was successful in the beginning, successful enough to marry a member of the prominent Jackson family and start his own. His well-bred wife was accustomed to an elaborate lifestyle and Emmerick was able to provide lavishly. Their children were presented to Charleston society at the proper ages, and the immensely wealthy Duquesne family were among the most esteemed families in the state. As Emmerick continued to prosper, he arranged for the construction of a new plantation house. One which would be the marvel of South Carolina, perhaps the entire south. Vanity took hold and the plans grew more and more elaborate, the cost of construction grew to astronomical figures. But Duquesne had the prestige and the credit to build whatever he desired.

"It was decided that while the home was being constructed, Emmerick would whisk his wife and children away to Europe as he expanded his shipping offices in the hopes of becoming international. He hired the most renowned architect in Charleston, who also happened to be his wife's brother. Emmerick, trusting his brother-in-law as well as his impeccable reputation as a builder, left the construction solely to his management while away. The architect hired crews to work around the clock, rushing the construction so that when Duquesne returned his masterpiece would be awaiting him."

"Sounds like the brother-in-law was a terrible architect from the design of the house," Echo commented, then felt bad for doing so. "Sorry, I don't mean to insult your home."

Thaddeuss gave a broad laugh, "Not at all, my boy. It is that specific part of the story I was coming up to...

"While touring Europe, Emmerick met another woman with whom he began a tumultuous affair. His wife was heartbroken. She was a Jackson, after all—a prize in America. To be so easily tired of and replaced was a humiliation to which she was not accustomed. A vindictive woman, Duquesne's wife never confronted her husband over it. It would not have mattered even if she had. Wives were powerless in those days to do anything about a husband's dalliances. However, she did confide her pain in letters to her brother back home. A plan was set in motion. As if fate were on her side in vengeance, a great hurricane hit Charleston while they were in Europe, destroying the bulk of Duquesne's ships back home. Having borrowed heavily to build a shipping empire in Europe, not to mention the house construction, Duquesne was over leveraged. With the South Carolina branch in ruins, he fell into bankruptcy. Emmerick's only income was the revenue from his plantation. His wife, humiliated by her husband's infidelity, had clung to their massive wealth as her only reason for living. With that wealth eradicated and her love destroyed, she killed herself before they sailed home. Emmerick, unmoved by her passing, wed his mistress, boasting to her of the fine new mansion awaiting them in Charleston. With debts mounting, his accounts emptied, and every reserve completely exhausted, Duquesne and his new bride, and their newborn child, sailed for home where at least he would have his newly constructed mansion as a beacon for future success.

"Emmerick Duquesne and his wife found their arrogance dashed the moment their carriage came through the gates. He was appalled at the monstrosity. The architectural design for the house which he had chosen before Europe, had been abandoned and replaced with an array of competing choices without order or logic. Stone, brick, plaster, wood, all thrown into a mix lacking perspective or craftsmanship. Chaotic hallways, unconventional materials, displeasing color schemes, unpredictable staircases; the horrible disfigurements to his plans enraged him. The monthly reports he had been receiving while away had all been deliberate fabrications. It had been his hope that his illustrious new home might spark confidence in the bankers of South Carolina to aid him in rebuilding his fortune. Those hopes were dissolved at first glimpse of the house. All his months of boasting, all his hopes of a better future, ruined forever by an architect's revenge.

"Laughing at Duquesne upon arrival, the architect explained his triumph. He had taken Duquesne's vast fortune and created an eyesore that would never erode away. It was his retribution for his sister's life. He said the house would stand as a reflection of the sin perpetrated upon her.

"Emmerick Duquesne was practically a pauper now. Only his farm remained. His house was unsellable—no way to recoup the money spent on it. Emmerick Duquesne had no choice but to stay and live within these monstrous walls with his whore."

"Wow!" Echo said after Thaddeuss finished the tale. "That is quite a story."

"Poetic justice, don't you think? When you take something from someone, you must pay a price for it. Never underestimate a brother's love for his sister," Thaddeuss said rather sinisterly.

Arielle shuddered a moment, unsure whether Thaddeuss' remark was meant to compliment her and Echo's relationship or if he were hinting at his residing rage over what happened to Atheidrelle.

"Of course," Thaddeuss continued, "Emmerick Duquesne had no alternatives. Later as the Duquesne family evolved, and a female heir married into the D'Angelo family—a witching family—money and power returned to the family line."

"May I ask why you remain here?" Echo asked. "Not to be insulting, but if you all hate this house so much, surely now you can afford to live anywhere."

"Roots, my boy. Roots," Thaddeuss bellowed. "Moreover, the house is now considered something of a showplace. It has been studied by architecture students for years. It is famous in its own right. Besides, the Duquesnes have always lived here. The D'Angelo/Duquesnes have always lived here."

Arielle looked meekly over her dinner plate and asked, "What happened to the architect?"

"Who?" Constance asked.

"The architect who got his revenge on Emmerick Duquesne. What happened to him?"

Taub answered, and with a chuckle. "His triumphant moment was short-lived. My great-great-grandfather killed him somewhere in this house. Nobody one-ups a Duquesne."

CHAPTER NINETEEN

Voices in the Walls

Once dinner was over, Arielle followed Cassandra back upstairs to her room for a last goodbye before she and Echo returned to Oleander. Arielle was taken aback by the confusing twists and turns of the house but quite impressed to see that her sister seemed to have memorized them.

"Just down this hallway and to the left," guided Cassandra around a corner. Suddenly she slapped directly into a wall. "Ouch!"

Arielle laughed out loud. "So much for your knowing the way."

Cassandra seemed perplexed, almost bothered. "Seriously, Ari, this wall was not here earlier. And do you smell that? It smells chemical."

"It does actually," Arielle noticed. "It smells a little like glue."

Cassandra reached down and touched the baseboard trim. "This board is lighter than the ones on the other wall. It's wet paint, see."

She took her fingernails and dug into the corner of the board where the wallpaper ended. With little effort she managed to pull the corner of paper upward.

"Freshly glued," Arielle observed. "This wall is new."

"Like two hours ago new," Cassandra said. "Why?"

Arielle made a funny face and shrugged, "Mara said the house changes itself sometimes."

Cassandra grimaced, "Houses do not change themselves little sister. We've been witches all our lives, and I have never found a house with a mind of its own."

"Well, something blocked this hallway."

"Yes, something did. But I know another route to my room. I really need to check on Alexandrea. This has me concerned."

Eventually, using a route through more complicated passages, Cassandra opened the door to her own bedroom. Arielle was busy admiring the room until her eyes stopped on the disconcerting portrait of Atheidrelle. Cassandra was already rushing through the connecting door to Alexandrea's chamber. Arielle followed her sister.

Alexandrea was not sitting in the chair where Cassandra left her and the housemaid, Betty, was nowhere in sight. The room was empty.

"Where is she?" Cassandra said to herself mostly, looking around the room frantically. "Betty wouldn't take her out of here." She opened the bathroom door and found it empty as well. A sudden breeze swept the room.

Arielle followed the path of the breeze, "Cassandra, the door to the balcony is open."

Cassandra dashed to the balcony where she found her patient standing at the rail, staring out into the night.

"What is she looking at?" Arielle asked.

"I have no idea," Cassandra said. "But she's always looking out here. I don't know what goes through her mind. Does she remember her life before? But what I want to know is where is the maid, Betty?"

"It doesn't matter as long as your patient is all right, I guess," Arielle said, helping her sister bring the catatonic woman indoors.

"She's bleeding," Arielle observed, lifting her arm up.

"That's an injection site," Cassandra explained. "Taub must have come up to give her nightly sedation. It keeps her from wandering."

"Why would she wander?" Arielle replied. "Ever see where she's trying to wander to?"

Cassandra could not believe the thought had not occurred to her before. Where was Alexandrea attempting to run off to when she wandered away? Perhaps it was worth finding out. Cassandra now pondered if discovering Alexandrea's agenda might unlock a clue as to get her mind back on track.

"Taub always gives her the injections. I don't know how I'd stop it."

"I do," Arielle smiled. "How fresh do you think this injection is?"

"Minutes probably," Cassandra considered. "He was with us through dinner, and we just left the dining room. We were only lost for about fifteen minutes."

"Good," Arielle said, taking Alexandrea's arm and turning it upright to expose the bloody pin prick. Arielle closed her eyes and focused her powers to move objects. Manipulating the air around her to operate as a sort of vacuum, she pressed the suctioning air above the tiny hole in the woman's flesh. Within seconds a small stream of blood, no larger than a thread, began to lift out and into the air. Cassandra captured it with a water glass.

"Oh my God, Arielle!" Cassandra cried. "You are a genius! You just took the medicine out of her."

"Watch her tonight, and see where she tries to go," Arielle suggested. "Let me know in the morning what happens. I really need to get back. I love you, sis."

"I love you, too." The Obreiggon girls hugged, and Arielle started for the door.

"Can you find your way back?"

"We will see," Arielle chuckled.

Arielle left her sister's bedroom the way they originally entered. Tracing their previous footsteps proved to be no use at all as Arielle found herself confused by the many sharp turns along the way. She reached a small, narrow set of stairs that led down to a mezzanine which overlooked an interior greenhouse. She definitely had not ventured this way before. *Well, it is not like I can get too lost. It is a house after all. Eventually I will find an exit.* She continued for a while past the greenhouse and discovered a narrow hallway with a circular staircase wedged between stone walls. She followed it down to the next level but paused halfway because she heard distinct voices coming from within the walls. Pressing her ear to the cold stone, she could make out a little of whatever was being said but the words were broken by the thick barrier.

"...visitors were here."

"anyone...importance...could use."

"God Strain."

Arielle popped her head back. The God Strain? Did they mean Beryl? Was Beryl here? Then it occurred to her that whoever was speaking was referring to Echo. They must have been referring to Echo. He was the direct descendant of Beryl. The only person with the God Strain blood in Duquesne House.

Then she heard something else which startled her again. Something she could not quite understand. Her name. Someone was whispering her name. It seemed to float on the air. *Arielle. Arielle. Arielle come to me.*

"You hear the voices, don't you?" Ashby said from the turn of the stairs above. "I was on my way to my room when I saw you paused here. You hear them too, don't you?"

Arielle whirled around to face her young cousin. "Yes. It is coming from the walls. Is it Uncle Thaddeuss and Aunt Constance?"

"No. It isn't anyone in the house that we know." Ashby said matter-of-factly.

"I have heard the voices all my life. They are not from anyone in the family. My grandparents are still downstairs. Father went to bed."

It could be Mara, or Echo or Thorne?"

Ashby shook her head. "No. It isn't them either. I think it is the voices of ghosts."

The girl was not afraid in any way. It seemed strange to Arielle how unaffected Ashby seemed to be by something rather unnerving.

"I heard my name called."

"Interesting," Ashby whispered. "If you are lost, I can lead you back to the entrance hall."

"Thank you so much. I did get lost. Earlier Cassandra and I found a wall where she claims a hallway was yesterday."

As the child guided Arielle down the stairs onto the floor below, she replied, "The house does like to change itself. I think the ghosts get bored."

"Being a witch, I thought nothing could ever surprise me," Arielle replied, making whatever conversation she could to fill the echoing silence—or perhaps to muffle the sounds of the voices if they were to begin again.

Ashby slanted her eyes Arielle's way as they continued and said, "Just one of the many secrets of the House of Duquesne. You know the poem, right?"

"I do. Somewhat."

"I find it fascinating..." Ashby whispered as she began to recite a portion of the rhyme:

"Truth is best left farthest from light
And answers are reasons you can't sleep at night
Old family wealth laced with old family name
Mixed with too many secrets in The House of Duquesne."

"What a heritage!" Arielle laughed.

Ashby successfully led Arielle back to the door of the drawing room before bidding her goodnight and returning upstairs. Arielle was so relieved to find Echo still inside with Thaddeuss, Constance, and Thorne. Echo and Arielle thanked the family for the hospitality and announced they had to leave. Thaddeuss tried to convince them to stay the night, but Arielle insisted they return to Oleander.

"Please do remember that this house is your home any time," Constance told them. "While you are in town on business, we expect to see more of you."

Echo nodded and replied, "We will definitely come back before we return to Alabama."

Thorne took a step forward, placing his back to his parents. "Perhaps we can meet in town for lunch one day as well," he suggested. He seemed to be saying this primarily to Echo, and Arielle noticed. "I know you will both be busy with work, but I have an art gallery on King Street I'd love to show you sometime while you are here."

"That'd be nice," Echo smiled as he and Arielle turned to leave.

On the drive off the estate, Arielle felt unnerved. She felt as if she were being watched from the forest. Echo was quiet as well, but for different reasons. Arielle told him about her moment on the stairs and how she could have sworn someone said her name. She also mentioned hearing the words *the God Strain*.

"I think there's a motive somewhere," Arielle warned. "They are being nice to us because they want you for something. They have never been this nice to me on my own. It's you they are wooing."

"Arielle, I think you are selling them short. I know your dad and Blackie distrust them, but they all seemed very friendly to me. Maybe you are just a little biased because your mother was so evil. I actually kind of like Uncle Thaddeuss."

"And Thorne?" Arielle grinned. "What was that about? He was practically silent through dinner but now wants to show you his gallery."

Echo grinned devilishly and said, "Oh Thorne is totally gay. I caught him checking me out earlier when I glanced in a mirror."

Arielle folded her arms in playful contemplation. "I see."

"He's kind of hot though, isn't he?" Echo added.

"Uh, he's also your cousin!"

"Yeah, but like what? Second or third cousin. Does that even count?"

"Oh my God, you like him!" Arielle exclaimed.

Echo blushed but was also unable to conceal a grin. "I didn't say I liked him, just that he's hot. I don't even know him. Yet. But I think I will check out that gallery."

"Oh my God, if you hook up with our cousin while we are in Charleston-"

"Look, Seth already messed up my only other opportunity. Then he gave me a long lecture on propriety." Echo said.

"My brother is very protective," Arielle laughed. "I had a date pick me up at Blanchard House once, and Seth grilled him like a steak over charcoal. That guy never asked me out again."

CHAPTER TWENTY

Alexandrea's Stroll

It was shortly after midnight when Alexandrea stirred from the chair. Cassandra was waiting on a nearby sofa, half asleep herself when she saw her patient rise without assistance. Alexandrea moved across the room like a ghost, never turning to look at anything other than blankly ahead. Making her way toward the door, she guided herself past furniture as if some internal radar knew where it stood. Cassandra followed her quietly as the zombie-like creature wandered the corridors. Up staircases, down staircases, around bends and twists into territories of the house Cassandra had not yet seen. Eventually, Alexandrea stopped at a door located on a hallway with high-arched windows and stone casements. She paused there for several moments as if awaiting orders. Then, as if some unheard signal rang, she opened the door and entered the room. As Cassandra followed, she could see very little in the darkness. Alexandrea seemed to have no need for light. It was as if she knew exactly where she was going. Tall, gothic windows allowed moonlight to enter the room in slender strips which cast onto the floor. It was a sparsely furnished room except for dozens of statues lining the circular wall. Centered in the room were five tables housing cases and shelving, each holding a particularly ornate bobble. Cassandra guessed this must be some kind of art collection room.

Alexandrea approached a section of wall near a statue of a Grecian woman holding an urn. She slowly knelt down and pressed a stone in the wall a few inches from the floor. Cassandra watched in absolute amazement as the stone began to push itself from the wall to form a two-foot slab protruding out. Alexandrea pressed another stone located about a foot away from the first and a foot higher on the wall. That stone came forward too. As Cassandra watched she witnessed Alexandrea pressing more stones, all protruding out as if on a kind of spring system. The stones were forming a staircase. Alexandrea began to climb the stone slabs, stopping to press higher stones ahead of her until a circular stair came forth, taking her to the top of the room. Cassandra followed, carefully stepping upon each stone, holding the wall with her right hand to balance herself from falling from the rail-less staircase. Alexandrea walked the stairs without issue as if she had done this a hundred times. Near the top of the room, she paused and pressed both hands to the wall. The stones pushed back revealing a doorway. Alexandrea went inside.

Cassandra looked down to the floor below. It would be quite a fall if she tripped. She followed through the doorway behind her patient. They were outside now, atop a parapet overlooking the water. Poking up from the water were tiny tips of grasses. It was high tide now. By daylight the marshland would be returned, but for now the ocean was claiming it. Cassandra stayed close to the door, out of Alexandrea's way but near enough to rush to her aid if her patient were to attempt to jump.

Alexandrea merely stood at the edge, staring out into the night, but at what Cassandra could not see. She waited for several minutes when suddenly she heard a scraping noise coming from beside her. Cassandra whirled around to see a separate panel of stone pushing forward as if another door to the parapet was opening. Cassandra pressed herself into the shadows against the outer wall of the house to remain unseen.

Someone stepped outside with Alexandrea. A man. At first Cassandra thought it might be Taub, until she heard the man speak. It was not Taub D'Angelo's voice. It was deeper. And sinister. He was wearing dark clothing, and the shadowy night made it difficult to make out his features. But as the moonlight hit the side of his face, Cassandra could tell he was no one she had met so far in the house.

"You have found your way at last, my beloved," the man said to Alexandrea.

She did not turn around. She did not react at all. Her catatonic state remained as she stared into the distance. The man gently lifted her hand into his own and kissed her wrist and forearm. Alexandrea did not seem aware at all of anyone's presence or touch.

"Now that you have managed to come to me, I can bring you back to what you once were, and so much more. They interrupted your evolution, but now I can finish what we started. Come with me now, my love."

The man pulled her arm gently toward him, and Alexandrea followed the command. She looked as though she would follow him through the door he exited. Suddenly Cassandra sprung to action, shaken out of her quiet observation. Someone was attempting to take her patient away, and she had to protect Alexandrea.

"Who are you?" she cried, stepping away from the darkness where she had hidden herself.

The man was startled. He had not expected Cassandra to be there. He faced her. His eyes were glaring; he looked menacing. He looked...evil. Suddenly he hissed at her. Actually hissed. As his lips parted, she saw two gleaming fangs illuminate under a shimmer of moonlight. A vampire! Only once in her life had she ever seen a vampire, or the beginnings of one, but she knew what he was the moment he hissed at her.

He charged toward Cassandra. Instinctively, she thrust her hands forward and sent a burst of energy forth. Her power surge smashed into the vampire, sending him hurdling over the parapet battlement. Cassandra rushed to the edge and looked down. He fell straight into the water and out of sight. She grabbed Alexandrea's arm and pulled her back inside the door they had entered from. Slowly she led her back down the stone steps. Though the vampire was now over the edge of the house into the marsh, Cassandra wasted no time getting Alexandrea back to her room. It took some time to find her way, but she managed. Once back inside, Cassandra locked the door and ran to the window to make sure no one was on the balcony waiting. Alexandrea returned to her chair and sat back down, staring out through the windows once again.

"A vampire," Cassandra said out loud. "That is what happened to you. You've been bitten by a vampire."

She could not wrap her mind around it. When this happened to Yasmine, Yasmine had not become comatose. But the man had said the transformation—no, the evolution—had been interrupted. Perhaps Alexandrea D'Angelo was hovering in some strange limbo state of not quite alive, but not yet undead. Cassandra wondered if Taub knew about this or was she perhaps the only person who really knew what happened to his wife.

She decided it was probably best to sleep with Alexandrea that night and not risk her wandering off again, although Cassandra got little rest. The fear of what she had seen and the possibility of that man returning kept her alert through the night. In the morning, she called her sister at Oleander and told her what had occurred the night before.

"This is insane!" Arielle gasped. "What should we do? Call the Consort? Tell Dad? I don't know if you should say anything to the D'Angelos. What if they are vampires?"

"If they were vampires, then we would be vampires," Cassandra pointed out. "Besides, I've seen them during the day. I don't know if they have any idea a vampire is stalking Alexandrea. I think I should tell Taub what I saw. It could be the key to helping her recover."

"That house is crazy," Arielle said. "A vampire on the loose. Ghostly voices. And the house itself is alive or seems to be. How could my mother have grown up in that place?"

"The poem is certainly correct," Cassandra said. "There are too many secrets in the House of Duquesne."

"What do you need me to do?"

"Tell Salem. She's on the Witches Council. I think she should know just in case. I'll talk to Taub and see what his reaction is. If he doesn't seem surprised, then we will know the family knows about this."

"I'm going to tell Echo, too," Arielle said. "He plans to see Thorne tomorrow. Maybe he can get something out of him if Thorne knows anything."

"And see what you can get from Mara," Cassandra suggested. "If she secretly lives in town, maybe this is the reason. Maybe she knows what's happening here and moved out for safety."

"All right," Arielle said. "I have her number. I'll see if she wants to have lunch later today after I meet with the buyer for the boat repair. Be careful, Cassandra. Be very careful. I love you."

"I love you too, Ari."

CHAPTER TWENTY ONE

Half Truths and Dark Conversations

Taub D' Angelo came into his wife's room as he usually did when he awoke each morning. He found Cassandra sitting with her on the sofa brushing her hair. He had a tray of coffee with him for his cousin, and she sat drinking it as he gave his wife her morning injection.

"You look as if you had little sleep last night," he commented.

"I didn't sleep," she admitted. "I should tell you why."

Cassandra began to recount the events of the last evening, beginning with Arielle's removal of the medication from Alexandrea's veins. Taub looked displeased, but he listened to the entire story before saying anything. When Cassandra finished, she listened to his reaction.

"Yes," he said. "I know. I have always known about the vampire. This is the true reason why Alexandrea is in the condition she is currently in. I hoped it would fade considering the transformation to vampire was not completed."

"Why have you kept this secret?"

"For many reasons," Taub explained. "I love my wife deeply. I did not want my girls to know what was happening with their mother unless I knew for certain it was irreversible. I also did not want my father or the rest of the family to know the real situation for fear they would want to end her life. This is why I have not contacted the Council. She is no threat. She poses no danger. She is not a killer. She is not technically a vampire. I interrupted the attack before the monster could drain her blood and replace it with his own. He has only bitten her. Contaminated her, but not changed her."

"Who is he?" Cassandra asked.

"His name is Gideon."

Cassandra sat her coffee aside and faced her cousin directly when she asked,

"How did he find her?"

Taub rose from his seat and walked to stand behind his wife. He made gentle strokes to her hair with his fingertips. She did not react. He leaned down and kissed the top of her head. Cassandra relaxed her demeanor a little seeing his loving affection. Sometimes she wasn't certain whether Taub's tenderness with Alexandrea was genuine or rehearsed. It seemed genuine to her today.

"Charleston is a very old place, Cassandra, as you well know." Taub began. "Ghosts, vampires, witches—this city is steeping in the supernatural. I suppose Gideon saw her and wanted her. I have no explanation. All I know is I walked in just in time to save her and expel him from the room. This room is charmed now, by the way. He cannot enter here. She is safe in this room."

"I have one more question," Cassandra said. "You and I both know how powerful the witching world is. I don't understand why you haven't tried spells or amulets or some magical way to restore her. Surely something can be done."

"Vampires are a race just as powerful in their own right as a witch. I've yet to find a magic that can counteract his damage to her system. I cannot risk the Council destroying her. Perhaps now that you know the truth, together we can save her."

"I will try. I promise you, cousin."

. . .

The waiter gave a funny look to Arielle and Mara's table when he dropped off the bill and overheard Mara exclaim "Vampires?" He lingered a moment to try and hear the rest of the conversation, but the girls stopped talking until he left the table. Once he was out of earshot, Arielle continued her question.

"Do you know of any vampires in Charleston, or on Wadmalaw Island?"

"What a crazy question!" Mara laughed. "No, I don't. I mean, are there even any vampires left around these days? I thought the last pocket of those creatures got wiped out 50 years ago. In fact, wasn't it one of the Blanchards that fought in that battle?"

"Yeah, I think Olympia and her coven took out some vampires in her youth. But surely there are still some out there somewhere."

"What makes you ask all this?"

"I don't know," Arielle replied. "Just wondering. I watched an old movie and saw a woman acting a little like your mom and it turned out a vampire had bitten her."

Mara laughed. "Well, that's a theory. But I'm pretty sure I'd know if my mother had been attacked by a vampire."

The waiter returned to the table and seemed to want to offer something up for the women to consider. He held a flyer in his hand and presented it to them upon his return.

"Couldn't help but hear y'all say something about vampires. My brother and I run a ghost tour at night if you're interested in those kinds of things. Not really got anything on vampires, but lots of ghost stops and stories about witches that live around here."

"Really?" Mara smirked, slanting her eyes at Arielle. "Witches?"

"Oh yeah," the waiter said. Presumptuously, he pulled a chair over to join them. "This city is full of ghosts and witches and all kinds of evil."

"Are witches evil?" Mara asked, playing along. "Aren't there any good ones?"

Arielle gave her a playful wink before looking at the waiter with wide, eager eyes to hear his response.

"Naw, a witch is a minion of the devil. No such thing as a good witch." He looked around to make sure his manager wasn't around. "You two in town long? I guess it's your first trip to Charleston. You should totally check out our ghost tour. I'll write a 10 percent discount on this flyer, and you just give it to my brother when you check in."

"Thanks," Arielle smiled.

As the waiter walked away to service another table, Arielle watched in a bit of shock as her cousin Mara waved her hand and sent a nearby chair hurdling across the floor in front of the irritating waiter. He toppled over the chair and smacked face down into the plates of two diners who had been enjoying their meal. The impact of his head smashing into the table sent glasses tumbling and shards of broken dishes splintering outward. As he righted himself, bits of plate stabbed into his cheek mixed with blood and sauce, with a few angel hair pasta noodles clinging to his hair.

"Oh my God, Mara!"

"What?" Mara sneered. "I thought he deserved that."

Arielle was no longer smiling at the innocent game they were playing with the waiter. It had now crossed a line. "Yeah, but we don't use our powers to exact punishment on regular people."

"Maybe you don't," Mara quipped. "But one of the few pleasures I have in life is messing with idiots like that guy."

. . .

Echo entered The Gallery D'Angelo and found himself intrigued by what he found. He'd assumed the place would be rather stuffy with paintings of the ocean, or the marsh, or those typical landscapes found in every wannabe gallery around. But that was not the case in Thorne's gallery. Pop art abounded along the walls of the front room. Colorful and quirky submissions from up-and-coming artists gave the place a young feel and a more avant guard offering. Mona Lisa reimagined with an image of Janice from The Muppets. The familiar Andy Warhol Tomato Soup can reimagined with a bottle of Cheerwine Cola.

"Not what I expected," Echo remarked as Thorne came over to greet him.

"Wait till you see the back. I have an entire series of religious paintings that all have the same drag queen assembled in the crowd."

"How funny."

"I'm so glad you called about seeing the gallery. I know you originally said tomorrow, but today works better. I have more time today for you. Tomorrow we change out some of the art."

"I'm glad we chose today, too."

Thorne led him through the gallery and showed him the artwork before leading him into a small courtyard in back to have coffee by a fountain. Thorne seemed more at ease in this setting, his own place. Echo found himself liking him more.

"So, you gotta tell me why you stay in that monstrosity of a house!" Echo chuckled trying to begin a conversation.

"It's free. It's home. And my parents basically demand it. When you live on family money, you have to do what family says."

"Surely you can live on your own?" Echo replied. "You have this business after all."

Thorne laughed out loud. "I see you know very little about old money families. Art galleries are the whim of bored housewives with rich husbands or children of rich fathers that have no idea what they want to do in life. This place makes little money. Tourists mostly. It just gives me something to do and someplace to go during the day."

Echo had not expected such honesty. "I guess it is hard to stand on your own if you never had to. I know a little about that myself. My father gave me a job and trained me on how to do it. I had no qualifications until he taught me. And I live in my great-grandmother's house for free, so we are in a similar boat."

"Here's to sponging off the family," Thorne said, raising his coffee mug.

Echo wasn't sure how to present his next question. But it was something he wanted to know, so he spit it out. "So...does your family know you're gay?"

"Oh sure, I suppose," Thorne answered. "However, it is a subject never broached. Charleston isn't a particularly progressive city. Few people live out and proud here. If you do things on the down low and society isn't talking about you, it gets a pass."

"What's the dating scene like around here?" Echo asked.

"There isn't one," Thorne replied. "There is a gay bar, but its tiny. Few people speak to anyone. And there is nobody around here like you."

Echo blushed and sipped his coffee. "Well, you're pretty attractive yourself."

Thorne grinned and confided, "I was hoping nobody saw me staring at you last night. But I couldn't help myself."

"Thanks."

Thorne made a face, "Am I making you uncomfortable? Maybe I read things incorrectly. I thought maybe you felt some kind of attraction to me, too."

Echo blushed a deeper shade of red. "Oh, no, I did. Definitely."

Thorne stood up and led Echo back inside, up a narrow staircase to his office above the shop. Without a word said, he shut the door and locked it. Taking Echo by the shoulders, he began kissing him. The passion was returned. Before long, shirts were peeling off as the two of them crashed down onto the plush sofa. Echo felt a tinge of nervousness as Thorne reached down and pulled Echo's pants off. Echo heard Seth in the background. His voice of caution was too much to tune out.

"Uh, do you have protection?" he asked Thorne.

Thorne made a face and replied, "I'm clean. Plus, I'm on Prep."

"My cousin told me I should take that. But I never went."

"It's okay. I'm on it."

"Does that mean..."

"It means you shouldn't worry about it," Thorne said, crawling on top of Echo.

Echo had never known passion like Thorne emitted. He found himself completely entranced and more excited than he had ever been in his life. They made love for an hour before falling back onto the sofa in each other's arms.

"That was intense," Echo panted. "And amazing. I've never experienced anything like that."

"One of my powers," Thorne chuckled.

Echo made a face poking fun at the arrogance.

"No seriously," Thorne replied. "I put off some kind of pheromone that just gets my partners caught up in the moment. It works."

"I'll say."

"Plus, I was really eager to see what you looked like naked. Thought about it all last night," Thorne grinned. "Did you think about me at all?"

Echo blushed again.

"What?"

"Actually," Echo explained. "I have the power to morph into the image of anyone I've been around the last few hours. When I got back to Oleander last night, I changed into you and checked you out in the mirror. I already knew what you looked like."

"Damn!" Thorne gasped. "What a fantastic power."

"Yeah," Echo grinned. "I know what every hot guy I ever run across looks like naked."

. . .

Thaddeuss D'Angelo was tucked behind the desk of his study, heavily focused on some old documents written on parchment. Taub did not ask his father what they were as he entered the study. He had more pressing concerns on his mind.

"I've instructed you to knock before entering this domain," Thaddeuss said gruffly without looking up.

"I'm sorry, Sir, but I have something to tell you."

"Get on with it."

"Cassandra knows."

"Cassandra knows what, Taub?" Thaddeuss asked. "Do be specific as there is much she hadn't known before. What has she discovered?"

"She knows about Gideon."

Thaddeuss looked up from his important papers. "I see."

"Gideon made a play for Alexandrea again."

"How did that manage to occur?" Thaddeuss asked. "I thought we were doing our utmost to keep that transition from happening until you could successfully impregnate that wife of yours."

"So far I've had no luck in that department. But I have a potion brewing that will almost guarantee results. I found Aunt Atheidrelle's old notes. The ones she used to cause Arielle's birth."

"The spell that went wrong?" Thaddeuss said disapprovingly.

"It only went wrong in the sense that Atheidrelle was not the one who got pregnant, but Aunt Blackie did—so it obviously works."

"All right," Thaddeuss commented. "It had better. But none of that matters if your wife is turned before she is with child."

"I understand," Taub replied. "Cassandra used magic to remove the medicine so that she could see what Alexandrea was being pulled toward. She followed her to a rendezvous with Gideon. She stopped him from finishing his transformation. But he will try again."

"She knows only about Gideon? Nothing more?" Thaddeuss asked his son.

"Correct. I explained about Gideon's obsession only."

"Then I would not worry much. I believe Cassandra will accept the inkling of truth supplied to her. Besides, her own ascension will occur soon enough. In fact, possibly tomorrow."

"That will be good," Taub said. "I am very tired of pretending to love my wife. The sooner we can dispose of her the better. After the baby is conceived and born of course."

"Of course," Thaddeuss grinned.

CHAPTER TWENTY TWO

Miranda's Love

"Hold your brother steady now, Hera," Miranda directed as she sat Titan in the tub of warm water and bubbles. Hera pulled him close to her where he could sit upright, his back against her chest while the foaming bubbles grew larger under the tap water.

"Add more!" Hera shouted gleefully.

Miranda smiled and poured the remainder of the bottle under the running faucet. Soon the tub was so full she could barely see the children. Titan giggled and grabbed at the elusive suds in an attempt to capture and eat them. Hera was busy piling them onto his head and dabbing some on his chin.

"He looks like Santa Claus!" she laughed.

"It'll be time for Santa in a few weeks. Won't that be exciting!" Miranda said, sitting herself down on the floor beside the tub to begin washing Hera's hair.

"I used to be scared of Santa Claus," Hera confessed.

"Scared of Santa!" Miranda exclaimed. "Why would anyone be afraid of Santa?"

"I dunno," the child said. "Just seemed scary to me, him coming into our house at night. Con said he isn't real. He said no man can bring that many presents to every boy and girl in the world in one night. But Hecate said Santa is an ancient witch with powers like Aunt Salem's. He just stops time and gets it done."

"I never thought of it like that before," Miranda smiled again as she gently massaged her fingers into Hera's thick hair. "Your hair is growing fast. I may need to give you a cut soon."

"Aunt Fable says it's turning red like Aunt Salem's."

"No, I don't think so," Miranda observed. "You have some coppery tones, but I think you'll look more like your mother."

Hera's face fell slightly. "Do you think Santa Claus could bring Mama back?"

Miranda removed her hands from the child's hair and wrapped her arms around both Hera and little Titan. Her blouse now soaked with moisture and bubbles, but she didn't care. She felt like crying for the child. Miranda was not aware that they were being watched. Standing in the children's bedroom, looking through the crack in the bathroom door, was Seth.

"I don't think Santa has that kind of power, my sweet angel," Miranda said, kissing Hera's sudsy forehead. "I'm so sorry you don't have your mother anymore. I wish I could bring her back to you."

"Did you like Mama?" Hera asked.

"Yes, I did. Very much," Miranda said. "I didn't really know your mother for very long. I didn't know her at all really. But I have never heard anything but wonderful things about her. Even though I didn't know her, I like her a lot. I think we would have been good friends."

"Bubbles!" Titan yelped as he smacked his hands down and splashed the foam all over the three of them.

Miranda laughed and picked him up into the air, raising him up and down so that his legs could splash into the water. He laughed and placed his hands on the sweet woman's face and said, "Momma".

Miranda froze, unsure what to say or whether to correct him. He was too young to know what he was saying. He had heard his sister talking about their mother, it was probably a simple mistake his little mind was not yet mature enough to figure out.

Hera seemed to pick up on Miranda's discomfort. She placed her little hand on Miranda's and said, "That's okay. You can be his Mama. He doesn't remember our real one. He loves you. It's okay Miranda."

Once the children were dried off and hair was blown dry, Miranda put them into their pajamas and right to bed. As she clicked on Hera's new favorite nightlight, a Halloween holdover decoration which cast witches flying on brooms around the room, she read the story of The Cobbler and the Elves, then tiptoed out into the hall. Seth was waiting in the hallway when she stepped outside.

"I was listening at the door," he confessed. "I guess we shouldn't be too surprised that Titan will grow up thinking of you as his mother."

"Seth, I haven't meant to—"

"No, no," he interrupted. "I know you haven't. It is only natural. My mother was out of my life from when I was six years old until a few years ago. Aunt Artemis was my mother in all the really important ways. Just like you'll be to my children."

"I hope it doesn't upset you."

He forced an understanding smile. It broke his heart to hear his children call someone else Mother, but he also knew they needed one, and their own was gone. "I wish Yasmine were here," Seth said. "But she isn't. And if she isn't here, I think my children are damn lucky that you are. You truly do love them, don't you?"

"I do," Miranda smiled. "I'm sure I'll never have any of my own. But in a way I feel like they are mine."

"They are," Seth said. "And I'm very grateful."

He gave her a hug and held it for a moment longer than was comfortable for either of them. With his arms around her waist, he noticed the difference. Miranda was an attractive woman. Any man would think so, but she was not his woman. She was not his Yaz. Seth's hands knew every nook and cranny of Yasmine's body. Every curve, every dip, every place she called a flaw and every place he called a masterpiece. His hands slowly explored Miranda's hips and back as if they were searching for some similarity, any similarity to feed their hungry need for Yasmine. Miranda looked up into his eyes; Seth kissed her. His lips noticed the difference as well. This was not his Yasmine. And his body—his soul—could not respond to anyone other than his Yasmine. He pulled away.

"I am sorry," he said.

"No, no need," Miranda replied. "I understand. You're lonely. You miss her. You see me with the kids and some part of you thinks if I can be a substitute for them, maybe I could be one for you."

"Something like that, I guess," Seth said.

"And Seth, I like you. I do," she admitted. "If I thought you could ever care for me—but you have had your one great love. And it wasn't me."

"I'm sorry."

"Nothing to be sorry about," Miranda smiled. "Kids are more resilient than grownups. I can step in and be what they need. I can never be what you need. But I appreciate you trying."

CHAPTER TWENTY THREE

The Spy Who Discovered Too Much

Cassandra felt more at ease knowing the truth about her patient, even more at ease knowing Taub knew the truth. Now she could go about trying to find a way to help Alexandrea. The question was how to go about it. She wasn't exactly sure. One concern kept nagging her. The vampire's proximity to Alexandrea. And the house. He had not swooped up from the forest to strike Alexandrea on the balcony. He had entered that parapet from another passage inside the house. She hadn't thought to tell Taub about that when they spoke. She now realized it was an important detail. Perhaps she should investigate the room Gideon entered from. It might provide some new information.

She was presented with the opportunity later that afternoon when Taub informed her that she could take the next few hours off. He wanted to have some private time with his wife. Cassandra liked that he still spent hours alone with the woman he loved. Brushing her hair. Holding her hand. Reading to her from the books they had once enjoyed together. It endeared Taub to her even more. He really did cherish his poor wife.

Cassandra seized the moment of freedom to explore the house and try to locate the passage Gideon the vampire had emerged from. Surprisingly enough, she managed to retrace the steps she took with Alexandrea the previous night. The house had not changed itself since, and when Cassandra opened the door to the statue room, she felt a sense of accomplishment. She remembered the exact places to press in the wall to extend the stone stepping slabs and soon found her way up top again standing in the open doorway to the parapet. It was late afternoon, almost dark, but still enough day-ending red and orange light from the setting sun to see her way. With some light available, she was able to find the hidden doorway Gideon used. The stones lining it were groutless in a perfect door-shaped rectangle. Pressing it firmly, she felt it unhinge and spring open to welcome her. Cassandra stepped inside.

A long corridor confronted her, lined with small arched windows allowing plenty of fading sunlight to show her the way. Following the hall slowly, she eventually ran across an alcove with a thin set of stairs descending downward. The thin iron railings were not dusty, nor were any signs of cobwebs lingering between the spokes. This stair was used regularly.

She ventured to the floor below. The room was elaborately furnished. Heavy tapestries hung on the wall between thin strips of windows. Ornately carved couches with dark green velvet cushions sat atop rich rugs laid over the stone floor. Dozens of candelabra stands stood around the room, all candles unlit at the moment. A small fireplace, much too small for such a large room, sat quite out of place in a corner. Charred wood lay among the ashes beneath a hanging cauldron pot. A smell emanated from the corner, and when Cassandra walked over to inspect it, she traced her finger inside along the residue of the pot. She smelled the dried reddish-brown substance on her fingertips. It looked a little like dried blood.

Does Gideon live here, in this house, without the family even knowing? The questions Cassandra hoped to solve were now multiplying tenfold. She moved forward to explore a corridor branching off from the chamber when suddenly she heard a noise coming from further down the hall. She hid herself behind one of the folds in the heavy tapestry and spied.

Constance D'Angelo appeared from the corridor and made her way into the large room. With her was a servant girl. The girl was carrying two rather large jugs. Cassandra observed as Constance withdrew several wood logs from a cupboard in the wall next to the fireplace and started a fire in the hearth. The servant girl uncapped the two jugs and poured the red contents into the cauldron. Cassandra knew at once by the consistency it was blood. They were heating blood. But why? For Gideon? Cassandra remained tucked away out of sight until Constance and the girl disappeared back into the corridor in which they had entered. She was just about to step out when a wooden panel of shelves on another wall began to creak open. A figure stepped into the room.

Cassandra could not make the person out very well. It was staying in the shadows for the most part, cautiously avoiding the flimsy rays of sunlight casting through the window slits from the setting sun. It was a female. Cassandra could tell right away. For a moment she suspected it might be Mara, but Mara's hair was black. This girl's hair was browner. Still there was something familiar about the person. Cassandra watched the figure as she tiptoed to the pot and smelled the contents.

"Old blood," she said, almost disapprovingly. "Why is it always from an old person? Yuck."

Cassandra knew that voice. But it couldn't be. There was no possibility. Then again, life had taught her almost anything was possible. She watched from the tapestry as the woman began to exit the room. If only she would turn around toward the dimming light from the windows. If only those damn candelabras were lit! Cassandra could not be sure. She needed to see the woman's face. But the woman disappeared the way she came in. Cassandra stepped from behind the tapestry once she felt safe doing so. Cassandra knew she had to follow her. She had to know.

The corridor was dark, but enough light shone in from the few windows that she could make her way through the winding turns. Up ahead, she saw the figure of the woman stop at a casement window and sit down on a padded cushion in the window seat. She stared out into the newness of the fresh night. Cassandra hid herself behind an edge of stone where the corner turned. She watched the woman from a safe distance. Another hallway must have lain beyond the window because the figure of a man appeared next to the woman.

"Good evening, my dear," he said.

"Hello, Elijah."

"The others are rising now. You appear to have been up sooner than the rest of us. Are you still troubled, my pet?"

"I feel so much," the woman said. "Yet I feel so little. I have become free of worldly problems. I have shed the weights of past life ties. Yet I cannot shed him. I cannot soothe this insatiable anguish."

"You need to feed," Elijah told her.

"Can mere blood heal an unbeating heart that yearns for another?"

The man caressed the woman's arm softly. "Your sustaining love is remarkable. Usually that dies when we transcend to our higher state. Yet your love remains in some rudimentary form. It is unusual to say the least. Perhaps it is because of your condition when you changed."

"Perhaps," she said. "I wish it to stop."

"It will in time," Elijah said. "You are here now. My family's home keeps you safely tucked away from those who might strive to harm us. We are fortunate. Much more so than the others of our kind roaming the world without such a fortress to protect them. You must embrace the new way. You must forget your old life and see this place as your world now. We need you for the coming war. We need you to be ready and unfettered by the past."

"I know I am not the woman I was. I can barely recall her, or him, or that life. Yet every night when I rise, I walk these halls longing for something I cannot remember."

"He would destroy you. They all would, my dear."

"I know. Yet I wait for something that will never come. I wonder if it is him?"

"Let's go into town tonight," Elijah suggested. "You always feel so much better when you make a fresh kill."

"It isn't my night," she said. "I am not on the list for the boat until next week."

"I am sure one of the others would be most willing to offer you their place tonight."

"Why?" the woman asked. "Why should one of the others do that? They live for their night in town."

"Because we like to keep you happy, Yasmine," Elijah smiled. "You are too important to our cause. I will arrange everything myself. I shall take you personally into the city. We will find delicious fare, and you will feel better."

Cassandra watched as he escorted Yasmine away. She suddenly found herself sliding slowly down the wall until her knees touched the floor. Cassandra could not believe everything she had just witnessed. How could this be possible? How could everyone have been so wrong? Yasmine was alive.

CHAPTER TWENTY FOUR

The Call That Changed Everything

Salem Blanchard was more than a little surprised during her late afternoon staff meeting at her new advertising agency when she reached down to silence her cell phone ringer only to see the name Cassandra Obreiggon on her caller ID. Though the animosity with her older half-sister had long been resolved, Cassandra was still not a person with which Salem had much contact. Only family gatherings or visits to Oleander ever brought the two of them together. They got along fine, rather stiffly at times, but no longer enemies. Still, they were not the type of sisters who called one another casually on the phone. Something inside urged Salem to take the call. If Cassandra was reaching out, there had to be a mighty important reason. She excused herself from the meeting, directing her partner Miles to take over, as she stepped into the hallway outside the boardroom.

"Cassandra?"

"Salem! I didn't know who else to call," Cassandra sounded frantic.

"What's wrong? Is it Dad?"

"No, nothing like that," Cassandra cried. "I only have minutes because I'm trying to get back to my room. I'm at the House of Duquesne."

"Yes, Mother told me you were staying there a while."

"Salem, listen to me. This is urgent. I don't know what to do. Yasmine is here. Yasmine. She is alive! Or, not alive—she is a vampire. But she is here inside the House of Duquesne."

Salem almost dropped the phone. It wasn't possible. Yasmine was dead. Artemis found her charred remains herself. But were they Yasmine's remains? The family naturally assumed...but what if they had been wrong.

"Are you certain? Absolutely certain?"

"Absolutely!" Cassandra exclaimed. "I could not see her face. I only heard the voice. But another man—a vampire I think—called her Yasmine. He said she was important to their cause. I don't know what's going on here. My patient, Alexandrea, is in a catatonic state. I found out it's due to a vampire attack—a vampire named Gideon, who was not able to complete her transition. That is why she is like a zombie now. While trying to find out how Gideon keeps getting into the house, I stumbled on an area of the house where I think he lives. Constance D'Angelo brings him blood. And I suppose it is for Yasmine, too. It's for all of them. There are many it sounds like. You must tell Seth. Or don't tell Seth. I don't know what to do or who to tell or not tell. You were the only person I could think of that I thought might know what to do."

"I cannot believe this," Salem gasped. "Cassandra, are you in danger right now?"

"I don't think so, but I am not sure."

"Get out of there as fast as you can!" Salem ordered. "Don't stop to tell anyone. Just get to the nearest door and run the hell out. I will be there as soon as I can. I will meet you at Oleander. Tell no one anything until I get to you. But Cassandra, leave that house now!"

. . .

Fable was finishing with a patient when her cousin walked into the clinic. Marty, Mrs. Filtcher's Pomeranian, had just finished his last heartworm treatment and was all ready to go. As she closed the office door behind them, she turned to Salem in surprise.

"You never come here to the clinic. What is going on now?"

"Yasmine may not be dead."

"What?"

Salem recounted Cassandra's phone call and then sat down on the examination table. "What do we tell Seth? Or do we tell him anything at all? I mean, Yaz was a vampire. Seth was all set to destroy her when she disappeared. Do we put him through that again? Do I tell the aunts? Or do I just go to Charleston and dispose of Yasmine myself and spare him? If it even is Yasmine."

"I have no idea," Fable said, feeling faint. "This is big. I mean, it's Yaz!"

"But it's not Yaz," Salem corrected. "It's Yaz's body. A body with fangs and the propensity to kill innocent people. But it is not our Yasmine. And remember we aren't sure it was even her at all. Cassandra couldn't see her face. But the voice sounded the same, and the name."

"Yazzy was like our own sister."

"But that Yasmine is long gone. This Yasmine is a killer," Salem said.

Fable thought about it for a moment and gave the best advice she could offer. "You have to tell Aunt Artemis. She is the Hecate. But you also need to get to Charleston ASAP."

"I'll have my father come get me. He can transport me there in a zap. Will you handle Artemis? I must get to Cassandra. I have a terrible feeling."

"I'll handle everything here," Fable promised. "You call your Dad and get to Oleander now."

Salem did exactly that. She took her phone from her pocket and called her father. Xander came to Fable's office seconds later and whisked his daughter back to Charleston. Fable cancelled her remaining appointments and headed home to Blanchard House.

Walking through the front door, Fable was immediately confronted with her son Romulus bounding down the stairs toward her with little Con in tow behind. She gave her sons a fast hello kiss and told them she would play with them very soon. She could see Artemis in the office off the foyer concentrating on paying the household monthly bills. Fable stepped in and closed the door. Once she finished catching her aunt up on the new events revealed that day, Artemis was dumbfounded.

"The burned body we found on that island may not have been Yasmine?"

"Possibly not," Fable said. "Not according to Cassandra. Salem is already in Charleston now and hopefully with Cassandra."

"I need to formulate a plan," Artemis said. "If it is really Yasmine, she must be found and destroyed. We cannot allow her to live in the condition she is currently in. We owe too much to the memory of the sweet girl we've loved."

"Do we tell Seth?"

Artemis pondered the thought a moment and shook her head. "Not as of now. He should be told, but not until we are absolutely sure. Not until we see Yasmine with our own eyes. Not to say that I distrust Cassandra, but as of now this is only hearsay."

"Not to mention she is Atheidrelle Obreiggon's daughter," Fable added. "I know she is supposed to be nice now, but I don't put anything past those people."

"I would agree with you except for one thing. If Cassandra were lying, she would have said she saw her face, not just heard a similar voice. I believe Cassandra Obreiggon is trustworthy now," Artemis said. "I need to get to Charleston myself. I will phone Xander and have him come for me, too. For now, you just keep moving along as though nothing is any different until you hear from me."

Two hours later, Artemis and Salem Blanchard were sitting impatiently in the parlor of Nacaria Obreiggon's home in Charleston. Cassandra had not shown up yet, and everyone was growing concerned.

"Are you sure she was leaving right away?" Xander asked Salem. "Perhaps she had to stall for some reason or wait until no one was around."

"I made it very clear that she should run out as fast as possible," Salem said. "Of course, she might have run into one of the D'Angelo's and have to wait until later tonight. If she does not turn up by bedtime, then I'll be really worried."

Artemis tapped her brother-in-law's arm and asked, "Can you zap over there and bring her out?"

Xander shook his head. "Not that house. It's much too large to know where she'd be, and it's protected with too many charms. I could get to the perimeter, but not inside."

Arielle was pacing the floor now. Frustration was building, as well as anxiety. She could not wait until morning. It was her sister. True she and Cassandra had not liked each other for most of their lives, but that was different now. Now they were friends. Now they were truly sisters. She could not risk Cassandra's safety. "I don't like this at all. Cassandra could be in real danger. I say Echo and I should pop over to the house and check on things."

"How do you just pop over without causing suspicion?" Nacaria asked.

"I've made friends with the family a bit," Echo said. "I think I could just show up, and they'd be happy to see me."

"I believe you overestimate their fondness of you," Xander replied.

Echo gave a wry grin and winked at Arielle. "Then I'll pay Thorne a visit. I'm sure if I texted him, he'd let me into the house."

"Why would he do that?" Xander asked.

"Well," Echo blushed. "We've become friends. I know he will be receptive to a late-night visit."

"Oh," Salem blushed. "I see."

Nacaria was not on board with the plan. She shook her head in protest and told Echo he could not do that. "Even if you were to get inside the house, there is no possible reason why you'd be paying Cassandra a visit while there," Nacaria pointed out. "I think it needs to be Arielle. Arielle should go first thing in the morning. You both said your business deal is wrapped up now. Arielle saying goodbye to her sister is a natural thing. No one would suspect anything."

"What about Yasmine?" Salem said. "As a Consort officer, I must investigate this claim. Never mind the fact that she is also my sister-in-law."

"First things first," Xander told his daughter. "We find Cassandra. Then we try to locate this woman that may be Yasmine. At present, it is all we can do."

...

Cassandra Obreiggon waited in her room in the House of Duquesne. She did not know what else there was to do. Why she had returned there before fleeing was a mistake she would never forgive herself for. Salem told her to leave immediately. Why hadn't she? Now she couldn't. For some inexplicable reason her door was now locked. Both doors actually, and no matter how hard she tried, her powers would not work on opening either of them. She could neither enter the hallway outside her room nor enter Alexandrea's bedroom. She was trapped inside her room, barred by doors too heavy to break through. She could not help but worry that someone in the house knew she had entered the secret area. Why else would she be locked in now? When would they let her out? Maybe once morning came, and the danger of the vampires was nullified by the light of day. Perhaps these locked doors were meant to keep her safe until dawn. She wished she had answers. She tried her cell phone, but no luck. Her screen said she had no service. She did not understand why.

Pacing the floor of her room she felt more and more uncomfortable, especially with her mother's portrait staring at her from above on the wall. Atheidrelle's eyes were invasive. Menacing. Cassandra could stand it no longer. She flung her bedsheet over the portrait to conceal that domineering face. Yet that did little to squelch her uneasiness. All her anxiety from being locked in her room was becoming overpowered by a growing fear that the painting of her mother was watching her... and planning something. It seemed to possess an energy now which she had not felt before. It became the only thing in the room she could focus on. And in the air, ever so faintly, almost so faint that she thought she was imagining it...the painting seemed to be speaking to her.

CHAPTER TWENTY FIVE

Reconnaissance

Arielle and Echo showed up bright and early to the house. Thorne met them at the door after receiving Echo's text. He let them inside. He seemed very eager to see Echo again. The family, he informed them, were having breakfast in the breakfast room and would expect to say goodbye to them before they left town—but there was plenty of time, he said with a wink to Echo.

Arielle left her brother with their cousin and sprinted upstairs to find her sister. It was frustrating to lose her way, yet again inside the house. It was hard to remember the complicated route, but she eventually found Cassandra's door. She burst inside without knocking and found her sister was not there. Nor was she in Alexandrea's room. Cassandra's patient was sitting motionless at the window alone. Arielle began to worry. She darted from the room, trying to retrace her steps back to the first floor.

"Not that way!" shouted a voice. As Arielle turned to see who had warned her, she saw it was Ashby. She wondered if Ashby ever did anything other than roam these corridors.

"Ashby! You scared me."

"If you are going to use that staircase, let me lead the way. It can be tricky," the young girl offered.

"Thank you," Arielle said following her lead. "I'm looking for my sister."

"Cassandra is down at breakfast with the family. I just left her there," Ashby said.

The staircase they took was a new one to Arielle. Somehow, she had made a mistake again in finding her way and taken a foreign corridor. The stair was long and narrow but led straight down to the floor below. It did not appear too terribly tricky to figure out. But soon Arielle understood what Ashby meant with her warning.

"This staircase is booby trapped," Ashby alerted. "The eleventh tread and the fourth tread breakaway on a hinge. You end up smashed up on the cellar floor. We've lost more maids that way."

Arielle cringed at the thought—not to mention the casual way the young girl expressed it. Carefully stepping over the eleventh and fourth treads, Arielle found herself on the second floor. After a turn or two, she recognized the path and found her way back to the lower level.

She had never seen the breakfast room before. It was located near the glass conservatory which one could see driving up to the house, but Arielle had never actually been inside while in the house. As Ashby opened the door to allow her in, Arielle heard the voices of her uncle and aunt come to a halt upon seeing her. Thaddeuss' serious face softened as what could only be described as an insincere smile replaced it.

"Arielle!" he exclaimed, rising from his chair. "What an exciting surprise. Won't you join us?"

Arielle returned her own faux smile and said, "I've already eaten, thank you. I came to say goodbye and to have a few minutes with my sister before I return to Alabama."

"What a shame your stay has been so short," Constance replied.

"Cassie, can you and I have a minute alone?"

"Wouldn't that be rather rude, Arielle?" Cassandra said tersely. "You've interrupted our morning meal. The least you should do is join us for a few moments while we complete it."

Arielle was shocked at her sister's admonishment. Cassandra had not treated her like that in years. But Arielle took a seat at the table and allowed the servant standing by to fill a cup of coffee for her. Arielle drank it quietly, observing.

"I take it your business has been concluded in Charleston?" Thaddeuss asked.

"Yes," Arielle answered. "Echo and I are leaving today. We came to say goodbye."

"And where is Echo?" Constance asked.

"He's with Thorne right now."

"I see," Constance said, giving her husband a stern eye. "I told you my suspicions on that matter, Thaddeuss."

"It is of no concern," Thaddeuss said. "We won't discuss it again."

Cassandra said nothing as she finished her omelet and wiped her mouth gently with the tip of her napkin. Her manners seemed rather stiff to Arielle. Overly refined. Almost like...

Once breakfast was consumed, Cassandra excused herself. Arielle joined her in the hall. Arielle grabbed her sister's wrist in desperation the moment they were alone. "Cassandra, I have to get you out of here!"

"Whatever for?" Cassandra asked, almost entertained by her sister's frenzy.

"Because of what you saw last night!" Arielle said. "Salem told us about your call."

"Salem?" Cassandra said as if the very name repulsed her.

"Yes, our sister Salem," Arielle repeated. "When you told her about the vampire and then the woman you saw that you thought was Yasmine—"

"Oh, that," Cassandra laughed. "Arielle, I was mistaken. Moments after I spoke with your sister I ran into the young lady once again. It was only a servant whom I had not yet met. It certainly was not Yasmine Blanchard. But it was good of you to come say goodbye to me. But you will excuse me. I have a rather busy day ahead of me. Have a safe trip home."

With that Arielle found herself standing alone in the hall as Cassandra left to her duties. Something inside Arielle was screaming. Cassandra was not herself. At least not the Cassandra of late. She seemed more like the old Cassandra who hated Arielle. And she called Salem "your sister" not "our sister". Though they would never be the best of friends, Salem and Cassandra had forged a kind of friendship over time. Cassandra's words reduced their progress callously. It unnerved Arielle. She could not help but find herself becoming frantic. Something had happened to Cassandra overnight, and Arielle had no idea what it was.

Arielle and Echo left the House of Duquesne and retreated to Oleander to recount what happened. Arielle told the others how strangely Cassandra had reacted and that something felt very off about her.

"They have her," Xander said, pained from the realization. "They have warped her mind again the way her mother did all of those years."

"I don't think so," Salem said. "How could they turn her cold again in only one night? The Cassandra I spoke with last night was worried. She also cared. She cared about Yasmine."

"She doesn't today," Arielle noted. "I haven't felt that kind of emptiness from her in a long time."

"Do you think they have drugged her, or put a spell on her to make her behave this way?" Nacaria asked. "There are spells which can change the personality rather quickly."

"That family has power unlike anything we will ever understand," Xander said. "I think it is very possible they've influenced her mind."

"If we could only keep an eye on things," Nacaria said.

"Maybe we can," Echo said. "Tess."

"Tess?" Salem repeated.

"Yes, what if Tess came? What if she and I moved into the house for a little while? Thaddeuss would probably jump at the chance. He clearly wants to know us better. What if I said I had more business here and needed to stay a while? If I could get them to allow me to stay there, Tess could join me. She could be invisible. She could explore the house and maybe uncover whatever is going on. She can find Yasmine if she is truly there."

"That's an idea," Arielle agreed. "But there's no reason for Tess to be here. She doesn't work with us."

"Maybe there's no need to tell anyone she's there," Salem offered. "If she can remain invisible for lengthy periods of time, no one at the House of Duquesne even has to know she's moved in. She can maneuver unseen and determine what is going on."

CHAPTER TWENTY SIX

Moving In

It all happened far more easily than anyone expected. The moment Echo reached out to Uncle Thaddeuss and explained he would be remaining in Charleston several more weeks on another venture, Thaddeuss immediately offered for him to stay with the D'Angelos. Echo accepted. When Echo entered the House of Duquesne front door, luggage in hand, no one suspected his invisible sister was trailing in his footsteps. Constance showed Echo to a large room on the second floor, nearest the main staircase as to make it easier for him to find his way. As she closed the door behind her to allow him to unpack and settle in, Tess rematerialized.

"You and I haven't shared a room in years," she laughed. "Do you still snore?"

Echo smirked a devilish grin and replied, "With Thorne here, I doubt I'll be sleeping in this room very often. At least I hope not."

"Oh my God, Echo. He is your cousin."

"From like a fluke of timeline shifts!" Echo snarked. "It's not like we will give our children birth defects."

...

Thorne was as happy as Echo had hoped he would be at the proximity of his new love interest. Thorne wasted no time pulling Echo to his room. Securing the bolt on the door, he turned to Echo and smiled. Neither said anything as they rushed into each other's arms and began to kiss.

Lying in bed together half an hour later, Echo snuggled onto Thorne's chest and rested his head. Thorne tucked his arms under Echo's and held him.

"I have been so lonely," Thorne admitted. "It is not easy being a D'Angelo. Add to that a witch. Add to that a gay D'Angelo witch, living in repressed Charleston.

I'm glad you're staying awhile."

Echo kissed Thorne's forearm. "I've been pretty isolated, too. The world I came from had little time for love. We were all too busy trying not to be devoured by vampires."

"Vampires!" Thorne exclaimed. "I knew you were from a different reality, but I didn't know about any vampires."

"Yeah, in my world America and the rest of the planet, had fallen into Armageddon thanks to a vampire population that destroyed the world." Echo was only explaining his experiences. It only occurred to him after he said what he said that if vampires were truly at the House of Duquesne, maybe Thorne might have a reaction.

"It sounds dreadful."

"It was. I saw almost everyone I ever cared about die at the hands of vampires. I never want to think about that happening here," Echo said.

"It won't," Thorne said, squeezing him. "And if it ever did, I'll protect you."

Echo was not reassured by that sentence. Was it an admission that the possibility existed, or was it just one of those sweet things lovers say to one another? He cautioned himself to not fall too hard for Thorne D'Angelo. He was still a bit of a questionable commodity. But there was also nothing wrong with enjoying him while the opportunity was presenting itself and possibly learning a little about the current situation in the house. That is, if Thorne was the type to let something slip.

Over the next few days when Echo was not pretending to be in town on business, he and Thorne spent much time together. While Echo was busy schmoozing with the family and having secret rendezvous with Thorne, Tess seized opportunities to explore the insane house.

The house was a maze of difficulty. Tess found many places of interest in the house, but it was on day three when she finally found Cassandra's room. Tess found the room on the third floor but there was no Cassandra staying in it. Alexandrea was alone in her connecting room, drugged as she normally was. No servant was with her, and Cassandra's old room was empty of her belongings. Whatever reasons she had been brought to the House of Duquesne were no longer what held her there. Cassandra was clearly no longer living as a hired nurse in the house, but as a full-fledged family member.

Tess sat with Alexandrea for quite a while, waiting to see if any vampire came in to see her. Nothing happened until late in the afternoon when the door opened and Taub entered with his mother. As gingerly as she could, Tess moved in soft baby steps out of the way, tucking herself against the wall beside a bureau chest. She watched as they went to Alexandrea's chair where Constance D'Angelo placed her hand upon the woman's belly and lowered her lids in concentration.

"Success!" Constance cried reopening her eyes. "You have accomplished the task, Taub. Your wife is with child. Your father will be pleased."

Taub looked relieved. "I cannot tell you how glad I am that I no longer have to come in here and be with her. Once this baby is born, I plan to end her life personally."

"All in good time, my son," Constance said. "We must wait until this child reaches fruition. Everything must be handled quite precisely. I have already successfully concocted a potion which will speed this pregnancy along."

"How fast?"

"Very, considering the average child takes nine months to gestate. I can have this baby ready in three. Of course, the spell will have dire repercussions on Alexandrea's body, but that is no matter to us."

"As long as the child gets here as quickly as possible."

"Yes," Constance said. "Your father hasn't much time left. We need this child urgently. If it turns out to be a male, it may be our backup strategy if Plan A doesn't work out."

"But if we can get the God Strain," Taub said. "Wouldn't that be the most powerful of all."

"Yes, but the God Strain is not yet assured for us. This child is our safety net. It has the power of the vampire with the blood of the D'Angelos. If we cannot get the God Strain, this will suffice."

As they exited the room, Tess was more confused than she had ever been in her life. What in the world had they been talking about? Nothing made any sense. One thing was for certain though, there was definitely something evil happening in the House of Duquesne.

CHAPTER TWENTY SEVEN

Mara's Morals

Echo met Mara in town for lunch the following Friday, careful to show up with a briefcase full of legal papers and dressed in a suit. He needed to continue to sell the façade that he was there on business for his father's firm. They met at a rooftop restaurant called The Pavilion Bar overlooking the old marketplace where now a series of booths sold trinkets and Charleston souvenirs to tourists. It was chilly for rooftop dining, but the warmth from the standing heaters placed near the tables kept most of the chill off.

"I bet in another month this rooftop won't be open anymore," Echo said looking around at the lovely, if not chilly patio.

"In summer it is wonderful," Mara said. "I like it up here. But you're right; they will be shutting the outside down in a few days."

"I have this suit on so I'm warm enough, but aren't you freezing in that little dress?"

"I make my own heat," Mara smiled. "Besides, it's the view I am here for."

"It is lovely."

The waitress took their order, shivering in the cold, giving all appearances that she wished her patrons would have opted for the indoor seating. Mara and Echo were the only diners outside, and this was clearly a bit of an irritation to the waitress. Once she walked away with their lunch order, Echo began idle chit chat with his cousin, noticing that she was paying him little attention. It did not take long to discover why Mara had chosen this rooftop restaurant.

Following her line of sight to the street two stories below, Mara could not take her eyes off a certain door. Echo nonchalantly glimpsed a few times to see what the significance was. She was watching an old church which did not appear to be a church any longer. Now it was a series of shops and restaurants. The restaurant doorway which held Mara's fascination had a sign over it labeled Five Church. They continued small talk for a while, sipping their cocktails, but by the time the meal was served, Mara's facial expression tensed, and she didn't try to hide her fascination with what was happening below. Echo looked over the railing to see a young man walking out of the building, his arm wrapped around a blonde girl. The girl was laughing exaggeratedly and flipping her hair every chance she could. The man looked to be the same man who had been ending things with Mara that first day Echo met her.

"Ah," Echo said. "Spying, huh? Is that guy your ex-boyfriend?"

"He is still my boyfriend, even if he doesn't quite understand that yet," Mara grimaced. "I knew he was seeing her."

"Who is she?" Echo asked.

"Carlee Turner. He dated her before me," Mara said with a mocking tone. "Doesn't she look exactly like someone named Carlee would?"

Mara reached her hand over the rail and flicked her finger. Echo looked out to see a faint trail of green mist now hovering in the exact spot the couple had been standing. As they walked away, the mist appeared to follow, leaving a residue in the air like a homing device.

"Can people see that?" Echo gasped.

"Witches can. No one else. I'll follow them after lunch."

"And do what?"

"I haven't decided yet," Mara said devilishly. "But it'll be fun."

The remainder of lunch was spent talking about Thorne. Mara seemed interested in whatever was developing between her new cousin and her uncle. As she spoke about Thorne, Echo got the feeling that Thorne was possibly her only friend in the house. He had not realized it before but there wasn't a huge gap in age between Mara and her uncle. Taub was substantially older than his younger brother.

"I like Thorne," Echo said. "Other than that, I have no idea where it will go. It may just be a fling we both need now."

"Thorne doesn't fling," Mara said. "My grandfather considers Thorne something of a family embarrassment. Someone to keep occupied and out of the line of sight."

"Uncle Thaddeuss doesn't seem to have a problem with me," Echo said. "Do you think it's a gay thing? Or does he just not like Thorne?"

"Oh, it is definitely a gay thing. Grandfather places a lot of stock in the family name, and he considers Thorne a blemish on that name. But he does not interfere. Basically, he treats Thorne as inconsequential. Everyone in the house knows the only

D'Angelo that matters is Grandfather. My grandmother and my father fall next to a much lesser degree. The only person who ever ranked as high as Grandfather was Aunt Atheidrelle, until she died. But even still he speaks of her with the highest reverence."

"Do you matter to Thaddeus?" Echo asked.

"Me?" Mara laughed. "I don't even matter to Taub. Believe me, my family is not anything like yours. We don't bond much."

"What about your mother?"

"Alexandrea was never very maternal, though before her condition changed, I suppose I did like her. At least in comparison to everyone else. I suppose I care about her, but she's been mindless for so long I honestly forget she exists."

"Well, your father seems dedicated to her."

"*Seems* is the key word," Mara stated. "I don't think you quite get it yet, Echo. My family doesn't love. They align. Thaddeuss and Atheidrelle were all that counted. Now that Atheidrelle is gone, Taub has been promoted to a sort of relevancy—but for what reason I don't know."

"So, you just exist in that house without any real ties to anyone?"

"Thorne and I are friends. I suppose I love Ashby, although she and I rarely see one another. I wouldn't call it a sisterhood by any means. She mostly wanders around the house keeping to herself. But I feel a connection to her which I do not feel with anyone else."

Mara stared down to her water glass. She began running her finger along the beaded droplets of condensation. Echo watched her without saying anything. He got the distinct impression she was lost in her thoughts as if only just now realizing her words were true. Perhaps it had never occurred to her until now how she felt about her sister and the rest of her family.

Finally, he broke the silence, "I wonder if my mother ever meant anything to Thaddeuss or Atheidrelle."

"Blackie?" Mara chuckled, wiping her moist finger on the tablecloth. "Oh, Blackie was written out years ago when she left the house and sought a life of her own far away from the D'Angelos. Blackie, Thaddeuss, and Atheidrelle are full siblings, but I don't think Blackie ever figured very much into the fold. I have heard stories how in the old days the three of them were pretty tight—the trifecta—but something happened that made Blackie flee. I hope to be like her one day and get as far away from the D'Angelos as humanly possible."

"I wonder why Thaddeuss is so kind to me, if he hates my mother."

Mara made a face and laughed again. "You really are such an innocent Echo. He has an agenda. I have no clue as to what it involves, but you play into it, I am certain. Otherwise, I assure you he would never have contacted you. Blackie is exiled as far as Grandfather is concerned. For him to express such interest in her children—there's a reason."

Once lunch was over, Mara made her way downstairs to the street to follow the green trace still lingering on the sidewalk. Echo walked with her, curious to see what she was up to. They walked several blocks, chatting here and there about inconsequential Charleston stuff. A church built on this date, a house with a particularly haunting ghost story, nothing of major consequence. Eventually the trace ended, and Echo looked up to see the man and woman standing in the window of a pastry shop. The sun caused a glare on the glass, but even with the glare, it was plain to see they were holding hands as they ordered a sweet treat from the counter.

Mara did not look pleased. In fact, she looked frightening. She said nothing, only stood watching. Echo was about to ask her if she was all right when suddenly his thought was interrupted when the loud rumble of a car muffler resounded down the narrow street. The sound garnered Mara's attention as well, and she turned her head to see what the commotion could be. Before Echo could comment on the irritating noise, he witnessed his cousin fling her hand toward the car and swerve her arm back toward the storefront. Without a second's hesitation, the rumbling car lost control and darted away from its course, careening up onto the sidewalk and directly into the plate glass window of the pastry shop.

Echo instinctively jerked Mara out of harm's way, even though—as he did so—he suspected she was the one who caused the tragedy in the first place. As they tumbled onto the pavement, they both heard the shriek from inside the store. Before they could fully stand up again, a crowd of people swarmed the doorway and window to see inside the shop. An elderly lady staggered backward in shock.

"That poor girl," she gasped, clutching onto a strange man's arm for support. "The car. The car has crushed her."

Inside the store you could hear a man's voice crying out for help for the girl, Carlee, who was beyond help now. The man rushed to the window where the car had careened through, desperate to enlist someone for assistance. His eyes locked onto Mara. Echo watched his expression turn to horror as he stared into the eyes of his ex-girlfriend. Backing away in disbelief or utter terror, the man disappeared back into the recesses of the store. Echo looked at Mara in shock.

"What?" she asked defensively.

"What do you mean, *what*?" Echo exclaimed. "Mara! You killed her!"

"You don't know that she is dead," she argued. "Maybe she's just paralyzed. Besides, she did it to herself."

Echo was astounded. It was unfathomable that she could be so unphased by what she'd done. "Mara, this is wrong. This is murder."

"Murder?" she laughed. "Oh, Echo, you are so cute. We are witches. We get to live by a different set of rules. Why else do we have powers?"

"Not for this!" Echo said, lowering his voice so as to not be overheard. "As witches, it is our job to protect people who can't protect themselves."

She laughed again and patted his cheek gently. "Adorable."

"I'm serious Mara, this isn't okay."

"This is Charleston, Echo. We live differently here. Maybe in Alabama you guys are the vestige of humanitarianism and decency. But here, we use what we've got to get ahead. Sometimes we have to punish those who transgress against us. You'll learn. You are a D'Angelo too, you know. Let loose a little. It makes life so much more fun."

"But why?" Echo cried. "Why would you do this?"

Mara tilted her head, gesturing toward the store. For the first time he noticed a tinge of insanity dancing in her eyes as she said, "Because Brandon belongs to me. He wanted to play with magic until it scared him. Well, you don't get to go around breaking this girl's heart. Not if I want you."

CHAPTER TWENTY EIGHT

Blackie's Confession

The moment Trix told Blackie D'Angelo the reason for Tess' absence, the woman became inconsolably agitated. Tess being in Charleston, especially in the House of Duquesne, sent Blackie into a frenzy. Shaking her head vigorously and making writing gestures until Trix relented and supplied her with a clipboard and pen, Blackie was insistent upon communicating her thought. She wrote one simple word scratched clumsily with her left hand.

Demitra.

Trix did not understand why but she knew Blackie had her reasons. Trix phoned her great-grandmother in Daihmler and asked her to drive to Birmingham as soon as possible. Demitra was there within an hour with Artemis at her side. Trix let them inside Blackie's castle and led them to the small room on the first floor which had been accommodated for Blackie's convalescence. The Blanchard sisters were taken aback at the sight in the bed. Blackie had always been a picture of beauty and refinement. Seeing her half crumpled, drawn to one side, made them pity her.

"Blackie," Demitra said, patting her friend's hand. "What is it I can help you with?"

Blackie could say nothing, but she lifted her hand toward Demitra and took Demitra's arm. Lifting Demitra's hand to the side of her head, Blackie pressed it there as if to instruct Demitra to hold it in place. Blackie then lifted Demitra's other hand and placed it on the other side of her head.

"Mother, Demitra cannot heal you," Trix said. "That was Beryl. But Beryl is gone."

"She isn't asking for a healing," Artemis pointed out. "She wants Demitra to read her mind."

Blackie blinked vigorously.

Demitra focused her mind, tuning out the noise of the room, tuning out the heartbeats and breaths. She centered only on Blackie and whatever secrets were locked in her mind. She expected to see visions—her customary way for foretelling events—but that was not what happened this time. This time things worked in a much different way than Demitra had ever experienced before. Perhaps it was because her subject was a willing participant, eager to convey much with no other means to do so. Perhaps it was because they were both witches and Blackie's power was the impetus for the new construct operating. Whatever the cause, Demitra did not read Blackie's mind. She entered it.

Demitra looked around the room. Her sister Artemis and her great-granddaughter Trix were still there, although faded somewhat, almost transparent, as if existing on a different plane. Only Blackie was clearly visible, and she was no longer the pitiful drawn creature rendered so from the stroke. She was as alive and beautiful as ever, seated in a wingback chair, far from the bed.

"Sit with me," Blackie said without issue. "We haven't much time."

Demitra took a seat on a small settee beside the chair and listened as Blackie explained.

"You must get my son and daughter out of that house before it is too late. I have spent my entire life running from the wickedness of that house. I thought if I moved away and distanced myself, I would be safe. I could avoid participation in the evil brewing there. But now they have my children. Please Demitra, get them out of that house."

"I will, Blackie. I promise you. But you must tell me what is going on there. What are you hiding? Or protecting?"

"I will tell you everything. The secrets no longer matter. My children's lives are all I care about now."

"I'm ready," Demitra said, taking a big breath. "Tell me about the House of Duquesne."

Blackie told her of the birth of the House of Duquesne. She told her all about the vengeful architect and Emmerick Duquesne's sins which caused it. She explained the horrific design of the house, but she added a detail to the tale which Thaddeuss had not included in his version told to Echo and Arielle.

"The house was always supposed to be a maze. It was always supposed to be confusing. The ugliness and the hideousness of the design was the architect's revenge. But the confusion of the interior was always planned."

"Why?" Demitra asked. "Why plan for a house to be that way?"

Blackie looked Demitra eye to eye and answered, "Because the House of Duquesne is actually two houses in one. One house for the world to see, and another within those walls no one ever sees."

Demitra gave a slight gasp and asked, "What lives there?"

"The Duquesnes live there."

Demitra was confused. "A different family resides in the same house?"

"It is the same family. There are no D'Angelos. We are all Duquesnes. Emmerick built the house to hide his son and daughter and all those they contaminated. They are vampires, Demitra."

"Vampires!"

"Vampires. Charleston was different then, full of many unnatural things. Emmerick and his first wife had children—a son, Gideon, and a daughter, Bianca. Gideon was bitten, turned. He then turned his sister. They then turned a cousin staying with the family. His name was Elijah. Emmerick loved his children and sought to protect them and their secret. He needed a place to hide them and their dastardly friends they sired to entertain themselves. Emmerick took his family to Europe while the house was under construction. Emmerick had business there. His children ravaged European society. And Emmerick indulged them. From London to Paris to Venice, they left a trail of dead far and wide. It was in Venice where Emmerick took a mistress. A witch with great power. He wanted that power to put him back on top financially. His wife committed suicide over the disloyalty as well as the horror of what her children had become."

"What happened next?"

"Emmerick and his new bride, the witch, returned home. She was with child. Angelo Duquesne."

"Angelo?" Demitra repeated.

"Yes," Blackie nodded. "As in D'Angelo. Angelo Duquesne...D'Angelo. Hugh D'Angelo was the first time the new moniker was used in Charlestonian records—separating the family from the rumors of Duquesne vampires."

"So, the family split. One side is undead, the other are witches. The secret of the House of Duquesne is vampires," Demitra sighed.

"No," Blackie frowned. "Just one of the secrets. Remember, *there are too many secrets in the House of Duquesne*."

Demitra was already mind blown. She was not sure she could handle any further revelations. But this was her only chance to get the answers. "Tell me the rest."

Blackie continued, knowing time was of the essence for how long Demitra and she could keep this synergy was unknown. "The family continued publicly as if it were a new family. Emmerick and his wife eventually died. Angelo took a wife of his own. It changed the D'Angelo family forever. It is the reason Atheidrelle cannot die. Nor can Thaddeuss. Nor can I."

The statement was a powerful one. Shocking, yet Demitra believed it. But with believing it came an assault of revelations she was not prepared to handle. Blackie said, *Atheidrelle cannot die*. Nevermind what she also said about herself and Thaddeuss—if Atheidrelle was immortal then what was the purpose of that great battle at Blanchard House years ago? Demitra's mother sacrificed herself to save her family from Atheidrelle's evil. They allowed Atheidrelle into Olympia's body. They shot her to death, even chopped her head off. Was that for nothing? Did Olympia give up her life months sooner than she had to for absolutely nothing?

"What do you mean Atheidrelle cannot die. Or you and your brother?"

"My mother is something else altogether. My father did not mate with her out of love—she chose him. He was wealthy and powerful among humans, and he could hide her successfully from those who would have sought to destroy her."

Demitra was thoroughly lost now. Nothing added up. Briefly she turned to look back at Trix and Artemis, to see if perhaps they could hear this conversation. They couldn't. They sat wide eyed, staring at the bodies of Demitra and Blackie in their state of trance. Demitra returned her attention to Blackie, "Blackie, you just said *your* mother. But Angelo and his wife were not your parents. Your father was Hugh D'Angelo."

Blackie ignored the comment and continued with what she felt was most important. "Angelo's wife was what changed everything in our family."

"Was she a very powerful witch?" Demitra asked. "Or another vampire?"

"Worse," Blackie warned. "Succubi."

Demitra was not certain she heard correctly. Such things were of fiction, or long dead lore no one placed any stock in.

"My mother was a succubus. She fed from men's souls until she discovered the witch she could not devour. She enchanted my father long enough to spawn three offspring, a triad of sorts to replenish her kind. But her husband being a witch and the merging of two such beings created something else altogether. Three witches who cannot die."

"But Hugh D'Angelo was your father."

"Hugh D'Angelo was just the name to mark a generation of record. There never was a Hugh D'Angelo. It has always been the same man. Immortal. Hugh D'Angelo is my brother Thaddeuss," Blackie revealed. "One day in the future he will go by another name. But it will always be the same man. Angelo and my mother had three children, and we are all immortal."

Demitra was not prepared for this. It was all so confusing. So unbelievable, yet somehow it made the most sense of all. It explained so much of the mystery regarding the D'Angelo family.

"Hugh and Thaddeuss are the same person? Is that what you are saying?" Before she even allowed time for an answer, Demitra shot another question. "What do you mean you cannot die? If so, why was Atheidrelle so desperate to possess Arielle, then leapt into my mother?"

"Our souls continue. We must find bodies to hijack. My sister has not always been called Atheidrelle. She has been many names, aging to certain points, and then, desiring youth and beauty again, she injects her spirit into someone young and takes over their existence, retaining all her witchy powers. If she takes over another witch, that witch's power melds into her own, making Atheidrelle almost unstoppable."

"And you?"

"I have not body-jumped as often as my siblings, this is merely my third."

"And what of Thaddeuss? How many times has he jumped bodies?"

"I have lost count."

"Hugh never died," Demitra repeated, trying to put it all together in her mind. "Thaddeuss and Hugh are the same man. Blackie, what happened to your mother?"

Blackie's eyes practically dilated, turning to an almost charcoal color. It was plain to see that the very subject of her mother sent her to dark places. "She is locked somewhere in the House of Duquesne, alone, a prisoner. For the only way we can die is if she does. As long as she lives, we live."

"Can anything kill her?"

"The only way to kill her is to chop off her head, and Thaddeuss keeps her well hidden in a crypt located inside the vampire domain. No one will ever find her because the Duquesne vampires guard her impeccably. The House of Duquesne protects the inner house where the vampires protect her crypt. Her name is Themis, and she is why you will never end Atheidrelle. Atheidrelle will always come back."

"And Arielle, Echo, Tess, Trix, Thaddeuss' children, Cassandra? What of them?"

"They are not the children of a succubus. They are not eternal. One day my children will grow old and die, and I will watch them perish because I cannot. I will have to choose a new vessel and see them all go before me. Just as I have with the children I bore before them."

"You have other children?" Demitra gasped.

"I have had several children in my day. When the last one died, I swore to never fall in love again, never bring another life into this world to watch grow old and die before me. I would not have had Arielle willingly."

"Is there vampire blood in your veins as well?" Demitra asked.

"No," Blackie answered. "That is Gideon's family. All we need to live forever is a fresh healthy body when the time comes. My original body was shed many years ago, this you see now is my third. We can leap into anyone we want and push their souls away, ultimately killing them and keeping their forms for ourselves."

"You possess other people?"

"Possession is temporary. We infiltrate and eradicate. Our minds are still our minds. Years and years of knowledge, power, wealth. It all amasses as we continue to live forever. When I met Nacaria all those years ago and we became friends, I was much older than she ever knew. I am 120 years old. Atheidrelle and I were older than even Olympia Blanchard back then."

Suddenly the past came rushing back to Demitra. Things that never made sense began to. With widened eyes she turned to Blackie and asked, "Is this why Nacaria's plan failed so many years ago? After Atheidrelle cursed Salem and Seth and Nacaria went back in time to undo Atheidrelle's birth..."

Blackie nodded. "All Nacaria would have succeeded in doing would have been erasing the birth of the body Atheidrelle possessed, but she would have only found another. Nacaria's attempt would have made no difference."

Demitra was aghast. She had never heard of anything like this before. But there was no time to hear her reaction. Blackie continued. "Babies work better, but they must be D'Angelo babies—Duquesne babies. This way the family power remains in the bloodline. Each newborn we inhabit makes our power grow. I have lived three lives. My brother and sister have lived far more, which makes them immeasurably stronger than me, than anyone. Atheidrelle did not want Arielle because of her love for Xander—though that love was real. She wanted to possess Arielle once Arielle was of adult age. So that she could continue to live youthfully, and powerfully."

"This is astounding."

"There is a reason Thaddeuss wants my children in that house. The house is the only place the transformation can take place. The succubus is there; her energy is the battery. The House of Duquesne is a battery that charges the D'Angelo bloodline. Thaddeuss wants my children's bloodline. He wants them to produce children. Children he can inhabit. Children he can allow Atheidrelle to inhabit—he has her soul. Her soul is in that house, waiting for a body."

"Why does Thaddeuss want your children? He has children and grandchildren of his own he could inhabit."

"He wants the triplets. The triplets are D'Angelos. The triplets are Duquesnes. They are Blanchards. That alone would be an epic combination. But my three children also have something else he wants. Something he needs to rule the world and all of the witching kind."

"What do they have?" Demitra asked.

Blackie raised a brow in disbelief that her friend had not yet figured it out. "The God Strain."

Demitra gasped.

"With Beryl's blood, the D'Angelos become gods. Imagine what would happen in a world where Thaddeuss and Atheidrelle had the power of God."

Demitra paused and raised a concerned brow. Something didn't jive. "But the triplets are just young witches. They have fantastic powers, yes, but they are not gods."

During their entire conversation, Blackie never exhibited a more serious face than she did now. "They are not Gods, like Beryl. Gods are chosen. But a fraction of that power does reside inside them, and in Howard. The triplets are far too young and inexperienced to know yet, but they are the most powerful witches we have ever met. Beryl's blood flows in them. They are gods, Demitra. And Thaddeuss wants that blood."

CHAPTER TWENTY NINE

Yasmine

Tess Blanchard wandered the twisting corridors of the House of Duquesne, trying to locate the statue room Cassandra had mentioned to Salem. Unfortunately, Cassandra had not been specific in her details, making it quite a wild goose chase for Tess. As she meandered down a dark hallway, she found herself facing a lengthy row of portraits. It was unlike the downstairs hall of portraits which seemed to be more modern—these on the four-floor corridor were very old. She paused at the portrait of a particularly beautiful woman with almost white, translucent hair. There was something mesmerizing about her. She wore a green dress, off the shoulder, and it looked to be almost antebellum.

"Her name was Themis," called a voice at the other end of the hallway.

"She was beautiful," Tess replied before remembering she was supposed to be invisible. She looked down to her hands and feet and could not see them. She *was* still invisible.

"I can see through charms and cloaking," said the young girl coming forward. "My name is Ashby. I'm Taub D'Angelo's daughter. Are you Tess or Beatrix?"

"I'm Tess," Tess said shakily, unnerved that she had been discovered.

"I knew that of course. I can read minds, too. I suppose I only asked who you were out of polite conversation. It did seem to be the most logical follow up sentence to say," Ashby continued. "Don't worry, I'm the only one who knows you are here in the house. I have seen you walking around for days. I assumed you had your reasons."

"Thank you for keeping my secret," Tess said smiling, more than slightly taken aback by this girl's manner. Not knowing herself what to say next, Tess simply added, "I think we are cousins."

"First cousins once removed," Ashby clarified. "Or sometimes referred to as second cousins although that is not really the appropriate terminology. Second cousins would be the relationship between my child and your child."

"I see," Tess said.

She was beginning to understand Ashby a little more. The child was different. Maybe on the autistic spectrum. There was an emotionless directness emanating from her, but nothing appeared to be malicious in intent. She simply spoke what she thought.

"May I ask you what you are looking for?" Ashby asked. "I may be able to help you."

Tess hesitated, but then drew the conclusion that if this child had seen her stalking the house all this time, she was probably a good secret keeper and could be trusted.

"I am looking for a certain room. It has statues inside it. It is an outer room overlooking the outside grounds. It has a secret staircase in the walls that go around the room."

"Are you trying to get into the other house?" Ashby asked.

"The other house?"

"Yes. If you follow those stairs to the parapet, you can access a secret door outside which will lead you to the house within this one. But that isn't the only access. There are other entrances."

Tess was taken by surprise. This was new information to her. "Let me get this straight—you mean there is another house inside this one?"

Ashby wrinkled her nose as she attempted an awkward laugh—something Tess could tell the child did not do very often. "Isn't that a strange expression? *Let me get this straight?* As if information is usually crooked. I would think saying something like, 'let me clarify or may I refine this information..." Ashby stopped talking and turned her eyes toward the ceiling, thinking again before she corrected herself. "On second inspection of the sentence, I suppose it isn't so odd a term. Especially regarding our topic of this house. Everything here is crooked in a manner of speaking. *Getting something straight* seems to fit."

Tess really did not know what to respond to this stream of thought falling from Ashby's lips, so she turned the subject back to what mattered. "There is another house somewhere inside this one?"

"Yes," Ashby said. "Every wall you see has another room behind it which isn't connected to the portion we live in. Other people live on that side. Dangerous people. I see them sometimes. I encountered one once when I stumbled into their area by accident. But my father ran in and pulled me out. I followed my mother there once as well. She used to be friends with them."

"Them?"

"The other people. I don't really know who they are. But Father says they are dangerous."

Tess knelt down beside Ashby and placed her hands on the girl's shoulders. "I really need to find that place. I may know someone who is in there."

"Is it the new lady?" Ashby asked.

"New lady?"

"She has long, brown hair. Approximately my sister's height. I see her at night walking around the grounds outside. My balcony has a great view of the water. I see all of them coming and going down to the pier and taking boats. They stay gone for hours sometimes and come back just before dawn."

"Can you show me?" Tess asked.

"Sure," Ashby said. "Follow me."

Ashby led Tess through the house with the skill of an ocean navigator. Twice a servant passed them, and once Constance passed, but never did Ashby reveal that she had company walking beside her. Tess' instinct to trust the child was proving to be correct. Ashby made only one mistake en route when she turned a corner and smacked into a wall.

"That's new," she said. "It wasn't here last time. But that is okay, I know another way."

Tess followed but was very perplexed. When the coast was clear to speak to the girl she asked her, "That wall back there...you said it was new?"

"Yes," Ashby said in a way which Tess was learning must be a character trait of the child's—a very nonchalant way of interacting with people. "Sometimes walls show up. Or stairs. Or rooms even sometimes. You get used to it."

"How could that happen?" Tess asked.

"I think the people in the other house do it. Maybe they need room and make more. Or sometimes they hide the way into their side. Once when I found a hidden door to one of their bed chambers, they sealed up the hallway to it the next day. You can hear them building sometimes through the walls."

When Ashby opened the door to her bedroom, Tess found it to be a rather typical room for a little girl. Decorated in pinks and lavenders, with frilly bedspreads and canopy. Toys sat on shelves that looked to have been ignored for years. An Xbox and television sat in the corner with an array of games laid very neatly in an organized line around the bean bag chair in front. The door to the balcony was open and Tess stepped outside to look. The sun was going down, but she could still see quite well down to the little boathouse at the edge of the pier over the grassy marsh water.

"Would you mind if I stay here a while and keep a lookout for the lady?" Tess asked.

"No," Ashby replied. "I have to go down to dinner anyway. Have you eaten anything while you've been here?"

"Yes," Tess said. "I did find the kitchen and helped myself a few times. And my brother has brought me food from town."

"All right," Ashby said as she exited the room.

Tess camped out on the balcony. What she was waiting for she was not sure, but something told her it was worth checking out. It did not take very long for her to see what Ashby had been describing. Just after dark, a small group of people crossed the back lawn from some lower door Tess could not view. They were not dressed particularly out of place, yet Tess felt a sense of old world about them. They walked down to the pier and stepped onto the little boat. They drove off into the night under the stars.

Tess had not seen anyone resembling Yasmine with them. She didn't know how long she should wait. If Ashby was correct these people would not return until almost morning. She could not expect the little girl to allow her to remain in her room through the night as she slept. If only she could find a similar vantage point like the one Ashby's balcony offered. But suddenly, Tess realized she needn't worry about that anymore. She could see what she was hoping to see. A woman crossed the lawn, heading into what looked like an ornate garden to the farthest side of the house, almost out of view. The woman fit Yasmine's general size and appearance, but of course so did a quarter of the female population. Tess needed to get closer.

Just as she was considering how she might use the balcony to get down to the ground below, Ashby returned to her bedroom. Tess asked the child if she could lead her outside to the back of the house quickly. Ashby said it was an easy thing to achieve. There was a staircase on a nearby hall that led straight outside. She showed Tess the way and as the door to the outside opened Tess cautioned Ashby to not follow her.

"It could be dangerous."

"All right," Ashby said without emotion and returned upstairs.

Tess crossed the dewy, wet grass of the lawn and found the entrance to the formal garden which lay inside a wall of hedges. Inside the garden, lit only from the moon and stars above, Tess saw many stone statues scattered among little seating areas housed by lower-cut shrubbery. In the distance she could see the lady with her back turned, staring off into the night. Tess crept as quietly as she could, still invisible, closer toward her. When she was within six feet of the lady, Tess hung back and remained still so as to not make any noise while she waited to see the lady's face. It didn't take long as whatever the woman was looking for in the night either was not there or did not hold her attention. She turned around to walk back to the house. She passed by within inches of Tess without noticing she was there. Tess was befuddled as the light hit the lady's face. It was Yasmine. Yasmine Blanchard was alive. Or at least Yasmine existed still. She had not been destroyed. She was walking the inner halls of the House of Duquesne...a vampire.

...

Artemis Blanchard had just walked through the door from Birmingham when her cell phone rang in her pocket. She pulled it out and said "hello" as she simultaneously mouthed a hello to Seth, Fable, and the children all playing a board game on the living room floor.

"Aunt Artemis, it's Tess. So much is going on here. Cassandra is acting strangely. I think they are changing her somehow. I think something in this house is possessing her. And she was right about her suspicion. It is Yasmine. Yasmine is here! I just saw her."

Artemis could not take her eyes off Seth and the children as she hung up her call with Tess. What was she supposed to do now? He had worked so hard to pick up the shattered pieces of his life and start over. Even now he was heartbroken. To know his wife was still walking the earth would be yet another hell to put him through. It was difficult enough the first time for him to make peace with losing her—with ending her miserable existence. To go through all of that again would be cruel. The kind thing would be to handle this matter herself and never say a word to him about it. He was the closest thing to a son she'd ever had. She loved Seth so damn much. Sparing him that kind of pain was an act of love.

But on the other hand, he was her son—or closest thing to. And that connection was owed respect. Honesty. As Hecate she should act logically and with only what was best for the family. But her love for Seth superseded that oath in her heart. She could not lie to him, even by omission. Ominously, she asked Miranda to take the children upstairs. Once they were out of sight, she sat down on the sofa with Seth and Fable.

"I have no way to say this other than just say it," Artemis began with her hands holding Seth's. "It was not Yasmine's body we found charred on that island. Yasmine still exists."

The color drained from Seth's face yet even still a twinkle of hope glimmered in his eye. Artemis recognized what it stood for.

"No, Seth," she said. "Yasmine is still a vampire. She is not our Yaz."

Fable reached out and grabbed her cousin's hand, "Nothing has changed. We still have to destroy her. Our Yaz would have wanted it that way."

Seth looked broken again. After months of slowly attempting to rebuild himself enough to rejoin the world and be there for his children, this news was reducing him back to his lowest of lows. "Where is she?" Seth asked his aunt.

"She is in the House of Duquesne."

"Why is she there, is the more important question," Fable remarked.

"There is so much we now know," Artemis began. "Blackie allowed Demitra into her mind. We know everything now. It is time for a family meeting. We have much to do."

Within a few hours the coven of Blanchard witches was assembled in the Blanchard family living room. Howard was included in the group as it involved his children. He was not pleased to discover the dangers they were placed in.

"Echo and Tess have to get pulled out of there. Now!" Howard yelled.

"And Cassandra," Salem added. "We have to save Cassandra."

"And we must find and destroy Yasmine, as well as all the other vampires," Trix said with her mother Blackie seated in a wheelchair beside her.

Seth flinched but said nothing. Artemis reassuringly patted his shoulder.

"The most urgent thing is getting Echo, Tess, and Cassandra to safety. We need to call them and tell them to leave ASAP," Howard said. "We can worry about Yaz after."

"We have attempted calling. We can't get through to them," Artemis informed them.

"The vampires cannot be ignored," Trix said firmly to Howard. "I know what happens to the world when they set upon it. If those creatures are roaming South Carolina, it is only a matter of time before this world becomes as mine was. I will not live through that again."

"We are not going to allow that to happen, Trix," Demitra said. "But we must get Echo and Tess out before anything else. Thaddeuss wants their offspring. He plans to—I don't know what he plans to do—but he wants their bloodline."

. . .

Tess Blanchard made her way back into Echo's room. He was laying on the bed trying to send Trix a text but kept receiving an *unable to send* error code. He'd tried a dozen times, each meeting the same response. He tried Fable and Seth...same thing. But as Tess rushed into the room and slammed the door behind her, Echo knew immediately his sister had discovered something.

"Yasmine is alive! And she's here in the house! I saw her tonight."

"What?" Echo shouted. "Are you sure?"

"Yes! I phoned Aunt Artemis and told the family. You and I must find Cassandra and get out of here. Tonight!"

"How did you get your phone to work? Mine won't."

"It doesn't matter," Tess replied. "We have to go."

"Your phone works because they don't know you are here," Echo said, half to himself. "Mine has been blocked somehow."

"Here use mine, but hurry!" Tess urged, tossing him her cell.

Echo typed out a fast text to their sister and clicked send. "You have the same error message now. We can't get through to anyone."

"That does it," Tess replied. "We absolutely have to find Cassandra and bolt, right now!"

"How do we find her?"

"We inherited a smidgeon of our great-grandmother's psychic ability, let's just try to sync up together and put Demitra's power to use. We will sort of trace Cassandra until we find her."

Cassandra was standing alone in the circular statue room when they found her. She seemed as if she were waiting for something, perhaps them.

"Cassandra!" Tess shouted rushing forward, making herself visible again. "We found you! We have to get out of here right now!"

Cassandra stared blankly back at her. Tess stopped in her tracks. The look on Cassandra's face was that of a total stranger. True, they did not know each other very well—but they did know each other. They shared a sister in fact. Echo stepped forth, and Cassandra smiled in recognition.

"Forgive me, Echo. You startled me."

Tess took a step closer, her intuition raging now. "Who am I?"

Cassandra glared menacingly toward her.

"What is my name, Cassandra?"

"Have you forgotten it?" Cassandra replied, attempting a smile she was not very skilled at presenting.

"I am either Trix or Tess. Cassandra would know which."

"You are correct my dear, she would," said Thaddeuss approaching from the corridor behind them. "I find it rather amusing that the two of you truly believed you could escape this house without my consent. Despite your best efforts you have ended up exactly where I needed you to be. How cooperative."

Thaddeuss did not seem so kind and welcoming any longer. There was an unnerving sneer on his face that frightened the Blanchard twins. Cassandra looked equally menacing as she walked over to a stone in the wall and pressed it. Suddenly stones began to protrude from the wall, all forming a circular stair rising high above.

"What's going on?" Echo asked nervously.

"The endgame," Thaddeuss grinned.

"Uncle Thaddeuss," Echo stuttered. "I don't understand."

"You can dispense with the Uncle Thaddeuss nonsense now. I don't have to continue with this charade any longer. You are not dear to me, and I find the very presence of my traitorous sister's children abhorrent."

"Why did you want me here then?" Echo asked.

"I wanted the three of you. All I got was you and that useless Arielle. But I figured sooner or later one of your sisters would show up, and I was pleased to learn from Ashby that one has."

"Ashby?" Tess asked in surprise. "I can't believe it. I thought she was—"

"A good guy?" Thaddeuss grinned. "Oh, my naive niece, your cousin is neither good nor bad. She has no motives or agendas. Ashby is simply Ashby. Emotionless, blunt, strictly realistic. But if it makes you feel better, she did not betray you. She merely mentioned seeing the nice invisible lady in the corridor. It was then I knew it was time to enact the plan."

"What plan?" Tess asked.

"Oh, that will soon be obvious."

"Tess! Look!" Echo grabbed his sister's arm and directed her to look above them.

Emerging from a door in the topmost section of the wall, was Yasmine. She stared down at them with a detached smile as she descended the stone slab stairs. Echo and Tess stood in shock as they watched her come closer to the ground, step by achingly slow step.

"Now would be a good time, my dear," Thaddeuss called to her.

In what could only be described as a reluctant obedience, Yasmine Blanchard raised her arms. The twins knew the moment she made the motion what was happening. Like a wave of cold air rushing their way, they felt their extremities harden within the milliseconds it took to process her reaction. Yasmine was freezing them, the way Salem could. As the wave of power rushed into them, Echo and Tess saw nothing after that. They knew nothing after that. They simply stopped. Yasmine took the final step to the floor and approached the two siblings with bewilderment in her dead eyes. She had only used her power once before and the sight of it at work still fascinated her.

"That baby of yours has an amazing power, my dear," Thaddeuss said proudly. "And how fortunate for us that you became a vampire before it could be born. It is a useful tool for a vampire, the ability to stop time for other people. Gives you quite an escape route when in a predicament. I assume it also comes in handy for feeding."

"It has its uses," Yasmine agreed.

"Thankfully your becoming undead has stopped another grandchild of Nacaria's from ever being born," Cassandra smiled wickedly.

"Oh my dear, Atheidrelle," Thaddeuss said to Cassandra. "We have larger aspirations than continuing to focus on your feud with that Blanchard woman. Now everyone leave me alone for a while with Tess and Echo. Yasmine, please keep them frozen until I say otherwise."

CHAPTER THIRTY

Hope and Grief

It was growing late at Blanchard House, and everyone was going to bed. Not that many would sleep well. Not with everything they learned that night about Yasmine and the fact that so far, no word had come from Oleander that the twins had made it there safely. Artemis sent everyone to bed knowing they would need rest for what was undoubtedly coming tomorrow. She did not retire herself, however—she had too much to do. She needed to formulate a plan for action. She was upstairs in her room, deep in thought. She didn't hear the footsteps in the hall or down the stairs as Seth Blanchard crept outside.

The crescent moon provided little illumination, but the stars were sufficient to light the way down the path to the cemetery. Seth stalked across the swaying grasses with a determination in his mind and a rage in his heart. Clutched in his right hand was a sledgehammer.

The iron gate squeaked in the silent night as he pushed it open to step into the Blanchard family graveyard. He was a man on a mission with no other thoughts in his head other than the futile task he'd assigned himself. He made his way to Yasmine's grave. Her grave, with someone else's charred remains buried beneath those six feet of earth. He'd dug the grave himself and laid his wife to rest there—what had been left of her. He needed her name to be scrawled in stone in that cemetery. He needed their children to have a place to come to whenever they needed to feel close to their mother. Only it wasn't her grave. He didn't know who rested there now beneath the surface. but it was not his beloved Yasmine.

Seth hoisted the sledgehammer high above his shoulders and crashed it down on top of the headstone. The thickness of the stone prevented much damage, but it did crack slightly a few inches. His next swing went to the front face of the stone, aimed directly at her name. Yasmine Blanchard. As the head of the hammer crushed in the first letters of her name, Seth felt exonerated from some of his grief. The headstone was a lie. His Yasmine was not dead. She was out there somewhere, existing in a different kind of state than she had before—but she was still out there.

Swing after swing, the thick stone crumbled with every blow until nothing remained but chunks of granite and rubble. Seth looked out into the night, skyward. She was out there somewhere, walking through this very night under that very crescent moon. She was probably killing someone. His sweet, innocent, beautiful Yasmine was probably killing someone. He felt powerless.

How could this be happening? How could she be out there somewhere without him? Why hadn't he felt her? He always had felt her. Seth had always saved her. It was only a few years ago when he'd dashed up those flights of stairs in downtown Tuscaloosa, with a werewolf on his heels, and faced down the monster Patric to saved Yasmine's life. She'd run into his arms. He'd been her hero.

Then last year, he'd literally searched through the channels of time to find her when she'd been lost in the past. She was losing strength, her soul merging with the younger version of herself. He'd rushed into that hotel room and swept her up in his arms, saving her once again and bringing her home. Seth always saved Yasmine... until those damn vampires grabbed her and there was nothing he could do.

But she was out there now, somewhere. He knew where. It didn't feel right not to try to save her once again. There had to be a way.

...

When the sun rose over Blanchard House, Artemis was at the kitchen table downing her third cup of coffee. She had not slept at all. She had hoped Nacaria or the kids would phone in the night to let her know they were safe. But no one called. It was very early, but if Nacaria or the kids didn't call soon, she would call Nacaria herself and wake her. Artemis was startled when she heard the front door open and close. For a moment she thought it might be Tess and Echo, until Howard entered the kitchen. He gave her a grieved smile, signaling he was as worried as she.

"This is going to be a war, isn't it?" he said.

"I think it is," Artemis admitted. "I have no idea how extensive this problem is or how easily we can handle it. But I fear something bigger than we expect is brewing. We are used to battles. One, maybe two and our problem is resolved. I fear this is larger than anything we've ever been through."

"You'll need all the Blanchard witches," Howard said.

"Yes, we will."

"I guess it's time you and I went out to the apple orchard."

Artemis smiled and gave her old friend a hug. He was right, it was time. And she was glad it had been his own idea and not her suggestion. She knew she would have been able to guilt him into complying, but it being his decision made things simple. It was time to restore the powers Olympia Blanchard bound from Howard at birth.

The orchard was a bounty of oranges and golds as the leaves fell from the spent limbs, some still harboring drying fruit. Artemis carried a hand shovel with her and knelt beneath the second apple tree and began to dig. Buried three feet down was a bottle, sealed in wax. Nothing appeared to be inside it, but they both knew something was—something very important.

"What if my power is something stupid, like making plants grow," Howard frowned. "What if it is not anything that can help."

"In battle, every power is important," Artemis said. "Imagine growing a vine so large it can wrap around and subdue an attacker. There are no unimportant powers."

"I hope so."

"Besides, you are the son of the God Strain. I imagine whatever is in this bottle is pretty powerful."

Howard lifted it in his hand. He raised his eyebrow and looked incredulously at Artemis, then smashed the bottle on the ground. As it shattered, he staggered backward, back arched, head raised, as if something unseen were entering his body. Artemis steadied him from falling and, within seconds, it was over.

"Wow," he said. "That was a rush."

"Anything?" Artemis asked. "Anything particular you feel you can do?"

"Not a clue."

"Try moving something," Artemis suggested. She laid the shovel on the ground. "Focus on the shovel. With your mind's eye, try to swipe it a few inches."

Howard had no idea what a mind's eye was, but he concentrated as hard as he could, but the shovel remained in place.

"Okay, maybe you're like Seth. Can you make it rain? Focus on drawing rain clouds overhead and give us a sprinkle. The grass needs watering anyway."

Howard did as requested, but nothing happened.

Artemis held her face in her hands and thought. "Okay, maybe it is something similar to your children. Try making the metal of the shovel form something else. Or try to turn yourself invisible. Or try to copycat me and turn yourself into me."

None of those things worked.

"Can you heal?" Artemis asked, stumped. "Maybe you have Beryl's ability." She took the tip of the shovel and scraped her finger until it bled. Extending it forward for Howard to heal, he focused his mind on the small wound. Nothing.

"I suppose it'll manifest itself when it's ready," Artemis said. "Usually, we have years of honing powers. But you missed all of that. Thanks to Mother."

"If only Olympia were here to tell us."

The moment he said the words, a glowing cloud of vaper began to materialize under the nearest tree. Artemis and Howard stood shell shocked as the mist took shape. Took shape in the form of Olympia Blanchard. It wasn't the young Olympia from the past which other members of the family had visited through time travel. This was their Olympia. Old Olympia. The Olympia they knew before she died.

"Mother?"

Olympia Blanchard, regal and vibrant again—although slightly transparent—clasped her hands together and proclaimed, "You have your powers, Howard."

Howard and Artemis turned to each other in disbelief then looked back at the apparition before them. "How? How are you here?" Artemis stuttered.

"Howard has the power to restore life to the dead," Olympia explained. "The immediate dead. I am only a shadow."

Howard had questions. So many questions. But it had been so long since he had heard his dear friend's voice. The questions faded from his mind as he focused solely on seeing the old woman again after so long.

Tearily, Howard looked her way and with a cracking voice said, "Olympia."

"Hello, my great grandson," she smiled lovingly at him. "Time is precious. Your ability lasts only a short while. I am beginning to fade again; listen closely to me. You can bring the immediate dead back to life if you get to them within a few minutes after death. For the long dead, you can only bring our souls back for counsel and only for the briefest of moments. Use your powers well, son. Know that I love you very much."

"Mother!" Artemis cried. "Wait! We have some real problems we need your help with."

"I am not really here, Artemis. I have left this world. As I said, I am merely a shadow. You are Hecate now. You do not need me to lead this family. But hear my warning...everything is about to change. Good and evil are going to war. Your leadership as Hecate of this family will be the most vital in Blanchard history. Lead them well, daughter."

And she was gone. Faded into the air as quickly as she had materialized. Howard slowly sank to the ground, exhaustion filling him all over. Artemis knelt to him, understanding his power had to be immensely draining. They sat together on the ground in silence, both on the verge of tears. Eventually, they gave into those tears, embracing one another as they mourned once again for the matriarch they never stopped grieving.

Pulling herself away and wiping the tears from her eyes, Artemis said, "Well, we know what you can do. And it is a remarkably useful and powerful gift. We will unquestionably need you in battle."

CHAPTER THIRTY ONE

Mara Tags Along

She hated being inside the walls of Duquesne House. Every moment within the monstrous structure filled her heart with dread. There was a pulse within the house, like a heartbeat, and if it were indeed a heart, it was black. Most of the time she could manage living with the feeling, but on nights like these when it was too much, she would do as she did now and take a walk down to the water's edge.

The marshland carried a putrid smell which most inhabitants of the barrier islands of Charleston were long accustomed to. But Mara was not. She'd lived here all her life, but the stench always assailed her. Perhaps it was because the walls of the House of Duquesne were thick and the windows never open, thus shielding her senses from the stagnant waters, making every time she experienced them new again. Perhaps it was not the scent of brackish waters which sickened her. Maybe it was trigger for her, a confrontation with truth—her family's and her own. Mara was as black at times as the heart of her family home. Yet she possessed a sparkle too. It was perhaps that sparkle which sometimes made her soul reject the ugliness around her even if on occasion she was as much as part of it as anyone else.

She settled herself on a large rock at the water's edge where discarded clam shells—abandoned by their owners—caused the water to make music as it slowly rolled over them. She stared out into the black night at the only illumination in sight. The lantern swinging on the approaching boat was coming toward the dock. Mara knew it was time for departure which was why she had walked to the water in the first place. She sometimes liked to see who would be going out for the evening.

As old man Macklereed brought his boat to a halt at the pier, two figures were walking down the worn grassy path from the house. Mara recognized the vampire Davidson immediately by his height against the backdrop of stars. Alongside him walked Elijah Duquense. Mara often thought Elijah rather handsome. It was rare for her to see him—none of the living inside the house were ever supposed to encounter the undead. However, Mara always defied rules and over her years grew to know some of the vampires a little in passing.

"Good evening, cousin," Elijah bowed as he passed Mara on the rock.

Mara nodded back. She was not afraid of him. Of any of them. The Duquesne vampires needed the D'Angelos' protection. They would never betray the trust. More than that, Elijah possessed that old world dignity where family was still revered—no matter how many generations separated them.

As Davidson passed, Mara stood up from her perch on the rock. He smiled her way knowing from her very presence how this night was going to go. "Bored again I see, Miss D'Angelo. May I assume you are joining us tonight?"

Mara smiled and clasped his arm. He guided her to the boat.

Elijah said nothing on the ride to town. He did not approve of her accompanying Davidson on his nights hunting, but it happened so occasionally that he never alerted her grandfather. Elijah understood Mara needed companionship sometimes and the youngish (in appearance that is) Davidson filled that need for her. Likewise, Davidson traded his youth years ago for immortal life as companion to the aged and weathered Aspasia. He longed sometimes for a fresher laugh, a newer experience, and a face which had no creases or texture.

Davidson and Mara were not lovers. Elijah knew this for a fact. Had they ever been he would have been compelled to inform Thaddeuss of the situation which would have certainly been the end of Davidson. Elijah recognized these two strange companions were merely sporadic friends, using each other for a distraction.

Mara waited patiently on Church Street while Davidson fed upon the woman he dragged into the twisting alleys of the Pirates Courtyard—a small cluster of apartments and courtyards which once housed and hid away ship raiders and their bounty. It is said Blackbeard himself stashed treasure somewhere in the cove after raiding ships in the Charleston harbor for five days.

After Davidson dumped his meal's body into the deep well in the center courtyard and pushed the heavy concrete cap back over it, he rejoined his friend.

"She was delicious," he smiled. "I thank you for the recommendation."

"You are welcome," Mara replied. "I accidentally bumped into her on the street a few days ago, and she was terribly rude. I apologized, but she continued to be hateful. I put a trace on her and found she lives here. I've been meaning to come back myself and show her what unkindness can lead to. But then when I saw you tonight, I thought she might make a perfect dinner for you instead."

Davidson gently kissed Mara's hand and smiled, "And I thank you for the thoughtfulness."

They walked together down to the Battery. Along the way, Davidson confided he and Aspasia were at odds once again. His aged lover was jealous he had requested to come into town without her once more.

"Well, you can't spend every excursion with her," Mara noted. "I'd think that would arouse suspicion if by chance anyone ever noticed you both in connection with a missing person."

"Precisely," Davidson agreed. "Not to mention I grew tired of her company decades ago."

Mara thought his statement very telling, perhaps even puzzling. In the handful of times they'd spent evenings in town together, she never thought to ask him much about himself. "I'm curious now," she began. "I cannot fathom a time when I would ever grow tired of the man I love. I think of him constantly. To have eternity with him would still not be enough."

"You are very young, my dear," Davidson frowned. "And I am afraid the absence of love in your formative years may have caused finding love to be an obsession for you now. I personally have known true love and been scorned by it. It is the very reason I exist the way I am now."

Mara was intrigued. She led him by the hand to a bench on the edge of Battery Park where they sat down facing the water. "Tell me your story."

Davidson's tale was a grim one. It had been 1944, France. Operation Dragoon called for American and French armies to land east of Marseille and Toulon. Retaking these cities from German control would open Allied supply capacity to the French mainland. Private Davidson Conway was only 24 years old when he was part of the American 7th Army under the leadership of General Alexander Patch. 94,000 men landed on the shores August 15 with only 395 casualties. While the French army freed Marseille and Toulon, the American army cut off the Germans near Montélimar. The people of Montélimar, elated at seeing the Germans flee their city, met the American army in the streets with glasses of wine, baskets of bread, and the occasional grateful kiss from a pretty girl.

Armandine was one such grateful young woman. Private Conway was covered in dust, dirt, and the dried blood of the wounded and dead when the beautiful Armandine swept him into her arms for a welcoming kiss. Davidson fell in love instantly. His stay in Montélimar lasted only a couple of weeks, but it was long enough for him to understand true love. He asked Armandine's father for her hand in marriage. It was immediately granted. Davidson had no great wealth, was from no great family. But he was an American and a hero to the people his regiment freed. The American army had to move on, but Davidson swore he'd return in a few weeks and the wedding would be immediate.

As it turned out Davidson was not the only soldier who would win Armandine's affection. Upon Davidson's return, he found his beloved married to another American soldier who'd remained in the village and stolen Armandine's heart. Angry, heartbroken, and feeling more foolish than a man ever should, Davidson fled Montélimar and found himself wandering the streets of Paris. Drinking heavily and fighting madness, he wandered straight into the clutches of a regal aristocrat named Aspasia DeFonblanque. And she was a vampire.

"And Aspasia turned you?" Mara asked after hearing the tragic story.

"She needed companionship," Davidson said. "I was young, handsome, and my mortal life held no meaning any longer. I gave myself to her willingly."

Mara wasn't sure if she should ask, but her curiosity got the better of her. "What happened to Armandine?"

Davidson turned to Mara with a devilish gleam in his eyes and allowed his pointy fangs to protrude, glistening in the lamplight. "I ate her."

...

As the night waned, Davidson and Mara strolled the Charleston sidewalks arm in arm making their way back to the dock where Macklereed awaited to return them to the Duquesne dock on Wadmalaw Island. As Mara turned them onto an alternate street from the more direct route to the dock, Davidson peered at his companion inquisitively.

"This is not the way, my dear."

"It will get us there all the same," Mara stated. "There is just something I must do first."

Davidson said no more and trusted his companion. Within a couple of blocks, they came across a row of modest townhouses, each painted its own muted pastel color. He immediately noticed the bluish smoke hovering before the door to Number 12. Though it was the dark of night, the streetlamps illuminated enough of the pale-yellow facade of the townhouse to allow the blue haze to be visible.

"May I ask what that is?" he asked.

"My tracing spell," Mara said rather nonchalantly. "I placed it on my Brandon earlier today."

Davidson's eyes followed the trail as it moved past two more townhouses to turn right around the corner of the block. "This is where your true love resides?"

Mara's face hardened. Through her quivering lips she replied, "No. It isn't. Brandon does not live here. He has obviously just left here."

Davidson studied Mara's disheartened expression and understood. This was the townhouse of another woman. A woman whom Brandon had recently said goodnight to. He gripped Mara's hand in solidarity. "A broken heart must be avenged. I understand completely, my dear."

Mara gave him a forced smile of thanks as she patted his reassuring hand before removing herself from his hold. "You should probably move to the other side of the street," she warned. "I would feel terrible if you were harmed."

Still eyeing her suspiciously, Davidson heeded her advice and walked across the two-lane road to the sidewalk across the street. He watched with fascination as Mara approached the far-left wall of the yellow townhouse. She placed the first two fingers of her left hand on the plastered facade and slowly walked to the other end where the next house began. As she went her fingers dragged in a line across the front of Number 12. Davidson watched in amazement as the surface area touched beneath her fingers ignited.

Within seconds the linear flame across the yellow townhouse rose to a height of ten feet. Mara crossed the street to join him at a safe distance. Whatever flame she'd managed to concoct from her magic was an unstoppable force. Before even a minute's worth of time passed, the entire structure was engulfed. Peculiarly, only Number 12. Number 10 on the left and Number 14 on the right suffered no damage—not even a smoky stain. As the yellow townhouse immersed within the inferno, Mara and Davidson heard the woman's scream pierce the silent night air from the upstairs window. Number 12 collapsed into its hellfire, bringing its fury down upon Mara's rival until the fevered screams stopped.

Sirens were ringing now, and lights were clicking on from surrounding townhomes. Davidson quickly escorted Mara to another street before anyone witnessed their presence. They walked in silence for a while, heading now to their proper destination, the dock. As the boat master came into sight, as well as Elijah now approaching from a connecting street, Davidson stopped walking and glanced down into Mara's eyes.

"You are mad, I believe."

"Am I?" she replied.

"We are all a little crazy," Davidson smiled. "Just be cautious my dear. Madness can consume you entirely. Do not become the thing I have become. I succumbed to my fury and lost my soul. Control your fury, Miss D'Angelo. I would be greatly saddened to discover one day that you had become as lost as me."

"I am not lost," Mara assured him. "I'm simply righting wrongs and cleansing the soul of the one I love."

CHAPTER THIRTY TWO

Seth's Wife

Seth Blanchard learned a great deal the night before. More than he ever wanted to know. He was only just beginning to make peace with his wife's death, and now she was alive again. Or a close facsimile of alive. He knew what he had to do, and it had to be done immediately. His sister and his aunt were formulating plans quickly. He had little time. Salem was calling a meeting with the Council of the Consort that very afternoon, using their father to zap all the Witches Association leaders to her office board room. Artemis was calling the Mobile Blanchards and aligning the family with their varying powers into an army. The march into the House of Duquesne was inevitable. But when, no one knew. Perhaps this very night. It all largely depended on the ruling of the Council.

Seth met Miranda outside of the elementary school after she had dropped Hera and Con off at class. She was more than surprised to see him standing by her car when she walked across the parking lot.

"I need you to do me the largest favor you've ever done anyone," he began. "A lot is going on and I have to go to Charleston, into dangerous territory."

"I know," Miranda said solemnly. "Fable told me last night. Yasmine still exists. I know that you must go find her and destroy her. I'm so sorry Seth."

"There is a lot to sort out and a lot to line up before we can act. But I have responsibilities to my children which must come first. Will you help me?"

"Of course, I will!" Miranda smiled. "You know I love those kids."

"I know you do. That's why I chose you."

An hour later, Seth and Miranda were standing before a judge at the Daihmler County courthouse. The ceremony was simple and transactional. Romance played no role at all, but after it was said and done and the judge signed the papers, Miranda Perkins was Miranda Blanchard, Seth's wife. As he drove her back to Daihmler

Elementary to retrieve her car, he told her all she needed to know.

"I may die in Charleston. I don't know what will happen to any of us. This is unlike anything we have ever faced. If Atheidrelle Obreiggon is truly back—well, we barely survived her the first time. The family may not make it. The children are now legally yours if something unforeseen happens. Yasmine owned Sinclair Industries. Now Howard handles it for the family, but the company belongs to Hera and Titan. You will always have everything you need to raise my children."

"Seth, you're scaring me. You talk as though you aren't coming back."

"I'm not."

Suddenly, Xander Obreiggon appeared out of thin air beside them. He gave a half smile to Miranda as he leaned forward to kiss her cheek. He said nothing except, "My daughter in law."

He reached out and took his son's hand. In a flash they vanished from sight. Miranda fell back against the side of her car, unable to process what was happening.

Xander stood with Seth outside the gates of the House of Duquesne. There was a somber tension between them as they stood beneath the dark canopy of trees. Only the sounds of rustling branches and rolling leaves carried across the air.

Xander spoke, "I don't agree with this."

"It doesn't matter," Seth said. "I appreciate your doing this for me. It is the way I want it to be."

"Son—"

"She is the love of my life. I must do this."

"You are planning on having her turn you, aren't you Seth?" Xander uttered the words but did not want to believe them.

Seth made a grim face, almost ashamed, "If she will."

"But son—" Xander gasped. "Your children! Your mother! Me, Salem! Everyone. How can you just walk away?"

"When I married Yasmine, I said 'forsaking all others'. I'm keeping that vow now."

"She will not recognize you," Xander cautioned. "Not the way you think. She has no soul now. She is a predator, and she will kill you, Seth."

"I also vowed 'till death do us part'. If it comes to that then I will die with the woman I love."

Xander was shaking now. He'd never been the strongest of men physically or emotionally. Courage was not in his wheelhouse. In his youth, when it counted the most, he had not risked everything for the woman he loved until it was too late. Seeing his son now, about to embark on this quest, Xander both admired and pitied him. But mostly, he pitied himself because he knew he was going to lose his son. "We've had such a short time together."

"It has been enough," Seth said. "You have proven your love to me, Dad. Now love my children. Show up for their lives and don't look back at any failures you feel over me. You did right by me when it counted. You became the father I needed. Your conscience is clean now. I love you, Dad. Thank you for this."

With that Seth walked through the open gate and disappeared around the bend of the road to Duquesne House. Xander looked to the sky. It was late morning now, but when night fell, Xander knew it would be the end of his son's life. One way or another.

. . .

"What?!" Fable screamed as Miranda rushed into Blanchard House with the news. Her cries brought Demitra and Artemis running as well. Arielle and Jerry were not far behind.

"Seth left."

"What do you mean, left?" Artemis exclaimed.

Miranda shrugged and tried to explain, "He took me to the courthouse, married me, gave me this letter, and then vanished with his father."

Artemis snatched the letter from her hand and tore it open. Immediately, tears welled in her eyes as she gasped for a breath that did not come. Demitra placed a hand of reassurance on her sister's shoulder and took the letter away to read aloud.

Dear family,

You should have known I couldn't do this. I've barely been alive these months without her. Now to find out she's still out there... I can't allow you to kill her. Not my Yaz. I laid awake all last night thinking about what matters and since every one of you matter so much, I had to revert to just what matters most. That's always been Yaz. Always will be. And since we can't cure her, I must join her. I'd rather be a creature of darkness with her at my side than live the rest of my life in light without her. I love my children more than anything in this world—except their mother. I love her more. I leave the children in Miranda's capable care. I have made her my legal wife. Their legal mother. She will raise them well and raise them here where they belong. When they are older, please tell them I did not leave them because I did not love them. I left them because I cannot live without their mother. Let our love be their legacy. Let them know how deeply the heart can run.

Salem, Arielle, Fable, Demitra, and Artemis— I am sorry I failed you. You always knew I was weak. But without Yaz I am nothing. I will find her. I will join her. And I will take her far away from that place where we can be together forever.

Yours eternally,

Seth

"That son of a bitch," Fable whispered. "He's left us. He's choosing to become a vampire."

"I can't believe it," Arielle wept. "We have to get to Charleston now to stop him!"

Artemis said nothing. She took the letter back into her hands and pressed it to her chest. Slowly she walked upstairs holding the letter in her arms the way she once used to hold Seth when he was little. Demitra stepped toward the stairs to follow, but Jerry grabbed her arm. When she looked at her husband's face, he was shaking his head. She stepped back down and collapsed into his arms.

CHAPTER THIRTY THREE

Prisoners

The room was unfamiliar as they suddenly became aware of their surroundings again. Echo looked to Tess. She seemed as puzzled as he. He heard a click and turned around to see the heavy oak door closing. Echo rushed it and tried to open it, but it would not budge.

"Where are we?" Tess asked, looking around the room.

The room was small, with only two single beds and a chest of drawers with their clothes neatly folded inside. A curtain hanging from a rod covered the door to a tiny bathroom. The floors were stone and bare and only one tiny window looked out to the marshland outside.

"It looks like we are at the top of the house," Echo observed from the window. "Maybe a tower."

"And they've locked us in," Tess said. "But why?"

"What happened? Why can't we remember?"

"I don't know," Tess said. "But we are getting out of here, brother."

She looked around the room for anything that might help. On her hands and knees, she peered under the bed. She lifted the mattress. Then she looked bewildered at her brother. He wasn't sure what she was thinking. Tess opened the drawers and inspected the bottoms as well as the treads they slid upon.

"What are you doing?" Echo finally asked.

"I was looking for something sharp to try and pick the door lock. Or something to use to hack the door with. But Echo, look around...there is no metal."

Echo joined Tess as they inspected the room more closely. The bed frames were made of wood. Only wood. Cross slats holding the mattress were made of thin wooden pieces. The legs and frame were adjoined by tongue and groove. There was not a single bolt, nail, or screw involved in its construction. The chest of drawers was the same. Even the drape over the bathroom door was held by a plastic rod and plastic curtain rings. The bathroom was the same. Plastic shower head. Plastic faucet handles. Even the toilet contained not even a half inch of metal.

"This room has been outfitted to protect against Trix," Tess observed. "No metal at all. Nothing she could draw from to forge a key or a weapon. It's like Thaddeuss was expecting to imprison all of us and prepared against her particular ability."

"Capturing us was his plan all along," Echo sighed.

"Maybe." Tess said, pressing a finger to her temple. "But if so, where is the third bed? Why only two? It's like he only needed two of us. But why?"

"It doesn't matter. All that matters is we are trapped."

Suddenly Tess made a peculiar face. "Something's wrong."

"Duh?" Echo scoffed sarcastically.

"No, Echo," she said with a frightened tone. "Something is wrong with me, down there."

She motioned to her lower body and rushed off behind the curtain, snatching it closed behind her. Echo heard her shuffling around, as if she were undressing. He tried to follow her in, but she pushed back against the curtain, making him stay back. In a few moments he heard her broken voice call out from the bathroom.

"There is semen."

"What?" Echo cried, snatching the curtain back and running to see his sister.

Tess stood there, tear stained face, utterly shocked and broken. "Someone had sex with me, Echo."

"What?" Echo cried. Seeing his sister's devastated face—the fear and revulsion now dawning upon her was like a dagger gutting his insides.

"I—I've been raped."

CHAPTER THIRTY FOUR

Forsaking All Others

He found his way into the house through an unlocked back side door. The house was astounding. Seth had never seen anything like it in his life. Yet somehow, he knew this place. Though he had never been there before, every step he took was the correct one. Despite the many opportunities for taking a wrong turn, Seth Blanchard took none. It was as if something inside his soul knew the way. Something was pulling him to her.

As he crept through the dark catacombs of the house, he could feel his love guiding him. Before he even heard the footsteps coming his way, his instinct pulled him to hide behind a door to wait as an elderly woman walked past. She did not appear to be a servant. Perhaps it was the Constance D'Angelo he'd heard about. He waited until her steps were no longer audible before he continued his way.

On the second floor he came across two staircases flanking an arched dome covering what appeared to be a rather large Faberge egg on a pedestal. From his vantage point, the two stairs twisted to a short mezzanine above, although they did not appear to connect to anything. Despite seeing nothing in sight to be accessed by the stairs, Seth somehow knew to take the left set of stairs. At the top he walked to the middle of the landing. His hands seemed to understand what to do. He pressed them into the stone wall which pushed open a hidden door in the brick. Stepping inside the tiny closet-sized alcove, he found a pulley. Tugging the ancient rope, the hidden door closed on him as it simultaneously opened another panel directly in the wall before him. A tiny hallway stretched out, lighted only by the dimmest bulbs. He followed the hall. He was now inside the walls of Duquesne House—the house within the house. He felt his tie to Yasmine growing stronger.

He could not imagine how a house, even this house, could be so extensive. But it was. He had been walking for nearly an hour when he finally opened up into a chamber of doors. The wallpaper was ornate in brilliant colors of golds, burgundies, dark blues, and forest greens. The light fixtures flanking the heavy wooden doors were gold leafed carvings of griffins and some kind of wildcat. There were nine doors in all, but his attention was on only one. The one he knew his wife was behind. He was about to open it, about to go to her, when he heard voices beyond the door.

"Are you ready, my dear?" a man could be heard saying.

A long pause followed his question, but Seth heard no response. The man began speaking again. "It's time for you to venture into the city. Everyone is waiting at the boat for you. Remember to return to the boat well before dawn. Enjoy your evening out, my dear."

Seth quickly retreated before the door opened. He stood no chance of reaching Yasmine emotionally if another vampire were around. It would surely kill him before he had the opportunity to talk with her. As Seth dashed back the way he came, his new plan formed. She was going into town, into Charleston. He would go back outside to the front gates and call an Uber to take him to the city. He would find her there.

...

He had been following her for many blocks now, from a safe distance of course. To a casual observer she blended well with the pedestrians wandering the streets of historic Charleston—tourists on vacation stopping to take pictures of the lavish hundreds-of-years-old homes with their long side porches. Yasmine turned down Church Street on the scent of a roaming couple admiring St. Philip's Church and its soaring steeple. Seth hid himself in the shadows of a doorway down the street. He knew what Yasmine knew, that the couple would naturally wander into the secluded graveyard to look at the old tombstones. With the brick wall and iron gate surrounding it, along with the lateness of the hour, no one else would be around. Something inside Seth wanted to step out under the streetlights and warn this oblivious couple who walked hand in hand, in love. He wanted to save them—alert them to the carnivorous predator stalking them. But he didn't. He waited. Watching. Watching the huntress biding her time. That huntress was his wife, whom he prized above all living creatures, or non-living as it were now.

Yasmine allowed the couple to pass through the gates and move deeper inside the perimeter before following them. When she moved, it was quite a sight to behold. A stream of light from the streetlamp cast over her face for the briefest moment. Seth could see the ravenous eyes fixed upon its prey. Her long canine teeth were fully protracted now, ready to feast. *She is so beautiful.* Even as he thought it, he knew it was wrong. How could something so evil be beautiful to him? But he knew the answer. *Because it's Yaz.*

Seth crept in very softly, always remaining around 20 feet behind her, shielding himself behind tall headstones whenever possible. He could hear the voices of the couple talking now, bouncing off the walls of the cemetery. The man was telling his girl about the ghost who supposedly haunts the cemetery. Seth listened to the story as he sidestepped leaves and twigs along the path. Sally had been a debutante leaving a grand ball in her long gown, wearing all her finery, when her friends dared her to enter St. Philip's graveyard to touch the haunted headstone in the furthest corner of the cemetery. The headstone itself is haunted by whoever was buried beneath its long worn and unreadable engraving. Sally, unable to resist the dare, made her way to the unknown grave whereupon she inadvertently caught her dress on something. Seth listened, finding himself intrigued by the tale even as he watched Yasmine inching closer to the unwitting couple. The man continued telling his girlfriend the legend. Sally heard a noise that startled her the moment her fingers touched the stone. She turned to run away, unaware her dress was caught. The tug of her gown snatched her back. Some say she fell and hit her head; others say her fear that the ghost had hold of her caused her heart to fail. Whatever the cause, Sally died on the spot. Now she roams the graveyard looking to warn unsuspecting curiosity seekers who might make the same error she made.

The girl was entertained by the story but feigned being afraid to nuzzle closer to her man. They stood staring down at the leaning tombstone in the back of St. Philip's, completely unaware of the danger approaching. Seth saw her as she lurched closer to the doomed lovers. Again, he wanted to shout a warning to the innocents, but his conscience betrayed him because his heart would not turn on Yasmine. With the agility of a lioness, Yasmine pounced onto the back of the man, instantly overpowering him, sinking him to the ground on his knees. The girl watched helplessly, crippled by her own terror, unable to do anything more than view the terrible scene playing out before her eyes. Seth was transfixed as well as Yasmine ripped into the man's throat, spitting out chunks of his flesh to make the blood flow faster as she drank him dry. The girl, frozen in horror, did nothing but scream the same word repeatedly as she watched her lover die.

"Sally! Sally! Sally!"

Yasmine tossed the lifeless man's body aside as though it were a simple bed pillow. His shell crashed against the side of a thick headstone. The velocity of the toss snapped his spine. Seth heard the crunch when it happened. Yasmine grasped the girl's arm and pulled her down as she twisted herself behind her victim, subduing her with a choke hold. Seth then watched as Yasmine's head lifted and her eyes locked onto him.

"Did you truly believe I didn't know you were here?" Yasmine asked her husband. "I could smell you in the halls back at the house. I could smell you the moment I stepped from the boat onto the dock. Every street, every twist and turn through this city, I knew exactly where you were behind me."

"And you didn't kill me," Seth smiled.

"That doesn't mean I am not going to," Yasmine sneered devilishly. "Once I rid myself of this girl."

The girl began pleading with Yasmine for release, but Yasmine wasn't listening. Her focus was on Seth now. She snapped the girl's neck, killing her instantly for the interruption.

Seth bristled but held his eye contact with his wife. "Aren't you going to eat her?"

"The blood is still warm for the next few moments," Yasmine replied.

A silence filled the air between them with only the gaze they shared uniting them. Seth could see nothing of the Yasmine he had loved inside those insatiable eyes. Nothing emanated from her other than her sheer instinct to kill. He knew she planned for him to be next. He did not care. Though nothing remained in her of the woman he loved, to die at her hand would be something at least. Something linking them again after such a long time apart.

She began to drink from her victim. It was a slow consumption. Never once did she break eye contact with Seth. There was something very sensual about the way she took her time feeding on her prey, as if Yasmine were dragging it out so that there was more time to look at her husband. Once she was finished, she dropped the girl's body to the cold ground and walked toward Seth. Seth didn't budge. He waited, eager to feel her presence close to him again.

Face to face, Seth and Yasmine Blanchard looked at each other with curiosity on both their parts. Whatever love they had shared was unrecognizable now, neither felt anything of it in the other one. Still, something tethered them together which neither understood. Seth was before her unguarded. He did not summon his powers to stop her or save himself. He was her willing victim if she so desired. Yasmine had every intention of killing him on the spot, yet she resisted the impulse. There was something about him. Something so different from everyone else she had killed. He was like someone from a dream she could not place. Yet in the empty hole where her soul once dwelled, she sensed he was important.

"Together now as foes, yet neither one of us can bring ourselves to strike," Seth said softly.

"But I will," Yasmine evilly assured him. "I'm merely fascinated in the moment by whatever this is I am feeling."

Seth looked more deeply into her eyes, deep enough to see the red vessels glowing inside her retinas. They were not Yasmine's eyes. Not his Yasmine. Still, he did not care. "I have not come to destroy you," he told her. "I have come to join you."

The parting clouds overhead uncovered the slender moon in the sky, a gray blue patch of light reached down, highlighting them. The both of them took notice of it and an unexpected sentiment passed between them, breaking through—however momentarily—the monster inside Yasmine. It was infinitesimal to the eye, but her shoulders relaxed, and the hardness of her features softened ever so slightly.

"You have come to me, my love," she whispered. "I can almost remember you. But that was another life, wasn't it?"

"We can build a new life, Yaz."

Gently, as if she almost cared for him, Yasmine reached up and stroked his cheek with the back of her delicate fingers. "You would lose that light which shines inside you. I think I used to love that light most of all. I think I built all of my dreams upon it."

"It went out, Yaz. It went out when you died."

Yasmine turned away from him and faced the moonbeam which quickly disappeared behind more rolling clouds the moment it saw her. "What you ask of me is a life which is not for you. What I am, though glorious to me now, is not the Yasmine Blanchard you knew."

"There is no me without you, Yaz."

Seth took an impulsive risk by taking hold of her arm. This beast might forget whatever minimal bond threaded between and strike him down at any moment. But he stopped worrying about his own death the moment he had been told she died.

Now with her so close again, he did not care what happened. He was touching her once more, and that was all that mattered. He pulled her close to him. She did not resist. He ran his fingers through her long, brown hair. It was only in that moment he realized she still had trickles of blood from her two victims dripping from the corner of her mouth. He wiped it away with his hand, smearing it a little across her chin.

"One more kiss before I die, Yasmine."

He leaned in and pressed his lips to hers. He did not know what to expect from her end. Would she kill him? Bite him? Reject his request? But as he felt her lips part and their kiss deepen into one resembling what they had before, he felt her arms lift to wrap around his neck, her fingertips caressing the hair on the back of his head. Her embrace was cold, stiff. But it was the warmest he had felt since losing her.

When she withdrew from the kiss, she was looking at him strangely—as if deliberating something. He could feel the conflict inside her. A monster, thirsty for the hunt against some residual recollection of a life she could barely remember.

"Can you love?" he asked her.

"I must," she said softly. "Why else have I not killed you by now. I don't understand anymore."

"You will, once we are the same again. And since I cannot save you, I have come to join you. Not to change you. Not to end you. But to join you."

She looked confused. The huntress became a little girl again as he looked into her eyes. Whatever recognition lurked inside her of who she used to be and what they once had been together was poisoning the drive of the beast she had become. Yasmine didn't know what to do.

"Trust what I am telling you, Yasmine," Seth beseeched. "It always comes down to the two of us. Time and time again. Everything always comes back down to just you and me. Turn me, Yaz. Turn me and you will feel it again. Make us one again."

Yasmine bit down hard. He flinched from the piercing pain. Sinking to his knees as she pressed her fangs into his jugular. He felt the collar and shoulder of his shirt go damp as spillover escaped her lips and ran down. Seth became lightheaded. Dizzy. He began to lose consciousness. In his final thoughts he said goodbye to the life he had lived, and he prayed she would do the thing he asked of her and not just let him die.

Seth Blanchard collapsed to the dirt of St. Philip's cemetery. Yasmine stood up and began to walk away. She was full now. Three meals in one evening was a record for her. She looked back to the crumpled body on the ground. It held no more fascination. She walked away from the foolish man.

Passing under the twisted gnarly branches of oaks older than Charleston itself, she saw the path before her illuminate as the moon revealed itself once again upon her. Suddenly she felt something unfamiliar. The man's blood had memories. All her meals had memories. She typically enjoyed them in the moments after dining. But his memories were different. His memories contained her in them. His memories were also her memories. A life she had forgotten. A life she had lost all connection to. The power of them caused her to stagger forward, grabbing a headstone for balance. Suddenly the flood of images from a life lived came rushing forward into her mind.

It was Christmastime. Seth was sitting on a couch grousing over tangled lights he had to separate so that they could be hung on the tree by the fireplace. Yasmine was spreading tinsel on the undecorated tree. He barked at her to stop and give him time to get the lights on. She dumped the tinsel on his head.

Sitting on the edge of a swimming pool deck, Seth in the water before her. He strolled through the waist level water to lay his head in her lap. She stroked his hair. He looked up into her eyes. They kissed.

A warehouse. A menacing beast gripped her by the shoulders gnashing his terrible teeth towards her. Seth burst in. He fought the beast to its death. "I will always come for you, Yaz."

Pumpkins were lit as banks of flowers hovered magically along an outdoor aisle while she marched toward his smiling face. "I have loved only once and for all of my life." They were being married.

Yasmine lay in bed, looking down on the baby in her arms. Seth stumbled into the room, out of breath as he ran to his wife's bedside. He looked down to her, then their daughter, then back to her. Such love in his eyes. "Are you okay?" he asked. She smiled at him and tilted the baby slightly in his direction, "We both are."

Another doorway. Seth bursting through it as well. Yasmine had been lost in her past timeline, dangerously close to having her soul merge with that of her younger self. Unable to return to her normal time, her grandfather had taken her to this hotel to place distance between herself and little Yasmine. Seth had traveled through time and found her. He scooped her up in his arms and didn't let go for the longest time. "Seth! Seth! I knew you'd come for me." He looked into her eyes as he held the sides of her face,

"I will always come for you Yaz." He kissed her passionately. "You are my life."

Another bed, many years earlier. Yasmine was little—no more than six years old. Her parents were dead, along with her brother. She'd come to live with her grandfather and his new family. Scared and lonely, she'd lain in the bed unable to sleep. Until the door of her new room opened and eight-year-old Seth Blanchard tiptoed in. With him was a pillow and a blanket. He laid on the floor beside her bed and reached up to take hold of her hand. He held it all night. And she was able to sleep. He did this for days until she felt like it was home.

"I will always come for you, Yaz."

Yasmine the vampire gripped the headstone so firmly it broke under her clutch. She turned around to look back at the fence where Seth's body lay drained of its blood. Their life together pulsed through her mind. He always comes for me. He always finds me. He loved me. We loved each other. *There is no me without you, Yaz.*

He was not dead yet. She could hear the last vestiges of whatever drops were left in his body attempting to pump the slowing heart. There was a chance. Yasmine darted straight to him—wasting no time going around the maze of headstones, she simply shoved them out of her way as she went. Ancient stone tablets fell or crumbled from her path as she moved. She scooped him up in her arms and whispered "I remember you. I love you," before sending her fangs plunging back into his throat. She sent forth her own blood to fill those empty veins. He jolted from the sensation, like someone had hooked a hosepipe to him and refilled what was lost. His tired muscles grew energized. His slumped head righted. He felt strong again. Not invincible, but good. She pulled back and looked at him as she wiped blood from her chin.

"Yaz," he muttered.

Yasmine smiled down to her husband, "I came for you this time."

"Yaz."

"I have known only one love for all of my life. I am sorry that for a time I forgot you. But now I remember everything we shared."

"And we can now share it forever," he replied.

He leaned up to kiss her. She returned the kiss. It was real now, passionate. More passionate than anything either of them had ever felt before. She loved him now. Again. Now she could feel it. She could tap into its beauty and its power. They were the same again. The beast inside him was waking up, it would match her own. There was an eagerness stirring within him. An excitement unlike any he had ever felt.

"You are ready," she told him. "Now let us go out into the night. You must be fed. Only then will you truly comprehend this glorious gift we now share."

"Lead the way, my love," Seth said, rising to his feet with her assistance. "I will follow you until the end of time."

CHAPTER THIRTY FIVE

Council Approval

The council of the Consort of the Witches Association filled a long oval table in the boardroom of Salem's advertising agency. It was afterhours and the office was closed. Xander Obreiggon had spent an hour zapping back and forth across the southeast, transporting the members of the council to the meeting.

Brimford Uding, Jason'te Barstow, Millicent Davis, Ursula Kraven, Dahlia Kinnesky, and King of the Consort, Geoffrey London, all faced Salem Blanchard as she explained the reason for the emergency meeting.

"The world may be in great peril," she began. "It has come to my attention that many things which pose a great danger to mankind are going on in Charleston in the D'Angelo house."

"The House of Duquesne?" Millicent replied.

"That place has always had a sinister reputation, but most of it is all nonsense," stalwartly Brimford said with a dismissive gruff.

"No, it isn't nonsense," Salem shot back.

"Forgive me, Salem," Millicent said snidely. "But it is no great secret how your family and the D'Angelo family have shared ill will for decades. Why should you involve the council in your personal family dramas?"

"Blackie D'Angelo herself has confessed to my family the truth behind those walls," Salem announced. "The D'Angelos have the power to regenerate themselves into new bodies—meaning that some of them have lived several lives at the expense of innocent people whose bodies they have commandeered."

The council members, upon hearing this accusation, looked at one another in disturbed silence. Being an intuitive businesswoman—or simply an intuitive woman in general—Salem picked up on the subtle nuances of glances passing between some members. This was not a new rumor to a couple of them. Whether tales told through the years or personal observations, Salem knew a few of the councilmen believed her.

"Can you prove this?" King Geoffrey asked. "It is a weighty accusation. It is effectively an accusation of murder."

"I am aware of that," Salem said. "But even that is not the worst of our problems. The D'Angelos are housing vampires in the House of Duquesne. According to Blackie, the Duquesne family is not extinct. They all still live, in vampire form, behind the walls of that house."

"Preposterous!" Brimford shouted. "If there were any vampire attacks in that part of the country the council would surely have heard."

"Not if they are clever," Salem stated. "Not if they are careful to leave behind no evidence—If their vampire cell is hidden deeply away on an island in the marshlands and they do not turn victims into more vampires. According to Blackie, the family has been doing this for generations. I took it upon myself to research the murder and disappearance rate in Charleston and the surrounding areas. The death rate in the Charleston area and all the districts accessible during the night hours, is astoundingly higher than those of communities outside the perimeter."

"What are you expecting to happen here today, Salem?" Ursula asked. "You have my full support in whatever you are endeavoring to do."

"As a council member, I am motioning that we investigate the House of Duquense. I have three family members there currently who we have lost contact with. And it is rumored my sister-in-law, who was sadly turned into a vampire a while ago and thought destroyed, has not been destroyed after all and is being held inside the House of Duquesne."

Jason'te Barstow looked up from his hands and directly into Salem's eyes. She had his attention now. It was no secret that Mr. Barstow held a special place in his heart for Yasmine Blanchard. He had even officiated at her wedding to Seth.

"I need to get inside that house," Salem continued. "I am asking for the council to declare an official infiltration mission to search the house for my relatives and to investigate the vampire claim. If the council cannot agree to that, I ask for you to turn your heads while the Blanchards take on the mission alone."

"This entire story is ludicrous," Millicent declared. "I will not support either motion." It was long known that Millicent Davis was an ally of the D'Angelos, particularly Atheidrelle. It was not surprising she should take this stance. It was doubtful she knew the truth about the family—Millicent was not an evil woman per se. She simply was not one for backing down and admitting mistakes.

"I second the motion," Ursula said, dismissing Millicent's protest. "I believe the council should allow the Blanchard witches to look into this matter, and I will join them. My presence will substantiate their claims if we find evidence any of this is true."

"If you are willing to participate in their investigation, Ursula," King Geoffrey said. "I will support this endeavor."

"Ursula reigned as queen for a number of years," Jason'te added. "If she is involved in the matter, it will lend more credibility to the claims. And I agree these claims must be investigated. I vote yes."

"As do I," Brimford said.

The newest member to the Council, Dahlia, had only been installed to the council at the last Consort meeting. This was her first official vote, and she sided with Salem and the others. Millicent was the sole opposing voice. The motion was carried. The Blanchards could legally forge a search and rescue mission without crossing any lines as far as the Witches Association was concerned.

As Xander Obreiggon returned the council members one by one to their homes, Jason'te approached Salem while he waited his turn.

"If Yasmine is alive—"

"I know," Salem said, touching his hand gently. "I will have to destroy her. I am already prepared emotionally. It is my duty to the Witches Association. And my duty to her memory."

"It will be a difficult duty to carry out," Jason'te said softly.

"But my responsibility is to keep the world safe. We cannot allow this world to end up like the alternate one my family encountered last year."

"I'm certain Artemis will be at your side," Jason'te said. "And your brother."

Salem flinched. Jason'te noticed.

"What are you not telling us, Salem?"

Salem sighed and pulled her friend aside. "Seth left Blanchard House the moment he heard about Yasmine. He left a note. He's gone to join her."

"Join her?!"

"I'm afraid Yasmine may not be the only loved one I will have to destroy." Her eyes were glassy now as she truly realized the gravity of the situation awaiting her. To destroy her own brother was not something she had allowed herself to think about until now.

"Seth and Yasmine shared a love very few of us get," Jason'te said solemnly. "If I really think about it, it makes perfect sense he would do such a thing. Rest in the comfort of knowing that if you find and destroy them, you are giving them the gift of going out of this world together. Together is all they have ever wanted to be."

Salem kissed Jason'te on the cheek and nodded her head in agreement. Xander reappeared and placed his hand on Jason'te's shoulder, popping him back home to Birmingham. Salem stood alone in her office board room, realizing that her entire world was about to become more complicated than it ever had been before.

CHAPTER THIRTY SIX

Seth and Yasmine Do Charleston

The Christmas decorations had gone up along the streets of Charleston since the last time Yasmine was in town on a hunt. Marion Square was flanked on every corner with tall, metal cone structures lined with hundreds of glimmering lights. Clustered in the middle were dozens of unadorned trees with a plaque explaining they would soon be decorated by various elementary school classrooms. As they passed by, Seth thought fleetingly of Hera and what decorations she might make in school this Christmas. He would not be there to see her hang them on the Blanchard living room tree this year. He felt a pang. He could not tell if it was sadness or hunger—it felt the same.

"I used to think of those children too, Seth."

"You did?"

"Of course," Yasmine admitted. "I assume they were once important to me. It is natural for you to hold some residual connection to the old life. It will become easier to endure. Blood makes it all go away. You'll soon free yourself from those thoughts. Now that we have each other again, we are all we need. Our children can live. Grow. Fall in love. Marry. Live their lives."

"Don't you miss them?"

"I'm not sure I do." Yasmine said. "I feel things differently now. You will see as time progresses. Maybe I was an awful mother, because you were the only thing I could not shake from the old life."

Seth looked into her dark eyes, twinkling with color from the reflections of the Christmas lights. "You were a wonderful mother."

"Perhaps we will go back one day," she said. "Once they have been allowed to grow up. To become who they will become. Perhaps we will go back and turn them and be a family again for all time. We have time now. All the time we want to figure out whatever we need."

"I don't feel well, Yaz," Seth said. "My stomach hurts. I feel sick."

"You need to eat," she said, taking hold of his hand. "Later we will dine on something lavish, for now, you need sustenance. Anyone will do."

In the distance she spied a young girl on foot, college age, crossing Calhoun Street. She was headed into the Chevron gas station. Yasmine directed Seth toward the station, her eyes focused not only on the structure, but past it, inside the glass window, to the counter where the girl was purchasing cigarettes and a Red Bull. After the girl paid and made her way back across Calhoun, Yasmine and Seth were fast on her heels. She didn't seem to notice. Headphones in her ears and a light tune on her lips made her oblivious to the danger only steps behind her.

Turning on Anson Street, Yasmine watched the girl continue her trek. Seth was growing sicker now, almost stumbling. To anyone watching he probably appeared drunk. But Yasmine had the strength to practically carry him on her right arm as she pushed him down the sidewalk behind the college student. Right at George Street, Yasmine saw the opportunity. No one was around. She lifted her hands and froze the girl in place. The student stopped with her foot in midair, as if paused on a television screen. Seth lifted his agonized face upward and saw what was happening in front of him. He was in disbelief at the sight of the girl frozen in place. He looked to his side, the cars on Anson were also stopped—freeze-framed it seemed. He looked at his wife in utter disbelief.

"Feed, my love," she urged, pushing him toward the girl. "Feed while no one can see."

Seth didn't know what to do. He was frightened. Repulsed even. Yet the closer he got to the girl the stronger the inclination became. He could smell the blood in her veins. It was sweet like a fresh cream pastry. She smelled of vanilla and buttery cake. He wanted to taste her. He moved close behind her, smelling her scent as he perched his chin close to her neck. She was going to be delicious. His desire heightened. Suddenly he felt the pointy fangs in his mouth protrude from his incisors. He placed his lips on her soft neck and clamped down. It was all encompassing. Like the most flavorful bite of food, mixed with the most sensual sexual pleasure, combined with the most delicious drink he'd ever tasted. Tasting her was euphoric. Every pleasure a man could experience all mixed fluidly into one single bite. If there was such a place as Heaven, it felt like this blood entering his body.

When he'd drained her dry, he looked back to his wife. His red eyes glared with a force she'd never seen in him before, yet she knew that force well because she had experienced it many times since her transformation.

"There is nothing but that feeling, am I right, my love?" she smiled.

Seth rushed forward and swept Yasmine up in his arms, swinging her in a circle as he laughed and covered her face and neck with kisses.

"Baby that is everything!" he cried out. "I had no idea! I had no idea what perfection could taste like. What perfection could feel like. I feel alive. I never knew I wasn't before now!"

"It is exhilarating in a way no mere mortal can ever understand. We are evolved, Seth. Higher than before. Our senses, our pleasures, our triumphs. Now you can understand me. Now you know!"

Seth took her in his arms and kissed her, "Now we can understand each other, forever."

Suddenly he felt consumed with passion for her, unlike anything he'd ever felt before. He had always found Yasmine attractive, but now, it was almost an insatiable lust raging inside him. It had been so long since he'd made love to his wife. He'd dreamed of a moment like this for months, but now that it had arrived, he found himself unable to take his time. Unable to savor the gentleness and romance. He thrust her against the wall of a vacant storefront. She threw her arms around his neck, just as caught up in the moment as he. They tore at each other, almost ripping their clothes as they shed them from each other's bodies. Seth took Yasmine up against the wall and drove into her with a forcefulness he had never treated to any woman before. She gave back at the same level. As Seth exploded inside her, he realized he had never had sex before, not like this. It was all embodying. They were truly one writhing entity forever linked, forever hungry for one another. Seth Blanchard never wanted his wife as he wanted her that night, and Yasmine had never behaved with such a wildcat ferocity as she did against that cold brick wall with the lifeless body of a dead girl at their feet.

Yasmine and Seth disposed of the girl's corpse in a way no one would ever locate it. Seth summoned a water tornado on the bay to carry the dead college student out to sea. He'd never been able to create something so effortlessly and so intensely. Even his powers were heightened to levels they had never been before.

"Yaz," he said with his arm around his wife as they stood off the Battery watching the waterspout whisk the girl away. "How did you freeze her? Can we do that now? It was almost as if you had Salem's powers."

"I do," Yasmine smiled. "Seth, I am a witch now, like you. And I always will be."

"How?"

"It must have happened after the vampires attacked me. Remember how we were all over each other that week when I was recovering?" Yasmine's eyes flared vibrantly. "All of that toxin coursing through my veins, slowly transforming me. I got pregnant before I completely turned."

"Pregnant!" Seth exclaimed. "We are having another baby?"

"No, my love," she frowned. "We will never have any more children. When I transitioned the baby ceased to be a viable lifeform. It is forever inside me now, a tiny embryo that can never be born or live. But its power is inside me. Just the way Hera and Titan's were before they were born. I am a vampire with the power to freeze people in time. Imagine how gloriously helpful that will be to us. And you will forever be a vampire with the power to control the weather. We will never fear the sunlight because you can cover it with clouds anytime we want. We will live forever, Seth. Undetectable, unkillable. We are perhaps the most powerful vampires who have ever lived."

"Is that why the D'Angelos had you?" Seth asked. "They wanted your power?"

"Yes. They are building an army. They have plans. But none of that involves us any longer."

"Will they come after you?"

"No," Yasmine smiled. "I made sure they had adequate replacements before we fled. No one will find us."

"Replacements?"

"Echo and Tess. Tess mainly, Echo was merely a means to the end."

Seth felt something now other than euphoria. Perhaps it was a holdover emotion from the old life not yet drained out of him. Echo. Tess. They were family. "You gave them Echo and Tess? They are Blanchards. They are our family."

"Are they?" Yasmine replied as though she cared very little. "We barely know them. They are only in this world by a fluke of magic. Let the D'Angelos have them. It matters very little to us now, Seth."

"It matters to me, Yasmine," Seth snapped back. "At least I think it does. I know you barely knew them, but I know them—Echo especially. I can't leave Charleston if he is in danger. We have to go back for him and for Tess."

"I don't understand," Yasmine said.

"I know you don't. And I don't know why I care still. Even now I can feel myself starting to not. Starting to lose my connections to everyone we knew. But for whatever reason, in this moment, I still care enough. We have to go back for them."

"It might be too late," Yasmine said. "The act has already taken place."

"The act?"

"Thaddeuss' child. He impregnated Tess last night. He means to transfer his soul into her child the moment it is born. It will come rapidly. As long as they remain inside that house, gestation will happen rapidly. When it is born, Thaddeuss will inhabit the child, retaining all his powers and memories. He will also add Tess' child's powers to his own as he absorbs the baby's soul. It is how he stays so powerful. His wife will administer the same rapid growth potion until Thaddeuss' new body reaches young adulthood. Then he will live his lifetime over again."

"Tess is pregnant by Thaddeuss?"

"He and Atheidrelle amassed all of their power this way. They are immortal."

Yasmine and Seth sneaked back into the House of Duquesne rather quietly by utilizing a secret door in the courtyard which led only to the vampire sector of the house. Seth was amazed at the intricacy of the house's design. Layers upon layers of corridors and chambers dedicated to housing the Duquense vampire nest within the confines of the D'Angelos house. Yasmine led her husband into a common room, lavishly decorated with old world furnishings and tapestries. There were no windows at all in the chamber, and it was lit dimly by an overhead iron chandelier and a fire burning in the hearth of a giant fireplace, large enough for a human to stand inside.

Several people were reclined on couches, chaise lounges and cushy velvet chairs. They all looked as if they'd had a hearty meal and were resting from the effort. As Yasmine and Seth entered, all attention turned toward the newcomer.

"Who is this?" cried a dapper young man rising from a chair as he extinguished a cigarette.

"No need to worry, Davidson," said a beautiful young woman, now gliding across the room to welcome them. "He is one of us." She had pearlescent skin, piercing blue eyes and black hair which hung straight to her neck.

"Seth, this is Bianca Duquense," Yasmine said, nodding to the woman.

"Hi," Seth nodded.

"This is the husband from your old life! Very enticing," Bianca laughed, formally shaking Seth's hand. "I could smell your transformation as you entered. Newly turned and only recently made your first kill. Tell me, what did you think of it?"

"It was electrifying," Seth grinned. "I can still taste her."

"I like him, Yasmine," Bianca said. "He is welcome to remain."

The others in the room came forward, five in all. Davidson, the only youthful one in the group other than Bianca, extended a courteous handshake to Seth. He introduced himself as the mate of Aspasia. Seth's newfound developing senses and intuition knew instantly with no other explanations that the dignified older woman in the satin evening gown, with the snow-kissed auburn hair underneath the pink veiled hat, was Aspasia. Seth knew without being told she was a very old vampire, French descent, probably once nobility, who'd taken Davidson as a companion not too many years ago. He was not as refined as she, probably just a Charlestonian she had taken a fancy to or turned to stave off loneliness. He was of no importance, but Aspasia was someone deserving deferential treatment.

"It is an honor, ma'am," Seth said, kissing the woman's hand.

Aspasia said nothing but smiled acceptingly. Seth could tell she appreciated the recognition she had once held an esteemed ranking over those she now dwelled among. Her sensibilities were from a world long dissolved, but she valued its acknowledgment.

Moving to side-sit on the sofa with her dainty white legs lifted to the cushions beside her, Bianca addressed Seth as if she were the hostess for the evening. "Aspasia came here many years ago as a guest to one of the D'Angelo New Year parties," Bianca informed Seth. "I turned her myself in order to infuse a little culture into our lives. She was a Baroness."

"Bianca is one of the original Duquesnes. She is Angelo Duquesne's daughter," Yasmine whispered to Seth.

"Unfortunately, Father was killed 185 years ago. Caught by an unexpected sunrise on the morning of Daylight Savings Time," Bianca explained. "Careless mistakes can prove fatal to our kind, Seth. I would advise you to always know the time when you are out in the world."

"I will remember that," Seth nodded gratefully.

"But of course, that shouldn't be a problem for you," Bianca stated. "I sense your great powers. You are like our lovely Yasmine, aren't you? You are a witch."

This revelation brought the other vampires to attention.

"Yes, I am," Seth nodded. "I control the skies. We will never need to fear the sun again."

"I knew I liked him for a good reason!" Bianca laughed, rising from the sofa and slapping Davidson in the back harder than he was ready for.

The dark man who had been observing from the back of the room, waiting for his introduction, stepped forward. He introduced himself as Gideon Duquesne, Bianca's brother, with him was their toe-headed cousin Elijah Duquesne. Gideon was older than Bianca and Elijah, but not much. He looked to have been made a vampire in his early thirties.

"Gideon is the patriarch of our little family," Bianca grinned. "And he enjoys the distinction."

Gideon gave a slight bow towards Seth. "Your wife has endeared herself to me during her time here. I admit I have taken her under my wing so to speak. I suppose I can now naturally return her to her husband's care."

Seth pulled Yasmine closer and smiled, "Until the end of time."

The vampires seemed genuinely agreeable to Seth's addition to their nest but of course he recognized it was only due to his miraculous powers to manipulate weather. However, Seth knew something they didn't. He wasn't staying. He was getting Yasmine out of there as soon as possible because he knew the Blanchards were coming for them. These vampires were doomed when the Blanchards arrived. Seth would leave them to their fate. His only priority was getting Yasmine safely away—once he found and freed Echo and Tess. Unfortunately, the sun was beginning to rise. The rescue would have to wait until nightfall.

Yasmine took Seth back to her chamber where he'd originally located her. They curled up together on the bed and drifted off into a kind of trancelike slumber the likes of which Seth had never experienced before. He felt almost as if his body were plugged into a wall socket recharging.

CHAPTER THIRTY SEVEN

Tess' Baby

"What is happening to me?" Tess shrieked as she clutched her belly. A definite baby bump had sprouted overnight.

"I don't get it," Echo exclaimed. "You look pregnant. But how? What in the hell is inside you?"

"I'm scared, Echo! I'm scared!"

The door unlatched as Thaddeuss entered. Echo charged forward instinctively, thinking he could overpower the older man and get himself and his sister to freedom. Thaddeuss simply lifted his hand and sent Echo smashing backward into the wall. Held there as if attached to it, Echo could not pull himself free from the stone.

With a look of self-satisfaction, Thaddeuss D'Angelo boasted, "I am a powerful witch, Dear Nephew. You will never best me."

"What have you done to me?" Tess frantically cried.

"You are having my child," Thaddeuss grinned devilishly. "You will remain here until its birth. It will not be too long a confinement, my dear. This house, uh, expedites things."

Tess could not believe her ears. Pregnant? By Thaddeuss? "You raped me?"

"Oh, my dear girl, rape is a nasty word," Thaddeuss said. "I simply used you to achieve a necessary goal. I assure you; you will not be harmed."

Tess Blanchard was mortified and now desperately afraid. "Why would you do this to me?"

"It was necessary," Thaddeuss explained. "It had to be you. You or your sister. You carry the God Strain. As will your baby."

His words resounded in their brains. All this deceit, all this wickedness perpetrated upon them was all for The God Strain. This unfathomable thing they possessed which could not be seen or touched. They weren't even sure what it was. He would do all of this to them for something so intangible.

Still straining to free himself from the wall, Echo nodded his head toward his sister and yelled, "Is that thing inside her even human?"

"Of course!" Thaddeuss laughed. "As human as you or I. But powerful. Oh, so very powerful. A witch. A Blanchard witch at that. A D'Angelo witch. A God Strain witch."

"What are you going to do with my baby?" Tess asked.

With a look of complete maniacal triumph Thaddeuss answered as though the answer should have been obvious, "Become it."

Tess looked at Echo, then clutched her baby bump. "Become it?" she repeated.

"After birth, my soul will leave this body and infiltrate the baby's. My spirit will have no problem overpowering an infant's. I will take over the vessel, and my wife will use old magic we have long mastered, to accelerate my new body's growth until I reach the wonderful age of twenty-one. A whole new life ahead of me."

There was a triumph in his tone, as if he half expected Tess and Echo to be happy for him. His achievement, in his eyes, was one of wonder which carried the expectation that anyone would be in awe, even the ones being used to carry it out.

"You will kill my baby and use its body to *live longer*?!" Tess said, tasting the ugliness of the putrid deed as she spoke the words.

Thaddeuss raised a playful brow. "If it is a boy that is. If it is a girl, I will allow Atheidrelle to inhabit it and you and I will try again in a few days."

"Atheidrelle?" Echo exclaimed.

"A few days?" Tess shouted.

Thaddeuss grinned devilishly as he stroked the sides of his cropped beard. "As I said, this house and my wife's magics accelerate things. If you were anywhere else your delivery would take the customary nine months. Alas, The House of Duquesne contains...properties, we shall say. I can breed you over and over until we have a son."

Echo was astonished yet still hung up on the other thing Thaddeuss divulged. "Your sister Atheidrelle is alive?"

Thaddeuss stepped closer to his trapped nephew and continued. "My sister's spirit is currently inhabiting her daughter's body until we are able to rebirth her. Cassandra is an adequate temporary replacement until we can manufacture a vessel far more powerful."

"You're crazy!" Echo shouted, straining against the invisible restraints holding him against the wall.

"No, Echo," Thaddeuss sneered. "I am eternal. Eternal because I have the power to live life after life retaining all my knowledge, all of my powers, and collecting more with every rebirth." Thaddeuss walked to Tess, gently lifting his hands to stroke her newly formed baby bump with the back of his fingers. She flinched at the touch, but Thaddeuss continued the caress her belly with delicate circles. "With this child I shall not only add Blanchard blood to my veins, but I will also have God's blood in my veins. My sister and I will be the most powerful beings who have ever lived."

"How?" Tess asked. "How are you able to live over and over? How do you just hijack another body?"

He did not immediately answer. Thaddeuss began pacing the room, eyeing the sparseness of it. He dragged his fingertips over the stone wall and stopped to grip the rickety wooden bed. His expression seemed disapproving. Perhaps this was the first time he had ever been inside this chamber and was finding its contrast to the rest of the house revolting. In a few moments, he snapped back into focus and continued the discussion.

"It's perfectly natural...for our family," Thaddeuss sneered. "I have lived many lives before. As have my sisters."

Tess and Echo shared the same expression. They were astounded.

Thaddeuss noticed their exchange and its meaning. "Yes, your mother...Barbara has done this as well."

"Blackie?"

"That dreaded nickname," Thaddeuss huffed. "Yes, *Blackie*. Your mother was not born in the body she currently holds. She has had a few in her time—that is until she developed some sort of consciousness and decided Atheidrelle and I were getting out of hand. Or perhaps it was caused by watching her final child grow elderly and die. She never could stomach the deaths of her children."

Tess beat Echo to the question, "Blackie has had other children?"

"We all have," Thaddeuss revealed. "I myself have had a dozen or more. Taub and Thorne are only the most recent. Constance is my fifth wife."

"Blackie had other children and watched them age and die." Tess said it more as a revelation sinking in than a question.

"And she vowed never to go through that again." Thaddeuss explained. "Perhaps it was because our father valued her less that motherhood meant more to her than a means to an end. Whatever her reason, when she left here, she vowed never to return, never to rebirth, and never to bear more children. Imagine her surprise when Atheidrelle's spell went awry, and it was Barbara who became pregnant with Arielle. And now here you two are, as well as your sister. For a woman rejecting motherhood, my sister certainly has a plethora of offspring."

Echo seemed proud now, the shock of this revelation waning. "Our mother chose to be human. Our mother walked away from this power because she wanted to repent from her wrongs."

Thaddeuss seemed less impressed with Blackie's choice. "She left this house and the source of its power. And you see where that has gotten her. Broken, twisted, crippled, unable to speak. Barbara D'Angelo, taken down by a common mortal's stroke. Had she been here we could have shed feeble body and supplied her with a stronger one. Your mother walked away from the only thing that can save her now."

"You people are monsters!" shouted Echo. "You cannot just breed my sister for bodies!"

"Actually, I can and have. And I will again," Thaddeuss replied. "And if you were not an abomination—a homosexual, I could have used you to impregnate Mara. You and my son Thorne are unforgivably useless to our family effort."

"Is Thorne...."

"No. This is Thorne's only life," Thaddeuss explained. "I am afraid our children do not have the luxury of sharing the gift Atheidrelle and Barbara and I share. My children's only uses are to provide us with new vessels when needed. Something my son failed to do by being born a useless degenerate who only can only respond sexually to men. Taub and Alexandrea now have a child on the way which could possibly be of use if needed. He at least did not fail me."

"Constance? Your wife? She is okay with all of this?" Echo asked.

"Lovely woman. Devoted to me. She is my favorite bride, so far. Of course, she will age and wither and die like the others before her. As will your precious Thorne and Taub. Mara and Ashby as well. I have seen countless children and grandchildren come and go through the years, but my sisters and I always remain."

A silence fell. Thaddeuss waited, watching his revelations dawn upon the young captives. Echo's mind wandered to Thorne. Had he been using him the entire time? Was Thorne as evil as the rest of the D'Angelos? But Tess' mind went strangely to other places. She thought of Constance. Thaddeuss said she was his fifth wife, so far. She wondered what happens once Thaddeuss is young again, yet his wife is old. How must that feel for his wives? What then happens to them? Do they live out their days holding some esteemed rank in the household? Are they quietly sent away to live out the rest of their lives elsewhere while a new, younger bride is chosen? Tess couldn't help but imagine the complexity involved in such a marriage. Then her thoughts reverted to herself and her baby. That was the only aspect in this insanity she needed to focus upon. How was she going to get herself and her baby to freedom?

"You won't get away with this," Tess said, breaking the quiet. "The Blanchards will come for us. They will stop you."

Thaddeuss laughed again, "The Blanchard's power is nothing compared to mine. I understand the world believes them to be among the most powerful witching families of the world, but then again the world doesn't know the depths of my family's capabilities."

"They will when this is over." Echo said. "We will make sure of that."

"You will be dead." Thaddeuss said. "Once my sister and I have our new bodies with your bloodlines surging through them, we can make all the new God Strain babies we ever desire. We will dominate this world. No one can stop us."

CHAPTER THIRTY EIGHT

Blanchards Past

Artemis Blanchard did not have much time to plan. She was not even sure what the plan was going to be. There was too much going on. Too much danger awaiting to contend with. She could not do this alone. Though she was the Hecate now, her experience was too limited to comprehend all of this. Her mother would have known what to do. So would her grandfather. Artemis had not lived the lives they lived or experienced the perils they experienced. She felt ill-equipped to lead her coven through this tumultuous time, but she had an idea of how to garner the knowledge she would require. Yet to do it, she needed Howard. He rushed right over and met her upstairs in the magic room. It was his first time ever seeing this room despite all his years with the Blanchards. No one else in the family was invited. It was only the two of them alone in the room.

"So, what do I do?" Howard asked. "Just summon Olympia again?"

Artemis shot him the most serious face she had ever shown him, "You summon *everyone*."

Howard Caldwell Blanchard was not accustomed to having powers. He found himself rather surprised at how easy it was to use once he focused his mind on the effort. Within the next few minutes, Artemis and Howard stood in the tower adorning the top of Blanchard House staring at the many translucent faces of Blanchards past. Olympia Blanchard. Pastoria Blanchard. Constantinople and Angharad Blanchard. And good old Zelda. Artemis could not help but pay the most attention to her grandfather. His mesmerizing eyes and dark beard made him seem like a kind of old-world magician. She had only ever seen him in photographs. His wife Angharad stood emotionless at his side. The lack of warmth from her told Artemis all she needed to know as to why Olympia never spoke of her own mother. Her gaze drifted to Olympia, who was smiling lovingly at her eldest daughter. Beside her was Pastoria...and good old Zelda looking as kooky and colorful as she had in life.

"Well, you got a shit ton of troubles ain't you, Arty?" Zelda chuckled, looking around the room. "I ain't seen these many dead witches in one place...ever, I guess."

"My dear granddaughter," Constantinople Blanchard said, coming forward, placing his strong hands on Artemis' shoulders. She could not feel the sensation of his touch since souls have no physical bodies. Still, she could see the gesture, and she felt all the closer to him for it.

"There is much to explain," Artemis said to the group. "Much to tell you so you can advise me."

"We know everything," Olympia told her daughter. "Part of Howard's power of reconstituting us is that his power imparts us with the knowledge of why we are being summoned. We are here to help you, but it will be you who must see it out. We cannot join you in battle. Our lives are over. We have no corporeal form. But we will guide you as you figure out what to do."

The next several minutes were spent in a whirlwind of Howard and Artemis listening to the many dead relatives speaking, advising, culminating plans and strategies. Some ideas were solid. Some were not. But all were helpful. Artemis felt like a novice surrounded by warriors, all with far more knowledge and experience than she would have ever held.

"It is coming to war," her grandfather warned. "Much larger forces are at work than any of you have experienced before. The world is in danger from all the evils our generations spent our lives combating. The House of Duquesne is the center of that evil, and the D'Angelo's are planning to take over the world."

Olympia stepped closer to her daughter. Her bright blue eyes shimmered as they had in life. Their radiance was not lessened by the fact that they, and she, were transparent. "You have the most difficult task before you that any Hecate in our family has ever faced." Olympia forewarned her. "I had hoped your reign as my replacement would be a smooth one. But that will not be the case now."

"What am I going to have to do?"

"Only you can know that, my darling. But I trust that you are the correct one to figure it out."

"You will need help," Pastoria added. "Lots of help. You need to alert my boys. They must come immediately to assist you. You will need the backup of all the Blanchards."

"And my girls," Zelda offered. "Stupid creatures though they are, you gone need them idiots! They got powers, and you need all you can get hold of."

The grim woman Artemis could not bring herself to think of as her grandmother, moved forward. "You will need more than that," Angharad Blanchard cautioned. "To combat dark forces, you must employ dark forces."

Artemis looked at her mother. Olympia gave a sorrowful nod of agreement.

"My daughters always walked on the side of light," Angharad said, gesturing toward Olympia and Pastoria. "But I come from darker places. I have walked through the shadows this world conceals. I have seen realities they never faced. I have known things no one else knows. To fight dark forces, you must join them."

"I don't understand."

Constantinople Blanchard stepped forward and placed his hands on his granddaughter's brow. His power was immense. It was as if he were embedding the library of his knowledge with the simple touch of his hands. All became clear. Artemis saw it all, everything she must do. Everything she must sacrifice to stand a chance. Tears fell from her eyes as she comprehended her fate.

"Fate is unmovable," he said, reading her thoughts. "My Olympia sacrificed herself for the sake of the family because it was her destiny to do so. Now you face your own set of circumstances which will test how far you are willing to go to save the Blanchard line."

Angharad gripped her arm. Again, Artemis could not feel her touch, but the harshness of the movement and the grim expression across Angharad's face, conveyed the urgency. "To save the world."

As everyone slowly faded into the oblivions from which they had been pulled, only Howard and Artemis remained in the magic room. Howard was spent. Totally exhausted from the energy it took to summon, and hold, those souls in place. He sat on the floor, too weak to stand. He did not know what to say about what transpired. He understood little of what went on. He only knew that Artemis, perhaps the one person he loved most in the world, was changed now. Changed by the weight on her shoulders.

"I know what I have to do," she said tearfully. "Nothing will ever be the same again."

"Hasn't everything changed enough already?" Howard cried. "A few years ago, I was only your family friend. Now I'm a Blanchard; I have kids; Beryl's off being a god somewhere; Yasmine is a vampire! We have had enough change Artemis! Why can't things just get fixed and go back to normal?"

"We are never going to go back to normal, Howard," she said. "They are right. The D'Angelos must be stopped before they are so powerful, they dominate the world. They have your children. They have Cassandra. They have Yasmine. Now Seth. That nest of vampires—Howard, we may be at the very cusp of what happened to that other world you went to. The world where vampires destroyed humanity. What if it was the D'Angelos who unleashed the evil there. And it is about to happen here now. We cannot allow it. We must stop it. I have to stop it."

"How?" Howard replied. "How are you going to stop it?"

"Like my grandmother said, I have to join it."

Artemis summoned the coven. She summoned all living Blanchards home. Seneca and Drake and their children were on their way up from Mobile. All they needed was her call to bring them home to assist. Soon Salem, Arielle, Trix, Blackie, and Fable were assembled in the living room, awaiting the arrival of the Mobile branch of the family. Melinda and Sarah, Zelda's daughters, were on their way over as well. Zelda's girls were willing to do anything they could to help Artemis. Miranda was upstairs with the children in the nursery, keeping the children occupied and out of the family's way.

"We forgot," Fable said, awkwardly breaking the tension of the room while they waited for Artemis to come downstairs and begin. "Today was Thanksgiving."

"It is, isn't it?" Salem frowned. "With everything going on, we just forgot."

"I didn't forget," rang a voice from the kitchen. It was Nacaria. "Xander and I brought food with us. After Artemis phoned telling us to get here as soon as possible, Xander zapped over to some take out places. We have Chinese food and pizza if anyone wants to eat. It's already in the kitchen."

Once Artemis joined them downstairs, the family filled the kitchen to eat their Thanksgiving meal buffet-style, standing around the kitchen island. It was nothing like the Thanksgivings of Blanchard House past. And as everyone consumed pizza slices, General Tso chicken, sweet and sour pork, and a bevy of rice, they all understood this might be their last together. Things were spinning out of control fast, and no one had any idea what would happen next.

As everyone was finishing up their meal, Artemis mindspoke to her sister, *Walk with me, Dee.*

Without attracting much attention, the sisters meandered into the foyer to withdraw their coats from the hall closet and went outside. Strolling arm in arm across the brown autumn lawn, Artemis led them out to their mother's now dormant rose garden. The stems were brittle from the growing cold, and small spent middles with spiky crowns poked out where long-fallen summer rose petals had departed.

"You will keep mother's garden up for me, won't you Dee?"

Demitra stared at her oldest sister and squeezed her hand. "Nothing is going to happen to you, Artemis. You will lead this family through this and fix everything. Just like you always do."

"We always do," Artemis corrected. "With every major turmoil I have ever faced, you have been there beside me, sister. You were my right hand in everything. I am counting on you now to be that for me again."

"With Mother's rose bushes?" Demitra said sarcastically, shielding herself from the fear that Artemis meant much more.

"With everything," Artemis said. She took a long breath and exhaled it out, fighting back the urge to cry. She turned to her sister and said, "I leave the family to you."

Demitra released Artemis' hand and began shaking her head aggressively. "No, Artemis! No! No! No! You will not do this to me—you will not give up! You will not sacrifice yourself! You will not leave me all alone!"

Artemis smiled at her sister and caressed her white cheek with the back of her hand. "Demitra, you've never been alone. You will never be alone. You have amassed quite a family for yourself, little sister. It is time to take your place as the head of it now."

"No, Artemis! You cannot leave me. I cannot do this without you. I can't live without you!"

Artemis stroked her best friend's wet cheek. "You will do just fine. I believe in you. You are the new Hecate, Demitra Blanchard. Lead this family well using all of the love, kindness, intelligence, and fortitude you display every single day of your life."

Demitra could not figure out where this was coming from. Why would Artemis be handing over the family's leadership to her now? She knew something much larger than the fear of dying in battle was brewing in Artemis' mind. She was up to something.

"Where are you going?" Demitra demanded. "You're not going to die on me, Artemis! I have lost too much. I cannot lose you."

"I'm not going to die, Dee. But I am not going to be here either. I know what must be done."

"I refuse to take over," Demitra argued. "I won't let you do whatever it is you're planning on doing."

Artemis kissed her cheek. "I love you so much, Demitra. You have been my partner in life. My best friend. You will do what I ask you because *I'm* asking it of you."

"Please, please don't leave me."

"You are the head of this family now—the head of this coven. You will do me proud, my sister. Now there are some things you must know before I go. Things Mother told to me when I took over."

Demitra could only cry and whisper "please". But she listened. She heard every word her sister told her, because she knew it was happening and it was necessary. Demitra Blanchard was going to have to lead the family, because Artemis Blanchard was going away to save them.

The family were all inside finishing the takeout Xander brought them when Demitra returned to the house. She said nothing to anyone, which was alarming enough as they looked into her tear-stained face. She motioned to her brother-in-law to come with her. Xander rose from the table and followed her into the foyer.

"Go out to the rose garden and wait for me. Artemis is there. We need your help with something. Go now."

As Xander obeyed in confusion, Demitra walked upstairs. A few moments later she returned with her grandsons in tow. She marched Con and Rom outside and into the rose garden where her sister waited.

"Grandma, what's going on?" Con asked as Rom paced on his haunches encircling Artemis.

"Boys, listen to Grandma," Demitra commanded. "I am Hecate now, and I have something I need you boys to do."

Xander looked on in utter bewilderment, not understanding anything transpiring before him. Artemis closed her eyes and reached her arms out slightly on each side. Demitra placed one of her sister's arms in Con's hands and the other she positioned in front of Rom's snout. Demitra then placed her own hands on each of her grandson's heads and told them, "Boys, I need each of you to bite Aunt Artemis."

Xander gasped, "What?"

"Grandma?" Con stuttered.

"It's all right," Demitra said gently.

Romulus began to emit a low growl of disapproval. He knew it was wrong to hurt people, especially people you love. Artemis knelt and stroked his ears and face. She told him it was okay. "This is what has to happen, boys," she said. "To save this family, I have to change." She stood back up and positioned her wrists before their mouths again. She looked to Demitra and nodded.

Demitra kissed her sister's cheek before planting a firm hand to both boys' heads. "You must both bite at the exact same moment," she instructed them. "Uniting both of your antibodies at the same time. You are each half of something powerful; we need both halves to rejoin inside Aunt Artemis."

Artemis looked down to her grandnephews one last time, giving them a loving smile. She closed her eyes and braced herself for the painful bites. As Demitra cried, "Now!" the boys clamped their teeth into Artemis's flesh, drawing blood which trickled down her wrists onto the cold, dry ground. Their saliva began entering her wounds.

"The power of the wolf," Demitra said. "The power of the wolf invades you."

The boys removed their teeth from their aunt's arm and stepped back behind their grandmother. Blood ran from Artemis' wrists as she caught a sharp breath escaping her lungs. Her veins burned slightly, as if a potent serum was rushing into her system. Artemis looked at Xander.

"Take me to the House of Duquesne."

Demitra returned to the house with the boys beside her. Everyone looked up from the table. Salem could tell something was wrong, something had changed. It was as if a sudden instinct kicked in, and she simply knew.

"You are Hecate now."

With a somber and crestfallen look, Demitra announced, "Yes, I am."

Fable jumped from the table, "Where is Aunt Artemis? Where is Xander? Mother, what is going on? Why aren't the boys up with Miranda?'

"Artemis has work to do," Demitra explained. "Work which will make it impossible for her to ever be part of us again. She is transcending."

"What do you mean transcending?" Fable cried. "And is that blood on Con's lips? And Rom's fur too! What is happening?"

Demitra gave a loving squeeze to her grandson's necks and explained, "Your sons have shared their gift with Artemis. They have sired her."

"What are you talking about?" Nacaria shrieked. "Sired? You mean they turned her into a werewolf?"

"Tonight is a full moon," Demitra noted. "By nightfall, Artemis will be a creature of the night."

Fable jumped up from the table, enraged. "My boys are not werewolves!" she screamed. "They are not creatures of the damn night! They are just a boy and a wolf."

Demitra nodded and explained, "Yes, but together, their bite reconstitutes the curse. They have both bitten Artemis together. Patric's virus now flows through her veins."

"Is that even possible?" Arielle whispered to Trix.

"I think it's not only possible," Salem answered. "I think it has already occurred. But why Aunt Demitra? Where is Artemis now?"

"On her way to find Yasmine, and if she is correct, Seth—who is probably already now a vampire as well. She will get one of them to bite her, to sire her with their disease. Artemis will have the strength of the witches, the vampires, and the wolves flowing through her. Artemis will be the Queen of Shadows. She will rule over the beasts of this earth and stop them from whatever dark plan they have aligned with."

"Artemis is a werewolf? And a vampire?" Nacaria shrieked. "But her soul! Her soul will grow dark. Her soul will become consumed by the evil flowing inside it! How will she stop any evil if she herself becomes evil?"

Demitra turned to Howard and Trix. "Because God will save her. Howard, it is time to call your mother."

CHAPTER THIRTY NINE

Beryl Returns

All eyes fell upon Howard and Trix. They looked to one another, unsure of exactly what they were supposed to do. Demitra explained to them how they carried Beryl Blanchard's bloodline, and if anyone could summon her back, it would be them. Howard linked hands with his daughter, and they began.

Nothing. Nothing happened.

"We aren't concentrating enough," Trix guessed. "Or maybe we need all of us. Maybe we can't summon her without Echo and Tess."

"I think she's right," Howard said to Demitra. "I can't get any link on Beryl. I'm trying, but there's nothing. Maybe Trix is right, and it takes all four of us who share the God Strain."

"Perhaps Xander can take you guys to the House of Duquesne once he returns," Nacaria suggested. "If you can locate Echo and Tess—"

"Or walk right into a D'Angelo stronghold and we lose everyone," Salem warned.

"I have an idea," Arielle said meekly.

"What is it, Arielle?' Demitra asked. "I'm open to anything."

"Beryl is God, right?"

"Or a fractional piece of Him," Demitra clarified.

"Well," Arielle began. "When people want to talk to God, they just...pray."

Everyone looked around the table at each other. It had not occurred to anyone that the answer could be so simple. That perhaps—just perhaps—they could have been talking to Beryl all this time through a simple prayer.

"Bow your heads," Demitra ordered. "Join hands."

Everyone did as she commanded. But before she began to speak the front door opened. Seneca, Drake, Ocean, Sage, and Sydney Blanchard walked in, right behind them were Melinda and Sarah. Demitra did not bother to explain. She simply directed them to stand around the table and join the rest. Within moments everyone in the house had linked hands as Demitra began a prayer.

"Dear Heavenly Father, we are in trouble down here. Your world is in peril, and it is up to us to save it. That is an arrogant statement I realize but nonetheless true as far as I can see. I am not a devout woman. I cannot even tell you when I last prayed. But now I must because we need you. We need my daughter. Beryl is a part of you, and we need that part right now. We need you, God. We need you to send Beryl to us for just a little while. We cannot save your work, your world, or your people without her. Please—I beg of you, Lord. We need the God Strain."

Prayers are probably never answered so quickly, but this one was. Before hands had even unclasped, the Blanchard House kitchen was flooded in the brightest, most blinding light imaginable. It obliterated everything except itself. As it slowly dimmed, Demitra looked across the table to see her daughter, Beryl, standing behind Howard and Trix. Beryl never looked so glorious. Her skin seemed to radiate light itself, as if it were made from a million suns. Her golden blonde hair glittered like it was comprised from strands of gold. The love, the warmth, the genuine goodness emanating from her was flowing through every crevice of the room and into the hearts and souls of every person there. Demitra could barely speak. All she wanted for the rest of her life was to stand in the presence of the god standing before them and feel the indescribable things she felt in her presence.

"You have asked for me, and I have come to you," Beryl said to her mother. Her voice reverberated as though made of brass instruments from a band.

It was difficult for anyone to form words to say to such a presence. Gone were the memories of the sister, or daughter, or cousin who had once been Beryl Blanchard. In the place of those recognizable attachments stood something astonishing. She was not the same. It felt like looking into the eyes of a personified holiness no one present was worthy of witnessing.

"Beryl," Fable said, finally breaking through her own captivation. She forced herself to speak by remembering this radiant being had once been her sister. "Beryl you are...you are...wondrous."

Beryl said nothing, she only smiled. The smile itself carried power—deep peace and abiding comfort.

"I have missed you," Fable said. I have missed you so much."

"I am never too far from you even when I am nowhere near."

"Mother," Howard said, rising and standing before her. "I-I-I, I am speechless in your presence."

Beryl's radiance grew exponentially brighter as she looked into his eyes. Placing one hand on Howard's chest, then her other on Trix's shoulder, she told them, "I live within you always, my children. But time grows short, and I have infinite responsibilities. Why have you summoned me?"

"Artemis has—"

"I know," Beryl smiled.

"We need you to find her before her curses take hold," Demitra requested. "Before she breaks the code of light and kills. I want you to restore her soul."

"It has never been done," Beryl said. "Once the beasts of the earth contaminate you, you are lost to darkness." Her words frightened the Blanchards, yet somehow they knew she had not completed her statement. As they watched what could only be described as predetermination flashing in her eyes, they understood Beryl was watching fate play out within her all-knowing mind. She then went on, "However, Artemis' deed was from a place of love—a place of humanity. A sacrifice of everything for the greater good. I shall do what you ask of me. I will give her back her soul."

"And Yasmine!" Fable shouted. "And Seth if he's been turned. You must save them too, Beryl!"

The glorious feeling of joy which streamed from Beryl's presence, dimmed slightly as a frown crossed her impeccable face. "I am afraid Seth and Yasmine are beyond reach. I will not contaminate light by touching it to darkness. However, Artemis is another story. She is still pure in the sight of God. She has not yet taken a life. She made the ultimate sacrifice for His works. She will be rewarded. She will be saved."

The explosive light which flooded the room as Beryl entered, flashed once more, sending everyone falling back out of chairs or shielding their eyes with their arms as Beryl vanished as quickly as prayer had brought her.

CHAPTER FORTY

You Will Never Get Away

Brandon attempted to slam the apartment door in Mara D'Angelo's face the moment he opened it to find her standing in the hall. With a thrust of her hand the door crashed open, knocking Brandon to the floor. He scooted to his feet quickly, backing away as he rose.

"That's not very welcoming, my love," she smiled. "I've only come to talk. To offer my condolences for your friend's passing and to let you know I'm here for you. I forgive you for betraying me."

"You killed her, Mara!" he cried. "I know you did. I don't know how you did it, but I know you did it."

"Which one has you so upset?" she asked rather innocently. There was no sarcasm in her tone. She genuinely was curious.

"What do you mean, which one?" Brandon shouted. "Carlee! Has there been more?"

Mara closed the door behind her and came into the apartment, taking a seat on the tweed sofa of the small living room. Brandon stood shaking against the half wall between his living room and his tiny dining area off the kitchen.

"You know she wasn't right for you, Brandon. You only went back to her because you allowed fear of commitment to me to stop you. You keep pushing me away when you know in your heart no one will ever love you as much as I do. But that is all over now. I forgive you, and I am ready to resume our relationship."

"Relationship?" Brandon scoffed. "Mara, I can't stand you! You are completely insane if you think we can be together. You are obsessed with me for some reason, and you have to stop. I don't want you. You make my skin crawl. Let me go."

She examined him with a puzzled, almost bemused expression. "I will never let you go," Mara informed him with a gentle smile. "And this obsession—as you call it—is the only thing keeping you alive. My love for you, Brandon, is what keeps you alive."

He threw his fists up to the air in frustration and shouted, "How arrogant can you be? You think I can't live a happy life if you aren't loving me? I don't need your love. Nor do I want it. I will be very happy without you in my life."

Mara shook her head and emitted a girlish chuckle, amused by his misinterpretation. "No, darling. What I am saying is that I am only allowing you to continue to live because I am so spectacularly in love with you."

Brandon's face froze. He understood the madness now. As he looked at her beautiful face—its soft, delicate features—he saw behind the innocence, into her delusion. "I don't love you, Mara," he said.

Mara gave him a disapproving look as she twisted her long hair into a ponytail behind her head. "There are prices to pay for not loving me, Brandon. You just paid one with the death of your friend. I would caution you to not pay another."

She was like a deranged little bird with a broken wing, unable to fly away to something more fulfilling. She was stuck, building a nest in a tree that did not want her. It was then that the pieces started pulling together in his mind. All the things this broken, little bird was capable of manifesting.

"Emily," he said. "A few months ago, my first girlfriend Emily drowned in Kiawah. You did that, didn't you?"

Mara sat up straighter, hands in her lap as she faced him with all seriousness. "Are we going to be honest now?" she asked him. "Should I speak the truth to you and end this coy little game of pretending to not be what I actually am?"

"I want the truth."

Mara sighed. "Fine—yes. I caused Emily's death. I caused Carlee's death. I also recently burned one of your little tramps alive in her townhouse. I am a witch, Brandon. A powerful one. And I can be of such help to you in life. We can be so happy if you will simply try."

Brandon could not believe what he was hearing, yet at the same time it was the only thing which made sense. He'd known from the start something was off with Mara. He derided himself constantly for not listening to his instincts and steering clear of the beautiful girl. Once she was in his life there was no shedding her. And at every turn strange and terrible things happened in her presence.

"A witch?" he repeated.

"You live in Charleston," she smiled. "You know the stories. They are true. We exist. I am proof. And because I love you, I erased those girls from our minds."

Brandon's face was broken by this confession. Sweet, kind Emily. His first love. "Why?"

"Because you belong to me, and I belong to you. I have saved myself for you. I was clean...pure. I gave myself to you because I loved you. We are bonded now. We are one."

"What? Just because you were a virgin? That doesn't mean you own me. I've been with other people, Mara. By your own definition I guess that means I was unclean."

"That's all right, my love," Mara smiled lovingly toward him. "I am cleansing you. Emily, Carlee, and that dancer you had that one night with. All of them. I'm cleaning you, darling, so that we can be one. Untainted. Unspoiled."

"Oh my God, Mara. You are unhinged."

"No, I'm just a woman in love," Mara replied. "I come from a place of great darkness and pain. A place where nothing good can thrive. I have grown up with evil behind every wall and madness in every conversation. I have never had anything clean and decent and true. Nothing that has been mine and mine alone. Everything I have has been spoiled by all those who came before me. You and I will build a life of happiness and love and purity."

"Mara, you cannot create love from murder."

"Of course, you can," she laughed. And she believed it. "Think of it as me simply taking out the trash. No one ever misses the trash. You will love me, Brandon. If you would just give it a chance, you would see that no one has ever loved you the way I can. The more you fight me, the more miserable you are going to be. Stop fighting and see what awesome things we can create together. I am the only person who can ever truly love you."

"And if I don't, what happens?"

Mara frowned again and traced her fingers along the pattern of a throw pillow. "Then I'm afraid you will never know a moment's peace in your life. My wrath will haunt you and hunt you until the day you finally find the sweet release of death. You will never get away from my love or my hatred—your choice."

Brandon said nothing. What more was there to say? In those few silent moments between them his life flashed through his mind. Years of hiding, running, trying to keep this madwoman from finding him. Anyone he would ever love could die at any moment because of her scorned heart. How many lives could she run through until he finally stopped fighting her? How much blood would be on his hands for denying her? There was no way out. He had seen her power. Unstoppable. But what if he gave in? What if he gave her what she wanted for a little while? She was undeniably beautiful. He had never had a problem being with her physically. And the emotional disconnect he'd felt was partially due to the mystery of her, what she might be hiding—what was that thing that was off about her? Now he knew the answer. Perhaps he could give her what she wanted for a while. Maybe she would grow bored eventually. Maybe he might have a chance to catch his breath and make an escape plan. He might even find a way to kill her when her guard was down.

Brandon slowly approached the sofa and knelt before her. He laid his head in her lap. Mara stroked his hair with her fingers gently. Reluctantly, but necessarily, Brandon lifted his arms and wrapped them around her waist. She leaned down to kiss his head.

"I forgive you, Brandon," she said softly. "We needn't ever discuss this matter again. It will be a happy life I assure you. But you must try to love me."

He looked up into her sparkling emerald eyes, so full of hope, so full of madness. "I will try."

CHAPTER FORTY ONE

The Other Vault

Demitra took Salem up to the magic room alone. The day was waning, and the orange glow shimmering through the tower windows carried with it an exhaustion from all they'd learned and endured this day. Demitra closed the door behind them and faced her niece. Salem was still shellshocked, but Demitra needed her help.

"Before Artemis left, when she made me her successor, she told me a secret only a Hecate can know. I am going to share the secret with you now, Salem, because I need your help to access it."

"Access it?"

"There is another vault inside Blanchard House."

Salem wasn't expecting this surprising fact. She grew up in that house. Ran through every hall, played in every room. Where could another hidden room possibly be?

Demitra continued explaining, "Only the coven leader is ever supposed to know about it. The door to it lies under this floor. Within that vault lies secrets and magics which should never be seen or used unless it is of earth-shattering consequence. I believe we face that now."

"And you need me to open it?"

"I could do it myself, with a crowbar and a lot of noise. But I think using you would be simpler."

It was Demitra's attempt at humor, but Salem wasn't laughing. She understood the serious overtones of the situation and knew there had to be more. And there was.

"I also show you this because if something happens to me during what is about to come, I make you my successor," Demitra informed her. "If I die Salem, you are to be the next Hecate. Because of this, I know I can trust you with this secret."

Salem wanted to say something. She wanted to impart some sort of emotion to the situation because it seemed to lack any. Demitra was already admitting a possibility of defeat by even telling Salem any of this. Everything was moving so fast, too fast. Salem wanted to stop time and simply sit with her aunt to take it all in. But there was no time for that. And Salem being a master of swallowing her feelings when her strength was required, did it again now. She'd process all this later, when there was time.

Demitra pointed toward the plank board floor and said, "Now concentrate your power and open that door."

Salem looked at the floor. She had no idea what she was doing or what she was supposed to focus upon, but she waved her hands at the floorboards and raised them from their position one by one. After a few were lifted out of place, a door became visible beneath the floor. Demitra lifted it open by the circular iron handle. The two of them proceeded down the hidden staircase running through the center of Blanchard House. The staircase was narrow—only the vaguest thread of light shone in from the trap door up above. Using their hands against the dusty plaster walls, the witches crept slowly down.

"Where are we, do you think?" Salem asked.

"I think Fable's bathroom wall maybe—probably the wall between her and Seth."

Seth, Salem thought. *My brother*. She had not allowed herself time to really think about things as they now stood. Her brother was gone. In her mind, she had envisioned his reunion with Yasmine as a rather joyous kind of thing. She sympathized with his happiness. She imagined his return to his beloved must have been quite a scene when it occurred. But now as they traversed this dark passage into the bowels of Blanchard House, she came to terms with what Seth's departure truly meant. He was now joined with darkness. That dreaded shadowy world she and her family had fought all their lives. And he'd just given himself over to it. Willingly. And for what? Love? Admirable as that may seem on the surface, it was in fact a terribly selfish thing to do. Seth had children. He knew what it was like to be left behind by parents too consumed with themselves to consider anything else. How many nights had Salem and Seth cried alone in their beds or to each other? When Nacaria went away, they learned what it was like to be orphaned. They had Artemis then, and Demitra, and of course Olympia. But it was not the same. Now Salem realized she was going to have to be the Artemis for Hera and Titan. It then dawned on her, *they are the same age we were*—or nearly. Her heart tore in two at the thought of her sweet, innocent niece and nephew now walking the exact same path as she and Seth once walked.

Demitra seemed to know her thoughts, the perk of having a clairvoyant aunt. "You will be there for them at every turn, Salem. They will persevere just as you did. And they have Miranda. She loves them. They will be alright."

"Why do the children in this family always seem to lose someone at every turn?" Salem whispered.

"I'll be here with you," Demitra said. "And Fable and Arielle. We are all with you. We are all here for those kids."

Salem looked at her with a raised brow, "Didn't you just tell me that if something happens to you, I am the new Hecate? How can you promise you'll not leave us too?"

"It's a precaution, that's all," Demitra smiled. "I have no intentions of deserting this family or you. It will be a long time before you become Hecate. This is just a safeguard. We have no idea what we are getting into."

The door at the bottom of the stairs presented itself the moment Demitra finished speaking. The door creaked open, offering them nothing but darkness beyond. Salem withdrew her phone from her pocket and turned the flashlight on. Not much illuminated in the darkness. Salem felt the wall for a light switch but found nothing.

"When was this built?" she whispered to Demitra.

"My grandfather's time, or his father's. I'm not really sure."

"Maybe before the house had electricity," Salem noted. "Probably back then the house was just one or two stories. I bet that staircase was added later when the house got bigger. Look over there, there seem to be lanterns."

"Got a match?"

"No, but maybe a spell?" Salem offered.

"I'm a psychic," Demitra said. "I don't really do spells very well."

"I freeze things or move them," Salem replied. "I'm not great at spells either."

"Wait a minute!" Demitra cried. "I have a lighter in my pocket. I found Hera and Con playing with it this morning."

"The kids were playing with a lighter?" Salem exclaimed.

"Not really our biggest concern right now Salem," Demitra scoffed as she flicked the lighter on and lit on of the lanterns. It lit right away.

"Good, there's still oil in it. I'll light the others."

Within a minute or two, Salem lit the several lanterns lining the walls and the room came into view. The room was massive, perhaps stretching the length of the entire first floor of Blanchard House. Several closed doors within sight told them that this was not the only room in this vault. A set of stairs led down about four feet to an area housing a dusty desk and two maroon couches. A glass case sat on the desk with a glowing ball inside vacillating among a multitude of colors. Whatever that thing was, Demitra and Salem did not need psychic abilities to know it was best left under that case. Rolled scrolls lay on surfaces throughout the room. Salem unfurled the one nearest her. It appeared to be a family crest and list of names of the Norwood family, ancestors of the Blanchards. Salem unrolled another. It was the same thing, only a ledger of the Blanchards.

"Aunt Demitra," Salem gasped in surprise. "This scroll has our family members on it. It even has Howard listed. And Olympus. And look, here's Hera, and Titan, Rom, and Con. Hell even Echo, Tess, and Trix? It has all of us. But how?"

Demitra joined her and glanced at the scroll. "That isn't Artemis' handwriting. It looks to be written in some sort of antique calligraphy."

"Maybe it automatically adds names as Blanchards are born?"

"Maybe so," Demitra replied, peering over Salem's shoulder, scanning the list. "Who is Theda?"

Salem shrugged, "Maybe a baby that died in childbirth?" She laid the scroll aside and continued to look around the room. "Any idea what we are looking for exactly?"

"I suppose we will know it when we find it."

Salem curiously walked to one of the closed doors and opened it. As the lantern light illuminated the tiny room, they saw that it was nothing but a small closet of shelves containing glass jars of a grayish powder. Each jar had a name etched on its lid. Blaze Blanchard. Griselda Blanchard. Victor Blanchard. Ora Mae Norwood. Zacharia Timmons.

"Bone dust," Salem said. "The remains of our ancestors."

Salem stepped backward to close the door again. As she moved, the light from one of the nearby lanterns hit something hanging from a nail on one of the shelves. The glass capsule on the chain flickered. It was a necklace. Salem lifted it closer to inspect. Five tiny capsule-shaped arms glimmered from the stone affixing them together. As she looked closer, she could see miniscule clasps atop each little encapsulated compartment.

"Looks like a hinge," she observed. Unfastening one of the clasps she noticed she was right, a tiny top lifted off one of the compartments. "Aunt Demitra, look at this. I think this necklace means something."

Demitra stepped over to the closet and looked for herself. "Where was this?"

"Just hanging here with the bone dust."

"Salem, I think it's supposed to be some sort of talisman or maybe a conduit to the powers of our dead ancestors. Imagine how powerful that could make a person in a battle!"

"You'd have the abilities of five other witches."

Demitra's face brightened. "I have no active powers in battle. This could be useful. Maybe we fill each of these capsules with the bone dust of five of our dead?"

"But who?"

"Whoever had impressive powers," Demitra replied.

"You keep looking around," Salem suggested. "I'll fill the necklace."

Demitra continued to poke around the expansive room, careful to look with her eyes and not her hands as Artemis had warned her of the dangers involved in handling artifacts she knew nothing about. Salem chose carefully from the store of remains of long dead witches of the family. Constantinople Blanchard was the first person she added into the necklace because Olympia always told of his great power. Next, she added his wife Angharad, whom the family knew scarcely little about except that she was a most powerful witch. Griselda Blanchard, Olympia's grandmother, was the next to be added because she too was known as being strong in her magics. A name caught Salem's attention from the shelves she hadn't thought about in years, Hemmerlick Jasper. He was a distant cousin of Olympia's whom Olympia mentioned once or twice over her years. Hemmerlick's power was the domination and control of wind power. Salem figured Demitra could use that kind of active ability.

. . .

Demitra was lost in the enormity of confusion of the room. Hundreds of books, talisman, bottles, and trinkets made it impossible to know what might be of help. It was then when she almost laughed at her own stupidity. *I'm freaking psychic.* She closed her eyes and felt the room with her mind, sending tendrils of thought out around the room hoping to pick up on something useful. Within a few seconds she began to get a tremor of thought. A long-faded memory of the room. She could see her grandmother, dark and ferocious looking, arguing with another woman, a woman who appeared almost as foreboding as she. The woman's dark hair was tainted with multiple streaks of gray swirling through like bad highlights. Demitra's sense homed in on this trace of the room's memory. It was a sister. Angharad's older sister.

"I know you have it," the older woman said pleadingly. "I know your husband took it from the nest when he slaughtered the Old Ones in France. I need it, Angharad. Please. I am begging you as your sister."

Angharad did not look the least concerned or beseeched. Her stoic hardness could have been a power in its own right. Demitra wondered what had happened in Angharad Blanchard's life to make her so callous.

"Magdara, I fear your use of the vial. Constantinople and I nearly perished wiping out the nest of vampires in Lourdes. To give you the vampire king's blood could prove catastrophic if misused."

"It will not be misused. I have no intention of resurrecting the undead. But my husband is still missing. That blood could protect me in my endeavor to find him. If I could swallow but even a drop, I could be undetectable. The vampires in Copenhagen would not sense that I am not one of them. By the time the drop wears off I may have located my husband. Please, sister, will you not help me?"

"No," Angharad said without emotion. "I am remorseful, Magdara, but the risk is too much. The greater cause of keeping the earth free of the plague outweighs any personal need. I cannot give you the vial."

The memory faded from Demitra's mind. At first her sympathy for her grandmother's sister held her captive. Had Magdara found another way to save her husband? Did Angharad ever give in and help her only sister? Demitra could not imagine a scenario in which she would not do her utmost to help Nacaria or Artemis in whatever they needed. But reality set in and Demitra realized there was no time to worry about dramas of 100 years ago. She now knew there was a vial in this room. A vial of vampire blood which, according to Angharad's conversation with Magdara, could trick a vampire into believing Demitra was one of them, at least temporarily.

Demitra focused her control on the vial's location. She trained her mind only to the vial. It was much the same way she often helped the police locate a missing person or a weapon in a crime. Blotting everything else out, she turned the world to blackness only allowing the one object she sought to emit any light at all. The location came to her, pulsing almost like a heartbeat. Suddenly she knew exactly where it lay. She walked over to one of the ornately carved bookshelves. The fleur-de-lis relief carving on the crown of the third shelf caught her immediate attention. She touched her finger to the design and twisted it around. A small panel opened behind it containing a glass vial about four inches long, filled with some reddish-brown liquid. Demitra had the vial of vampire blood.

"What will that do?" Salem asked as she handed over the necklace to her aunt.

"Hopefully if I drink a drop of this and wear that necklace, I can enter the battle pretty strongly."

"Battle?'

"Oh, there is definitely going to be a battle, Salem. We are not only going to rescue Echo, Tess, and Cassandra. We are going to take down the House of Duquesne once and for all."

CHAPTER FORTY TWO

Ties That Unbind

Thaddeuss, Constance, Atheidrelle, and Taub were gathered in the drawing room of the House of Duquesne when Thorne and Mara entered.

"It is about time the two of you made an appearance," Thaddeuss declared disapprovingly. "Everything is coming to a head now. I believe the Blanchards may come looking for their family members soon. We must all be prepared."

"What have you done, Father?" Thorne asked. "Have you done something to Echo?"

Thaddeuss smirked and dismissed the question with the wave of a hand.

"It's all over then?" Mara asked. "If they come here, they will find out all about this place. They have surely spoken to the Witches Council. This family's secrets will be exposed. Maybe now we can all be free of this awful place."

Atheidrelle Obreiggon stepped forth and slapped Mara hard across the face. "How dare you? This house is our sanctuary. It is our refuge. It is the center of our survival."

"Cassandra?"

Atheidrelle's shrill laugh coming from Cassandra's mouth unnerved Thorne and Mara. Atheidrelle turned to her brother, "Thaddeuss, your granddaughter is a not very intelligent."

"This is Atheidrelle, Mara," Constance informed her. "She has stepped into her daughter's shell until a new body can be generated. This will occur in due time."

"So, you've done it then?" Thorne said. "You've taken poor Tess. What have you done with Echo?"

"Your fondness for your cousin is not only sickening, but also grossly inconsequential," Thaddeuss replied. "Echo is disposable. As disposable as you are, my son. I caution you to remember that."

Thorne bristled. "I wouldn't say I am exactly disposable. I am still a man. I could produce a child."

"Then by all means produce one and be of some use to us!" Taub shouted at his brother. "We need bodies. Don't you worry about what will happen to you?"

Thorne looked incredulously at Taub. "You forget brother that you and I and Mara and Ashby do not have the privilege of regenerating. We are merely bystanders to our father's eternal life. We have no dog in this hunt."

Taub waved his hands in frustration at his brother's lack of comprehension. "In the past, that is a true statement. However, our new cousins' bloodline changes the game. With the addition of the God Strain, Brother, perhaps we too could become immortal. We may be the last of Father's children to grow old and die. Father will be capable of amazing things when their blood mixes with his collective powers. He may be able to bestow life to us as well. It is worth a chance. The only one we have."

"I'm still young, Taub," Thorne quipped. "I have years before I need to worry about rebirth."

"Yes, but the world is changing now," Taub reminded. "There are more powerful beings out there than D'Angelos now. Now there are gods. I have Alexandrea's child gestating. It will be born within three months. It has the blood of the vampire flowing through it. That will make me vastly more powerful than I am now if I am able to leap into it."

"If it is male," Atheidrelle corrected. "If Alexandrea's child is female, I may choose to trade in my daughter's virtually useless form to gain the power of the vampire. Of course, I am still holding out hope Tess will produce both a boy and a girl. Thaddeuss and I could both have the God Strain if that occurs."

Mara laughed, "As Thorne so properly put it, we have youth already. We are in no hurry. It is only the three of you who are so desperate."

"Just you remember, Mara, you are part of us," Thaddeuss said. "Useless as you and your uncle are to the cause, you, Thorne, and Ashby are still D'Angelos. If the Blanchards come for one of us, they come for all of us."

Mara digested this statement as she walked to the fireplace hearth and stole a steady glance at her reflection. She was young. She was beautiful. But in time it would fade. What was she if she were neither of these things? Her gaze moved away from her toned, smooth face and momentarily glimpsed her own eyes. A sliver of something humane quivered from them. *But what am I if I kill to stay young?* In the briefest of seconds while she looked at her image, she pondered this question. Mara considered herself a fairly good person. Yes, sometimes she killed people who were in her way—but that was more on them for being in her way. Brandon for instance. He belonged to her. If other girls tried to interfere with that, their ends lay at their own feet. But innocent lives being taken merely for Mara to stay young or amass power—that seemed evil. That was going too far. Still...this was her family. The only one she had. Crossing them would be burning a bridge too necessary for survival.

"Decide where you stand Brother," Taub directed to Thorne. "You as well, Daughter." Mara removed herself from her reflection to return her attention to her father as he continued. "You both live quite a luxurious life off our backs. And despite whatever either of you believe, one day you will grow old. You will become sick. And you will die as have the many siblings which came before us. Now we have the chance to stop their fate from becoming ours. With the God Strain, we too might possibly become immortal. Choose your allegiance."

Thorne didn't say anything. He did not have to. Taub's words of truth rang through his mind, and he knew a time would come when the D'Angelo's plans would indeed benefit him. He did care for Echo. But he cared for himself more. His own vanity. His own freedoms. His own decadent lifestyle. He gave a nod toward his father. Thaddeuss gave a slight bow of the head to acknowledge the loyalty. Mara did not say anything. She still wasn't sure.

...

Never in her 50 plus years of life had Artemis Blanchard's senses felt so acute. Every fiber of her awareness was heightened at peak level. She could smell the vampires the moment she stood at the gates of Duquense House. Her nephews' wolf venom coursing through her body enhanced everything. She could hear the swampy creatures swimming below the water's surface 1,000 yards away. She could hear the squirrels scampering along bare limbs. She could hear the choir of tree frogs, crickets, cicadas, and birds resounding through the night for miles. The black sky above was of no consequence to her now. Her eyes narrowed into slits and dilated into night-vision clarity. The power of the wolf flowed through her, and she felt more invulnerable than she had ever felt in her life. She fully expected to walk unnoticed across the Duquense lands to the house, but she didn't walk. She ran. She ran, she jumped, she leapt from tree branches. It took her no time at all to reach the house. To soar from the highest limb onto the steepest roofline pitch of the House of Duquesne. And she never needed to take a wolf form to do it. The beast's speed and agility were in her wiring now. Artemis Blanchard was no mere human any longer, and the witch within her felt even more powerful than before as she utilized her mindspeak and summoned the one she sought.

Seth. Come to me.

And he did.

Within minutes of Artemis reaching the parapet on the eastern face of the house, the secret door in the stone of the house pushed open. Seth Blanchard—vampire—came outside.

"I see," he grinned malevolently. "I am not the only one enjoying a few changes in body chemistry."

"You are not."

"Have you come for me, Artemis? Have you come to kill me and Yasmine?"

Artemis smiled under the black sky where thick clouds blotted out the full moon. In such darkness, no human would have seen the glint in her large eyes nor the restored elasticity of her aging flesh. But Seth did. He could see everything just as capably as she.

"I have come to join you Seth," she said. "Bite me. Turn me."

Seth took a step backward, distrusting his ears. "What are you attempting to pull, Artemis? This is not a life you would seek out unless you had some greater plan at work."

"Can you not feel how I am changed?"

"That is quite clear," Seth said suspiciously. "But I have to wonder why? You are too powerful to fall victim to a werewolf's bite. Unless it was by your own volition. And since I can only think of two who could have provided you with this transformation, I can only guess you had the boys do this purposefully. Now you want me to infuse you with yet another dark force. Why?"

"That is irrelevant," Artemis said. "I simply need you to do it."

Seth looked out into the night, away from her wanting gaze. "I don't think so."

Artemis took a step closer to her nephew. The night wind whipped her long, raven hair like a cape behind her. "You owe me Seth," she said. "I have given my life to you. All I ask is this one final gesture between us."

Seth was not a fool. He might have been one once—before Yasmine gave him the gift. But now Seth Blanchard understood cunning. He understood the dark majesty of a black soul. He knew his aunt had a method to her madness, and he felt apprehensive supplying her with anything she asked for.

"You wish me to turn you," Seth summarized, "So that you can become the most powerful creature on earth. I don't think that bodes well for Yasmine or myself. I have given up too much to be with her. Giving you the leverage of that much power—it would be signing our death warrants."

Artemis' canine eyes flared red. "I am not here for you. But I do need you. I promise to let you and Yasmine go, for now. But only if you share your gift with me."

"You will simply let Yasmine and I walk out of here?" Seth asked suspiciously.

"I will."

"Take a Vow."

Artemis smiled. *Good boy*, she thought. *I taught you well.* A witch's Vow, if broken, would relinquish that witch's powers forever. Artemis was proud he had not taken her word for it. She would have expected no less from him.

"I Vow to you Seth, that you and Yasmine are free to leave unharmed—if you leave now. After this night ends, I will no longer honor the agreement. I Vow merely one night of safety. Plenty of time for you two to get away."

"But you will come for us...eventually," he deduced.

"Of course," Artemis smiled. "And as your mother, I promise I will destroy you. I will not allow you to roam this earth killing innocents for sport and pleasure. I will come for you. But I will give you a head start."

"And if I refuse to help you?"

"Then I shall kill you now. And you know that I can. Especially now that I have the wolf inside me."

"You have the witch and wolf," Seth smiled. "I have the witch and vampire. I'd say we are evenly matched, wouldn't you? It could be anyone's game to win or lose."

"Feel like risking it, boy?" she asked. "I am one powerful witch. Is your life with Yasmine worth the chance? All I ask is for you to turn me. In return you will have one night's head start."

"I want a year," Seth bartered.

Artemis smiled again. She expected a counter and was pleased to find it was a hefty one. She had indeed trained him well. Now it was she who turned away to face the cool crisp night below them. Taking a moment to consider his bargain and the ripple effect to the world accepting it might cause. Seth, perhaps more anxious than she, couldn't wait the deliberation out without further pleading the case.

"What's worth more to you, Artemis? Destroying Yasmine and myself or ending the evils inside this house? Which poses the greater threat?"

"I will give you one month," Artemis said. "That is all you'll get. Otherwise, I will take my chances and end you now."

Seth flinched. He knew she would give no more ground. "Agreed. One month. I will take Yaz and go the moment you turn."

"I'd expect no less."

Seth stepped forward to his aunt. As she twisted her neck around to expose herself to him, both looked into the other's eyes, knowing that this was the last moment ever on earth they would be allies. A lifetime of love between them. A lifetime of caring about each other, having each other's backs. And this was the last time they would ever not be enemies. Like a last kiss blown in a parting love's direction, Seth offered a reverential smile before he sank his fangs into her flesh and drank.

It was all there. The life they had shared together. It flooded into him like a tidal wave of love, loss, pain, and joy. *Where are they taking my Mama?* Artemis held the little boy tightly in her arms as he wept. *I will never leave you, Seth. I'll take care of you.* Baseball games. Football games. Homework. Broken hearts. Bad report cards. *Please let me borrow the car, Aunt Artemis! I have a date.* The speeding tickets waved in his face. *Seth, why can't you drive at a normal speed?! You want me to buy you a truck for your birthday, but all you do is act irresponsibly.* Baby Michael's death. Artemis consoling Seth after the loss of his nephew. Seth's love for Yasmine. Artemis' support of it. The fight with Patric. The wedding. The birth of Titan. Olympia's death. Everything. Everything felt all at once between them. Seth had loved this woman. This woman had loved him. And as he injected his toxin into her bloodstream, he knew that everything which ever passed between them was dying now. It felt as if the bond were snapping physically, forever parting them from the special kinship they'd always shared. Now and forever, or as long as he would be able to evade her, they would be adversaries. The hunter and the hunted. As Seth killed his aunt and sired a queen, he understood their bond was now ended. A deep sadness swelled inside him as she crumpled to the ground to die.

He did not wait to see what happened next. Seth Blanchard darted back into the house, running through the twists and turns of those confusing catacombs in desperation to find his wife—to get Yasmine out while they had the chance. Before all literal Hell broke loose.

On the parapet, Artemis Blanchard lay crumbled on the cold stone floor, blood trickling down her neck onto her chest and dampening the end strands of her black hair. The cold wind surged around her. She felt sick. Sicker than any sickness she had ever known. It was if her very soul was shriveling up inside her—all the goodness and purity of her heart was dying. Suddenly her half-closed eyes felt a burning sensation as a painfully bright light began to grow from nowhere. She had no strength to lift her head to look at where it was coming from, but she knew it was there. The magnificence of that light seemed to fill the empty places inside where her soul was dying. She did not want the light to ever extinguish.

"I'm here, Artemis," Beryl said. "Hold on. I have come to help you."

Artemis felt herself lifted effortlessly from the floor. She hovered in the cold air but felt nothing other than all-encompassing warmth and love. Her sight was blinded by whatever radiance was swelling around her, but she didn't care. She never wanted this feeling to end. Never had Artemis felt such sheer happiness—ubiquitous peace—emanating all around her. *I feel the presence of God.*

"Your sacrifice was a noble one," Beryl's incandescent voice rang out. "Your love for the greater good has baptized you clean from the darkness inside you. You are worthy. You are purely true. I restore your soul, Artemis Blanchard. Take your place at a helm where no one has ever reigned. You are the only one of your kind. Fail your God not in the honor He has bestowed upon you."

"Are you God?" Artemis managed to softly mutter as the majesty of the moment swept into her soul like a glittery lightning.

"I am but His finger. It is His light which regenerates you. You are now His sword. Use His gift wisely and with the purity of your heart."

In the very instant the sentence was said, Beryl was gone. The light was gone. Artemis Blanchard stood alone on the parapet, reverberating with something from within. It had worked. The ancient Blanchard coven leaders' plan had been a success. Artemis Blanchard was no longer a witch. No longer a werewolf. Not a vampire. She was a triad of power. Something else all together now.

I am the Sword.

CHAPTER FORTY THREE

Gathering Forces

Gideon Duquesne gathered his clan together in the common room they shared. Bianca, Elijah, Aspasia, and Davidson sat along the tufted sofas and chairs waiting to understand why they were not venturing into the city for the evening.

The moment the stone panel in the wall slid open and none other than Thaddeuss D'Angelo entered the room, the vampires knew something serious was transpiring.

"Hello nephew," Gideon acknowledged as he entered. "I believe you remember Aspasia. This is Davidson, her companion. Davidson, this is my nephew, Hugh Duquesne. Of course, he is more modernly known as Thaddeuss D'Angelo."

Bianca approached. It had been years since Thaddeuss ventured into the inner sanctum of the vampire lair. He had forgotten how wickedly beautiful his aunt was. "Bianca, my dear, you are a vision."

"What brings you to our part of the house, cousin?" Elijah asked.

"Where is our newest member of the household?" Thaddeuss asked, looking around but not finding Yasmine.

Bianca positioned herself atop a chaise lounge and curled her red stiletto heels under her legs as she reclined. With a playful smile, she informed him, "She has sired a mate. Undoubtedly they are occupied at the moment. She was not in her room."

Thaddeuss did not look pleased. "She created a companion?" He turned to Gideon in displeasure. "How did this happen? Was it someone from town?"

Gideon did not like being spoken to as if he were an underling. "Caution, nephew. I do not serve you."

"We serve each other," Thaddeuss asserted. "Your very safety and sustenance relies upon my generosity..."

"And we guard your mother which keeps you alive," Gideon countered. "A mutual exchange of favors."

"Who did Yasmine sire?"

Aspasia spoke up with an air of frivolity in her European accent. "Why, her own earthly spouse no less. Her husband came in search of her and now he has joined our ranks."

"Seth?" Thaddeuss said excitedly. "Seth Blanchard is here? He is a vampire now?"

"And rather enjoying it too I might add," Bianca laughed.

Thaddeuss put his finger and thumb to his chin in contemplation, "This could be a good thing for us. Seth has great power as well. With he and Yasmine at our sides, we stand a much better chance of winning."

"You seem to be the possessor of information we are not," Elijah observed. "Care to share with us Hugh?"

"The Blanchard witches are coming here. Coming to rescue three of their own. My nephew Echo, his sister Tess, and my niece Cassandra. They will not be successful. I suspect they will also attempt to vanquish Yasmine and her husband now as well. But we will be ready for them. You will come out of your realm and into ours for battle."

Gideon considered the idea. He knew he could not refuse. He required Thaddeuss for survival and could not afford to displease him. Moreover, if witches infiltrated the house, they would surely find a way into the vampire domain, which could spell doom for his little family.

"Elijah, I believe we will require reinforcements," Gideon directed his cousin. "Unleash the lesser creatures."

"Lesser creatures?" Thaddeuss replied.

It amused Gideon as to how little Hugh Duquesne knew about the inner workings of his house. Living in his luxury with all its decadent finery, blissfully unaware of the preventative measures employed behind the walls to secure the House of Duquesne. Hugh, under the guise of Thaddeuss D'Angelo, might present himself to the world as the master of the family, but Gideon was its general.

Thaddeuss repeated his question, "What are these lesser creatures of which you speak, cousin?"

Gideon grinned malevolently, "Those unfortunate souls we have drained, but not turned. A dozen or so poor souls who wandered onto these lands by error. Fishermen coming ashore on our property, hikers exploring the terrain, stranded motorists seeking help. Over the years we have amassed individuals we... partook in... yet we did not take them to the point of death. Neither did we bestow the gift of eternal life to them. You see, Nephew, we too hedge our bets. I foresaw a day like this when we might require a front-line battalion."

"Where are these creatures?" Thaddeuss asked.

"Lining the chambers around your mother's crypt. They are ravenous by now I am most certain. We will unleash them upon your witches."

Thaddeuss was astounded by the information, yet pleased. Another line of defense would be very fortuitous. "And find Yasmine!" he demanded. "Without her freezing power, it may be a hopeless battle."

"One thing, nephew," Gideon beckoned before Thaddeuss departed to his portion of the house. "After this night is over, I want Alexandrea. I have waited far too long for the mate I have chosen."

"She is with child," Thaddeuss informed his vampire uncle. "Once the child is born, she is yours for the rest of eternity."

CHAPTER FORTY FOUR

Battle for The House of Duquesne

Since becoming mistress of Oleander, Nacaria had led many visitors into the house and shown them the grandeur of the Obreiggon estate. She rather enjoyed giving tours and showcasing the restorations she and Xander made to the centuries-old plantation. There was no time now to indulge those who had never seen the magnificent home. Time was of the essence. Sarah and Melinda, Zelda's daughters, walked, mouths open, through the majestic entrance along with Pastoria's sons and grandchildren. Demitra assembled her army before her and began her reign as Hecate with the most difficult mission of their lives.

"We will have no time for mistakes once we get inside the house," Demitra began. "We will need teams. Each team will have their own mission. No one can stray from that mission. Everything hinges upon every team's success." She looked at the faces before her, her family and friends, she knew not all of them were coming back to Oleander at the end of this night. This was the first time the thought occurred to her. With everything happening so fast the monumental significance of the fight was lost in the mad rush. Demitra felt nauseous as she realized this. The woman in her wanted to take a moment and freeze-frame everyone's faces in her mind—to pay a kind of homage to their place in her life. But the Hecate in her had no time for such sentimental meanderings. Too much was at stake and time was running out.

Interrupting Demitra's thoughts, Ursula interjected, "If we are dealing with vampires, shouldn't we be going in there during the day?"

It was a reasonable question. In fact, a logical one. However, things being what they were, it rendered the luxury of waiting impossible. Demitra conveyed why, "I would say yes if it were not for Tess and Echo. We cannot waste a moment's time getting to them."

Demitra scanned those gathered before her and quickly ran through their individual gifts and talents, forming her teams in the only seconds she had to consider them. "Ursula, I would like you to team with Drake, Sydney, Fable, and Melinda to search out the vampires. Locate their domain, but do not engage them. We just need to know where they are to report to the council. However, if they attack, you have adequate powers between you to fight and escape. Ursula possesses the power to send energy bursts. Drake can manifest forcefields. Sydney has the strength of a hundred men, Fable can summon animals to help, and Melinda has keen psychic abilities.

"Salem, I need you to head the rescue team to find Echo and Tess. Take Arielle, Trix, and Ocean with you. Seneca, I need you with me as I go after Thaddeuss. Nacaria, you take Sarah to find Cassandra. Sarah's razor-sharp instincts and your mastery of spells should make it easy. Xander, your job is to zap us there in groups, then you remain with Howard. If anyone goes down—anyone gets killed—someone from that team mindspeak to Xander so that he can zap Howard to them and revive them while there is time. And lastly, Blackie...if what you say is true, the moment you get inside that house you should begin to heal. Sage, you stick with Blackie, once she is back to her old self, I need the two of you to try and find her mother's hidden chamber. But do not enter, only locate it."

Everyone had their orders. Within a few minutes, Xander Obreiggon had successfully zapped everyone by twos to the front lawn of the House of Duquesne. The house towered over them like a behemoth. A living monster of stone and mortar. It was more than anyone who had never seen it was prepared for. It felt alive and it meant to destroy them all.

Standing back several yards from the door, the group watched as Salem tossed out her hands and blew the thick oak door to Duquesne House. The explosion was loud, and the fiery embers of the ancient oak splintered off onto the stone steps and into the entrance hall.

"Go!" Demitra commanded as every individual team, except Fable's, sprinted through the front doors. Fable's team had other instructions. They would infiltrate from another location, throwing the enemy off guard.

With lightning speed, Demitra's teams charged inside. The explosion of the front door brought the running feet of servants into the hall. Arielle swiped them all to the side, parting the way for the Blanchard coven to move to their designated missions. With Sage's assistance, Blackie moved slowly but deliberately into a nearby parlor she knew very well.

As the invaders burst into the house, eyes were watching. Standing out of sight atop the grand staircase, Thaddeuss witnessed the assault on his home. His son Taub rushed to his side in frantic fury.

"What's happening, Father?"

"The Blanchard's are attacking," Thaddeuss scowled. "I expected their attack to be forthcoming, however, I did think we'd have more time. Still, we are prepared. I prepared the vampires. They stand ready to aid us. Go open the portals. Let them out."

Thaddeuss D'Angelo touched his index finger to his temple and sent out a message to his family in *mindspeak*. "The House of Duquesne is under attack by the Blanchard family. Ready yourselves for battle. Kill them all."

Thaddeuss stood sentry at the top of the stairs. Salem, taking the stairs three at a time, did not see him until it was too late. She flung out her hands to inflict a melee toward him, but he was faster than she, sending a propulsion of power at her which knocked her backward against the rail and over it. She plunged downward toward the deadly stone floor below. In the brief seconds she experienced the deadly floor coming closer and closer to her face, she knew this might be the end for her. But a mere two feet from the floor she stopped abruptly midair. The shock of coming so close to death was made more evident when she saw her long auburn tresses sprawled out on the stone before her eyes. *That was close.* Tossing her hair from her face she caught sight of Arielle on the other side of the hall, holding her in place with her levitation power. Salem gave her sister a thankful wink and righted herself back onto her feet. Arielle grabbed Trix's hand as Ocean and Salem joined them to charge forth down a corridor into the bowels of the house in search of Tess and Echo.

Seneca and Demitra dashed up the stairs where Salem had been tossed. Thaddeuss was still there, undeterred by their approach. He seemed emboldened by either his own arrogant sense of unmatched power or his determination to hold the Blanchards at bay. He swatted a hand sideways and rendered a burst of power onto the staircase itself, splitting it into two sections, causing his aggressors to lose balance and topple downward. As Seneca began to lose footing, he heroically grabbed his cousin Demitra by the arm, slinging her to safety against the staircase wall—his quick reflexes saving her from falling through the crack in the stairs. Once she was secure, Seneca managed to leap into the air to grasp the iron railing of the other side of the splitting stairs. He swung himself back onto the treads safely. Demitra focused her eyes on the balustrade beside Thaddeuss. Clutching the necklace of power around her neck, she wielded a force to break the railing from its anchors and smash into Thaddeuss. The blow sent him tumbling backward into the second-floor corridor.

. . .

Nacaria and Sarah were now running through the downstairs hall behind Salem, Ocean, Trix, and Arielle. Sarah was already huffing as she moved—her weight being quite an issue in her agility. But adrenaline was helping, and she was able to ignore the pain in her joints as she maneuvered along with Nacaria, never missing a beat. In the main entrance hall, more servants were coming to the defense of the house, darting down the corridor hard on the heels of Nacaria, Sarah, Salem, and the others. Xander acted fast, hoping to cut off as many servants as he could from infiltrating the hall after his wife and daughters. He used his powers to grab heavy furniture pieces and zap them into the corridor entrance, building a barricade of unmovable objects to keep the human opposition blocked, rendering the servants unable to stop the rescue team in their quest to locate Echo and Tess. The few servants who had made it through before his blockade, were now brandishing guns and long knives aimed directly at the rescue team. A gun fired at Sarah, but her impeccable magical instincts anticipated the shot well before the servant's finger squeezed the trigger. She had already dodged it before it zipped by. Nacaria whirled around to face the charging servants and cast a spell into the air.

"Bones crack and fall to dust!" Nacaria bellowed. She stopped sprinting and turned to watch her spell take effect as the half dozen male servants' legs simply shattered beneath them. It was a spell which would have never worked on a witch—witches being too powerful—but for an average regular person, it was impeccably effective. The D'Angelo family's loyalist servants sank to the ground unable to walk or stand with only muscle and tissue for support. Cries of agony rang through the air as bone from the pelvis down shattered to dust beneath their flesh.

. . .

Back on the stairs in the entrance hall, Thaddeuss D'Angelo—more powerful than anyone imagined—manifested a long jagged-edged dagger from thin air and hurled it straight at Demitra. Seneca leapt forward, knocking his cousin out of harm's way.

The sharp blade sailed into his neck, slicing his jugular. Seneca landed hard on the stone steps, blood spewing from the wound. Screaming in horror, Demitra ran to the aid of her cousin.

Demitra clasped her hands over the wound, but it was too wide and too deep. Her hands pushed past flesh and moved inside the neck to the sliced muscle beneath. There was nothing to be done. Seneca was losing too much blood. There was no way to close the wound. But then from the corner of her eye, Demitra spotted Howard below. She sent another blast of power Thaddeuss' way, knocking him for a second time into the upstairs hallway. She then aimed another blast as he tried to stand. Howard knew what to do. While Demitra kept Thaddeuss at bay, Howard dashed onto the broken staircase and went to work. But nothing was happening. Howard was frantic. His hands were firmly pressed onto Seneca's body—his concentration fixed upon healing him—but nothing was happening. Seneca Blanchard lay there choking on blood—the dagger still protruding from his throat.

"He's not dead, Howard," Demitra exclaimed, understanding the issue. "You can't heal people the way Beryl could. You can only reverse death."

Howard stared at Demitra strangely. He didn't understand.

"Kill him, Howard!" she demanded. "Then bring him back."

Howard balked. He'd never harmed anyone in his life. Now she was expecting him to kill Seneca? Seneca was family—in a way. Howard didn't exactly understand how he and Seneca were related, maybe second cousins twice removed or something, but they were family. Howard was ambivalent to act, but Demitra continued to yell for him to do it. Howard relented. As Demitra shot another blow to Thaddeuss, Howard pulled the dagger from Seneca's throat and stabbed it into his heart as hard as he could. Seneca's eyes rolled back as blood spurted out in what seemed to Howard to be gallons. In moments, Seneca was gone. Howard placed his hands to Seneca's chest and began.

What happened next was something Howard Caldwell could hardly understand or articulate. The light, the warmth—the power of God—poured from some hidden place within him and radiated from his hands. It was more than merely a surging power...it was a soul awakening. For the first time in Howard's life, he knew God existed and he never wanted to forget what it felt like to connect to even the smallest fraction of that truth. As he felt the Holy connection, a white-silver stream swirled from his fingertips, emitting a dazzling glow. It enveloped Seneca like a shimmery cocoon. As it faded away from sight, Seneca lay before Howard fully healed. His eyes were closed, appearing to be unconscious. Demitra knelt beside Howard. Thaddeuss was gone now, retreating somewhere on the second floor. Seneca began to stir. He opened his eyes. Demitra smiled at Howard as she gripped his arm and shook it with excited pride. Howard had used his new power successfully. Seneca Blanchard was coming back around.

. . .

Deep into the bowels of the first-floor halls, Arielle—knowing more routes in the House of Duquesne than anyone else—led the charge pulling Trix and Salem with her around corners and into rooms looking for their siblings.

Ocean hung back, waiting to block the way if more attackers pursued after them. Arielle and her sisters needed time to check as many rooms as they could. Nacaria had taken care of the first line of attackers, but Ocean was sure there would be more storming the corridor soon. Deciding it was best to let the girls move ahead without him, Ocean outstretched his arms and cupped his hands inward, summoning his power. He could feel the water around him—in the pipes hidden above, in the floors below, in the walls. Of the four magical elements in the world (fire, water, earth, air) water was not merely Ocean's element, it was part of his physical composite. Ocean Blanchard and water itself were almost the same thing. He sent his summoning power forth and called to his elemental friend. The water rushed through the pipes, obeying its master. Within moments several holes burst open overheard and from the sides of the walls as torrents of water from the plumbing system streamed forth to do his bidding. Ocean waved his hands in a circular motion creating a swirling blockade before him. He kept his hands spinning, powering the liquid force to even stronger depths. A typhoon of dense liquid racing in a circle, ready to smash into anyone who dared attack.

Meanwhile, Salem, Arielle, and Trix checked room after room down the winding, confusing hallways. With every empty chamber they moved to the next. Nacaria and Sarah caught up to them along the way, having needed to rest a moment for Sarah to calm her breathing.

"Arielle," Nacaria told her stepdaughter, "They won't be in any ordinary room. Thaddeuss will have them locked away somewhere. Find a chamber that is fortified. Sarah and I will continue on and try to find Cassandra."

Suddenly, someone came running around a corner almost smacking directly into Arielle. It was Mara D'Angelo. Mara looked ready to attack yet stopped the moment she saw her cousin. Neither woman spoke a word, they only stared briefly at one another, surveying the other's intention. Arielle broke the silence.

"Mara, I don't want to fight you. I know you don't like this family. I know you understand what they are doing is wrong. You are not like the other D'Angelos. Help us, cousin. Please."

"I don't know what I should do?" Mara admitted. "Why are you attacking us?"

"They have my brother and my sister, Mara," Arielle explained. "Echo and Tess are somewhere in this house. You must know what Thaddeuss is planning. Where are they? Where is Cassandra? Please help us save them."

Mara weighed her options for a moment. She analyzed the other two women with Arielle, wondering if they meant her harm. She decided to speak openly and take her chances. "I have known what they were planning to do. I did not think it affected me, so I didn't care very much. But I do not want Echo hurt...or you. Why I care about you I don't know, but for some reason I find that I do. I can help you find them, but then I am leaving. I will not fight you or your family. And I will not aid mine. I only want to find Ashby and get back to the city. I leave the D'Angelos and the Blanchards to fight their own battle without me or my little sister."

"Fair enough," Arielle agreed. "Just please help us find Echo, Tess, and Cassandra."

Mara gave Arielle a troubled look. She did not know whether she should divulge what she knew. Mara did not want harm to come to her cousins, but she also feared betraying her father and grandfather. Arielle could tell there was something else Mara was not saying. She pressed her for the details.

"Tell me whatever you know, Mara," Arielle said. "I Vow to you that if you are honest with me—if you do nothing to cause harm to us or our family—I will not allow you or Ashby to be harmed while you make your getaway."

Mara knew escaping this battle would mark her forever to her family as a traitor. And there would be consequences in that. She knew she should stay and fight, but going to war with the Blanchards was too risky. All Mara could think about was Brandon and the second chance she had at happiness with him. He was afraid of her enough now to not struggle against their future. He was all she ever wanted from life. If she were ever going to have a life with Brandon, Mara had to walk away from the House of Duquesne. He was all she cared about. The only thing she felt obligated to do was take Ashby with her.

She chose her side and decided to disclose everything to Arielle. "Cassandra is not Cassandra. She is Atheidrelle. Thaddeuss brought Cassandra here so that Atheidrelle could possess her body until they forge a more powerful one."

A wave of nausea hit Arielle. She knew Mara spoke the truth. She felt the change in Cassandra when they last met. Arielle wanted to cry. *Cassandra.* The sister she had finally built a true and meaningful relationship with. If Cassandra was possessed by Atheidrelle, that meant that Cassandra was lost forever...unless they could find a way to exercise Atheidrelle from her body the way Olympia did for Arielle years ago. Suddenly a frightening thought entered her mind. Nacaria was searching for Cassandra, unaware it was really her ultimate nemesis. Arielle whirled around to warn her stepmother, but it was too late. Nacaria and Sarah were already gone, off on their own mission to find Cassandra.

Arielle turned back to Mara, "Where would Thaddeuss be holding Echo and Tess?"

"I don't know," Mara replied. "But like I said, I can help you find them."

Mara took a step away from Arielle and engaged her tracing power to locate Echo. A faint bluish mist appeared in the corridor. It seemed to stretch out of sight around a corner. Salem and Trix watched in amazement as the mist hovered lightly in the air.

"I don't know Tess. Never met her," Mara said. "I can't trace her. But this will lead you to Echo. That's all I can do for you, cousin. I am sorry. I will not stop your family, but I also cannot turn on my own. I'm going to find my sister and get us out of here. I have a life awaiting me outside of this house, and I will not risk losing it."

Arielle clutched her cousin's arm gently in gratitude. "I understand," she nodded. "Thank you."

Mara returned the affectionate moment with her own hands placed over Arielle's. "One more thing," she cautioned. "If you are attacking this house, you need to know there are vampires here. My grandfather will have been sure to open their doors now. They are the Duquenses. They are strong and old. Beware of them."

"Thank you, Mara. We know," Arielle said. "Now go find Ashby and get yourself to town where you'll be safe."

As Mara disappeared into the distance, Salem questioned the situation. "Arielle, are you sure that was wise?"

"She won't harm us," Arielle said. "I think I can trust her. We have to follow this mist and find Echo and Tess. We will figure out a way to save Cassandra after."

The three women followed the mist around a bend and discovered it stopped directly into a wall facing. No doorway stood where the mist entered, it simply looked as if it were stretching into a paneled wall. Trix stepped toward the wall and inspected it for a moment. She then took a step backward and lifted her hand. Closing her eyes, she focused her power on the wall face. Within seconds dozens of tiny nails streamed out of the heavy wooden panels. As each nail removed itself from its position in the wall, Trix forged the metal into a medium-sized sledgehammer. Once she could feel that every bit of metal had evacuated the wall, she swung the hammer as hard as she could toward the paneling. Without fasteners affixing the panels to joists, the wall fell to the floor the moment her hammer struck.

Arielle turned to Salem and whispered, "Doesn't she know you could have just blown a hole through that?"

Salem gave her little sister a disapproving head shake and whispered back, "Let her play her part. Besides, it's a pretty cool power to watch in action."

With the wall panel now removed, the blue mist was hovering on the other side stretching down another corridor. Salem, Arielle, and Trix stepped through the hole in the wall and continued to flow the trail.

. . .

Outside the House of Duquesne, Fable Blanchard and her group had made their way around the house and were standing on the furthest eastern side of the great manor. The enormous stone walls towered above Fable. There were no doors in sight. Fable's team of Ursula, Drake, Sydney, and Melinda stood off to the side, quietly and patiently waiting. They had been waiting a while for Fable to assemble her other army. She'd kept her eyes closed, and her concentration honed on its one endeavor. She had spent the last several minutes sending out distress messages to the animal kingdom as far as her beacon could reach. During the time she waited, an army of woodland creatures crept out of their habitats around the property to lend their service to her. Badgers, squirrels, rats, a few snakes, and even a bobcat waited patiently at the edges of the lawn. Fable needed more, and she was waiting on the rest of her other battalions to make their way to the house.

The sounds emanating around her formed a chorus of crunches, howls, squawks, chirps, and growls. After several more minutes, Fable opened her eyes to see a brigade lining up for their orders. Possums, squirrels, badgers, wildcats, bobcats, snakes, scorpions, feral cats, and wild dogs took their places among the rodents and beasts as six alligators slinked up to join the ranks.

Ursula, Drake, Sydney, and Melinda marveled at the assistance Fable conjured. With Fable's forces now assembled, the group were ready to wage attack from the back of the house. Salem had handled the front entrance, now Fable's team would take the house by surprise from behind. Fable gave the nod to Sydney. Sydney Blanchard walked to the nearest exterior wall of the house and pushed. It was a struggle at first, something Sydney was not accustomed to. Usually her strength never failed her, but this house was massive and so were its stone walls. But soon the brick and stone began to budge. Old mortar began to disintegrate against the friction of shifting stones. Finally, the rock lost hold as Sydney pushed a portion of wall into the interior of the house. Drake threw a forcefield around Sydney to save her from the crumbling debris now falling from the top of the hole she'd made. Once the dust and crumbling rock settled, a thinly opened entrance stood leading into the monstrous structure. The team filed in behind Sydney.

...

Back inside the house, in the front parlor, Blackie was tucked away in a corner with Sage. She was panicking at being back inside the evil house she worked so hard to free herself from. Guilt infiltrated her as she waited for the house to do its thing and heal her. All her many years—her many lifetimes—spent in that house were playing out in her mind as she looked out onto the familiar room which never changed. So many other incarnations of her life, other women's bodies she had stolen and taken over—including this one which was now failing her as it aged. But Blackie did not have time to think about that now. She had to let the house heal her. Already she could feel her left side begin to twitch. Movement of any kind was a welcome gift. Blackie D'Angelo was not accustomed to being helpless. These last weeks had been torture for her, but it was more than the need to be whole again. Her children were in peril, real peril somewhere inside this house which had almost destroyed her life. She had to get them out before her brother used them up for his own diabolical needs. And for that, she needed to be whole again. Slowly she could feel the transformation beginning. Her drawn and twisted face began to right itself. Her left side began to move. She was regaining her strength, regaining the use of her stroke-ravaged body. Sage looked on in fascination as Blackie D'Angelo healed before him.

"How?" he stammered.

"My mother," Blackie said, hearing her voice again for the first time since her stroke. "My mother's force saturates these walls. In her presence, I am invincible."

...

Ocean had not been able to rejoin Arielle's group. He had his hands full in an inner corridor holding back several D'Angelo servants. The servants looked more like guards in stature and strength, almost as if the family knew one day their home would fall under attack and had hired mercenaries. Ocean directed his wall of water at the guerillas with a massive velocity. Unleashing a river through the corridor, he watched the D'Angelo's hired army crash back through the catacombs of the house as if they were no more than children on a water slide.

...

Fable was rushing through the house now, a horde of creatures in tow behind her. The others in her team were running up ahead, twisting through the catacombs of the confusing halls. Fable stopped in her tracks as she heard a loud explosion combust behind her head. Bits of wood flitted down around her. The others were already down the hall and out of sight when Fable turned to investigate the explosion. A cabinet had exploded into splinters behind her. Obviously, someone was aiming for Fable and missed. She followed the trajectory and saw that the strike came from an older woman standing in the center of a large painting frame. The team had run by the secret passage without knowing it was there, and now this vile looking woman was standing in the passage door.

"Why are you in my house!" the woman cried, sending another blast of energy toward Fable. Before Fable had time to react, three brave wildcats leapt in front of her, absorbing the blow themselves to save her. The cats were sent tumbling onto their backs, dead. Fable gasped. She wanted to run to them, these steadfast creatures who sacrificed their lives for their master. But there was no time to honor their devotion. The woman was readying herself for another melee.

Fable had never seen Constance D'Angelo before, but she was now well acquainted with her power. As Constance reared herself for another attack, more of Fable's protectors streamed into action. A flock of blackbirds, hawks, and bats now zipping through the hall behind Fable winged to her defense. The birds swarmed Constance in the doorway. She blasted energy at them repeatedly, sending many feathery carcasses crashing into the wall but there were too many winged warriors. Fable watched as Constance raised her arms to protect her eyes and face to no avail. The birds and bats still managed to scratch and bite at her flesh. Constance staggered back through the painting face, retreating into the room in which she had emerged. She slammed the painting shut behind her.

Fable was in no mood for another surprise attack, and she had no intention of letting this woman escape so easily. She raised her knee and kicked in the painting face.

Constance D'Angelo was far into the secret room attempting to open another door to flee. Fable's entry startled her, but she continued onward until she had the door handle in her grasp.

"The fuck you are!" Fable Blanchard screamed, stepping aside for her animal army to pour through the painting frame behind her.

Constance shrieked and yanked the far door open to escape. Two coyotes sailed over her head smashing into the door face, slamming it shut before she could go through. They snapped at her legs, dropping her to the ground. Her legs were bleeding. Bits of flesh torn away by the powerful jaws of Fable's devotees. Constance was whimpering, backing away on her elbows, trapping herself against the wall.

Fable's eyes hardened in fury. Slowly, she stalked forward to the cowering woman. "You thought you could steal members of my family!" Fable howled. Constance stared ahead at the approaching Fable, but her eyes lowered to Fable's feet where a dozen fanged snakes slithered closer, moving around several swamp possums standing on their hind legs with their sharp claws raised for attack. Buzzards and crows rushed over Fable's head. They circled the ceiling, their flapping wings moving the still air like a high-powered fan. Fable stood triumphant among her animal friends as her hair blew behind her. "You thought you could use my niece and my nephew. Thought you could best the Blanchards! Well, bitch, it is time for you to eat crow!"

Fable clapped her hands loudly as the snakes rushed Constance D'Angelo, biting their painful fangs into her sides. The coyotes took an arm in each mouth as two alligators tromped forward to each take one of her legs, their powerful jaws snapping bone as they closed down. Constance was pulled outstretched by the beasts, as the birds overhead all shot like missiles toward the woman's face and mouth. Constance's agonizing cries were drowned out by the flapping of wings before dying altogether as the feathered beasts tore out her tongue, pecked out her eyes, and ripped away her ears. Constance D'Angelo writhed in silent screaming.

The birds, snakes, and possums retreated from their work once Constance drew her last pained breath. Fable smiled down to the coyotes and alligators, "Eat up, my lovelies. Dinner is served."

CHAPTER FORTY FIVE

Attack of the Vampires

Gideon Duquesne found Alexandrea D'Angelo seated as she always was, in her bedroom, staring out into the dark of night. He approached lovingly. His bargain with Thaddeuss was over after tonight. He would no longer honor their pact to wait for Alexandrea to give birth. Gideon would not risk losing the one thing he cherished in this empty existence. Slowly he sank his fangs into her neck and injected her with his gift. Her empty eyes fluttered. Her head turned toward him. Gideon then saw the one thing he had not seen in months. Her smile returned to that beautiful face.

"My love," she said.

He lifted her from the chair and held her in his arms. "We have been released from the confines of our stronghold within these walls. The D'Angelos need us for their fight. A great battle is commencing. I must join it and protect our home and our insured safety within these walls."

Alexandrea did not understand. But she didn't need to. She only knew he had come for her. He had finally made her like himself, freeing her from the prison Taub held her inside.

"We fight?" she asked.

"No, my love," Gideon smiled. "I will see this war through. You, my darling, must leave this place. Run. Go out into the forest. Wait for me to find you. Once the interlopers are dealt with and the House of Duquesne is cleansed of those who mean us harm, I will bring you home."

He walked her to the door and pulled it open for her. "Go. Go fast. If you find a victim to feed upon, take them quickly for sustenance. Then flee to the forest. I will come for you before dawn, once I have killed the enemies who have infiltrated our sanctuary."

. . .

The trail of blue mist Mara set out for them in the corridors was still glowing brightly as Salem, Trix, and Arielle made their way up a long twisting staircase somewhere on the fourth floor. A strange sight met them halfway up the stairs. The mist did not continue up the winding stone stairs; instead, it trailed into and through the rock stone wall. Salem and Arielle clenched hands, drawing their powers together just as they had many times in the past to blast out that part of the wall. The stones blew outward into the passage behind the wall, although a cloud of debris hovered in the air obscuring their line of sight until it settled. The trio were covered in a layer of mortar dust as they passed through the hole into a modest bedroom. Broken rock and dust covered the bed and the tops of the dresser and nightstand, but the trail of mist shone through the trickling soot showing them the way to finding Echo. Just beyond the room, the mist stretched down a slim unimpressive hallway turning directly into a thick door of oak where the blue mist stopped. However, the pathway to the door was not clear and the sight of what was obstructing it, terrified them. Between the door and the Blanchards stood four of the most revolting creatures Salem and Arielle had ever seen. But Trix had seen such beings. She knew all too well what lurked there before the door guarding Echo and Tess. Ghoulish beings with limbs drawn inward as though atrophied, skin withered, yet tautly constricted as if shrink-wrapped to the bone and muscle and sinew. They looked like dehydrated meat—starved, dry, shriveled. Their emaciated arms outstretched toward Trix, Arielle and Salem in a starved eagerness to satiate their denied hunger. Staring at their prey with lifeless black eyes, their twisted faces displayed a yearning unlike anything Arielle and Salem had ever seen. But Trix knew. They were hungry. They had been purposely kept this way, the zombie-like by-products of the vampires. A pitiful army of ravenous creatures whose only desire was to drink.

"What are those things?" Arielle screamed, backing herself down the hall several feet as she pulled her sisters with her.

"The vampires made them," Trix explained. Trix was prepared. She pulled herself from Arielle's grasp and readied herself. She'd fought these things all her life. She turned her hand over, palm up, and focused her mind. Within seconds a stream of metal began to move toward her from all directions. Disintegrating nails sent wall hangings crashing to the floor of the hall. Hardware from locked doors melted and joined the flow as the doors they held dipped down to the floor, held now only in place by the wooden doorframes. Strands of what once might have been candlesticks, mirror frames, or bed posts flowed beneath baseboard cracks to join the rest of liquid metal now forming a long scythe in Trix's right hand.

The monsters approached slowly, reaching for the living prey yet seeming hesitant to move too far from the door they obscured.

"They are guarding Echo and Tess' chamber," Salem said. "That must be where they are."

Trix charged forward without warning and deftly swung her scythe around her body, bringing its razor-sharp blade upward to meet the nearest creature's middle section. The blade sliced with ease through the *almost*-vampire starting at his right hip and cutting up to his left shoulder. His upper torso plopped to the floor rendering him incapable of moving, although not dead.

Salem finished the next one by blowing him to pieces. Trix was fast on the next strike, beheading the third, as Salem sent another detonation to the fourth, splattering the wall with his body parts. Arielle watched from several yards back allowing her more heroic sisters to clear the way.

Sidestepping the mess on the floor, Salem slammed her forearms together, combusting the wall housing the door. A large hole now provided not only an entrance to them room, but the ability to now hear inside. Tess and Echo's voices rang clear now through the wall, and within moments, Arielle and Trix were helping them climb out to freedom.

A rush of relief swept Trix now that she could finally lay her eyes on her siblings and see for herself they were alive and safe. She swept them into her arms. Her elation lasted only seconds before her mind absorbed the new reality her extreme relief had kept her from noticing.

Moving her hands to her sister's belly, she cried, "Tess! Are you—"

"Thaddeuss did this to her!" Echo shouted. "He's trying to make a baby with the God Strain so he can possess it and live his life all over again."

Trix removed her eyes from Tess' stomach and looked into her twin's eyes. The pain...the humiliation...the dehumanization of her being, was all there in those eyes. Trix thrust her arm around her sister's neck and pulled her into an embrace. Tess began to cry as Trix stroked the back of her head as she held her.

"I didn't believe anyone could be this evil," Trix said through gritted teeth.

Thaddeuss would pay for doing this to her sister. She would make sure of it. She thought about what Tess must be going through. The impact of this assault and now the everlasting reminder of a baby—But she didn't have the time to think about that now. That would have to be processed later. She had to get Tess out of there and to safety.

"This entire family is insane," Salem warned. "The D'Angelos are pure evil. Every one of them except Blackie."

. . .

Downstairs Seneca and Demitra found themselves ambushed by Taub and Thorne who were backed up by two people who were clearly not servants. Elijah Duquesne and Aspasia looked upon the intruders with an almost amused excitement. The vampires were unafraid of the witches. Assured of their superiority by hundreds of years of existence, they did not share the panic nor the desperation of their D'Angelo cousins. Taub, Thorne, and the vampires marched toward Demitra and Seneca, who were slowly backing up as they tried to formulate a plan. Seneca was doing his best to bombard their stalkers by using his telekinesis to draw heavy furnishings across the floor to crash into them. But Thorne, sharing the same power, was quick to offset the melee by redirecting each piece to the side.

Demitra and Seneca had now backed themselves into the mouth of a tall fireplace hearth. Suddenly a horde of blood thirsty vampire zombies charged in from an open doorway. The invading creatures did not appear to be there to assist the D'Angelos. They were starving and out for themselves. Their addition provided a distraction giving Demitra the seconds she needed to touch her amulet and draw upon her grandmother's vast powers. She sent a burst of energy forth, knocking the fiendish monsters back against the stone walls. The ferocity of the blast left them stunned on the ground momentarily. Next, she waved her hands above her head and dropped the heavy tapestries from the upper walls to crash down upon Elijah and Aspasia. It only preoccupied the vampires momentarily, but it gave Demitra time. She summoned a powerful wind current from outside which burst through the tall gallery windows. The force of the glass shattering sent some of the fragments slicing Thorne and Taub as they flew. But Taub was too quick; he waved his hand in a circular motion, lifting the shards of glass from the floor and sending them shooting, like bullets, through the air toward his prey.

Trapped by the interior confines of the fireplace, Demitra and Seneca had no place to run, no left or right to sidestep to. Suddenly Demitra saw a flash before her eyes as a thin transparent barrier appeared in front of her, like a bubble. It was a shield. She glanced in the direction of the shattered windows to see Ursula and Drake climbing through the remnants of where the stained glass had been. Drake was propelling a forcefield their way to stop the glass from slicing them to bits. The shards hit the bubble protecting Demitra and Seneca and pulverized into finer bits.

Seneca charged forward, ready to attack the D'Angelo brothers. Taub levitated into the air, rearing his arms behind him and allowing a black vapor to pour from his chest. It was as if he were manifesting some deadly toxin from within his cavity. The black mist swirled around Seneca, growing more and more solid as it twisted round him. Soon Seneca was completely encased by what now appeared to be black cords. Demitra could only watch in horror as she saw the cords choke her cousin further. She knew he would soon be dead. Yet without warning, another door burst open as Xander bound forth, leaping into the air, and reaching the end of his fingertips as high above him as he could. The moment his index finger touched Seneca's shoe, both Xander and Seneca disappeared. Xander successfully zapped him to freedom.

Demitra sighed in short-lived relief before witnessing something truly horrific. The black ectoplasm which Taub had created from his insides had now detonated, sending multiple layers of black matter spreading through the room. Demitra dove to the floor as one of the layers shot toward her head. When she lifted, she saw that the black matter sliced through the fireplace wall behind her, leaving crumbling dust and shifting brick. She jumped free of the falling rubble only to see a nightmare scene before her. Drake Blanchard was on the ground, sliced into four halves from the burst of matter. There was no blood—no spilling of his insides. It was as if his open wounds had cauterized instantly from whatever composed that black matter. As Demitra looked down upon her fallen cousin, she was pummeled with the memory from years ago when Drake's nephew, Forest Blanchard, was dealt a similar fate at the hands of Atheidrelle. Just as it was with Forest, there was nothing she could do. Drake was dead.

Demitra scanned the room. Taub was pleased with himself, grinning vilely at his handiwork. Thorne seemed shaken. Backed away near a corner, he appeared to be disturbed by his brother's victory. The vampires were watching the scene as well; however, they appeared to be more preoccupied by Drake's remains on the floor—paused in place as if waiting for blood to eventually spill. None did, but the creatures waited for it regardless.

Demitra screamed through her mind for Howard. Howard had to come. Xander, from wherever he had gone with Seneca, must hear her cries and come forth with Howard in tow to save her cousin. But Howard never came. Ursula rushed to Demitra's side, grabbing her arm to flee before Taub struck again, but there was no place to go. Demitra stood with Ursula alone in the room as the vampire monsters snapped from their fascination and began stalking forward. Taub marched on them as well, as did Thorne, now stirred from his repulsion and refocused on the enemies before him. Demitra and Ursula stood together, back-to-back as Taub, Thorne, Aspasia, Elijah, and the vampire creatures encircled.

Demitra reached for her amulet to send forth another burst, but it was gone. A quick glance back at the fireplace revealed its whereabouts. In her rush to duck the black matter, the amulet must have fallen from her neck. It was out of reach, and she was powerless as the murderous D'Angelo brothers, and their vampire cousins, as well as the vampire's zombie creatures, crept closer.

. . .

Dashing down the twisting hallways of the house, Arielle led the way, taking the group down a path she remembered from her last visit. It should have led to the grand entry hall. However, Arielle was taken by surprise when she turned a sharp corner and smacked straight into a wall.

"That wasn't there last time!" she shouted, rubbing her nose to make sure she hadn't broken it. "This damn house."

"What do we do now?" Trix said, looking around and finding no noticeable alternate pathways.

A sound, muffled but grating, grew in the distance. Salem, Arielle, Tess, Trix, and Echo looked at each other in confusion. It was getting closer, but no one knew its origin. Salem thrust her arms out, shielding her family from the unseen danger like a mother slams an arm over a child in the passenger seat when she brakes abruptly. All eyes focused on the far wall, which was now shaking slightly. The sounds were growing louder. The plaster on the wall began to shake and crack, as dust sprinkled from the growing cracks. Salem took her fight stance, prepared to freeze or blast whatever came through the wall. She gave a startled flinch as the plaster loosened its hold and crashed to the ground. Behind the falling plaster tumbled several large cement blocks, pushed by some unseen force from behind. The settling dust revealed a comforting sight as a familiar sneeze rang out. Salem lowered her hands from their battle position as Sydney stepped through the newly formed doorway, Fable behind her. Fable was fanning the air as she twitched her nostrils.

"Oh my God, Fable!" Arielle exclaimed. "Y'all scared us to death."

Fable slapped Sydney on the back and remarked, "It's really handy having a Wonder Woman in the family. We were lost so Sydney just started making her own path. She must have knocked holes in a half dozen walls to get here."

. . .

Xander had zapped Seneca to the entrance hall, the only place Xander could think of in the second's time he had to save him. The split grand staircase was still teetering on collapse but held on above them by the few stubborn wall bolts remaining.

"Xander!" shouted the voice he most wanted to hear. He whirled around to see Nacaria on the floor, clutching Sarah in her arms. "Xander, where is Howard? She's dying!"

Xander ran to his wife and knelt beside Zelda's daughter Sarah. Sarah was bleeding profusely. A scorched hole lay dead center in her chest as the poor woman gasped for the last breaths of life.

"What happened to her?" Xander asked.

"A male servant cornered us with a gun, but he was meant to be a distraction. Sarah got hit from behind with a burst of some sort of fireball from Thaddeuss. He hurled it at me, but she jumped in the path. The servant fired the gun at me but missed, badly. It was then I saw Blackie behind him. She had hypnotized him to not be able to see me. But when I grabbed Sarah to help her, Thaddeuss went after Blackie. I have no idea where they are. We need Howard. Sarah is dying."

Xander looked into his wife's beautiful eyes, so tender, so compassionate. He hated to say the words. "I'm sorry, my darling. Sarah is already dead."

Nacaria clutched the brave woman close to her chest and wept. She had only really known Zelda's daughter when they were little, but she was still family...and she died to save Nacaria. She was about to tell Xander again to fetch Howard, in case there was still time to revive her, but the moment was abruptly interrupted by a voice shouting at the top of the staircase landing.

"You are all dead!" said the exquisite pale woman with shoulder-length straight, black hair. It was Bianca Duquense. She bared her sharp fangs and hissed at them. Taking a giant leap over the banister, she landed deftly on her feet with little strain. Seneca swung at her, but she grasped him by the throat and threw him into the air. As his body came flailing back down, his head smashed against the thick stone stair treads of the staircase. Bianca walked with a speed none of them expected her kind to possess. She lifted Seneca's stunned body with one hand, the blood still oozing from his head wound as she stabbed him onto one of the exposed broken stair rail posts, impaling him through the heart.

Nacaria screamed. As Bianca darted toward them, Xander zapped Nacaria away.

CHAPTER FORTY SIX

Requiem for the Blanchards

Demitra and Ursula knew they were trapped, as Taub and Thorne, Elijah, Aspasia, and the vampire creatures drew closer. For a split second Demitra thought there was no chance for escape. She would never again see Jerry or her grandsons. She hoped Salem would make a great Hecate after her death. But then something fortuitous happened. Ursula had an idea which proved to be a good one. Though she didn't possess enough power to strike all of their approaching adversaries, she did have enough firepower for one good hit. She sent a powerful energy burst from her hand, aimed directly at Drake's fallen and quartered corpse on the floor. His four sections burst, freeing the trapped blood within their singed, cauterized sections. The red liquid spilled forth across the floor. For a split second Demitra was appalled at the defilement of her cousins body, until she understood Ursula's intention. As the vampire's ravenous creatures moved toward them, the call of Drake's blood proved too compelling for their starved animalistic impulses to ignore. The creatures stopped their approach upon Demitra and Ursula to cluster around Drake's remains with ravenous intent in their red gleaming eyes. It was a nauseating sight to behold as the undisciplined monsters fell to their knees, tearing into his body with their bare hands. As more blood poured from the new wounds, they began scooping it from the floor with their bony hands, feasting on as much as they could gather. Some even dipped their mouths to the ground and slurped what they could intake through their rotting lips. Pushing and swatting at one another for access, they looked like children fighting for candy from a birthday pinata.

The cringeworthy moment provided the opportunity for Demitra and Ursula to dart clear of the circle they were trapped within and position themselves against a nearby wall. Taub, Thorne, Aspasia, and Elijah recharted their course and moved closer, pinning them in.

Ursula thrust her hands forward, mimicking a pushing motion, and magically inserted a force of pressure between herself and Demitra and the encroaching enemy. But there were four of them and only one of her, and Ursula was not strong enough to hold them at bay long. But a reprieve presented itself, as Sage Blanchard darted into the room. Seeing his cousin cornered, he grabbed the first thing he could reach, a large sofa. Using his super strength—a power he shared with his twin sister Sydney—he hurled it straight at Taub and Thorne. The confusion provided a quick escape as Demitra and Ursula rushed toward the doorway where Sage stood, now wielding and tossing a large desk through the air. The women dashed out of the room and back into the entry hall. They waited for Sage to join them before dashing down an adjacent corridor. But Sage didn't move. He stood very still, looking up at the top of the half-demolished staircase. Demitra's eyes followed her cousin's to see a vampire standing at the top of the gallery. It was Aspasia's companion, Davidson. His fangs were sharp, and he was about to make a move.

"Go!" Sage yelled to Demitra and Ursula. "Go! I'll stop him from following you."

"We can't leave you!" Demitra shouted back.

A familiar voice shouted out from behind, "I've got his back! You two go!"

It was Ocean. He was running forward to assist his cousin, a tide of water rushing at his feet, directly under his control. He reached Sage and together they readied themselves for the fight.

Demitra hesitated but decided to trust the boys. Ocean was already wielding a current, ready to send it forth. Sage was strong and could handle himself. Without the talisman, Demitra was powerless to assist in battle. She clasped Ursula's hand and they disappeared down the corridor. The vampire leapt from the gallery to follow, but Ocean's wall of water rushed forth and blocked the hallway, protecting Demitra and Ursula from attack. Taub and Thorne were now back in play, rushing the entrance hall ready for a kill. Sage was ready. Instead of rushing the enemy, he rushed the cracked pillar under the gallery. Using his massive strength, he ran shoulder-first into the pillar, sending it crashing down and the compromised staircase with it. The entire structure smashed to the entry hall, completely covering Davidson with rubble, and blocking Taub and Thorne's path. Ocean released his wall of water, before he and Sage dashed down the corridor to follow the path Ursula and Demitra had taken.

...

Xander and Nacaria barely escaped the murderous clutches of the vampire Bianca Duquesne. The moment Bianca killed Seneca and came rushing toward them, Xander zapped himself and his wife away to a large ballroom in the center of the House of Duquesne. Xander had not been in the ballroom for many years. He was shocked he even remembered it.

Nacaria was falling apart. In a matter of minutes, she had seen Thaddeuss blast poor Sarah with a fireball to the chest, killing her. She saw him take off after Blackie to God knows where. Then she watched one of the vampires slaughter her cousin before her eyes. Nacaria was not accustomed to battles. It was too much for her delicate heart to stand.

"Everyone's dying, Xander," she wept in her husband's arms. "Everyone's dying."

Xander held his wife, pressing her head onto his shoulder. There was no time for this, he knew it, but she was breaking. Nacaria was a stranger to such evil in the world, having lived apart from the world for so many years. She needed to catch her breath, and he held her until she did. Once she recovered, he looked into her eyes and smiled. She understood its meaning. *I love you. We will be okay.*

"Now darling, we need to go find our children," he told her.

All at once the doors to the ballroom burst open. Xander was just about to zap them away again to safety when he saw, with much relief, the flutter of red and auburn hair bouncing through. His daughters. Salem and Arielle came running in with Trix, Tess, Echo, Fable, Ocean, and Sydney behind them.

"Salem!" Nacaria cried out, rushing toward her daughter, sweeping her into a powerful embrace. Nacaria reached an arm free and dragged Arielle into the hug as well. Xander sprinted forth and joined them from behind.

"My God Tess," Nacaria exclaimed, as she pulled free from the embrace with her children. "What have they done to you?"

"We have to get her out of here," Echo insisted. "They want the baby to rebirth them as gods."

Xander grabbed Tess' arm. "I'll get her back to Blanchard House."

Without warning, an explosion reverberated through the ballroom before Xander had the chance to do anything. Everyone fell to the ground for cover as the walls combusted inward from all sides. Stones thrust forward, hitting the little group, doing no real damage other than scrapes and bruises. Dust and dirt covered everyone. The heavy cloud of smoky debris hung in the air, obliterating the ability to see for a few moments. As the dust drifted down to the parquet floor, the Blanchards and Obreiggions looked up to see themselves surrounded. Thaddeuss, Taub, and Thorne flanked one side of the room. Bianca, Elijah, and Gideon covered another. On the third side stood a half dozen of the horrendous creatures the vampires controlled. And on the fourth side of the room...stood Yasmine and Seth Blanchard.

For a fleeting moment Salem felt rescued, until her eyes locked onto her brother's. Seth Blanchard's eyes were dead. The blackest eyes she had ever seen. It was not her brother. He pulled his lips apart and through the grimy air she saw the fangs. Yasmine had them too. No, these two people were no longer her family. Salem's heart felt ripped in two. Seth. Her only brother. The person who had gone through everything she had gone through in life. The joys, the heartaches, the losses. There was no thread to bind them any longer. Seth Blanchard was not human anymore. Just as the realization was dawning, Salem saw another sight which took her breath. Standing just behind Yasmine and Seth, barely in view, was Howard.

"None of you are going anywhere," Thaddeuss snarled, "Not until I have Tess...and Trix. Present them to me now or watch their beloved father ripped to shreds before your eyes."

Seth and Yasmine stepped aside to show a closer view of Howard Caldwell. He was not moving. He was not speaking. He was frozen. Frozen the way Salem froze people. Helpless, suspended in a state of nothingness. But how, Salem wondered? Who among them had the same power as she?

"Howard!" Arielle screamed.

"Seth what's wrong with you!" Fable roared. "Do something! Help us! We are your family."

One of the vampires laughed. Gideon Duquesne presented a devilish smile, "You were his family. Until our sweet Yasmine baptized him into ours."

Xander reached his hands behind him; he opened and closed them swiftly, alerting the others to join hands and clasp him for a quick getaway. But that did not happen. Thaddeuss was prepared.

"I wouldn't make any hasty retreat if I were you, Xander," Thaddeuss cautioned. "You see, I have your other daughter as well."

Gideon and Elijah stepped aside, revealing Cassandra held in the grips of two servants, each with a gun placed to her temple.

"Cassandra!" Xander bellowed. "Let my children go, Thaddeuss! You can have us. Just let my children go free."

Thaddeuss smiled devilishly, "Only after you give me back my child. The one inside Tess. Give me Tess and her sister, and you are all free to leave."

Arielle stared straight ahead into her captive sister's eyes. "That isn't Cassandra," she whispered.

But no one heard Arielle's warning. In the same moment Nacaria—thinking fast on her feet—shouted a disarming spell which caused the pistols in the servants' hands to send an electric shock. They each dropped their weapon as Nacaria screamed, "Cassandra run!"

Cassandra bolted forward, hands still behind her back. Nacaria dashed toward her to pull her to safety.

"That's not Cassandra!!!!" Arielle screamed at the top of her lungs.

As Nacaria grabbed Cassandra by the arms, to pull her to the safety provided by the group, her eyes widened in horror as Cassandra outstretched her arms—which had not been bound at all—and brandished a long, sharp sword. Smiling diabolically at Nacaria's shell shocked expression, Cassandra plunged the sword toward Nacaria's chest.

Acting on sheer instinct to save his beloved, Xander Obreiggon zapped himself forward and wrapped his arms around Nacaria from behind, his intention to whisk her to safety before the fatal blow struck. What happened, however, was something no one expected. The sword made contact. As Atheidrelle Obreiggon, using her daughter's body as her disguise, stabbed the sword into and through Nacaria Blanchard...the sword also stabbed through Xander's chest, impaling them both together, through their hearts. As the tip of the sharp edge burst from Xander's back, blood and tissue spurted from the wound. All anyone needed to see was the look on Atheidrelle's face. With one blow she had finally killed her nemesis, the woman she hated above all creatures, but in doing so she also killed the only man her wicked soul had ever wanted. Nacaria and Xander Obreiggon fell dead to the floor, together.

"Nnnooo!!!!!!" Salem wailed, running toward her parents.

Atheidrelle stood motionless, staring to the ground. Xander, her beloved Xander, was dead. And in some sort of karmic insult, he was dead with his arms around the woman who had always stood between them.

"Atheidrelle!" Arielle shouted. "Howard can save them! He can save your precious Xander! Tell them to release him!"

It was a good tactic on Arielle's part. But Atheidrelle did not send a command to release Howard from his catatonic state. Staring down at her beloved Xander entwined with her enemy, Atheidrelle chose to leave them there. Xander never loved her. And she would rather lose him forever than allow Nacaria Blanchard to live and have him.

Salem sank to her knees between her parents. She lifted her mother's lifeless face into her lap as she pulled her father closer to her. Arielle staggered forward, numb, unbelieving of the sight before her. She stood above her sister, looking down at their parents below. Salem began stroking Nacaria's long blonde hair as a mother would a child. She didn't understand why, but she did. Then something unexpected happened. Seth slowly staggered forward.

He wore a peculiar look on his face, as if he could not comprehend something. He felt as if he should feel something for the people lying dead at his feet, but he didn't. Still the sight of them was compelling him somehow. He looked back to Yasmine as if she might hold the answers to whatever he was feeling. She shrugged. Her unsympathetic face felt nothing for the fallen couple. Seth was confused. A voice lost deep inside seemed to be trying to connect him to the sight, but it wasn't getting through.

Salem glanced up into the dead eyes of her emotionless brother. He was lost too. Everything was lost. She had lost everyone now. A burning rage welled up inside her. A fury she had not felt in years, not since the death of her husband and son. It was volcanic and powerful, and it was bubbling like lava to the surface. Shaking with an energy more potent than she had ever known before, Salem thrust her hand out and grabbed Seth's cold, unfeeling fingers. Seth appeared dumbfounded as the surge emanating from Salem raced into and through him, connecting with some hidden force inside which he could no longer access himself. Arielle understood what Salem was doing. They'd done this very thing when they took down Patric the werewolf years ago. Arielle, grabbed Seth's other hand, at once feeling the surge race into her own being, uniting with the force between them all. Salem, Arielle, and Seth began to shake with the raging power. Arielle looked to her sister as Salem gave the nod. Instantaneously, Salem and Arielle slapped their free hands together, drawing the swelling force through the three Obreiggon siblings and pushing it outward like a sonic boom in every direction. The magnitude of the force was unstoppable...bringing down the house. The House of Duquesne fell. Ripped apart in one catastrophic blast as if it had been constructed of matchsticks. The entire magnificent structure burst all at once in flying projectiles all around. Then it suddenly stopped. Almost like pausing footage of an atomic bomb mid-blast, everything simply halted.

Block, rock, stone, wooden rafters, shattering glass, and ricocheting splinters all paused mid fall—hovering like a canopy of Armageddon above everyone. Shaken by the chaos, Seth looked to the women who'd taken his hand. One wasn't moving, she stood completely still. The other people behind them stood in the same suspended state. Everyone in all directions had stopped moving, except Yasmine who sent her husband a mischievous wink, signaling she'd stopped the motion in action. But Yasmine was not the only person unaffected by the spell. The auburn-haired woman moved her head now, turning to look at Seth with her large green eyes. Yasmine crossed the ballroom floor ducking and dodging the hovering debris as she came to Seth's side.

She observed the auburn-haired woman's bewilderment and giggled.

"Yaz?" the woman asked her. "Did you do this? You froze this?"

Yasmine returned a blank expression. It was as if she did not know Salem at all.

"How are you still moving?" Seth asked. "My wife's power should have immobilized you as well."

Salem gasped, unable to comprehend anything any longer. "I have the power to freeze, too. I'm immune to it."

Seth simply and nonchalantly replied, "Oh."

He took Yasmine's hand in his own and kissed her cottony cheek.

"This is where we depart, my sweetheart," she told him. "Leave these people to fight their war. It does not affect us."

Salem could not believe the coldness of Yasmine's tone. "We are your family, Yasmine. Don't you remember us?"

Yasmine gripped Seth's arm and answered, "He is my only family." Yasmine looked into Seth's eyes, her own beginning to sparkle as an idea swelled in her head. "Seth, should we eat her before we go?"

Salem bristled. *This isn't happening.*

Seth gave Yasmine a mild chuckle. "Leave her. We will dine in town. We must be off now before the fighting commences. I will not risk you coming to harm."

Salem grabbed Seth's arm. Yasmine thrust it away and hissed at Salem—her long fangs obliterating everything Salem once thought beautiful about her cousin. "Seth, our parents are dead. Our family needs your help. Doesn't any of that register with you?"

Seth was not moved. He wrapped his arm around his wife and directed her through the maze of the mid crumbled house. Salem watched as they disappeared beyond a falling archway. They were gone. Her brother was lost to her now forever.

Salem only had moments to act. With the scene frozen she could make her way to Thaddeuss and Atheidrelle and end them once and for all—if indeed they could be ended. According to Blackie, they were immortal. But Salem didn't have the time to act upon them, for through the thick haze she spotted a figure just beyond the safety of the ballroom. Caught under a falling corridor, Salem saw Sage frozen mid-crunch beneath rock which had been a half second from crushing him. She darted to the corridor and grabbed his arm, pulling him to the ballroom out of harm's way. Before she could return to killing her enemies, everything suddenly unfroze. The house continued its demise. As if God sent His finger forward Himself to smash the evil structure, the House of Duquesne finished splitting apart at every twisted evil seam. Floor after floor, wall after wall, corridor after corridor, crashed down all around. The only thing left standing was the ballroom. It took several minutes for the thunderous sounds of crumbling rock and brick and wood to subside. Steam and water sprayed out into the night air from broken gas and plumbing lines. The House of Duquesne stood no more. Only a massive pile of rubble remained, blocking everyone, good and evil, in the center like a Roman arena. Everyone was aware now, locked together for one final showdown in the ring of debris.

Sage sprang to life, darting to his sister Sydney and cousin Ocean. In the one fleeting second available between them, they shared a look around, then back to each other, all realizing they were all that was left of their branch of the family. With the house now in devastation, the absence of their fathers revealed they were the last of the Mobile Blanchards.

Salem and Arielle stood facing the D'Angelos, the Duqeusnes, and the horde of vampire monsters. Salem did not have time, nor desire to worry about Seth now. Her only focus was the physical form of her sister Cassandra, who Salem now knew emphatically to be the one and only Atheidrelle D'Angelo Obreiggon.

The spell over Howard was broken with Yasmine's departure. Coming to his senses, he saw the destruction around and rushed to his children. Tess, Trix, and Echo pulled him to protection behind them as they, Fable, and Ocean inched closer to Salem and Arielle.

Astounded by the colossal wasteland around him, Thaddeuss surveyed the wreckage of his ancestral home. His fortress was demolished. The vampire sanctum was disintegrated. The House of Duquesne was gone. Leveled to nothing. His rage was palpable. His chest heaved with fury. He would have his revenge. But before he could gather himself to strike out, his eyes saw beyond the wall of rubble to the one remaining unbroken feature sitting atop it. A large square enclosure of ancient stone stood intact, tilted askew atop the tons of stone and wood beneath it. The box was unharmed in the collapse, yet now it was quivering, swelling. An energy pounded inside, trying to escape. And as he panicked for a mere second, Thaddeuss then saw his worst fears realized. Stepping from behind the one remaining room of the House of Duquesne, came Blackie D'Angelo. She stumbled amid the mountain of debris from the fallen house as she crept forward to the box.

Blackie stood before the square citadel, the last bastion of the Duquesne family. Placing her hands upon its outer face, she shouted. "Mother, come out. It is time. You can be free now. Your guards are gone. The defenses are down. Mother...come out."

"Barbara! NO!" Thaddeuss shouted, attempting to run toward the stronghold, but the barrier of rubble proved too daunting an obstacle. He shot a fire burst at the barricade, but its thickness and density made it impenetrable. He only managed to move the blockade a few measly feet. Thaddeuss gave up using his powers and began to frantically climb the rocky remains of his house. The rocks were too jagged, too unstable. He toppled back down to the ground, his arms and torso scraped from the effort.

"Blackie!" Atheidrelle screamed from the center of the circle of wreckage. "You cannot do this! You cannot free her!"

The Blanchards were intrigued by whatever struck such fear in the D'Angelos. The vampires Gideon, Elijah, and Bianca looked as frightened as their D'Angelo kin. Collectively, everyone looked above to the top of the wall of ruins, as Blackie reached her open palm out to a piece of serrated rock and sliced her hand. Blood poured from the gash as she slapped her red-soaked palm to the ancient stone of the box. As if her D'Angelo blood were some sort of acid—or more likely, a key—the particles of stone began to disintegrate at the touch. Captivated faces watched as the outer face of the prison crumbled.

Slowly a figure emerged. Long flowing hair, colorless, whipped in the dirt-laden breeze. It stretched to the figure's feet and further. Centuries uncut. Not white, not grey, not describable in any way other than devoid of pigment. As the woman from the box approached, no eye could look away from her. It felt as if everyone's soul was drawn to her, and she owned all in sight.

Blackie looked below into the remains of the ballroom, which was now merely a cauldron within the rock. Blackie eyed her children standing with Howard and announced, "I present to you my mother...Themis!"

Suddenly the ancient woman lifted into the air, her hair flowing behind her like a comet's tail. She outstretched her arms and shot forward until she hovered above them all atop the encircling rubble encasing them.

"My son, you hold me captive no longer. I will punish you greatly for the transgression. You and your sisters have syphoned my power from me long enough."

"We protected you, Mother!" Atheidrelle shouted from below.

Themis roared in fury, "You imprisoned me to ensure your own immortality! As long as I lived, you could not die. My life has been excruciating. Not a life at all. You've kept me caged for centuries. Now I am free, and you cannot stop me as I bring a reckoning upon this world and take my place among the gods again."

Themis reached out her arms and began to rise higher, as if about to make an exit but suddenly something toppled her. She crashed down to the rocky top of the wall. To the amazed eyes watching below, three figures appeared in the skyline, soaring through the air atop something no one could make out. Then as the figures grew closer, the door they were gliding upon came into view. The center figure leapt off, landing on the remains of the house, as the door glided downward allowing Demitra and Ursula to step off into the pit with the others.

The Blanchards, the D'Angelos, and the vampires stared upward to see the center figure, Artemis Blanchard, who was now standing only yards from Blackie and Themis. Behind her, stalking over the shards of stone and rock, was a sea of wolves, backing up their queen. Above their heads swarmed thousands of feathered creatures great and small. Fable's friends; hawks, buzzards, crows, eagles, cranes, sea gulls, owls, and vultures.

Fearing now that the balance of power was out of his control, Thaddeuss waged one final strike to take out as many foes as his army could. He shrieked something no one could decipher as suddenly his vampires and their fiends charged the Blanchard clan in the pit.

Artemis raised her right arm upward, clenching her hand into a fist above her head. It was a signal to end the chaos below. The vampire's fiendish zombies fell to their knees, bowing to her understood command. She was their queen as well now. The wolves crept forward, peering over the stone piling, growling their warning below to the vampires who now understood their minions obeyed a new master.

Artemis called out into the night, "I am Artemis, the Huntress. Obey me or die at my hand."

Gideon Duquesne looked upon the night's new empress before him, weighing the dangers of noncompliance. Bianca and Elijah looked to him for instruction. Aspasia and Davidson looked to Bianca. All waiting to see which option served them best. Gideon slowly, crouched to one knee. The other vampires followed his lead.

"Get up!" Thaddeuss commanded his army. "Get up you fools! Kill her! Kill them all!"

"They know I am their master," Artemis bellowed down to Thaddeuss, her voice now carrying a treble and countenance it never had before. It made him shudder. "They fear *my* wrath, not yours."

"What are you!" Atheidrelle demanded, moving to stand shoulder to shoulder with her brother. "We have the power of hundreds of years and dozens of witches. How dare you assume to be greater than us."

From the 30-foot height above, Artemis dropped to the ground as if it were one simple step. Now only inches from Atheidrelle's face, Artemis pronounced, "I am the Queen of the Beasts."

"We beseech you to spare us," Elijah Duquesne asked. "We will do no more harm to your kinship."

Artemis gave a mighty laugh. Demitra, Fable, Salem, and Howard had never seen her so frightening, so powerful. They were not exactly sure if they should feel protected or fearful of her presence themselves.

"I am your queen," Artemis smiled. "And your executioner!"

Suddenly the wolves pounced, ripping and tearing into the vampire zombies, shredding their pathetic frail bodies to pieces as though they were made of paper. As the last extremity was torn away and the zombies fell, the wolves encircled Gideon, Elijah, Bianca, Aspasia, and Davidson.

Thaddeuss clasped Atheidrelle's hand and pulled her closer to him, backing away slowly from Artemis. Something slammed to the ground behind them. They whirled around to see Themis staring ahead, past them, her eyes blazing with the intensity of a warrior. Thaddeuss and Atheidrelle sprinted to the side, out of the way. Themis and Artemis stared at one another wordlessly for the longest time. Each evaluating the other. Who was the stronger between them? Who would win in this matched fight? Themis made a slight tilt of her head as she mentally measured the foe before her. Artemis stood unflinching, almost amused. There was a darkness emanating from her, yet concealed within that darkness lurked a shred of warmth. Hope. Something almost holy beneath the dread.

Artemis, likewise, examined Themis with the same intensity. The translucence of the ancient creature appeared to almost glow within the dark pit of the fallen house. Themis emitted her own power, her own radiance. Yet it was a sickly glow. A greenish, yellowy, glow around the pearlescence of her skin and flowing hair. Whatever Themis projected from within, did not provide hope or warmth.

As the two divinities continued to appraise each other, one of them broke the silence.

"Do you truly believe you are capable of ending the likes of me or my children?" Themis asked with mocking hubris. "I am not one of the beasts of the earth."

"But you are one of the evils of it," Artemis stated. "And I have made a vow to God to rid His world of its evils."

"Best of luck," Themis laughed as she waved her arms, lifting her offspring by surprise from their feet and hurtling to cover behind her. Blackie was snatched from the top of the wall, crashing to the ground. Atheidrelle and Thaddeuss flung from their place on the edge of the standoff to crash into Blackie behind their mother. As the three D'Angelos rose to a stand again, Themis stood in front of them, placing herself between them and Artemis.

"Centuries," Themis began, looking directly at Artemis. "We have centuries coursing through us. My children have displeased me, but I will attend to them later. For now, we will stand together and wipe you and your kind from this earth. We are immortal."

"Are you?" Demitra smirked, stepping forward. She sent a wink to her great granddaughter Trix and a nod to Ursula. Picking up the cue, Ursula pushed a burst of energy forward, toppling the D'Angelos and Themis to the ground. Arielle waved her hand and sent Trix flying forward toward Themis.

Trix Blanchard was ready, her hand already outstretched, her power already in action as she summoned every piece of nearby metal laying amid the pile of rubble from The House of Duquesne. Part of how her power worked was instinctively knowing how much metal was within range to obey her call. She could feel the supply as her hand reached out to take hold of whatever weapon was forming. With only seconds to forge, there was no time to manifest anything as large as a sword. As the liquid stream of bolts, nails, and pipe shot out from their hidden places amid the wreckage, she improvised, forming the strongest sharpest ax ever made. In one fell swing, Trix swung her ax at her opponent's neck, slicing through every tendon, muscle, and vertebrae. For all her boasted power and lengthy lifespan, the succubus Themis had not been prepared for the sudden strike. Her head dislodged and fell to the side, held only by one remaining strand of muscle, dangling off the left shoulder. Reverberating through the arena of stone was a fading shrill cry like that of a banshee. The last sound Themis ever made.

The entity so formidable that it could empower three beings for centuries was bested in seconds by a being so much less powerful than she. The irony was not lost on the D'Angelos. The battery was dead. Freed from its prison to be eradicated by an angry sister for the crimes perpetrated upon her twin.

Thaddeuss, Atheidrelle, and Blackie felt the death of their mother as if experiencing it themselves. It reached deep within their physical beings, stunning them internally. They stumbled—wobbly from the loss as their very immortality spewed out from them. They were vulnerable now. Now, they could die. And they knew it. Thaddeuss righted himself. He motioned to his son, Taub. Taub sent out his black tether which wrapped around Tess, Trix, and Echo. They struggled to free themselves, but his hold was too strong.

"You may have killed the source of our immortality," he growled at the Blanchards. "You may have stolen the ability for our souls to remain earthbound, but you have not killed us. As long as we live, we still possess the power to jump into new life. And with the God Strain blended into the powers I have collected, life after life, I will be the most powerful witch who ever lived. I only have to wait for the birth. And Xander Obreiggon was not the only person who knows how to Leap!"

Thaddeuss grasped his son Taub's arm as Taub began to propel Tess, Trix, and Echo forward toward them. Thinking fast, Ocean Blanchard focused his power, utilizing the broken plumbing pipes spewing their wasted water all around the crumbled house. A wall of water rose before him which he whipped around Tess, Trix and Echo, breaking Taub's tether and protecting them in a shield of swirling liquid.

But Thaddeuss was equally as clever, sending a large fireball hurdling into the water wall, evaporating it into mist the moment the two elements collided. As the water vaporized, he and Atheidrelle witnessed a confusing sight. Tess stood before them clutching her baby bump. Beside her stood another Tess doing the same. Then another. Within the confines of the water shield, Echo had used his power to clone his sister. Now he and Trix were also Tess.

"Try to figure out who's who now, asshole!" Ocean quipped arrogantly.

With that Thaddeuss demonstrated a not before seen power. His eyes flared and instantly Ocean burst into flames. Ocean screamed in agony, falling to the ground writhing as his burning flesh seared and melted off within the inferno.

Arielle screamed. Howard darted to the poor man but could do nothing against the flames. He couldn't get his hands through. Arielle waved her hand and sent a powerful wind forward, blowing out the flames to reveal Ocean's charred, dead body singed beyond recognition. Howard jumped into action. The palms of his hands scorched as he grabbed the boy's sizzling remains.

Interpreting the present situation as evidence the balance of power might be changing, the vampires rose from their obedient stance to Artemis and roared into action. Elijah the vampire pounced onto Fable, placing his steely hands around her throat, choking the life from her. They fell to the ground, Fable writhing to free herself but unable to break the vampire's grip. Struggling to remain conscious, she directed her army in the sky to attack. The sky emptied of its winged warriors as hundreds of birds swooped down, tearing into the back of Elijah with their sharp claws. The vampire released his stranglehold on Fable to fight against the birds. Sydney darted forward and snatched her to safety as Fable gasped for air. Elijah struggled against the bird attack, but there were far too many. Soon no one could see Elijah's at all as he was encased by the winged predators swirling him around the enclosure. Flapping wings, squawking beaks, and slicing claws were completely immobilizing him.

Bianca panicked as she watched her cousin being sliced to shreds. With the enclosure occupied by the chaos, no one noticed as she attempted to climb her way out of the cauldron. Rock by rock, step by step, she made it nearly halfway up but fell to the ground as the angle proved too steep to manage. If she could have only reached two feet higher, she could have grabbed a small ledge of stone and possibly made it to freedom. She tried to step backward a few yards hoping to give herself launching room to use her vampire dexterity to leap higher, but her one attempt was met with a sweeping slap from Artemis, knocking her back to the ground once more.

Elijah was continuing to move around the ballroom enclosure with frantic pace, unable to free himself from the regiment of claws and beaks assailing him. Banging into a rock he ricocheted back past Thorne. But Thorne D'Angelo had stopped watching the vampire's torment, his eyes focused on the three Tess figures ahead. One of those figures was Echo. His Echo. As he observed each one, searching every move, every gesture to conclude which Tess was his lover, he saw a Tess look his way. He knew then. Though her eyes were her eyes, and the face was her face, Thorne knew that particular turn of the head. And when their eyes met, he knew it was Echo returning his stare. Despite the chaos around them and the allegiances between them, Thorne saw the glisten in those eyes. Teary, disappointed. Eyes mourning a loss. Thorne shared that loss. Fate was a dastardly jokester. It had dangled something real in their reach, then snatched it away. They were foes now—each aligned to their own. Inside that fleeting stare, the two men said their goodbyes to whatever they might have had and resigned themselves to their positions. Thorne knew he would kill any Blanchard he had to in this war, but he would not reveal Echo. His final gift to the man who might have made him a better person. Thorne would not alert his father as to which Tess was the only male.

The birds suddenly let go of their hold on Elijah, dropping his shredded carcass to the ground. He was not dead, but he was beyond help. His eyes were torn from the sockets. His ears were missing. His nostrils torn in flaps at the sides. His attempt at shielding his face from the predators resulted in three fingers now missing from his left hand and four from his right. His torso was gutted, his entrails spewing forth to his feet like grotesque dangling cords. An undead creature in unfathomable agony yet unable to experience the sweet peace of death. He stumbled around the remains of the ballroom floor, unable to do anything other than stagger and fall. It was a pitiful sight, even to those who recognized him as the monster he was. Blind, disfigured, missing digits and his stomach hanging open—his undead body would never find release from that torture.

Howard was finished reviving Ocean from death. The moment life sprang back into his young body, Ocean jumped to his feet and directed a wave of water toward Thaddeuss, smacking him into the rock wall. It achieved little harm, but he enjoyed doing it. As Thaddeuss slammed into the jagged rock wall, Ursula directed a magical blast in his direction, pinning him to the sharp edges of the rock. She made a pushing motion with her hands, her power pressing Thaddeuss into the serrated rocks. Increasing her force of energy, his body began slowly piercing itself into the jagged stone, impaling him from the back onto the remnants of the fallen house.

Atheidrelle reacted with lightning speed, sending a blast of her decimating power Ursula's way. Ursula Kraven, icon of American witches, long standing member of The Witches Association, and revered former Queen of the Consort was ripped apart instantly before everyone's eyes. It was the same death strike Atheidrelle rendered upon Ocean's brother Forest years ago. Ursula's body shredded before everyone's eyes. Tissue, muscle, bone, and blood plopped to the ground as her torso divided in half and her arms and legs broke away. Demitra released a bone-chilling screech as she ran to her longtime friend. Howard immediately joined her and began his attempt to restore Ursula to life.

"Hurry Howard!" Demitra cried.

"I'm trying," he panted. "I'm weak, Demitra. I think I'm running out of steam."

Howard heard more commotion around. He looked up momentarily to see the vampire Davidson tussling with Salem. They were rolling on the ground as his powerful bite snapped toward her neck. She was dodging his attack with acute agility, but the succession of his snaps was fast and getting much too close. Arielle leapt onto Davidson's back and tried to pull him from her sister. Howard returned his attention to Ursula, placing each of his hands upon her two divided parts while summoning his new power. His eyes glanced up to Demitra's as he heard a strange sound emit from close by. Demitra looked funny. Her eyes were glassy. She was not looking at him or Ursula any longer. She was not looking at anything. Staring straight ahead as if in shock, Demitra wore a pained expression. Howard then watched in horror as she collapsed on top of Ursula's mangled body. Howard jumped back to see Thaddeuss D'Angelo with his hand outstretched. He looked back down to Demitra. Dead center of her back was a scorched hole, the exposed insides of her cavity were sizzling and cauterizing. Howard could see her blackened spine within. She had been hit. Demitra was dead.

"No!!!" Howard shrieked as he withdrew his hands from Ursula and dragged Demitra to safety behind the melee. "Ocean! Cover us!" Howard shouted.

Ocean sprang into action, swirling another wall of water around himself, Howard and Demitra as Howard went to work. Tears streamed down his face. *Not Demitra. Not Demitra.* She was his friend. She was his family, even before he knew how true that was. They'd grown up together. Next to Artemis, she was the most important figure of his life, and maybe even above Artemis these days. Demitra wasn't only his friend, she was his grandmother. Ursula could wait. Demitra took precedence.

Sydney was now grabbing broken chunks of the house from the encircling barricade and hurling them at Thaddeuss and Atheidrelle. They were not subdued by the action, using their far greater powers to pulverize the boulders before they struck. It didn't matter, Sydney was succeeding in keeping them occupied while Ocean kept Howard and Demitra protected.

One of the Tesses was now brandishing a scythe. It was Trix, and she was charging toward Thaddeuss. Atheidrelle sent a blast her way, not to kill her, only to hold her at bay with a powerful forcefield. She and Thaddeuss needed Tess, and they could certainly use Trix to make another child to give them the all-consuming power they craved. Of everyone in the fight, Tess and Trix were the only ones they could not afford to kill. Atheidrelle swept the other two Tesses into her field, encasing the three of them with an inescapable shimmering barrier. She was certain it was Trix wielding the scythe, but she couldn't be sure which of the other two Tesses was the real Tess or Echo. She would keep them quartered off until the battle was over.

Thorne came dashing forth to attack Fable, emitting some reddish burst her way. Her birds, sensing the coming attack, encircled her, absorbing the blow. Dozens of birds disintegrated under the blast. Fable dove for cover behind a small piling of rock before the next strike. Thorne aimed for the rock, pulverizing it with his blast. Fable was exposed. He sent another reddish burst her way, but the confounded body of Elijah—still stumbling blindly and deafly—happened into the path of the strike and was assailed with Thorne's power burst. The impact sent Elijah smashing backward over Fable's back and into the rock pilings.

Artemis directed her wolves Thorne's way. The man was instantly consumed with fending off the predators. He shot blast after blast toward the animals, directly hitting most of them, but he was not fast enough to get them all. Three beasts seized him, biting and snapping as he fought off their fangs. Their jaws were too strong; Fable watched as the left side of Thorne's neck ripped away in the teeth of one of the powerful canines. Another went for the abdomen, taking a huge chunk from it, exposing his ribcage and lungs. Thorne was meeting an agonizing end, being devoured now by the beasts of the earth. Confined behind Atheidrelle's shimmery barrier, Echo could only see blurred images of what was taking place. As he realized it was Thorne being devoured alive by the wolves, he was almost grateful to be inside Atheidrelle's trap.

Artemis knew there was nothing Thorne could do to stop her attacking beasts. He would die eventually from his wounds, but her army of beasts hadn't finished with him yet. Thorne was now like Elijah—floundering through the enclosure, screaming in agony in everyone's way. Artemis sent a gust of wind toward the floundering nuisances, scooping them up and catapulting them high into the air, crashing down somewhere outside the perimeter where more of her beasts would be waiting to finish them off entirely.

As Arielle continued tussling with Davidson, successfully freeing Salem from his choke hold, Salem was able to send a freezing burst his way, stopping him in motion as Arielle straddled his back. Once Arielle jumped clear of him, Salem sent a fiery blast incinerating him on the spot. Davidson crumbled to dust.

Sage and Sydney now had their hands full as the vampires Aspasia, Bianca, and Gideon had waged an attack on them. The vampires were not expecting the twins to possess the superhuman strength they did. Their underestimation proved humiliating as Sage was now slamming Aspasia and Bianca into each other repeatedly. Each relentless blow stunning them so severely they were unable to react. Sydney's super strength had Gideon pressed to his knees under her clutches. In vain he tried to bite her arms but found even his centuries of strength was not enough to pull out from under the powerful hands pressing him to the ground.

Trix ran to their aide, scythe in hand. She swung hard as Sage whirled Aspasia toward her. With a clean swipe, Trix beheaded the regal European vampire and righted herself to take her next swing at Bianca. But Bianca was quick. She wrenched free of Sage by ducking between his legs, forcing him to flip to the ground as he tried to hold on to her. Once free, Bianca charged forward directly at one of Artemis' wolves now charging toward her to enter the fray. The powerful beast lurched at the beautiful vampire, but Bianca was banking on such a move from the approaching animal. At just the right moment, she jumped, planting sure-footed onto the wolf's back with her right leg and used the momentum to propel herself high enough on the wall facing to finish the climb she was unable to manage before. With age-old prowess and dexterity, Bianca spidered up the remaining few feet of the circular prison reaching freedom at the top. Without haste she sprinted away. Seeing the escape, Artemis directed her wolves to follow. Soon the wolves were scraping up the sides of rock and debris, toppling dislodged stones as they made their way up. Sydney, distracted by the sight, lost her grip on Gideon. He sprang to his feet and lurched himself toward the last wolf making its way up the enclosure. Wrapping his arms around the great beast's back, the wolf unwittingly carried Gideon up the wall far enough for the vampire to reach his own freedom atop it. Bianca, Gideon, and the wolves were out of sight now.

Artemis didn't go after them. Not yet certain if Howard's attempt to revive her sister was successful, she could not leave. She only hoped her sergeants would catch the monsters and tear them to shreds. Artemis understood that Howard was losing strength. After so many restorations already that night, he was drained. His power was too new, too untested for him to have mastered unyielding stamina. She watched stone-faced, straining to see behind the water wall Ocean was projecting, as Howard tried to muster enough energy to bring Demitra back.

Behind the water wall, Howard reached success. Demitra bolted upright, coughing horribly as her lungs breathed in the much-needed air. Howard snatched her into his arms and hugged her more tightly than he had ever hugged anyone. He cried into her soft black hair as she wrapped her arms around him in response.

"It's alright Howard," she smiled. "You did it. You saved me. It is okay."

"It's not okay," Howard cried. "You were dead, Dee! I almost lost you."

"But you didn't lose me. You're a Blanchard. And you saved me."

Ocean dropped the wall of water. Demitra surveyed the battle. She saw Arielle and Salem standing with Fable and Artemis beside them. Ursula was gone. The window of time already passed where she could have been revived. Howard made his choice and Demitra's life had been it.

Blackie was tossing bluish energy at Atheidrelle's forcefield, trying to release her children from her evil sister's hold. But Atheidrelle was much too powerful.

"Let go of my children Atheidrelle!" Blackie shouted. "You will not take them. You will not harm my children. Your reign of evil is over now!"

Atheidrelle gave a hearty laugh. "I have long grown weary of your pious demeanor, Sister. You think yourself superior because you walked away from your birthright. I think you are a fool. I also think you forget all the misdeeds you caused others in your early years. Turning your back on your family does not undo your own sins. I find your very existence tiresome."

With that Atheidrelle released her forcefield on the triplets so that she could direct the brunt of her force toward her sister. With one swift swipe of her hand, Blackie D'Angelo was sent hurtling at record speed toward the wall of rock, pipe, wood, and steel. Blackie slammed face first into the wall at such a velocity, her body shattered against it. Obliterated. Nothing was left. Bone was pulverized, laying in broken bits on the ground. Shreds of muscle, tissue, and her long black hair were pressed between the cracks of stone and rock, and blood covered the face of the impact zone. Nothing remained of Blackie D'Angelo.

Arielle fell to her knees in horror. The three Tesses ran to her. All Blackie's children now devastated by the sight their eyes could not pull away from. The bloody splatter which was once their mother.

"Dad, bring her back!" Echo shouted from behind his Tess façade.

Howard ran to the gruesome wall but there was nothing left to hold. No body parts remained for him to grasp to resurrect.

"Now this bedlam ends," Thaddeuss announced with Atheidrelle and Taub at his side.

Thaddeuss lifted his hand and sent a burst of energy toward Howard just as Taub sent out his black tendrils to wrap around the three Tesses. Thaddeuss' attack didn't have the chance to hit Howard. Artemis pounced directly between them, blocking Howard from Thaddeuss' reach. His burst hit Artemis and did nothing but awaken a wicked smile across her face. Atheidrelle sent her body-ripping spell Artemis' way—but again, no effect. Atheidrelle looked curiously at the new Artemis. Their eyes faced off and Atheidrelle could see the strange glow emitting from her opponent. Artemis the witch, Artemis the vampire, Artemis the wolf, Artemis the Hunter. Artemis, the Immortal. Her eyes glowed the most piercing metallic silver, and for the first real time in Atheidrelle's long unnatural life, she was genuinely afraid.

Artemis outstretched her hand, as if waiting to catch something, and held it there.

"You are defeated, Thaddeuss," Demitra Blanchard announced, stepping up to stand at her sister's side. "We have brought down the House of Duquesne. We have slayed the source of your immortality. And now in the name of the Council of the Witches Association, in protection of the Natural Order of Life, I, Hecate of the Blanchard Coven of Daihmler, end you!"

Thaddeuss D'Angelo—Hugh D'Angelo—presented a smile to meet his end. Perhaps he found the arrogance of the Blanchards amusing. Perhaps he knew they stood no chance of defeating him. Demitra Blanchard was a psychic, possessing no real active powers. The audacity in her voice assuming she would be the one to bring him down must have been the reason for his sinister smile. But then something happened. His smile switched to abject terror as the realization dawned that he was indeed about to die. Sailing through the air at the warp speed of lightning came a long, slender object landing directly in Artemis Blanchard's grip. She tossed it to her sister. Demitra grabbed it midair and swung her grandfather's sword with the might of a thousand warriors. Thaddeuss D'Angelo barely had time to register what was happening. Opening his mouth to scream "No!" was his last act upon the earth, as Constantinople Blanchard's blade sliced his head clean from the shoulders of the last body he would ever possess.

Atheidrelle watched in terror as her brother's head clumped to the ground, eyes still wide open in panic. Demitra stood triumphant, sword still in hand, and faced her family's last enemy.

"And now it comes down to us," Salem said, taking a step closer to the figure who had once been her half-sister Cassandra. Demitra tossed Salem the sword. Salem approached her enemy. "Atheidrelle Obreiggon, you have taken everything from me. My husband, my son, my grandmother, my mother, my father, my sister. You will now answer for what you have wrought onto the Blanchard family!" Salem froze Atheidrelle in place and readied herself to strike. "She is mine."

Salem lifted the sword to swing. As her hands glided the sword through the air, a sea of faces flashed through her mind. All the loved ones she'd lost due to this woman. This was Salem's vengeance upon them. The blade cut cleanly. Atheidrelle's head met the ground, rolling three feet until it was stopped in place by her brother's. Atheidrelle's headless torso fell backward, landing atop Thaddeuss'. Two bodies and two heads meeting death together on the dirty, bloody ground.

A silence fell, as everyone took in the scene, collectively exhaling their relief that the end of the D'Angelos evil was ended.

"It is all finally over," Salem sighed, dropping the sword to the ground.

"Not quite yet," Taub D'Angelo snarled.

In all the chaos they had almost forgotten about his presence. Looking now to his wicked sneer, fear rose again as he made a sudden movement with his hand. It was much too fast for the Blanchards to prepare for. The Blanchard sword wrenched from Salem's unprepared hand, sailing through the air at warp speed. The Blanchards looked on in horror as the sword stabbed directly through the three Tesses standing side by side. It penetrated the first Tess through the chest, continuing its trajectory through her back where it stabbed into a second Tess. Plunging through her chest cavity, it exited the back to and gored directly into the third. The piercing blade plunged through all three hearts before the sword's handle ripped through rib cages, lungs, and shattered spines upon exit. It all happened within the blink of an eye, like a rifle cartridge shot from a canon. As the sword tore from the back of the final Tess, all three lay decimated on the carnage laden ground.

"No!!!!!" Demitra shrieked, running toward her family. Howard was hard on her heels behind her.

Taub was laughing maniacally at the sight of the dead Blanchards. "You destroyed my family. Now I have destroyed yours. I'll be back one day for the rest of you!" Then, as Xander Obreiggon had been able to do, Taub D'Angelo vanished—escaping to parts unknown.

The shock of his exit was broken by Demitra's scream! "Howard, use your power!" she screeched. "Save your children!"

Howard sprang into action despite his exhaustion. Having used this gift so many times had taxed his energy. He prayed he could manifest enough power to save his children. He grabbed the body of the first Tess and went to work, struggling to summon the light within and wield it to use. The light was there. It was not as strong as before, but enough was left to see the healing through. Within a few seconds, the first Tess was breathing, her body restored. The hole through her cavity was gone. Only ripped clothing reflected any injury had ever taken place. She struggled for air, her physical self reeling from the sensation of having her lungs torn apart. But air was coming. Fable knelt beside her, steadying her as she drank the air in.

Howard moved to the second Tess and struggled again to engage the power. It was harder now, the light within him was faint, yet he managed to grab it and pull it forth into her, although its frequency was perilously diminished.

The sudden thought crossed Arielle's mind—what if they couldn't all be revived? What if only one survived? Or possibly two? What if Echo was dead? Could the survivors ever be morphed back to their original form without him? She looked back to the splatter on the rock facing where her mother died. She then looked to Howard, undeniably struggling to resurrect the second Tess. What if she lost her siblings as well? Ocean, sensing her thoughts, silently put his arm around her as they watched, breath held, hoping Howard had the strength to keep going.

The second Tess revived. Like the first, she was struggling to refill her lungs with sweet, sweet oxygen. But it was coming. Sydney stabilized this Tess while she recovered.

"Who is who?" Salem cried. The looked at the survivors hoping for a response. The two Tesses were still struggling to breath. Speech was not yet possible.

"It doesn't matter!" Demitra shrieked. "Just save them all and it won't matter, Howard. We will sort out who is who once they regain consciousness. Echo can change everyone back once they're awake."

"Only one to go," Fable whispered, clutching Salem's hand as tightly as she could. "Come on Howard. Come on."

Howard had his hands on the final remaining Tess. Nothing was happening. The bright light from within him was going dormant. Nothing was coming forward. He could not even feel a trace of it anywhere inside him. "No, no, no, no, no!" he bellowed. "No. One more. Give me one more!"

Demitra felt the tears streaming down her face. "One more, please, one more."

Nothing happened.

"Beryl!!!!" Demitra screamed into the night air. "We need one more! Please help your grandchildren! Please help your son save just one more!"

Silence hovered like a denied prayer. It seemed even the birds in the sky and the crickets in the forest were silent. Nothing came forward.

Demitra fell to her knees, Howard pulled her into his arms as he clutched the last remaining lifeless Tess in his arms. She wasn't coming back.

Artemis stepped forward; her silver eyes shed silvery tears. Sage, Salem, Arielle, and Ocean all fell to their knees. The two other Tesses were coming around now in Sydney and Fable's arms. They found their lungs in time to feel their hearts sink as they looked onto the dead body of their loved one. Then, instinctively, the two living Tesses looked at one another in complete bewilderment. They each knew their own identity, but who were the other two they were staring at? Who was alive and who was lying dead at their knees?

CHAPTER FORTY SEVEN

Snow

Seth and Yasmine Blanchard drove along the icy Colorado roads in the Pathfinder they'd stolen from their dinner victim earlier in the evening. Passing through the snow-covered mountains of Loveland, Colorado, Yasmine was astounded by the beauty. The road twisted and turned, winding around mountain peaks and valleys. Icy streams and lakes, tall aspens and evergreens poking their green bodies out from the snowy ground.

"Look at all of this, Seth! Have you ever seen anything so majestic?"

Seth smiled at his wife's fascination. Her sweet innocence had not completely gone away even though her humanity had. "We didn't get winters like this in Alabama. It's really something to see."

It was dark outside, but the moon was bright against the blanket of white on the mountain—and their vampire eyes carried a new depth of vision that even the blackest of night couldn't obscure.

"Do you think Artemis will find us here?" Yasmine asked her husband.

"I think Artemis and the rest of the family, if they survived their battle with the D'Angelos, will have their hands full for a while. But Artemis will come after us eventually. Still, she will honor our agreement. Which gives us plenty of time to get good and thoroughly lost."

"And who would look for us in Breckinridge?" Yasmine replied. "That's about the last place any of the family would ever expect us to go."

It was almost 11 p.m. when the stolen car pulled up to a complex of ski cabins on the hill. Just below, the town of Breckenridge glowed with Christmas lights strung among the many tall cedars and fir trees. Seth smiled at the glistening snowbanks and long runs of ski trails.

"It's beautiful, isn't it Yaz?"

He placed his arm around her shoulders and gave her a playful kiss. "Man, I'm hungry."

Yasmine smiled to her husband, as a little family of four passed over a wooden bridge a few feet away, headed to their cabin on the other side. The father held his young daughter, slumped over his shoulder asleep. The mother held tightly to their little boy's hand as his tired feet struggled to complete the journey.

"Look, baby," Yasmine smiled. "Dinner."

ABOUT THE AUTHOR

Micah House lives in Birmingham, Alabama with his husband and son. He is a former columnist turned fiction writer. His first novel in The Blanchard Witches saga is titled *The Blanchard Witches of Daihmler County*. The follow-up novel is *The Blanchard Witches: Prodigal Daughters*. The third in the series is *Stitches in Time.*

Printed in the USA
CPSIA information can be obtained
at www.ICGtesting.com
LVHW020144121123
763661LV00108B/5575

9 781736 508664